DETECTIVE & MYSTERY

W9-BVO-398

3 2487 00097 8925

Large Print Per
Perry, Anne.
The face of a stranger

WITHDRAWN

DUE IN 28 DAYS

14 DAY
LOAN

NEWARK PUBLIC LIBRARY
NEWARK, OHIO

THE FACE
OF A
STRANGER

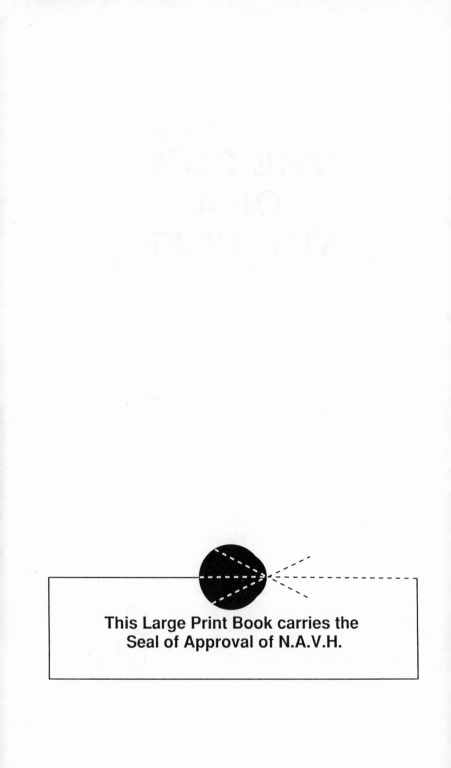

**This Large Print Book carries the
Seal of Approval of N.A.V.H.**

THE FACE
OF A
STRANGER

Anne Perry

Thorndike Press • Thorndike, Maine

Library of Congress Cataloging in Publication Data:

Perry, Anne.
   The face of a stranger / Anne Perry.
      p. cm.
   ISBN 1-56054-113-X (alk. paper : lg. print)
   1. Large type books. I. Title.
[PR6066.E693F3   1991]   91-6286
823'.914—dc20   CIP

Copyright © 1990 by Anne Perry.
All rights reserved.

Thorndike Press Large Print edition published in 1991
by arrangement with MBA Literary Agents, Ltd.

Cover design by Michael Anderson.

The tree indicium is a trademark of Thorndike Press.

This book is printed on acid-free, high opacity paper. ∞

To Christine M. J. Lynch, in gratitude
for old friendship renewed.

CHAPTER
ONE

He opened his eyes and saw nothing but a pale grayness above him, uniform, like a winter sky, threatening and heavy. He blinked and looked again. He was lying flat on his back; the grayness was a ceiling, dirty with the grime and trapped fumes of years.

He moved slightly. The bed he was lying on was hard and short. He made an effort to sit up and found it acutely painful. Inside his chest a fierce pain stabbed him, and his left arm was heavily bandaged and aching. As soon as he was half up his head thumped as if his pulse were a hammer behind his eyes.

There was another wooden cot just like his own a few feet away, and a pasty-faced man lay on it, moving restlessly, gray blanket mangled and sweat staining his shirt. Beyond him was another, blood-soaked bandages swathing the legs; and beyond that another, and so on down the great room to the black-bellied stove at the far end and the smoke-scored ceiling above it.

Panic exploded inside him, hot prickling through his skin. He was in a workhouse! God in heaven, how had he come to this?

But it was broad daylight! Awkwardly, shifting his position, he stared around the room. There were people in all the cots; they lined the walls, and every last one was occupied. No workhouse in the country allowed that! They should be up and laboring, for the good of their souls, if not for the workhouse purse. Not even children were granted the sin of idleness.

Of course; it was a hospital. It must be! Very carefully he lay down again, relief overwhelming him as his head touched the bran pillow. He had no recollection of how he had come to be in such a place, no memory of having hurt himself — and yet he was undoubtedly injured, his arm was stiff and clumsy, he was aware now of a deep ache in the bone. And his chest hurt him sharply every time he breathed in. There was a thunderstorm raging inside his head. What had happened to him? It must have been a major accident: a collapsing wall, a violent throw from a horse, a fall from a height? But no impression came back, not even a memory of fear.

He was still struggling to recall something

when a grinning face appeared above him and a voice spoke cheerfully.

"Now then, you awake again, are you?"

He stared upwards, focusing on the moon face. It was broad and blunt with a chapped skin and a smile that stretched wide over broken teeth.

He tried to clear his head.

"Again?" he said confusedly. The past lay behind him in dreamless sleep like a white corridor without a beginning.

"You're a right one, you are." The voice sighed good-humoredly. "You dunno nuffin' from one day ter the next, do yer? It wouldn't surprise me none if yer didn't remember yer own name! 'Ow are yer then? 'Ow's yer arm?"

"My name?" There was nothing there, nothing at all.

"Yeah." The voice was cheerful and patient. "Wot's yer name, then?"

He must know his name. Of course he must! It was . . . Blank seconds ticked by.

"Well then?" the voice pressed.

He struggled. Nothing came except a white panic, like a snowstorm in the brain, whirling and dangerous, and without focus.

"Yer've fergot!" The voice was stoic and resigned. "I thought so. Well the Peelers was 'ere, day afore yesterday; an' they said as you was 'Monk' — 'William Monk.' Now wot 'a you gorn an' done that the Peelers is after yer?" He pushed helpfully at the pillow with enormous hands and then straightened the blanket. "You like a nice 'ot drink then, or suffink? Proper parky it is, even in 'ere. July — an it feels like ruddy November! I'll get yer a nice 'ot drink o' gruel, 'ows that then? Raining a flood outside, it is. Ye're best off in 'ere."

"William Monk?" he repeated the name.

"That's right, leastways that's wot the Peelers says. Feller called Runcorn, 'e was; Mr. Runcorn, a hinspector, no less!" He raised scruffy eyebrows. "Wot yer done, then? You one o' them Swell Mob wot goes around pinchin' gennelmen's wallets and gold watches?" There was no criticism in his round, benign eyes. "That's wot yer looked like when they brought yer in 'ere, proper natty dressed yer was, hunderneath the mud and torn-up stuff, like, and all that blood."

Monk said nothing. His head reeled, pounding in an effort to perceive anything in the mists, even one clear, tangible memory. But even the name had no real significance. "William" had a vague familiarity but it was a common enough name. Everyone must know dozens of Williams.

"So yer don't remember," the man went on, his face friendly and faintly amused. He

10

had seen all manner of human frailty and there was nothing so fearful or so eccentric it disturbed his composure. He had seen men die of the pox and the plague, or climb the wall in terror of things that were not there. A grown man who could not remember yesterday was a curiosity, but nothing to marvel at. "Or else yer ain't saying," he went on. "Don't blame yer." He shrugged. "Don't do ter give the Peelers nothin' as yer don't 'ave ter. Now d'yer feel like a spot of 'ot gruel? Nice and thick, it is, bin sitting on that there stove a fair while. Put a bit of 'eart inter yer."

Monk was hungry, and even under the blanket he realized he was cold.

"Yes please," he accepted.

"Right-oh then, gruel it is. I suppose I'll be a'tellin' yer yer name termorrer jus' the same, an' yer'll look at me all gormless again." He shook his head. "Either yer 'it yer 'ead summink 'orrible, or ye're scared o' yer wits o' them Peelers. Wot yer done? You pinched the crown jools?" And he went off chuckling with laughter to himself, up to the black-bellied stove at the far end of the ward.

Police! Was he a thief? The thought was repellent, not only because of the fear attached to it but for itself, what it made of him. And yet he had no idea if it might be true.

Who was he? What manner of man? Had

11

he been hurt doing something brave, rash? Or chased down like an animal for some crime? Or was he merely unfortunate, a victim, in the wrong place at the wrong time?

He racked his mind and found nothing, not a shred of thought or sensation. He must live somewhere, know people with faces, voices, emotions. And there was nothing! For all that his memory held, he could have sprung into existence here in the hard cot in this bleak hospital ward.

But he was known to someone! The police.

The man returned with the gruel and carefully fed it to Monk, a spoonful at a time. It was thin and tasteless, but he was grateful for it. Afterwards he lay back again, and struggle as he might, even fear could not keep him from deep, apparently dreamless sleep.

When he woke the following morning at least two things were perfectly clear this time: his name, and where he was. He could remember the meager happenings of the previous day quite sharply: the nurse, the hot gruel, the man in the next cot turning and groaning, the gray-white ceiling, the feel of the blankets, and the pain in his chest.

He had little idea of time, but he judged it to be somewhere in the mid-afternoon when the policeman came. He was a big man, or he appeared so in the caped coat and top hat of Peel's Metropolitan Police Force. He had a bony face, long nose and wide mouth, a good brow, but deep-set eyes too small to tell the color of easily; a pleasant enough countenance, and intelligent, but showing small signs of temper between the brows and about the lips. He stopped at Monk's cot.

"Well, do you know me this time, then?" he asked cheerfully.

Monk did not shake his head; it hurt too much.

"No," he said simply.

The man mastered his irritation and something that might even have been disappointment. He looked Monk up and down closely, narrowing one eye in a nervous gesture as if he would concentrate his vision.

"You look better today," he pronounced.

Was that the truth; did he look better? Or did Runcorn merely want to encourage him? For that matter, what did he look like? He had no idea. Was he dark or fair, ugly or pleasing? Was he well built, or ungainly? He could not even see his hands, let alone his body beneath the blankets. He would not look now — he must wait till Runcorn was gone.

"Don't remember anything, I suppose?" Runcorn continued. "Don't remember what happened to you?"

"No." Monk was fighting with a cloud totally without shape. Did this man know him, or merely of him? Was he a public figure Monk ought to recognize? Or did he pursue him for some dutiful and anonymous purpose? Might he only be looking for information, or could he tell Monk something about himself more than a bare name, put flesh and memory to the bleak fact of his presence?

Monk was lying on the cot clothed up to his chin, and yet he felt mentally naked, vulnerable as the exposed and ridiculous are. His instinct was to hide, to conceal his weakness. And yet he must know. There must be dozens, perhaps scores of people in the world who knew him, and he knew nothing. It was a total and paralyzing disadvantage. He did not even know who loved or hated him, whom he had wronged, or helped. His need was like that of a man who starves for food, and yet is terrified that in any mouthful may lurk poison.

He looked back at the policeman. Runcorn, the nurse had said his name was. He must commit himself to something.

"Did I have an accident?" he asked.

"Looked like it," Runcorn replied matter-of-factly. "Hansom was turned over, right mess. You must have hit something at a hell of a lick. Horse frightened out of its wits." He shook his head and pulled the corners of his mouth down. "Cabby killed outright, poor devil. Hit his head on the curb. You were inside, so I suppose you were partly protected. Had a swine of a job to get you out. Dead weight. Never realized you were such a solid feller. Don't remember it, I suppose? Not even the fright?" Again his left eye narrowed a little.

"No." No images came to Monk's mind, no memory of speed, or impact, not even pain.

"Don't remember what you were doing?" Runcorn went on, without any real hope in his voice. "What case you were on?"

Monk seized on a brilliant hope, a thing with shape; he was almost too afraid to ask, in case it crumbled at his touch. He stared at Runcorn. He must know this man, personally, perhaps even daily. And yet nothing in him woke the slightest recall.

"Well, man?" Runcorn demanded. "Do you remember? You weren't anywhere we sent you! What the devil were you doing? You must have discovered something yourself. Can you remember what it was?"

The blank was impenetrable.

Monk moved his head fractionally in negation, but the bright bubble inside him stayed. He was a Peeler himself, that was why they knew him! He was not a thief — not a fugitive.

Runcorn leaned forward a little, watching him keenly, seeing the light in his face.

"You do remember something!" he said triumphantly. "Come on, man — what is it?"

Monk could not explain that it was not memory that changed him, but a dissolving of fear in one of the sharpest forms it had taken. The entire, suffocating blanket was still there, but characterless now, without specific menace.

Runcorn was still waiting, staring at him intently.

"No," Monk said slowly. "Not yet."

Runcorn straightened up. He sighed, trying to control himself. "It'll come."

"How long have I been here?" Monk asked. "I've lost count of time." It sounded reasonable enough; anyone ill might do that.

"Over three weeks — it's the thirty-first of July — 1856," he added with a touch of sarcasm.

Dear God! Over three weeks, and all he could remember was yesterday. He shut his eyes; it was infinitely worse than that — a whole lifetime of how many years? And all he could remember was yesterday! How old was he? How many years were lost? Panic boiled up inside him again and for a moment he could have screamed, Help me, somebody, who am I? Give me back my life, my self!

But men did not scream in public, even in private they did not cry out. The sweat stood cold on his skin and he lay rigid, hands clenched by his sides. Runcorn would take it for pain, ordinary physical pain. He must keep up the appearance. He must not let Runcorn think he had forgotten how to do his job. Without a job the workhouse would be a reality — grinding, hopeless, day after day of obedient, servile, pointless labor.

He forced himself back to the present.

"Over three weeks?"

"Yes," Runcorn replied. Then he coughed and cleared his throat. Perhaps he was embarrassed. What does one say to a man who cannot remember you, who cannot even remember himself? Monk felt for him.

"It'll come back," Runcorn repeated. "When you're up again; when you get back on the job. You want a break to get well, that's what you need, a break till you get your strength. Take a week or two. Bound to. Come back to the station when you're fit to work. It'll all come clear then, I dare say."

"Yes," Monk agreed, more for Runcorn's sake than his own. He did not believe it.

Monk left the hospital three days later. He was strong enough to walk, and no one stayed in such places longer than they had to. It was not only financial consideration, but the sheer danger. More people died of cross-infection than of any illness or injury that brought them there in the first place. This much was imparted to him in a cheerfully resigned manner by the nurse who had originally told him his name.

It was easy to believe. In the short days he could remember he had seen doctors move from one bloody or festering wound to another, from fever patient to vomiting and flux, then to open sores, and back again. Soiled bandages lay on the floor; there was little laundry done, although no doubt they did the best they could on the pittance they had.

And to be fair, they did their utmost never knowingly to admit patients suffering from typhoid, cholera or smallpox; and if they did discover these illnesses afterwards, they rectified their error. Those poor souls had to be quarantined in their own houses and left to die, or recover if God were willing. There they would be of least peril to the community. Everyone was familiar with the black flag hanging limply at the ends of a street.

Runcorn had left for him his Peeler's coat and tall hat, carefully dusted off and mended after the accident. At least they fitted him, apart from being a trifle loose because of the weight he had lost lying on his back since the injury. But that would return. He was a strong man, tall and lean muscled, but the nurse had shaved him so he had not yet seen his face. He had felt it, touching with his fingertips when no one was watching him. It was strong boned, and his mouth seemed wide, that was all he knew; and his hands were smooth and uncallused by labor, with a scattering of dark hairs on the backs.

Apparently he had had a few coins in his pocket when they brought him in, and these were handed to him as he left. Someone else must have paid for his treatment — presumably his police salary had been sufficient? Now he stood on the steps with eight shillings and eleven pence, a cotton handkerchief and an envelope with his name and "27 Grafton Street" written on it. It contained a receipt from his tailor.

He looked around him and recognized nothing. It was a bright day with fast-scudding clouds and a warm wind. Fifty yards away there was an intersection, and a small boy was wielding a broom, keeping the crossing clear of horse manure and other rubbish. A carriage swirled past, drawn by two high-stepping bays.

Monk stepped down, still feeling weak, and made his way to the main road. It took him five minutes to see a vacant hansom, hail it and give the cabby the address. He sat back inside and watched as streets and squares flickered by, other vehicles, carriages, some with liveried footmen, more hansoms, brewers' drays, costermongers' carts. He saw peddlers and vendors, a man selling fresh eels, another with hot pies, plum duff — it sounded good, he was hungry, but he had no idea how much the fare would be, so he did not dare stop.

A newspaper boy was shouting something, but they passed him too quickly to hear above the horse's hooves. A one-legged man sold matches.

There was a familiarity about the streets, but it was at the back of his mind. He could not have named a single one, simply that they did not seem alien.

Tottenham Court Road. It was very busy: carriages, drays, carts, women in wide skirts stepping over refuse in the gutter, two soldiers laughing and a little drunk, red coats a splash of color, a flower seller and two washerwomen.

The cab swung left into Grafton Street and stopped.

" 'Ere y'are, sir, Number Twenty-seven."

"Thank you." Monk climbed out awkwardly; he was still stiff and unpleasantly weak. Even that small exertion had tired him. He had no idea how much money to offer.

He held out a florin, two sixpences, a penny and a halfpenny in his hand.

The cabby hesitated, then took one of the sixpences and the halfpenny, tipped his hat and slapped the reins across his horse's rump, leaving Monk standing on the pavement. He hesitated, now that the moment was come, overtaken with fear. He had not even the slightest idea what he should find — or whom.

Two men passed, looking at him curiously. They must suppose him lost. He felt foolish, embarrassed. Who would answer his knock? Should he know them? If he lived here, they must know him. How well? Were they friends, or merely landlords? It was preposterous, but he did not even know if he had a family!

But if he had, surely they would have visited him. Runcorn had come, so they would have been told where he was. Or had he been the kind of man who inspires no love, only professional courtesy? Was that why Runcorn had called, because it was his job?

Had he been a good policeman, efficient at his work? Was he liked? It was ridiculous — pathetic.

He shook himself. This was childish. If he had family, a wife or brother or sister, Runcorn would have told him. He must discover each thing as he could; if he was fit to be employed by the Peelers, then he was a detective. He would learn each piece till he had enough to cobble together a whole, the pattern of his life. The first step was to knock on this door, dark brown and closed in front of him.

He lifted his hand and rapped sharply. It was long, desperate minutes with the questions roaring in his mind before it was opened by a broad, middle-aged woman in an apron. Her hair was scraped back untidily, but it was thick and clean and her scrubbed face was generous.

"Well I never!" she said impulsively. "Save my soul, if it in't Mr. Monk back again! I was only saying to Mr. Worley this very morning, as 'ow if you didn't come back again soon I'd 'ave ter let yer rooms; much as it'd go against me ter do it. But a body 'as ter live. Mind that Mr. Runcorn did come around an' say as yer'd 'ad a haccident and bin terrible 'urt and was in one 'o them 'orstipitals." She put her hand to her head in despair. "Gawd save us from such places. Ye're the first man I've seen as 'as come out o' there on 'is own two feet. To tell you the truth, I was expectin' every day to 'ave some messenger boy come and say as you was dead." She screwed up her face and looked at him carefully. "Mind yer does still look proper poorly. Come in and I'll make yer a good meal. Yer must be starved, I'll dare swear yer 'aven't 'ad a decent dish since yer left 'ere! It were as cold as a workhouse master's 'eart the day yer went!" And she whisked her enormous skirts around and led him inside.

He followed her through the paneled hall-way hung with sentimental pictures and up the stairs to a large landing. She produced a bunch of keys from her girdle and opened one of the doors.

"I suppose you gorn and lorst your own key, or you wouldn't 'ave knocked; that stands ter reason, don't it?"

"I had my own key?" he asked before realizing how it betrayed him.

"Gawd save us, o' course yer did!" she said in surprise. "Yer don't think I'm goin' ter get up and down at all hours o' the night ter let yer in and out, do yer? A Christian body needs 'er sleep. 'Eathen hours yer keeps, an' no mistake. Comes o' chasin' after 'eathen folk, I expec'." She turned to look at him. " 'Ere, yer does look ill. Yer must 'ave bin 'it summink terrible. You go in there an' sit down, an' I'll bring yer a good 'ot meal an' a drink. Do you the world o' good, that will." She snorted and straightened her apron fiercely. "I always thought them 'orstipitals din't look after yer proper. I'll wager as 'alf o' them wot dies in there dies o' starvation." And with indignation at the thought twitching in every muscle under her black taffeta, she swept out of the room, leaving the door open behind her.

Monk walked over and closed it, then turned to face the room. It was large, dark brown paneling and green wallpaper. The furniture was well used. A heavy oak table with four matching chairs stood in the center, Jacobean with carved legs and decorated claw feet. The sideboard against the far wall was similar, although what purpose it served he did not know; there was no china on it, and when he opened the drawers, no cutlery. However the lower drawers did contain table linen and napkins, freshly laundered and in good repair. There was also an oak desk with two small, flat drawers. Against the near wall, by the door, there was a handsome bookcase full of volumes. Part of the furniture? Or his own? Later he would look at the titles.

The windows were draped rather than hung with fringed plush curtains of a mid shade of green. The gas brackets on the walls were ornate, with pieces missing. The leather easy chair had faded patches on the arms, and the pile on the cushions was flat. The carpet's colors had long since dimmed to muted plums, navies and forest greens — a pleasant background. There were several pictures of a self-indulgent tone, and a motto over the mantelpiece with the dire warning GOD SEES ALL.

Were they his? Surely not; the emotions jarred on him and he found himself pulling a face at the mawkishness of the subjects, even feeling a touch of contempt.

It was a comfortable room, well lived in, but peculiarly impersonal, without photographs or mementos, no mark of his own taste. His eyes went around it again and again, but nothing was familiar, nothing brought even a pinprick of memory.

He tried the bedroom beyond. It was the same: comfortable, old, shabby. A large bed stood in the center, made up ready with clean sheets, crisp white bolster, and wine-colored eiderdown, flounced at the edges. On the heavy dresser there was a rather pleasant china washbowl and a jug for water. A handsome silver-backed hairbrush lay on the tallboy.

He touched the surfaces. His hands came away clean. Mrs. Worley was at least a good housekeeper.

He was about to open the drawers and look further when there was a sharp rap on the outer door and Mrs. Worley returned, carrying a tray with a steaming plate piled with steak and kidney pudding, boiled cabbage, carrots and beans, and another dish with pie and custard.

"There yer are," she said with satisfaction, setting it down on the table. He was relieved to see knife, fork and spoon with it, and a glass of cider. "You eat that, and yer'll feel better!"

"Thank you, Mrs. Worley." His gratitude was genuine; he had not had a good meal since . . . ?

"It's my duty, Mr. Monk, as a Christian woman," she replied with a little shake of her head. "And yer always paid me prompt, I'll say that for yer — never argued ner was a day late, fer ought else! Now you eat that up, then go ter bed. Yer look proper done in. I don't know what yer bin doin', an' I don't want ter. Prob'ly in't fit fer a body to know anyway."

"What shall I do with the . . ." He looked at the tray.

"Put it outside the door like yer always does!" she said with raised eyebrows. Then she looked at him more closely and sighed. "An' if yer gets took poorly in the night, yer'd best shout out, an' I'll come an' see to yer."

"It won't be necessary — I shall be perfectly well."

She sniffed and let out a little gasp, heavy with disbelief, then bustled out, closing the door behind her with a loud click. He realized immediately how ungracious he had been. She had offered to get up in the night to help him if he needed it, and all he had done was assure her she was not needed. And she had not looked surprised, or hurt. Was he always this discourteous? He paid — she said he paid promptly and without quibble. Was that all there was between them, no kindness, no feeling, just a lodger who was financially reliable, and a landlady who did her Christian duty by him, because that was her nature?

It was not an attractive picture.

He turned his attention to the food. It was plain, but of excellent flavor, and she was certainly not ungenerous with her portions. It flickered through his mind with some anxiety to wonder how much he paid for these amenities, and if he could much longer afford them while he was unable to work. The sooner he recovered his strength, and enough of his wits to resume his duties for the police, the better. He could hardly ask her for credit, particularly after her remarks, and his manners. Please heaven he did not owe her already for the time he was in the hospital!

When he had finished the meal he placed the tray outside on the landing table where she could collect it. He went back into the room, closed the door and sat in one of the armchairs, intending to look through the desk in the window corner, but in weariness, and the comfort of the cushions, he fell asleep.

When he woke, cold now and stiff, his side aching, it was dark, and he fumbled to light the gas. He was still tired, and would willingly have gone to bed, but he knew that the temptation of the desk, and the fear of it, would trouble even the most exhausted sleep.

He lit the lamp above it and pulled open the top. There was a flat surface with inkstand, a leather writing block and a dozen small closed drawers.

He started at the top left-hand side, and worked through them all. He must be a methodical man. There were receipted bills; a few newspaper clippings, entirely of crimes, usually violent, and describing brilliant police work in solving them; three railway timetables; business letters; and a note from a tailor.

A tailor. So that was where his money went — vain beggar. He must take a look through his wardrobe and see what his taste was. Expensive, according to the bill in his hand. A policeman who wanted to look like a gentleman! He laughed sharply: a ratcatcher with pretensions — was that what he was? A somewhat ridiculous figure. The thought hurt and he pushed it away with a black humor.

In other drawers there were envelopes, notepaper, good quality — vanity again! Whom did he write to? There was also sealing wax, string, a paper knife and scissors, a number of minor items of convenience. It was not until the tenth drawer that he found the personal correspondence. They were all in the same hand, to judge from the formation of the letters a young person, or someone of slight education. Only one person wrote to him — or only one whose letters he had considered worth keeping. He opened the first, angry with himself that his hands were shaking.

It was very simple, beginning "Dear William," full of homely news, and ending "your loving sister, Beth."

He put it down, the round characters burning in front of him, dizzy and overwhelmed with excitement and relief, and perhaps a shadow of disappointment he forced away. He had a sister, there was someone who knew him, had always known him; more than that, who cared. He picked up the letter again quickly, almost tearing it in his clumsiness to reread it. It was gentle, frank, and yes, it was affectionate; it must be, one did not speak so openly to someone one did not trust, and care for.

And yet there was nothing in it that was any kind of reply, no reference to anything he had written to her. Surely he did write? He could not have treated such a woman with cavalier disregard.

What kind of a man was he? If he had ignored her, not written, then there must be a reason. How could he explain himself, justify anything, when he could not remember? It was like being accused, standing in the dock with no defense.

It was long, painful moments before he thought to look for the address. When he did it came as a sharp, bewildering surprise — it was in Northumberland. He repeated it over and over to himself, aloud. It sounded familiar, but he could not place it. He had to go to the bookcase and search for an atlas to look it up. Even so he could not see it for several minutes. It was very small, a name in fine letters on the coast, a fishing village.

A fishing village! What was his sister doing there? Had she married and gone there? The surname on the envelope was Bannerman. Or had he been born there, and then come south to London? He laughed sharply. Was that the key to his pretension? He was a provincial fisherman's son, with eyes on passing himself off as something better?

When? When had he come?

He realized with a shock he did not know how old he was. He still had not looked at himself in the glass. Why not? Was he afraid of it? What did it matter how a man looked?

And yet he was trembling.

He swallowed hard and picked up the oil lamp from the desk. He walked slowly into the bedroom and put the lamp on the dresser. There must be a glass there, at least big enough to shave himself.

It was on a swivel; that was why he had not noticed it before, his eye had been on the silver brush. He set the lamp down and slowly tipped the glass.

The face he saw was dark and very strong, broad, slightly aquiline nose, wide mouth, rather thin upper lip, lower lip fuller, with an old scar just below it, eyes intense luminous gray in the flickering light. It was a powerful face, but not an easy one. If there was humor it would be harsh, of wit rather than laughter. He could have been anything between thirty-five and forty-five.

He picked up the lamp and walked back to the main room, finding the way blindly, his inner eye still seeing the face that had stared back at him from the dim glass. It was not that it displeased him especially, but it was the face of a stranger, and not one easy to know.

The following day he made his decision. He would travel north to see his sister. She would at least be able to tell him his childhood, his family. And to judge from her letters, and the recent date of the last, she still held him in affection, whether he deserved it or not. He wrote in the morning telling her simply that he had had an accident but was considerably recovered now, and intended to visit her when he was well enough to make the journey, which he expected to be no more than another day or two at the outside.

Among the other things in the desk drawer he found a modest sum of money. Apparently he was not extravagant except at the tailor, the clothes in his wardrobe were impeccably cut and of first-quality fabric, and possibly the bookshop — if the contents of the case were his. Other than that he had saved regularly, but if for any particular purpose there was no note of it, and it hardly mattered now. He gave Mrs. Worley what she asked for a further month's rent on account — minus the food he would not consume while he was away — and informed her he was going to visit his sister in Northumberland.

"Very good idea." She nodded her head sagaciously. "More'n time you paid her a visit, if yer ask me. Not that yer did, o' course! I'm not one to interfere" — she drew in her breath — "but yer in't bin orf ter see 'er since I known yer — an that's some years now. An' the poor soul writes to yer reg'lar — although w'en yer writes back I'm blessed if I know!"

She put the money in her pocket and looked at him closely.

"Well, you look after yerself — eat proper and don't go doin' any daft caperin's around chasin' folk. Let ruffians alone an' mind for yerself for a space." And with that parting advice she smoothed her apron again and turned away, her boot heels clicking down the corridor towards the kitchen.

It was August fourth when he boarded the train in London and settled himself for the long journey.

Northumberland was vast and bleak, wind roaring over treeless, heather-darkened moors, but there was a simplicity about its tumultuous skies and clean earth that pleased him enormously. Was it familiar to him, memories stirring from childhood, or only beauty that would have woken the same emotion in him had it been as unknown as the plains of the moon? He stood a long time at the station, bag in his hand, staring out at the hills before he finally made move to begin. He would have to find a conveyance of some kind: he was eleven miles from the sea and the hamlet he wanted. In normal health he might well have walked it, but he was still weak. His rib ached when he breathed deeply, and he had not yet the full use of his broken arm.

It was not more than a pony cart, and he had paid handsomely for it, he thought. But he was glad enough to have the driver take him to his sister's house, which he asked for by name, and deposit him and his bag on the narrow street in front of the door. As the wheels rattled away over the cobbles he conquered his thoughts, the apprehension and the sense of an irretrievable step, and knocked loudly.

He was about to knock again when the door swung open and a pretty, fresh-faced woman stood on the step. She was bordering on the plump and had strong dark hair and features reminiscent of his own only in the broad brow and some echo of cheekbones. Her eyes were blue and her nose had the strength without the arrogance, and her mouth was far softer. All this flashed into his mind, with the realization that she must be Beth, his sister. She would find him inexplicable, and probably be hurt, if he did not know her.

"Beth." He held out his hands.

Her face broke into a broad smile of delight.

"William! I hardly knew you, you've changed so much! We got your letter — you said an accident — are you hurt badly? We didn't expect you so soon —" She blushed.

"Not that you aren't very welcome, of course." Her accent was broad Northumberland, and he found it surprisingly pleasing to the ear. Was that familiarity again, or only the music of it after London?

"William?" She was staring at him. "Come inside — you must be tired out, and hungry." She made as if to pull him physically into the house.

He followed her, smiling in a sudden relief. She knew him; apparently she held no grudge for his long absence or the letters he had not written. There was a naturalness about her that made long explanations unnecessary. And he realized he was indeed hungry.

The kitchen was small but scrubbed clean; in fact the table was almost white. It woke no chord of memory in him at all. There were warm smells of bread and baked fish and salt wind from the sea. For the first time since waking in the hospital, he found himself beginning to relax, to ease the knots out.

Gradually, over bread and soup, he told her the facts he knew of the accident, inventing details where the story was so bare as to seem evasive. She listened while she continued to stir her cooking on the stove, warm the flat-iron and then began on a series of small children's clothes and a man's Sunday white shirt. If it was strange to her, or less than credible, she gave no outward sign. Perhaps the whole world of London was beyond her knowledge anyway, and inhabited by people who lived incomprehensible lives which could not be hoped to make sense to ordinary people.

It was the late summer dusk when her husband came in, a broad, fair man with wind-scoured face and mild features. His gray eyes still seemed tuned to the sea. He greeted Monk with friendly surprise, but no sense of dismay or of having been disturbed in his feelings, or the peace of his home.

No one asked Monk for explanations, even the three shy children returned from chores and play, and since he had none to give, the matter was passed over. It was a strange mark of the distance between them, which he observed with a wry pain, that apparently he had never shared enough of himself with his only family that they noticed the omission.

Day succeeded day, sometimes golden bright, sun hot when the wind was offshore and the sand soft under his feet. Other times it swung east off the North Sea and blew with sharp chill and the breath of storm. Monk walked along the beach, feeling it rip at him, beating his face, tearing at his hair, and the very size of it was at once frightening and comforting. It had nothing to do with people;

it was impersonal, indiscriminate.

He had been there a week, and was feeling the strength of life come back to him, when the alarm was called. It was nearly midnight and the wind screaming around the stone corners of the houses when the shouts came and the hammering on the door.

Rob Bannerman was up within minutes, oilskins and seaboots on still almost in his sleep. Monk stood on the landing in bewilderment, confused; at first no explanation came to his mind as to the emergency. It was not until he saw Beth's face when she ran to the window, and he followed her and saw below them the dancing lanterns and the gleam of light on moving figures, oilskins shining in the rain, that he realized what it was. Instinctively he put his arm around Beth, and she moved fractionally closer to him, but her body was stiff. Under her breath she was praying, and there were tears in her voice.

Rob was already out of the house. He had spoken to neither of them, not even hesitated beyond touching Beth's hand as he passed her.

It was a wreck, some ship driven by the screaming winds onto the outstretched fingers of rock, with God knew how many souls clinging to the sundering planks, water already swirling around their waists.

After the first moment of shock, Beth ran

upstairs again to dress, calling to Monk to do the same, then everything was a matter of finding blankets, heating soup, rebuilding fires ready to help the survivors — if, please God, there were any.

The work went on all night, the lifeboats going backwards and forwards, men roped together. Thirty-five people were pulled out of the sea, ten were lost. Survivors were all brought back to the few homes in the village. Beth's kitchen was full of white-faced shivering people and she and Monk plied them with hot soup and what comforting words they could think of.

Nothing was stinted. Beth emptied out every last morsel of food without a thought as to what her own family might eat tomorrow. Every stitch of dry clothing was brought out and offered.

One woman sat in the corner too numb with grief for her lost husband even to weep. Beth looked at her with a compassion that made her beautiful. In a moment between tasks Monk saw her bend and take the woman's hands, holding them between her own to press some warmth into them, speaking to her gently as if she had been a child.

Monk felt a sudden ache of loneliness, of being an outsider whose involvement in this passion of suffering and pity was only chance.

He contributed nothing but physical help; he could not even remember whether he had ever done it before, whether these were his people or not. Had he ever risked his life without grudge or question as Rob Bannerman did? He hungered with a terrible need for some part in the beauty of it. Had he ever had courage, generosity? Was there anything in his past to be proud of, to cling to?

There was no one he could ask —

The moment passed and the urgency of the present need overtook him again. He bent to pick up a child shaking with terror and cold, and wrapped it in a warm blanket, holding it close to his own body, stroking it with soft, repetitive words as he might a frightened animal.

By dawn it was over. The seas were still running high and hard, but Rob was back, too tired to speak and too weary with loss of those the sea had taken. He simply took off his wet clothes in the kitchen and climbed up to bed.

A week later Monk was fully recovered physically; only dreams troubled him, vague nightmares of fear, sharp pain and a sense of being violently struck and losing his balance, then a suffocation. He woke gasping, his heart racing and sweat on his skin, his breath rasping, but nothing was left except the fear, no thread to unravel towards recollection. The need to return to London became more pressing. He had found his distant past, his beginnings, but memory was virgin blank and Beth could tell him nothing whatsoever of his life since leaving, when she was still little more than a child. Apparently he had not written of it, only trivialities, items of ordinary news such as one might read in the journals or newspapers, and small matters of his welfare and concern for hers. This was the first time he had visited her in eight years, something he was not proud to learn. He seemed a cold man, obsessed with his own ambition. Had that compelled him to work so hard, or had he been so poor? He would like to think there was some excuse, but to judge from the money in his desk at Grafton Street, it had not lately been finance.

He racked his brains to recall any emotion, any flash of memory as to what sort of man he was, what he had valued, what sought. Nothing came, no explanations for his self-absorption.

He said good-bye to her and Rob, thanking them rather awkwardly for their kindness, surprising and embarrassing them, and because of it, himself too; but he meant it so deeply. Because they were strangers to him, he felt as if they had taken him in, a stranger, and offered him acceptance, even trust. They looked confused, Beth coloring shyly. But he did not try to explain; he did not have words, nor did he wish them to know.

London seemed enormous, dirty and indifferent when he got off the train and walked out of the ornate, smoke-grimed station. He took a hansom to Grafton Street, announced his return to Mrs. Worley, then went upstairs and changed his clothes from those worn and crumpled by his journey. He took himself to the police station Runcorn had named when speaking to the nurse. With the experience of Beth and Northumberland behind him he began to feel a little confidence. It was still another essay into the unknown, but with each step accomplished without unpleasant surprise, his apprehension lessened.

When he climbed out of the cab and paid the driver he stood on the pavement. The police station was as unfamiliar as everything else — not strange, simply without any spark of familiarity at all. He opened the doors and went inside, saw the sergeant at the duty desk and wondered how many hundreds of times before he had done exactly this.

" 'Arternoon, Mr. Monk." The man looked

up with slight surprise, and no pleasure. "Nasty haccident. Better now, are yer, sir?"

There was a chill in his voice, a wariness. Monk looked at him. He was perhaps forty, round-faced, mild and perhaps a trifle indecisive, a man who could be easily befriended, and easily crushed. Monk felt a stirring of shame, and knew no reason for it whatever, except the caution in the man's eyes. He was expecting Monk to say something to which he would not be able to reply with assurance. He was a subordinate, and slower with words, and he knew it.

"Yes I am, thank you." Monk could not remember the man's name to use it. He felt contempt for himself — what kind of a man embarrasses someone who cannot retaliate? Why? Was there some long history of incompetence or deceit that would explain such a thing?

"You'll be wantin' Mr. Runcorn, sir." The sergeant seemed to notice no change in Monk, and to be keen to speed him on his way.

"Yes, if he's in — please?"

The sergeant stepped aside a little and allowed Monk through the counter.

Monk stopped, feeling ridiculous. He had no idea which way to go, and he would raise suspicion if he went the wrong way. He had a hot, prickly sensation that there would be little allowance made for him — he was not liked.

"You o'right, sir?" the sergeant said anxiously.

"Yes — yes I am. Is Mr. Runcorn still" — he took a glance around and made a guess — "at the top of the stairs?"

"Yes sir, right w'ere 'e always was!"

"Thank you." And he set off up the steps rapidly, feeling a fool.

Runcorn was in the first room on the corridor. Monk knocked and went in. It was dark and littered with papers and cabinets and baskets for filing, but comfortable, in spite of a certain institutional bareness. Gas lamps hissed gently on the walls. Runcorn himself was sitting behind a large desk, chewing a pencil.

"Ah!" he said with satisfaction when Monk came in. "Fit for work, are you? About time. Best thing, work. Good for a man to work. Well, sit down then, sit down. Think better sitting down."

Monk obeyed, his muscles tight with tension. He imagined his breathing was so loud it must be audible above the gas.

"Good. Good," Runcorn went on. "Lot of cases, as always; I'll wager there's more stolen in some quarters of this city than is ever bought or sold honestly." He pushed away

43

a pile of papers and set his pen in its stand. "And the Swell Mob's been getting worse. All these enormous crinolines. Crinolines were made to steal from, so many petticoats on no one can feel a dip. But that's not what I had in mind for you. Give you a good one to get your teeth into." He smiled mirthlessly.

Monk waited.

"Nasty murder." He leaned back in his chair and looked directly at Monk. "Haven't managed to do anything about it, though heaven knows we've tried. Had Lamb in charge. Poor fellow's sick and taken to his bed. Put you on the case; see what you can do. Make a good job of it. We've got to turn up some kind of result."

"Who was killed?" Monk asked. "And when?"

"Feller called Joscelin Grey, younger brother of Lord Shelburne, so you can see it's rather important we tidy it up." His eyes never left Monk's face. "When? Well that's the worst part of it — rather a while ago, and we haven't turned up a damned thing. Nearly six weeks now — about when you had your accident, in fact, come to think of it, exactly then. Nasty night, thunderstorm and pouring with rain. Probably some ruffian followed him home, but made a very nasty job of it, bashed the poor feller about to an awful state. Newspapers in an outrage, naturally, crying for justice, and what's the world coming to, where are the police, and so on. We'll give you everything poor Lamb had, of course, and a good man to work with, name of Evan, John Evan; worked with Lamb till he took ill. See what you can do, anyway. Give them something!"

"Yes sir." Monk stood up. "Where is Mr. Evan?"

"Out somewhere; trail's pretty cold. Start tomorrow morning, bright and early. Too late now. Go home and get some rest. Last night of freedom, eh? Make the best of it; tomorrow I'll have you working like one of those railway diggers!"

"Yes sir." Monk excused himself and walked out. It was already darkening in the street and the wind was laden with the smell of coming rain. But he knew where he was going, and he knew what he would do tomorrow, and it would be with identity — and purpose.

CHAPTER TWO

Monk arrived early to meet John Evan and find out what Lamb had so far learned of the murder of Lord Shelburne's brother, Joscelin Grey.

He still had some sense of apprehension; his discoveries about himself had been commonplace, such small things as one might learn of anyone, likes and dislikes, vanities — his wardrobe had plainly shown him those — discourtesies, such as had made the desk sergeant nervous of him. But the remembered warmth of Northumberland was still with him and it was enough to buoy up his spirits. And he must work! The money would not last much longer.

John Evan was a tall young man, and lean almost to the point of appearing frail, but Monk judged from the way he stood that it was a deception; he might well be wiry under that rather elegant jacket, and the air with which he wore his clothes was a natural grace rather than effeminacy. His face was sensitive, all eyes and nose, and his hair waved back from his brow thick and honey brown. Above all he appeared intelligent, which was both necessary to Monk and frightening. He was not yet ready for a companion of such quick sight, or subtlety of perception.

But he had no choice in the matter. Runcorn introduced Evan, banged a pile of papers on the wide, scratched wooden table in Monk's office, a good-sized room crammed with filing drawers and bookcases and with one sash window overlooking an alley. The carpet was a domestic castoff, but better than the bare wood, and there were two leather-seated chairs. Runcorn went out, leaving them alone.

Evan hesitated for a moment, apparently not wishing to usurp authority, then as Monk did not move, he put out a long finger and touched the top of the pile of papers.

"Those are all the statements from the witnesses, sir. Not very helpful, I'm afraid."

Monk said the first thing that came to him.

"Were you with Mr. Lamb when they were taken?"

"Yes sir, all except the street sweeper; Mr. Lamb saw him while I went after the cabby."

"Cabby?" For a moment Monk had a wild hope that the assailant had been seen, was known, that it was merely his whereabouts that were needed. Then the thought died immediately. It would hardly have taken them six weeks if it were so simple. And more than that, there had been in Runcorn's face a challenge, even a kind of perverse satisfaction.

"The cabby that brought Major Grey home, sir," Evan said, demolishing the hope apologetically.

"Oh." Monk was about to ask him if there was anything useful in the man's statement, then realized how inefficient he would appear. He had all the papers in front of him. He picked up the first, and Evan waited silently by the window while he read.

It was in neat, very legible writing, and headed at the top was the statement of Mary Ann Brown, seller of ribbons and laces in the street. Monk imagined the grammar to have been altered somewhat from the original, and a few aspirates put in, but the flavor was clear enough.

"I was standing in my usual place in Doughty Street near Mecklenburg Square, like as I always do, on the corner, knowing as how there is ladies living in many of them buildings, especially ladies as has their own maids what does sewing for them, and the like."

Question from Mr. Lamb: "So you were there at six o'clock in the evening?"

48

"I suppose I must have been, though I carsen't tell the time, and I don't have no watch. But I see'd the gentleman arrive what was killed. Something terrible, that is, when even the gentry's not safe."

"You saw Major Grey arrive?"

"Yes sir. What a gentleman he looked, all happy and jaunty, like."

"Was he alone?"

"Yes sir, he was."

"Did he go straight in? After paying the cabby, of course."

"Yes sir, he did."

"What time did you leave Mecklenburg Square?"

"Don't rightly know, not for sure. But I heard the church clock at St. Mark's strike the quarter just afore I got there."

"Home?"

"Yes sir."

"And how far is your home from Mecklenburg Square?"

"About a mile, I reckon."

"Where do you live?"

"Off the Pentonville Road, sir."

"Half an hour's walk?"

"Bless you, no sir, more like quarter. A sight too wet to be hanging around, it was. Besides, girls as hang around that time of an evening gets themselves misunderstood, or worse."

49

"Quite. So you left Mecklenburg Square about seven o'clock."

"Reckon so."

"Did you see anyone else go into Number Six, after Mr. Grey?"

"Yes sir, one other gentleman in a black coat with a big fur collar."

There was a note in brackets after the last statement to say it had been established that this person was a resident of the apartments, and no suspicion attached to him.

The name of Mary Ann Brown was written in the same hand at the bottom, and a rough cross placed beside it.

Monk put it down. It was a statement of only negative value; it made it highly unlikely that Joscelin Grey had been followed home by his murderer. But then the crime had happened in July, when it was light till nine in the evening. A man with murder, or even robbery, on his mind would not wish to be seen so close to his victim.

By the window Evan stood still, watching him, ignoring the clatter in the street beyond, a drayman shouting as he backed his horse, a coster calling his wares and the hiss and rattle of carriage wheels.

Monk picked up the next statement, in the name of Alfred Cressent, a boy of eleven who swept a crossing at the corner of Mecklenburg

Square and Doughty Street, keeping it clear of horse droppings principally, and any other litter that might be let fall.

His contribution was much the same, except that he had not left Doughty Street until roughly half an hour after the ribbon girl.

The cabby claimed to have picked Grey up at a regimental club a little before six o'clock, and driven him straight to Mecklenburg Square. His fare had done no more than pass the time of day with him, some trivial comment about the weather, which had been extraordinarily unpleasant, and wished him a good night upon leaving. He could recall nothing more, and to the best of his knowledge they had not been followed or especially remarked by anyone. He had seen no unusual or suspicious characters in the neighborhood of Guilford Street or Mecklenburg Square, either on the way there or on his departure, only the usual peddlers, street sweepers, flower sellers and a few gentlemen of unobtrusive appearance who might have been clerks returning home after a long day's work, or pickpockets awaiting a victim, or any of a hundred other things. This statement also was of no real help.

Monk put it on top of the other two, then looked up and found Evan's gaze still on him, shyness tinged with a faint, self-deprecating humor. Instinctively he liked Evan — or could it be just loneliness, because he had no friend, no human companionship deeper than the courtesies of office or the impersonal kindness of Mrs. Worley fulfilling her "Christian duty." Had he had friends before, or wanted them? If so, where were they? Why had no one welcomed him back? Not even a letter. The answer was unpleasant, and obvious: he had not earned such a thing. He was clever, ambitious — a rather superior ratcatcher. Not appealing. But he must not let Evan see his weakness. He must appear professional, in command.

"Are they all like this?" he asked.

"Pretty much," Evan replied, standing more upright now that he was spoken to. "Nobody saw or heard anything that has led us even to a time or a description. For that matter, not even a definitive motive."

Monk was surprised; it brought his mind back to the business. He must not let it wander. It would be hard enough to appear efficient without woolgathering.

"Not robbery?" he asked.

Evan shook his head and shrugged very slightly. Without effort he had the elegance Monk strove for, and Runcorn missed absolutely.

"Not unless he was frightened off," he answered. "There was money in Grey's wallet, and several small, easily portable ornaments of value around the room. One fact that might be worth something, though: he had no watch on. Gentlemen of his sort usually have rather good watches, engraved, that sort of thing. And he did have a watch chain."

Monk sat on the edge of the table.

"Could he have pawned it?" he asked. "Did anyone see him with a watch?" It was an intelligent question, and it came to him instinctively. Even well-to-do men sometimes ran short of ready money, or dressed and dined beyond their means and were temporarily embarrassed. How had he known to ask that? Perhaps his skill was so deep it was not dependent on memory?

Evan flushed faintly and his hazel eyes looked suddenly awkward.

"I'm afraid we didn't find out, sir. I mean, the people we asked didn't seem to recall clearly; some said they remembered something about a watch, others that they didn't. We couldn't get a description of one. We wondered if he might have pawned it too; but we didn't find a ticket, and we tried the local pawnshops."

"Nothing?"

Evan shook his head. "Nothing at all, sir."

"So we wouldn't know it, even if it turned up?" Monk said disappointedly, jerking his hand at the door. "Some miserable devil could walk in here sporting it, and we should be none the wiser. Still, I daresay if the killer took it, he will have thrown it into the river when the hue and cry went up anyway. If he didn't he's too daft to be out on his own." He twisted around to look at the pile of papers again and riffled through them untidily. "What else is there?"

The next was the account of the neighbor opposite, one Albert Scarsdale, very bare and prickly. Obviously he had resented the inconsideration, the appalling bad taste of Grey in getting himself murdered in Mecklenburg Square, and felt the less he said about it himself the sooner it would be forgotten, and the sooner he might dissociate himself from the whole sordid affair.

He admitted he thought he had heard someone in the hallway between his apartment and that of Grey at about eight o'clock, and possibly again at about quarter to ten. He could not possibly say whether it was two separate visitors or one arriving and then later leaving; in fact he was not sure beyond doubt that it had not been a stray animal, a cat, or the porter making a round — from his choice of words he regarded the two as roughly equal. It might even have been an errand boy who had lost his way, or any of a dozen other things. He had been occupied with his own interests, and had seen and heard nothing of remark. The statement was signed and affirmed as being true with an ornate and ill-natured signature.

Monk looked across at Evan, still waiting by the window.

"Mr. Scarsdale sounds like an officious and unhelpful little beggar," he observed dryly.

"Very, sir," Evan agreed, his eyes shining but no smile touching his lips. "I imagine it's the scandal in the buildings; attracts notice from the wrong kind of people, and very bad for the social reputation."

"Something less than a gentleman." Monk made an immediate and cruel judgment.

Evan pretended not to understand him, although it was a patent lie.

"Less than a gentleman, sir?" His face puckered.

Monk spoke before he had time to think, or wonder why he was so sure.

"Certainly. Someone secure in his social status would not be affected by a scandal whose proximity was only a geographical accident, and nothing to do with him personally. Unless, of course, he knew Grey well?"

"No sir," Evan said, but his eyes showed his total comprehension. Obviously Scarsdale still smarted under Grey's contempt, and Monk could imagine it vividly. "No, he disclaimed all personal acquaintance with him. And either that's a lie or else it's very odd. If he were the gentleman he pretends to be, he would surely know Grey, at least to speak to. They were immediate neighbors, after all."

Monk did not want to court disappointment.

"It may be no more than social pretension, but worth inquiring into." He looked at the papers again. "What else is there?" He glanced up at Evan. "Who found him, by the way?"

Evan came over and sorted out two more reports from the bottom of the pile. He handed them to Monk.

"Cleaning woman and the porter, sir. Their accounts agree, except that the porter says a bit more, because naturally we asked him about the evening as well."

Monk was temporarily lost. "As well?"

Evan flushed faintly with irritation at his own lack of clarity.

"He wasn't found until the following morning, when the woman who cleans and cooks for him arrived and couldn't get in. He wouldn't give her a key, apparently didn't trust her: he let her in himself, and if he wasn't there then she just went away and came another time. Usually he leaves some message with the porter."

"I see. Did he go away often? I assume we

know where to?" There was an instinctive edge of authority to his voice now, and impatience.

"Occasional weekend, so far as the porter knows; sometimes longer, a week or two at a country house, in the season," Evan answered.

"So what happened when Mrs. — what's her name? — arrived?"

Evan stood almost to attention. "Huggins. She knocked as usual, and when she got no answer after the third attempt, she went down to see the porter, Grimwade, to find out if there was a message. Grimwade told her he'd seen Grey arrive home the evening before, and he hadn't gone out yet, and to go back and try again. Perhaps Grey had been in the bathroom, or unusually soundly asleep, and no doubt he'd be standing at the top of the stairs by now, wanting his breakfast."

"But of course he wasn't," Monk said unnecessarily.

"No. Mrs. Huggins came back a few minutes later all fussed and excited — these women love a little drama — and demanded that Grimwade do something about it. To her endless satisfaction" — Evan smiled bleakly — "she said that he'd be lying there murdered in his own blood, and they should do something immediately, and call the police. She must have told me that a dozen times." He pulled a small face. "She's now convinced she has the second sight, and I spent a quarter of an hour persuading her that she should stick to cleaning and not give it up in favor of fortune-telling — although she's already a heroine, of sorts, in the local newspaper — and no doubt the local pub!"

Monk found himself smiling too.

"One more saved from a career in the fairground stalls — and still in the service of the gentry," he said. "Heroine for a day — and free gin every time she retells it for the next six months. Did Grimwade go back with her?"

"Yes, with a master key, of course."

"And what did they find, exactly?" This was perhaps the most important single thing: the precise facts of the discovery of the body.

Evan concentrated till Monk was not sure if he was remembering the witness's words or his own sight of the rooms.

"The small outer hall was perfectly orderly," Evan began. "Usual things you might expect to see, stand for coats and things, and hats, rather a nice stand for sticks, umbrellas and so forth, box for boots, a small table for calling cards, nothing else. Everything was neat and tidy. The door from that led directly into the sitting room; and the bedroom and utilities were off that." A shadow passed over his extraordinary face. He relaxed a little and half unconsciously leaned against the window frame.

"That next room was a different matter altogether. The curtains were drawn and the gas was still burning, even though it was daylight outside. Grey himself was lying half on the floor and half on the big chair, head downward. There was a lot of blood, and he was in a pretty dreadful state." His eyes did not waver, but it was with an effort, and Monk could see it. "I must admit," he continued, "I've seen a few deaths, but this was the most brutal, by a long way. The man had been beaten to death with something quite thin — I mean not a bludgeon — hit a great many times. There had pretty obviously been a fight. A small table had been knocked over and one leg broken off, several ornaments were on the floor and one of the heavy stuffed chairs was on its back, the one he was half on." Evan was frowning at the memory, and his skin was pale. "The other rooms hadn't been touched." He moved his hands in a gesture of negation. "It was quite a while before we could get Mrs. Huggins into a sane state of mind, and then persuade her to look at the kitchen and bedroom; but eventually she did, and said they were just as she had left them the previous day."

Monk breathed in deeply, thinking. He must say something intelligent, not some fatuous comment on the obvious. Evan was watching him, waiting. He found himself self-conscious.

"So it would appear he had a visitor some time in the evening," he said more tentatively than he had wished. "Who quarreled with him, or else simply attacked him. There was a violent fight, and Grey lost."

"More or less," Evan agreed, straightening up again. "At least we don't have anything else to go on. We don't even know if it was a stranger, or someone he knew."

"No sign of a forced entry?"

"No sir. Anyway, no burglar is likely to force an entry into a house when all the lights are still on."

"No." Monk cursed himself for an idiotic question. Was he always such a fool? There was no surprise in Evan's face. Good manners? Or fear of angering a superior not noted for tolerance? "No, of course not," he said aloud. "I suppose he wouldn't have been surprised by Grey, and then lit the lights to fool us?"

"Unlikely sir. If he were that coolheaded, he surely would have taken some of the valuables? At least the money in Grey's wallet, which would be untraceable."

Monk had no answer for that. He sighed

and sat down behind the desk. He did not bother to invite Evan to sit also. He read the rest of the porter's statement.

Lamb had asked exhaustively about all visitors the previous evening, if there had been any errand boys, messengers, even a stray animal. Grimwade was affronted at the very suggestion. Certainly not: errand boys were always escorted to the appropriate place, or if possible their errands taken over by Grimwade himself. No stray animal had ever tainted the buildings with its presence — dirty things, stray animals, and apt to soil the place. What did the police think he was — were they trying to insult him?

Monk wondered what Lamb had replied. He would certainly have had a pointed answer to the man on the relative merits of stray animals and stray humans! A couple of acid retorts rose to his mind even now.

Grimwade swore there had been two visitors and only two. He was perfectly sure no others had passed his window. The first was a lady, at about eight o'clock, and he would sooner not say upon whom she called; a question of private affairs must be treated with discretion, but she had not visited Mr. Grey, of that he was perfectly certain. Anyway, she was a very slight creature, and could not possibly have inflicted the injuries suffered by the dead man.

The second visitor was a man who called upon a Mr. Yeats, a longtime resident, and Grimwade had escorted him as far as the appropriate landing himself and seen him received.

Whoever had murdered Grey had obviously either used one of the other visitors as a decoy or else had already been in the building in some guise in which he had so far been overlooked. So much was logic.

Monk put the paper down. They would have to question Grimwade more closely, explore even the minutest possibilities; there might be something.

Evan sat down on the window ledge.

Mrs. Huggins's statement was exactly as Evan had said, if a good deal more verbose. Monk read it only because he wanted time to think.

Afterwards he picked up the last one, the medical report. It was the one he found most unpleasant, but maybe also the most necessary. It was written in a small, precise hand, very round. It made him imagine a small doctor with round spectacles and very clean fingers. It did not occur to him until afterwards to wonder if he had ever known such a person, and if it was the first wisp of memory returning.

The account was clinical in the extreme, discussing the corpse as if Joscelin Grey were a species rather than an individual, a human being full of passions and cares, hopes and humors who had been suddenly and violently cut off from life, and who must have experienced terror and extreme pain in the few minutes that were being examined so unemotionally.

The body had been looked at a little after nine thirty A.M. It was that of a man in his early thirties, of slender build but well nourished, and not apparently suffering from any illness or disability apart from a fairly recent wound in the upper part of the right leg, which might have caused him to limp. The doctor judged it to be a shallow wound, such as he had seen in many ex-soldiers, and to be five or six months old. The body had been dead between eight and twelve hours; he could not be more precise than that.

The cause of death was obvious for anyone to see: a succession of violent and powerful blows about the head and shoulders with some long, thin instrument. A heavy cane or stick seemed the most likely.

Monk put down the report, sobered by the details of death. The bare language, shorn of all emotion, perversely brought the very feeling of it closer. His imagination saw it sharply, even smelled it, conjuring up the sour odor and the buzz of flies. Had he dealt with many murders? He could hardly ask.

"Very unpleasant," he said without looking up at Evan.

"Very," Evan agreed, nodding. "Newspapers made rather a lot of it at the time. Been going on at us for not having found the murderer. Apart from the fact that it's made a lot of people nervous, Mecklenburg Square is a pretty good area, and if one isn't safe there, where is one safe? Added to that, Joscelin Grey was a well-liked, pretty harmless young ex-officer, and of extremely good family. He served in the Crimea and was invalided out. He had rather a good record, saw the Charge of the Light Brigade, badly wounded at Sebastopol." Evan's face pinched a little with a mixture of embarrassment and perhaps pity. "A lot of people feel his country has let him down, so to speak, first by allowing this to happen to him, and then by not even catching the man who did it." He looked across at Monk, apologizing for the injustice, and because he understood it. "I know that's unfair, but a spot of crusading sells newspapers; always helps to have a cause, you know! And of course the running patterers have composed a lot of songs about it — returning hero and all that!"

Monk's mouth turned down at the corners.

"Have they been hitting hard?"

"Rather," Evan admitted with a little shrug. "And we haven't a blind thing to go on. We've been over and over every bit of evidence there is, and there's simply nothing to connect him to anyone. Any ruffian could have come in from the street if he dodged the porter. Nobody saw or heard anything useful, and we are right where we started." He got up gloomily and came over to the table.

"I suppose you'd better see the physical evidence, not that there is much. And then I daresay you'd like to see the flat, at least get a feeling for the scene?"

Monk stood up also.

"Yes I would. You never know, something might suggest itself." Although he could imagine nothing. If Lamb had not succeeded, and this keen, delicate young junior, what was he going to find? He felt failure begin to circle around him, dark and enclosing. Had Runcorn given him this knowing he would fail? Was it a discreet and efficient way of getting rid of him without being seen to be callous? How did he even know for sure that Runcorn was not an old enemy? Had he done him some wrong long ago? The possibility was cold and real. The shadowy outline of himself that had appeared so far was devoid of any quick acts of compassion, any sudden gentlenesses or warmth to seize hold of and to like. He was discovering himself as a stranger might, and what he saw so far did not excite his admiration. He liked Evan far more than he liked himself.

He had imagined he had hidden his complete loss of memory, but perhaps it was obvious, perhaps Runcorn had seen it and taken this chance to even some old score? God, how he wished he knew what kind of man he was, had been. Who loved him, who hated him — and who had what cause? Had he ever loved a woman, or any woman loved him? He did not even know that!

Evan was walking quickly ahead of him, his long legs carrying him at a surprisingly fast pace. Everything in Monk wanted to trust him, and yet he was almost paralyzed by his ignorance. Every foothold he trod on dissolved into quicksand under his weight. He knew nothing. Everything was surmise, constantly shifting guesses.

He behaved automatically, having nothing but instinct and ingrained habit to rely on.

The physical evidence was astonishingly bare, set out like luggage in a lost-and-found office, ownerless; pathetic and rather embarrassing remnants of someone else's life, robbed now of their purpose and meaning — a little like his own belongings in Grafton Street, objects whose history and emotion were obliterated.

He stopped beside Evan and picked up a pile of clothes. The trousers were dark, well cut from expensive material, now spotted with blood. The boots were highly polished and only slightly worn on the soles. Personal linen was obviously changed very recently; shirt was expensive; cravat silk, the neck and front heavily stained. The jacket was tailored to high fashion, but ruined with blood, and a ragged tear in the sleeve. They told him nothing except a hazard at the size and build of Joscelin Grey, and an admiration for his pocket and his taste. There was nothing to be deduced from the bloodstains, since they already knew what the injuries had been.

He put them down and turned to Evan, who was watching him.

"Not very helpful, is it, sir?" Evan looked at them with a mixture of unhappiness and distaste. There was something in his face that might have been real pity. Perhaps he was too sensitive to be a police officer.

"No, not very," Monk agreed dryly. "What else was there?"

"The weapon, sir." Evan reached out and picked up a heavy ebony stick with a silver head. It too was encrusted with blood and hair.

Monk winced. If he had seen such grisly

things before, his immunity to them had gone with his memory.

"Nasty." Evan's mouth turned down, his hazel eyes on Monk's face.

Monk was conscious of him, and abashed. Was the distaste, the pity, for him? Was Evan wondering why a senior officer should be so squeamish? He conquered his revulsion with an effort and took the stick. It was unusually heavy.

"War wound," Evan observed, still watching him. "From what witnesses say, he actually walked with it: I mean it wasn't an ornament."

"Right leg." Monk recalled the medical report. "Accounts for the weight." He put the stick down. "Nothing else?"

"Couple of broken glasses, sir, and a decanter broken too. Must have been on the table that was knocked over, from the way it was lying; and a couple of ornaments. There's a drawing of the way the room was, in Mr. Lamb's file, sir. Not that I know of anything it can tell us. But Mr. Lamb spent hours poring over it."

Monk felt a quick stab of compassion for Lamb, then for himself. He wished for a moment that he could change places with Evan, leave the decisions, the judgments to someone else, and disclaim the failure. He hated failure!

He realized now what a driving, burning desire he had to solve this crime — to win — to wipe that smile off Runcorn's face.

"Oh — money, sir." Evan pulled out a cardboard box and opened it. He picked up a fine pigskin wallet and, separately, several gold sovereigns, a couple of cards from a club and an exclusive dining room. There were about a dozen cards of his own, engraved "Major the Honorable Joscelin Grey, Six, Mecklenburg Square, London."

"Is that all?" Monk asked.

"Yes sir, the money is twelve pounds seven shillings and sixpence altogether. If he were a thief, it's odd he didn't take that."

"Perhaps he was frightened — he may have been hurt himself." It was the only thing he could think of. He motioned Evan to put the box away. "I suppose we'd better go and have a look at Mecklenburg Square."

"Yes sir." Evan straightened up to obey. "It's about half an hour's walk. Are you well enough for it yet?"

"A couple of miles? For heaven's sake, man, it was my arm I broke, not both my legs!" He reached sharply for his jacket and hat.

Evan had been a little optimistic. Against the wind and stepping carefully to avoid peddlers and groups of fellow travelers on the footpath, and traffic and horse dung in the streets, it was a good forty minutes before they reached Mecklenburg Square, walked around the gardens and stopped outside Number 6. The boy sweeping the crossing was busy on the corner of Doughty Street, and Monk wondered if it was the same one who had been there on that evening in July. He felt a rush of pity for the child, out in all weather, often with sleet or snow driving down the funnel of the high buildings, dodging in among the carriages and drays, shoveling droppings. What an abysmal way to earn your keep. Then he was angry with himself — that was stupid and sentimental nonsense. He must deal with reality. He squared his chest and marched into the foyer. The porter was standing by a small office doorway, no more than a cubbyhole.

"Yes sir?" He moved forward courteously, but at the same time blocking their further progress.

"Grimwade?" Monk asked him.

"Yes sir?" The man was obviously surprised and embarrassed. "I'm sorry, sir, I can't say as I remember you. I'm not usually bad about faces —" He let it hang, hoping Monk would help him. He glanced across at Evan, and a flicker of memory lit in his face.

"Police," Monk said simply. "We'd like to take another look at Major Grey's flat. You have the key?"

The man's relief was very mixed.

"Oh yes, sir, and we ain't let nobody in. Lock's still as Mr. Lamb left it."

"Good, thank you." Monk had been preparing to show some proof of his identity, but the porter was apparently quite satisfied with his recognition of Evan, and turned back to his cubbyhole to fetch the key.

He came with it a moment later and led them upstairs with the solemnity due the presence of the dead, especially those who had died violently. Monk had the momentarily unpleasant impression that they would find Joscelin Grey's corpse still lying there, untouched and waiting for them.

It was ridiculous, and he shook it off fiercely. It was beginning to assume the repetitive quality of a nightmare, as if events could happen more than once.

"Here we are, sir." Evan was standing at the door, the porter's key in his hand. "There's a back door as well, of course, from the kitchen, but it opens onto the same landing, about twelve yards along, for services, errands, and the like."

Monk recalled his attention.

"But one would still have to pass the porter at the gate?"

"Oh yes, sir. I suppose there's not much point in having a porter if there's a way in

71

without passing him. Then any beggar or peddler could bother you." He pulled an extraordinary face as he pondered the habits of his betters. "Or creditors!" he added lugubriously.

"Quite." Monk was sardonic.

Evan turned and put the key in the lock. He seemed reluctant, as if a memory of the violence he had seen there still clung to the place, repelling him. Or was Monk projecting his own fancies onto someone else?

The hallway inside was exactly as Evan had described it: neat, blue Georgian with white paint and trims, very clean and elegant. He saw the hat stand with its place for sticks and umbrellas, the table for calling cards and so forth. Evan was ahead of him, his back stiff, opening the door to the main room.

Monk walked in behind him. He was not sure what he was expecting to see; his body was tight also, as if waiting for an attack, for something startling and ugly on the senses.

The decoration was elegant, and had originally been expensive, but in the flat light, without gas or fire, it looked bleak and commonplace enough. The Wedgwood-blue walls seemed at a glance immaculate, the white trims without scar, but there was a fine rime of dust over the polished wood of the chiffonier and the desk and a film dulling colors of the carpet.

His eye traveled automatically to the window first, then around the other furniture — ornate side table with piecrust edges, a jardiniere with a Japanese bowl on it, a mahogany bookcase — till he came to the overturned heavy chair, the broken table, companion to the other, the pale inner wood a sharp scar against its mellowed satin skin. It looked like an animal with legs in the air.

Then he saw the bloodstain on the floor. There was not a lot of it, not widespread at all, but very dark, almost black. Grey must have bled a lot in that one place. He looked away from it, and noticed then that much of what seemed pattern on the carpet was probably lighter, spattered blood. On the far wall there was a picture crooked, and when he walked over to it and looked more carefully, he saw a bruise in the plaster, and the paint was faintly scarred. It was a bad watercolor of the Bay of Naples, all harsh blues with a conical Mount Vesuvius in the background.

"It must have been a considerable fight," he said quietly.

"Yes sir," Evan agreed. He was standing in the middle of the floor, not sure what to do. "There were several bruises on the body, arms and shoulders, and one knuckle was skinned. I should say he put up a good fight."

Monk looked at him, frowning.

73

"I don't remember that in the medical report."

"I think it just said 'evidences of a struggle,' sir. But that's pretty obvious from the room here, anyway." His eyes glanced around at it as he spoke. "There's blood on that chair as well." He pointed to the heavy stuffed one lying on its back. "That's where he was, with his head on the floor. We're looking for a violent man, sir." He shivered slightly.

"Yes." Monk stared around, trying to visualize what must have happened in this room nearly six weeks ago, the fear and the impact of flesh on flesh, shadows moving, shadows because he did not know them, furniture crashing over, glass splintering. Then suddenly it became real, a flash sharper and more savage than anything his imagination had called up, red moments of rage and terror, the thrashing stick; then it was gone again, leaving him trembling and his stomach sick. What in God's name had happened in this room that the echo of it still hung here, like an agonized ghost, or a beast of prey?

He turned and walked out, oblivious of Evan behind him, fumbling for the door. He had to get out of here, into the commonplace and grubby street, the sound of voices, the demanding present. He was not even sure if Evan followed him.

CHAPTER THREE

As soon as Monk was out in the street he felt better, but he could not completely shake the impression that had come to him so violently. For an instant it had been real enough to bring his body out in hot, drenching sweat, and then leave him shivering and nauseous at the sheer bestiality of it.

He put up his hand shakily and felt his cheek wet. There was a hard, angular rain driving on the wind.

He turned to see Evan behind him. But if Evan had felt that savage presence, there was no sign of it in his face. He was puzzled, a little concerned, but Monk could read no more in him than that.

"A violent man." Monk repeated Evan's words through stiff lips.

"Yes sir," Evan said solemnly, catching up to him. He started to say something, then changed his mind. "Where are you going to begin, sir?" he asked instead.

It was a moment before Monk could collect his thoughts to reply. They were walking along Doughty Street to Guilford Street.

"Recheck the statements," he answered, stopping on the corner curb as a hansom sped past them, its wheels spraying filth. "That's the only place I know to begin. I'll do the least promising first. The street sweeper boy is there." He indicated the child a few yards from them, busy shoveling dung and at the same time seizing a penny that had been thrown him. "Is he the same one?"

"I think so, sir; I can't see his face from here." That was something of a euphemism; the child's features were hidden by dirt and the hazards of his occupation, and the top half of his head was covered by an enormous cloth cap, to protect him from the rain.

Monk and Evan stepped out onto the street towards him.

"Well?" Monk asked when they reached the boy.

Evan nodded.

Monk fished for a coin; he felt obliged to recompense the child for the earnings he might lose in the time forfeited. He came up with twopence and offered it.

"Alfred, I am a policeman. I want to talk to you about the gentleman who was killed in Number Six in the square."

The boy took the twopence.

"Yeah guv, I dunno anyfink what I din't tell ve ovver rozzer as asked me." He sniffed and looked up hopefully. A man with twopence to spend was worth pleasing.

"Maybe not," Monk conceded, "but I'd like to talk to you anyway." A tradesman's cart clattered by them towards Grey's Inn Road, splashing them with mud and leaving a couple of cabbage leaves almost at their feet. "Can we go to the footpath?" Monk inquired, hiding his distaste. His good boots were getting soiled and his trouser legs were wet.

The boy nodded, then acknowledging their lack of skill in dodging wheels and hooves with the professional's condescension for the amateur, he steered them to the curb again.

"Yers guv?" he asked hopefully, pocketing the twopence somewhere inside the folds of his several jackets and sniffing hard. He refrained from wiping his hand across his face in deference to their superior status.

"You saw Major Grey come home the day he was killed?" Monk asked with appropriate gravity.

"Yers guv, and vere weren't nob'dy followin' 'im, as fer as I could see."

"Was the street busy?"

"No, wicked night, it were, for July, raining summink 'orrible. Nob'dy much abaht, an'

77

everyone goin' as fast as veir legs'd carry 'em."

"How long have you been at this crossing?"

"Couple o' years." His faint fair eyebrows rose with surprise; obviously it was a question he had not expected.

"So you must know most of the people who live around here?" Monk pursued.

"Yers, reckon as I do." His eyes sparked with sudden sharp comprehension. "Yer means did I see anyone as don't belong?"

Monk nodded in appreciation of his sagacity. "Precisely."

" 'E were bashed ter deaf, weren't 'e?"

"Yes." Monk winced inwardly at the appropriateness of the phrase.

"Ven yer in't lookin' fer a woman?"

"No," Monk agreed. Then it flashed through his mind that a man might dress as a woman, if perhaps it were not some stranger who had murdered Grey, but a person known to him, someone who had built up over the years the kind of hatred that had seemed to linger in that room. "Unless it were a large woman," he added, "and very strong, perhaps."

The boy hid a smirk. "Woman as I saw was on the little side. Most women as makes veir way vat fashion gotta look fetchin' like, or leastways summink as a woman oughter.

Don't see no great big scrubbers 'round 'ere, an' no dollymops." He sniffed again and pulled his mouth down fiercely to express his disapproval. "Only the class for gennelmen as 'as money like wot vey got 'ere." He gestured towards the elaborate house fronts behind him towards the square.

"I see." Monk hid a brief amusement. "And you saw some woman of that type going into Number Six that evening?" It was probably not worth anything, but every clue must be followed at this stage.

"No one as don't go vere reg'lar, guv."

"What time?"

"Jus' as I were goin' 'ome."

"About half past seven?"

"S' right."

"How about earlier?"

"Only wot goes inter Number Six, like?"

"Yes."

He shut his eyes in deep concentration, trying to be obliging; there might be another twopence. "One of ve gennelmen wot lives in Number Six came 'ome wiv another gent, little feller wiv one o' vem collars wot looks like fur, but all curly."

"Astrakhan?" Monk offered.

"I dunno wot yer calls it. Anyway, 'e went in abaht six, an' I never sawed 'im come aht. Vat any 'elp to yer, guv?"

"It might be. Thank you very much." Monk spoke to him with all seriousness, gave him another penny, to Evan's surprise, and watched him step blithely off into the thoroughfare, dodging in between traffic, and take up his duties again.

Evan's face was brooding, thoughtful, but whether on the boy's answers or his means of livelihood, Monk did not ask.

"The ribbon seller's not here today." Evan looked up and down the Guilford Street footpath. "Who do you want to try next?"

Monk thought for a moment. "How do we find the cabby? I presume we have an address for him?"

"Yes sir, but I doubt he'd be there now."

Monk turned to face the drizzling east wind. "Not unless he's ill," he agreed. "Good evening for trade. No one will walk in this weather if they can ride." He was pleased with that — it sounded intelligent, and it was the merest common sense. "We'll send a message and have him call at the police station. I don't suppose he can add anything to what he's already said anyway." He smiled sarcastically. "Unless, of course, he killed Grey himself!"

Evan stared at him, his eyes wide, unsure for an instant whether he was joking or not. Then Monk suddenly found he was not sure himself. There was no reason to believe the cabby. Perhaps there had been heated words between them, some stupid quarrel, possibly over nothing more important than the fare. Maybe the man had followed Grey upstairs, carrying a case or a parcel for him, seen the flat, the warmth, the space, the ornaments, and in a fit of envy become abusive. He may even have been drunk; he would not be the first cabby to bolster himself against cold, rain and long hours a little too generously. God help them, enough of them died of bronchitis or consumption anyway.

Evan was still looking at him, not entirely sure.

Monk spoke his last thoughts aloud.

"We must check with the porter that Grey actually entered alone. He might easily have overlooked a cabby carrying baggage, invisible, like a postman; we become so used to them, the eye sees but the mind doesn't register."

"It's possible." Belief was strengthening in Evan's voice. "He could have set up the mark for someone else, noted addresses or wealthy fares, likely-looking victims for someone. Could be a well-paying sideline?"

"Could indeed." Monk was getting chilled standing on the curb. "Not as good as a sweep's boy for scouting the inside of a house,

81

but better for knowing when the victim is out. If that was his idea, he certainly mistook Grey." He shivered. "Perhaps we'd better call on him rather than send a message; it might make him nervous. It's late; we'll have a bit of lunch at the local public house, and see what the gossip is. Then you can go back to the station this afternoon and find out if anything is known about this cabby, what sort of reputation he has — if we know him, for example, and who his associates are. I'll try the porter again, and if possible some of the neighbors."

The local tavern turned out to be a pleasant, noisy place which served them ale and a sandwich with civility, but something of a wary eye, knowing them to be strangers and perhaps guessing from their clothes that they were police. One or two ribald comments were offered, but apparently Grey had not patronized the place and there was no particular sympathy for him, only the communal interest in the macabre that murder always wakens.

Afterwards Evan went back to the police station, and Monk returned to Mecklenburg Square, and Grimwade. He began at the beginning.

"Yes sir," Grimwade said patiently. "Major Grey came in about quarter after six, or a bit before, and 'e looked 'is usual self to me."

"He came by cab?" Monk wanted to be sure he had not led the man, suggested the answer he wanted.

"Yes sir."

"How do you know? Did you see the cab?"

"Yes sir, I did." Grimwade wavered between nervousness and affront. "Stopped right by the door 'ere; not a night to walk a step as you didn't 'ave to."

"Did you see the cabby?"

" 'Ere, I don't understand what you're getting after." Now the affront was definitely warning.

"Did you see him?" Monk repeated.

Grimwade screwed up his face. "Don't recall as I did," he conceded.

"Did he get down off the box, help Major Grey with a parcel, or a case or anything?"

"Not as I remember; no, 'e didn't."

"Are you sure?"

"Yes I am sure. 'E never got through that door."

That theory at least was gone. He should have been too old at this to be disappointed, but he had no experience to call on. It seemed to come to him easily enough, but possibly most of it was common sense.

"He went upstairs alone?" He tried a last time, to remove every vestige of doubt.

"Yes sir, 'e did."

"Did he speak to you?"

"Nothing special, as I can think of. I don't remember nothin', so I reckon it can't 'ave bin. 'E never said nothin' about bein' afraid, or as 'e was expecting anyone."

"But there were visitors to the buildings that afternoon and evening?"

"Nobody as would be a-murderin' anyone."

"Indeed?" Monk raised his eyebrows. "You're not suggesting Major Grey did that to himself in some kind of bizarre accident, are you? Or of course there is the other alternative — that the murderer was someone already here?"

Grimwade's face changed rapidly from resignation through extreme offense to blank horror. He stared at Monk, but no words came to his brain.

"You have another idea? I thought not — neither have I." Monk sighed. "So let us think again. You said there were two visitors after Major Grey came in: one woman at about seven o'clock, and a man later on at about quarter to ten. Now, who did the woman come to see, Mr. Grimwade, and what did she look like? And please, no cosmetic alterations for the sake of discretion!"

"No wot?"

"Tell me the truth, man!" Monk snapped. "It could become very embarrassing for your tenants if we have to investigate it for ourselves."

Grimwade glared at him, but he took the point perfectly.

"A local lady of pleasure, sir; called Mollie Ruggles," he said between his teeth. " 'Andsome piece, with red 'air. I know where she lives, but I expec' you understand it would come real gratifyin' if you could see your way clear to bein' discreet about 'oo told yer she was 'ere?" His expression was comical in its effort to expunge his dislike and look appealing.

Monk hid a sour amusement — it would only alienate the man.

"I will," he agreed. It would be in his own interest also. Prostitutes could be useful informants, if well treated. "Who did she come to see?"

"Mr. Taylor, sir; 'e lives in flat number five. She comes to see 'im quite reg'lar."

"And it was definitely her?"

"Yes sir."

"Did you take her to Mr. Taylor's door?"

"Oh no, sir. Reckon as she knows 'er way by now. And Mr. Taylor — well . . ." He hunched his shoulders. "It wouldn't be tactful, now would it, sir? Not as I suppose you 'as ter be tactful, in your callin'!" he added meaningfully.

"No." Monk smiled slightly. "So you didn't leave your position when she came?"

"No sir."

"Any other women come, Mr. Grimwade?" He looked at him very directly.

Grimwade avoided his eyes.

"Do I have to make my own inquiries?" Monk threatened. "And leave detectives here to follow people?"

Grimwade was shocked. His head came up sharply.

"You wouldn't do that, sir! They're gentlemen as lives 'ere! They'd leave. They won't put up with that kind o' thing!"

"Then don't make it necessary."

"You're an 'ard man, Mr. Monk." But there was a grudging respect behind the grievance in his voice. That was small victory in itself.

"I want to find the man who killed Major Grey," Monk answered him. "Someone came into these buildings, found his way upstairs into that flat and beat Major Grey with a stick, over and over until he was dead, and then went on beating him afterwards." He saw Grimwade wincing, and felt the revulsion himself. He remembered the horror he had felt when actually standing in the room. Did walls retain memory? Could violence or hatred remain in the air after a deed was finished, and touch the sensitive, the imaginative with a shadow of the horror?

No, that was ridiculous. It was not the imaginative, but the nightmare-ridden who felt such things. He was letting his own fear, the horror of his still occasionally recurring dreams and the hollowness of his past extend into the present and warp his judgment. Let a little more time pass, a little more identity build, learn to know himself, and he would grow firmer memories in reality. His sanity would come back; he would have a past to root himself in, other emotions, and people.

Or could it be — could it possibly be that it was some sort of mixed, dreamlike, distorted recollection coming back to him? Could he be recalling snatches of the pain and fear he must have felt when the coach turned over on him, throwing him down, imprisoning him, the scream of terror as the horse fell, the cab driver flung headlong, crushed to death on the stones of the street? He must have known violent fear, and in the instant before unconsciousness, have felt sharp, even blinding pain as his bones broke. Was that what he had sensed? Had it been nothing to do with Grey at all, but his own memory returning, just a flash, a sensation, the fierceness of the feeling long before the clarity of actual perception came back?

He must learn more of himself, what he had

been doing that night, where he was going, or had come from. What manner of man had he been, whom had he cared for, whom wronged, or whom owed? What had mattered to him? Every man had relationships, every man had feelings, even hungers; every man who was alive at all stirred some sort of passions in others. There must be people somewhere who had feelings about him — more than professional rivalry and resentment — surely? He could not have been so negative, of so little purpose that his whole life had left no mark on another soul.

As soon as he was off duty, he must leave Grey, stop building the pattern piece by piece of his life, and take up the few clues to his own, place them together with whatever skill he possessed.

Grimwade was still waiting for him, watching curiously, knowing that he had temporarily lost his attention.

Monk looked back at him.

"Well, Mr. Grimwade?" he said with sudden softness. "What other women?"

Grimwade mistook the lowering tone for a further threat.

"One to see Mr. Scarsdale, sir; although 'e paid me 'andsome not to say so."

"What time was it?"

"About eight o'clock."

Scarsdale had said he had heard someone at eight. Was it his own visitor he was talking about, trying to play safe, in case someone else had seen her too?

"Did you go up with her?" He looked at Grimwade.

"No sir, on account o' she'd bin 'ere before, an' knew 'er way, like. An' I knew as she was expected." He gave a slight leer, knowingly, as man to man.

Monk acknowledged it. "And the one at quarter to ten?" he asked. "The visitor for Mr. Yeats, I think you said? Had he been here before too?"

"No sir. I went up with 'im, 'cos 'e didn't know Mr. Yeats very well an' 'adn't called 'ere before. I said that to Mr. Lamb."

"Indeed." Monk forbore from criticizing him over the omission of Scarsdale's woman. He would defeat his own purpose if he antagonized him any further. "So you went up with this man?"

"Yes sir." Grimwade was firm. "Saw Mr. Yeats open the door to 'im."

"What did he look like, this man?"

Grimwade screwed up his eyes. "Oh, big man, 'e was, solid and — 'ere!" His face dropped. "You don't think it was 'im wot done it, do yer?" He breathed out slowly, his eyes wide. "Gor' — it must 'a' bin.

When I thinks of it now!"

"It might have," Monk agreed cautiously. "It's possible. Would you know him if you saw him again?"

Grimwade's face fell. "Ah, there you 'ave me, sir; I don't think as I would. Yer see, I didn't see 'im close, like, when 'e was down 'ere. An' on the stairs I only looked where I was goin', it bein' dark. 'E 'ad one o' them 'eavy coats on, as it was a rotten night an' rainin' somethin' wicked. A natural night for anyone to 'ave 'is coat turned up an' 'is 'at drawn down. I reckon 'e were dark, that's about all I could say fer sure, an' if 'e 'ad a beard, it weren't much of a one."

"He was probably clean-shaven, and probably dark." Monk tried to keep the disappointment out of his voice. He must not let irritation push the man into saying something to please him, something less than true.

" 'E were big, sir," Grimwade said hopefully. "An' 'e were tall, must 'ave bin six feet. That lets out a lot o' people, don't it?"

"Yes, yes it does," Monk agreed. "When did he leave?"

"I saw 'im out o' the corner o' me eye, sir. 'E went past me window at about 'alf past ten, or a little afore."

"Out of the corner of your eye? You're sure it was him?"

" 'Ad ter be; 'e didn't leave before, ner after, an' 'e looked the same. Same coat, and 'at, same size, same 'eight. Weren't no one else like that lives 'ere."

"Did you speak to him?"

"No, 'e looked like 'e was in a bit of an 'urry. Maybe 'e wanted ter get 'ome. It were a beastly rotten night, like I said, sir; not fit fer man ner beast."

"Yes I know. Thank you, Mr. Grimwade. If you remember anything more, tell me, or leave a message for me at the police station. Good day."

"Good day, sir," Grimwade said with intense relief.

Monk decided to wait for Scarsdale, first to tax him with his lie about the woman, then to try and learn something more about Joscelin Grey. He realized with faint surprise that he knew almost nothing about him, except the manner of his death. Grey's life was as blank an outline as his own, a shadow man, circumscribed by a few physical facts, without color or substance that could have induced love or hate. And surely there had been hate in whoever had beaten Grey to death, and then gone on hitting and hitting him long after there was any purpose? Was there something in Grey, innocently or knowingly, that had generated such a passion, or was he merely the catalyst of something he knew nothing of — and its victim?

He went back outside into the square and found a seat from which he could see the entrance of Number 6.

It was more than an hour before Scarsdale arrived, and already beginning to get darker and colder, but Monk was compelled by the importance it had for him to wait.

He saw him arrive on foot, and followed a few paces after him, inquiring from Grimwade in the hall if it was indeed Scarsdale.

"Yes sir," Grimwade said reluctantly, but Monk was not interested in the porter's misfortunes.

"D' yer need me ter take yer up?"

"No thank you; I'll find it." And he took the stairs two at a time and arrived on the landing just as the door was closing. He strode across from the stair head and knocked briskly. There was a second's hesitation, then the door opened. He explained his identity and his errand tersely.

Scarsdale was not pleased to see him. He was a small, wiry man whose handsomest feature was his fair mustache, not matched by slightly receding hair and undistinguished features. He was smartly, rather fussily dressed.

"I'm sorry, I can't see you this evening," he said brusquely. "I have to change to go out for dinner. Call again tomorrow, or the next day."

Monk was the bigger man, and in no mood to be summarily dismissed.

"I have other people to call on tomorrow," he said, placing himself half in Scarsdale's way. "I need certain information from you now."

"Well I haven't any —" Scarsdale began, retreating as if to close the door.

Monk stepped forward. "For example, the name of the young woman who visited you the evening Major Grey was killed, and why you lied to us about her."

It had the result Monk had wished. Scarsdale stopped dead. He fumbled for words, trying to decide whether to bluff it out or attempt a little late conciliation. Monk watched him with contempt.

"I — er," Scarsdale began. "I — think you have misunderstood — er . . ." He still had not made the decision.

Monk's face tightened. "Perhaps you would prefer to discuss it somewhere more discreet than the hallway?" He looked towards the stairs, and the landing where other doorways led off — including Grey's.

"Yes — yes I suppose so." Scarsdale was now acutely uncomfortable, a fine beading of sweat on his brow. "Although I really cannot tell you anything germane to the issue, you know." He backed into his own entranceway and Monk followed. "The young lady who visited me has no connection with poor Grey, and she neither saw nor heard anyone else!"

Monk closed the main door, then followed him into the sitting room.

"Then you asked her, sir?" He allowed his face to register interest.

"Yes, of course I did!" Scarsdale was beginning to regain his composure, now that he was among his own possessions. The gas was lit and turned up; it glowed gently on polished leather, old Turkey carpet and silver-framed photographs. He was a gentleman, facing a mere member of Peel's police. "Naturally, if there had been anything that could have assisted you in your work, I should have told you." He used the word *work* with a vague condescension, a mark of the gulf between them. He did not invite Monk to sit, and remained standing himself, rather awkwardly between the sideboard and the sofa.

"And this young lady, of course, is well known to you?" Monk did not try to keep his own sarcastic contempt out of his voice.

Scarsdale was confused, not sure whether to affect insult or to prevaricate because he could think of nothing suitably crushing. He chose the latter.

"I beg your pardon?" he said stiffly.

"You can vouch for her truthfulness," Monk elaborated, his eyes meeting Scarsdale's with a bitter smile. "Apart from her . . . *work*" — he deliberately chose the same word — "she is a person of perfect probity?"

Scarsdale colored heavily and Monk realized he had lost any chance of cooperation from him.

"You exceed your authority!" Scarsdale snapped. "And you are impertinent. My private affairs are no concern of yours. Watch your tongue, or I shall be obliged to complain to your superiors." He looked at Monk and decided this was not a good idea. "The woman in question has no reason to lie," he said stiffly. "She came up alone and left alone, and saw no one at either time, except Grimwade, the porter; and you can ascertain that from him. No one enters these buildings without his permission, you know." He sniffed very slightly. "This is not a common rooming house!" His eyes glanced for a second at the handsome furnishings, then back at Monk.

"Then it follows that Grimwade must have seen the murderer," Monk replied, keeping his eyes on Scarsdale's face.

Scarsdale saw the imputation, and paled; he was arrogant, and perhaps bigoted, but he was not stupid.

Monk took what he believed might well be his best chance.

"You are a gentleman of similar social standing" — he winced inwardly at his own hypocrisy — "and an immediate neighbor of Major Grey's; you must be able to tell me something about him personally. I know nothing."

Scarsdale was happy enough to change the subject, and in spite of his irritation, flattered.

"Yes, of course," he agreed quickly. "Nothing at all?"

"Nothing at all," Monk conceded.

"He was a younger brother of Lord Shelburne, you know?" Scarsdale's eyes widened, and at last he walked to the center of the room and sat down on a hard-backed, carved chair. He waved his arm vaguely, giving Monk permission to do so too.

"Indeed?" Monk chose another hard-backed chair so as not to be below Scarsdale.

"Oh yes, a very old family," Scarsdale said with relish. "The Dowager Lady Shelburne, his mother, of course, was the eldest daughter of the Duke of Ruthven, at least I think it was he; certainly the duke of somewhere."

"Joscelin Grey," Monk reminded him.

"Oh. Very pleasant fellow; officer in the Crimea, forgotten which regiment, but a very distinguished record." He nodded vigorously. "Wounded at Sebastopol, I think he said, then invalided out. Walked with a limp, poor devil. Not that it was disfiguring. Very good-looking fellow, great charm, very well liked, you know."

"A wealthy family?"

"Shelburne?" Scarsdale was faintly amused by Monk's ignorance and his confidence was beginning to return. "Of course. But I suppose you know, or perhaps you don't." He looked Monk up and down disparagingly. "But naturally all the money went to the eldest son, the present Lord Shelburne. Always happens that way, everything to the eldest, along with the title. Keeps the estates whole, otherwise everything would be in bits and pieces, d'you understand? All the power of the land gone!"

Monk controlled his sense of being patronized; he was perfectly aware of the laws of primogeniture.

"Yes, thank you. Where did Joscelin Grey's money come from?"

Scarsdale waved his hands, which were small, with wide knuckles and very short nails. "Oh business interests, I presume. I don't believe he had a great deal, but he didn't appear in any want. Always dressed well. Tell a lot from a fellow's clothes, you know." Again he looked at Monk with a faint curl of his lip, then saw the quality of Monk's jacket and the portion of his shirt that was visible, and changed his mind, his eyes registering confusion.

"And as far as you know he was neither married nor betrothed?" Monk kept a stiff face and hid at least most of his satisfaction.

Scarsdale was surprised at his inefficiency. "Surely you know that?"

"Yes, we know there was no official arrangement," Monk said, hastening to cover his mistake. "But you are in a position to know if there was any other relationship, anyone in whom he — had an interest?"

Scarsdale's rather full mouth turned down at the corners.

"If you mean an arrangement of convenience, not that I am aware of. But then a man of breeding does not inquire into the personal tastes — or accommodations — of another gentleman."

"No, I didn't mean a financial matter," Monk answered with the shadow of a sneer. "I meant some lady he might have — admired — or even been courting."

Scarsdale colored angrily. "Not as far as I know."

"Was he a gambler?"

"I have no idea. I don't gamble myself, except with friends, of course, and Grey was not among them. I haven't heard anything, if that's what you mean."

Monk realized he would get no more this evening, and he was tired. His own mystery was heavy at the back of his mind. Odd, how emptiness could be so intrusive. He rose to his feet.

"Thank you, Mr. Scarsdale. If you should hear anything to throw light on Major Grey's last few days, or who might have wished him harm, I am sure you will let us know. The sooner we apprehend this man, the safer it will be for everyone."

Scarsdale rose also, his face tightening at the subtle and unpleasant reminder that it had happened just across the hall from his own flat, threatening his security even as he stood there.

"Yes, naturally," he said a little sharply. "Now if you will be good enough to permit me to change — I have a dinner engagement, you know."

Monk arrived at the police station to find Evan waiting for him. He was surprised at the sharpness of his pleasure at seeing him. Had he always been a lonely person, or was this just the isolation from memory, from all that might have been love or warmth in himself? Surely there was a friend somewhere — someone with whom he had shared pleasure and pain, at least common experience? Had there been no woman — in the past, if not now — some stored-up memory of tenderness, of laughter or tears? If not he must have been a cold fish. Was there perhaps some tragedy? Or some wrong?

The nothingness was crowding in on him, threatening to engulf the precarious present. He had not even the comfort of habit.

Evan's acute face, all eyes and nose, was infinitely welcome.

"Find out anything, sir?" He stood up from the wooden chair in which he had been sitting.

"Not a lot," Monk answered with a voice that was suddenly louder, firmer than the words warranted. "I don't see much chance of anyone having got in unseen, except the man who visited Yeats at about quarter to ten. Grimwade says he was a biggish man, muffled up, which is reasonable on a night like that. He says he saw him leave at roughly half past ten. Took him upstairs, but didn't see him closely, and wouldn't recognize him again."

Evan's face was a mixture of excitement and frustration.

"Damn!" he exploded. "Could be almost anyone then!" He looked at Monk quickly. "But at least we have a fair idea how he got in. That's a great step forward; congratulations, sir!"

Monk felt a quick renewal of his spirits. He knew it was not justified; the step was actually very small. He sat down in the chair behind the desk.

"About six feet," he reiterated. "Dark and probably clean-shaven. I suppose that does narrow it a little."

"Oh it narrows it quite a lot, sir," Evan said eagerly, resuming his own seat. "At least we know that it wasn't a chance thief. If he called on Yeats, or said he did, he had planned it, and taken the trouble to scout the building. He knew who else lived there. And of course there's Yeats himself. Did you see him?"

"No, he wasn't in, and anyway I'd rather find out a little about him before I face him with it."

"Yes, yes of course. If he knew anything, he's bound to deny it, I suppose." But the anticipation was building in Evan's face, his voice; even his body was tightening under the elegant coat as if he expected some sudden action here in the police station. "The cabby was no good, by the way. Perfectly respectable fellow, worked this area for twenty years, got a wife and seven or eight children. Never been any complaints against him."

"Yes," Monk agreed. "Grimwade said he hadn't gone into the building, in fact doesn't think he even got off the box."

"What do you want me to do about this Yeats?" Evan asked, a very slight smile curling his lips. "Sunday tomorrow, a bit hard to turn up much then."

Monk had forgotten.

"You're right. Leave it till Monday. He's been there for nearly seven weeks; it's hardly a hot trail."

Evan's smile broadened rapidly.

"Thank you, sir. I did have other ideas for Sunday." He stood up. "Have a good week-end, sir. Good night."

Monk watched him go with a sense of loss. It was foolish. Of course Evan would have friends, even family, and interests, perhaps a woman. He had never thought of that before. Somehow it added to his own sense of isolation. What did he normally do with his own time? Had he friends outside duty, some pursuit or pastime he enjoyed? There had to be more than this single-minded, ambitious man he had found so far.

He was still searching his imagination uselessly when there was a knock on the door, hasty, but not assertive, as though the person would have been pleased enough had there been no answer and he could have left again.

"Come in!" Monk said loudly.

The door opened and a stout young man came in. He wore a constable's uniform. His eyes were anxious, his rather homely face pink.

"Yes?" Monk inquired.

The young man cleared his throat. "Mr. Monk, sir?"

"Yes?" Monk said again. Should he know this man? From his wary expression there was some history in their past which had been important at least to him. He stood in the middle of the floor, fidgeting his weight from one foot to the other. Monk's wordless stare was making him worse.

"Can I do something for you?" Monk tried to sound reassuring. "Have you something to report?" He wished he could remember the man's name.

"No sir — I mean yes sir, I 'ave something to ask you." He took a deep breath. "There's a report of a watch turned up at a pawnbroker's wot I done this arternoon, sir, an' — an' I thought as it might be summink ter do with your gennelman as was murdered — seein' as 'e didn't 'ave no watch, just a chain, like? Sir." He held a piece of paper with copperplate handwriting on it as if it might explode.

Monk took it and glanced at it. It was the description of a gentleman's gold pocket watch with the initials J.G. inscribed ornately on the cover. There was nothing written inside.

He looked up at the constable.

"Thank you," he said with a smile. "It might well be — right initials. What do you know about it?"

The constable blushed scarlet. "Nuffink much, Mr. Monk. 'E swears blind as it was one of 'is reg'lars as brought it in. But you can't believe anyfink 'e says 'cause 'e would say that, wouldn't 'e? He don't want ter be mixed up in no murder."

Monk glanced at the paper again. The pawnbroker's name and address were there and he could follow up on it any time he chose.

"No, he'd doubtless lie," he agreed. "But we might learn something all the same, if we can prove this was Grey's watch. Thank you — very observant of you. May I keep it?"

"Yes sir. We don't need it; we 'as lots more agin 'im." Now his furious pink color was obviously pleasure, and considerable surprise. He still stood rooted to the spot.

"Was there anything else?" Monk raised his eyebrows.

"No sir! No there in't. Thank you, sir." And the constable turned on his heel and marched out, tripping on the doorsill as he went and rocketing out into the passage.

Almost immediately the door was opened again by a wiry sergeant with a black mustache.

"You o'right, sir?" he asked, seeing Monk's frown.

"Yes. What's the matter with — er." He waved his hand towards the departing figure of the constable, wishing desperately that he knew the man's name.

" 'Arrison?"

"Yes."

"Nothin' — just afeared of you, that's all. Which in't 'ardly surprisin', seein' as 'ow you tore 'im off such a strip in front o' the 'ole station, w'en that macer slipped through 'is fingers — which weren't 'ardly 'is fault, seein' as the feller were a downright contortionist. 'Arder to 'old then a greased pig, 'e were. An' if we'd broke 'is neck we'd be the ones for the 'igh jump before breakfast!"

Monk was confused. He did not know what to say. Had he been unjust to the man, or was there cause for whatever he had said? On the face of it, it sounded as if he had been gratuitously cruel, but he was hearing only one side of the story — there was no one to defend him, to explain, to give his reasons and say what he knew and perhaps they did not.

And rack and tear as he might, there was nothing in his mind, not even Harrison's face — let alone some shred about the incident.

He felt a fool sitting staring up at the critical

eyes of the sergeant, who plainly disliked him, for what he felt was fair cause.

Monk ached to explain himself! Even more he wanted to know for his own understanding. How many incidents would come up like this, things he had done that seemed ugly from the outside, to someone who did not know his side of the story?

"Mr. Monk, sir?"

Monk recalled his attention quickly. "Yes, Sergeant?"

"Thought you might like to know as we got the magsman wot snuffed ol' Billy Marlowe. They'll swing 'im for sure. Right villain."

"Oh — thank you. Well done." He had no idea what the sergeant was talking about, but obviously he was expected to. "Very well done," he added.

"Thank you, sir." The sergeant straightened up, then turned and left, closing the door behind him with a sharp snick.

Monk bent to his work again.

An hour later he left the police station and walked slowly along the dark, wet pavements and found the way back to Grafton Street.

Mrs. Worley's rooms were at least becoming familiar. He knew where to find things, and better than that, they offered privacy: no one would disturb him, intrude on his time to think, to try again to find some thread.

After his meal of mutton stew and dumplings, which were hot and filling, if a little heavy, he thanked Mrs. Worley when she collected the tray, saw her down the stairs, and then began once more to go through the desk. The bills were of little use; he could hardly go to his tailor and say "What kind of man am I? What do I care about? Do you like, or dislike me, and why?" One small comfort he could draw from his accounts was that he appeared to have been prompt in paying them; there were no demand notices, and the receipts were all dated within a few days of presentation. He was learning something, a crumb: he was methodical.

The personal letters from Beth told him much of her: of simplicity, an unforced affection, a life of small detail. She said nothing of hardships or of bitter winters, nothing even of wrecks or the lifeboatmen. Her concern for him was based on her feelings, and seemed to be without knowledge; she simply translated her own affections and interests to his life, and assumed his feelings were the same. He knew without needing deeper evidence that it was because he had told her nothing; perhaps he had not even written regularly. It was an unpleasant thought, and he was harshly ashamed of it. He must write to her soon, compose a letter which would seem rational, and yet perhaps elicit some answer from her which would tell him more.

The following morning he woke late to find Mrs. Worley knocking on the door. He let her in and she put his breakfast on the table with a sigh and a shake of her head. He was obliged to eat it before dressing or it would have grown cold. Afterwards he resumed the search, and again it was fruitless for any sharpening of identity, anything of the man behind the immaculate, rather expensive possessions. They told him nothing except that he had good taste, if a little predictable — perhaps that he liked to be admired? But what was admiration worth if it was for the cost and discretion of one's belongings? A shallow man? Vain? Or a man seeking security he did not feel, making his place in a world that he did not believe accepted him?

The apartment itself was impersonal, with traditional furniture, sentimental pictures. Surely Mrs. Worley's taste rather than his own?

After luncheon he was reduced to the last places to seek: the pockets of his other clothes, jackets hanging in the cupboard. In the best of them, a well-cut, rather formal coat, he found a piece of paper, and on unfolding it carefully, saw that it was a printed sheet for a service of Evensong at a church he did not know.

Perhaps it was close by. He felt a quickening of hope. Maybe he was a member of the congregation. The minister would know him. He might have friends there, a belief, even an office or a calling of some sort. He folded up the paper again carefully and put it in the desk, then went into the bedroom to wash and shave again, and change into his best clothes, and the coat from which the sheet had come. By five o'clock he was ready, and he went downstairs to ask Mrs. Worley where St. Marylebone Church might be.

His disappointment was shattering when she showed complete ignorance. Temper boiled inside him at the frustration. She must know. But her placid, blunt face was expressionless.

He was about to argue, to shout at her that she must know, when he realized how foolish it would be. He would only anger her, drive from himself a friend he sorely needed.

She was staring at him, her face puckered.

"My, you are in a state. Let me ask Mr. Worley for yer; he's a rare fine understanding o' the city. O' course I expect it's on the Marylebone Road, but ezac'ly where I'm sure I wouldn't know. It's a long street, that is."

"Thank you," he said carefully, feeling foolish. "It's rather important."

"Going to a wedding, are yer?" She looked at his carefully brushed dark coat. "What you want is a good cabby, what knows 'is way, and'll get you there nice and prompt, like."

It was an obvious answer, and he wondered why he had not thought of it himself. He thanked her, and when Mr. Worley had been asked, and given his opinion that it might be opposite York Gate, he went out to look for a cab.

Evensong had already begun when he hurried up the steps and into the vestry. He could hear the voices lifted rather thinly in the first hymn. It sounded dutiful rather than joyous. Was he a religious man; or, it would be truer to ask, had he been? He felt no sense of comfort or reverence now, except for the simple beauty of the stonework.

He went in as quickly as he could, walking almost on the sides of his polished boots to make no noise. One or two heads turned, sharp with criticism. He ignored them and slid into a back pew, fumbling for a hymnbook.

Nothing sounded familiar; he followed the hymn because the tune was trite, full of musical clichés. He knelt when everyone else knelt, and rose as they rose. He missed the responses.

When the minister stepped into the pulpit

to speak, Monk stared at him, searching his face for some flicker of memory. Could he go to this man and confide in him the truth, ask him to tell him everything he knew? The voice droned on in one platitude after another; his intention was benign, but so tied in words as to be almost incomprehensible. Monk sank deeper and deeper into a feeling of helplessness. The man did not seem able to remember his own train of thought from one sentence to the next, let alone the nature and passions of his flock.

When the last amen had been sung, Monk watched the people file out, hoping someone would touch his memory, or better still, actually speak to him.

He was about to give up even that when he saw a young woman in black, slender and of medium height, dark hair drawn softly back from a face almost luminous, dark eyes and fragile skin, mouth too generous and too big for it. It was not a weak face, and yet it was one that could have moved easily to laughter, or tragedy. There was a grace in the way she walked that compelled him to watch her.

As she drew level she became aware of him and turned. Her eyes widened and she hesitated. She drew in her breath as if to speak.

He waited, hope surging up inside him, and a ridiculous excitement, as if some exquisite realization were about to come.

Then the moment vanished; she seemed to regain a mastery of herself, her chin lifted a little, and she picked up her skirt unnecessarily and continued on her way.

He went after her, but she was lost in a group of people, two of whom, also dressed in black, were obviously accompanying her. One was a tall, fair man in his mid-thirties with smooth hair and a long-nosed, serious face; the other was a woman of unusual uprightness of carriage and features of remarkable character. The three of them walked towards the street and waiting vehicles and none of them turned their heads again.

Monk rode home in a rage of confusion, fear, and wild, disturbing hope.

CHAPTER
FOUR

But when Monk arrived on Monday morning, breathless and a little late, he was unable to begin investigation on Yeats and his visitor. Runcorn was in his room, pacing the floor and waving a piece of blue notepaper in his hand. He stopped and spun around the moment he heard Monk's feet.

"Ah!" He brandished the paper with a look of bright, shimmering anger, his left eye narrowed almost shut.

The good-morning greeting died on Monk's tongue.

"Letter from upstairs." Runcorn held up the blue paper. "The powers that be are after us again. The Dowager Lady Shelburne has written to Sir Willoughby Gentry, and confided to the said member of Parliament" — he gave every vowel its full value in his volume of scorn for that body — "that she is not happy with the utter lack of success the Metropolitan Police Force is having in apprehending the vile maniac who so foully murdered her son in his own house. No excuses are acceptable for our dilatory and lackadaisical attitude, our total lack of culprits to hand." His face purpled in his offense at the injustice of it, but there was no misery in him, only a feeding rage. "What the hell are you doing, Monk? You're supposed to be such a damn good detective, you've got your eyes on a superintendency — the commissionership, for all I know! So what do we tell this — this ladyship?"

Monk took a deep breath. He was more stunned by Runcorn's reference to himself, to his ambition, than anything in the letter. Was he an overweeningly ambitious man? There was no time for self-defense now; Runcorn was standing in front of him commanding an answer.

"Lamb's done all the groundwork, sir." He gave Lamb the praise that was due him. "He's investigated all he could, questioned all the other residents, street peddlers, locals, anyone who might have seen or known anything." He could see from Runcorn's face that he was achieving nothing, but he persisted. "Unfortunately it was a particularly foul night and everyone was in a hurry, heads down and collars up against the rain. Because it was so wet no one hung around, and with the overcast it was dark earlier than usual."

Runcorn was fidgeting with impatience.

"Lamb spent a lot of time checking out the villains we know," Monk continued. "He's written up in his report that he's spoken to every snout and informer in the area. Not a peep. No one knows anything; or if they do, they're not saying. Lamb was of the opinion they were telling the truth. I don't know what else he could have done." His experience offered nothing, but neither could his intelligence suggest any omission. All his sympathy was with Lamb.

"Constable Harrison found a watch with the initials J.G. on it in a pawnbroker's — but we don't know it was Grey's."

"No," Runcorn agreed fiercely, running his finger with distaste along the deckle edge of the notepaper. It was a luxury he could not afford. "Indeed you don't! So what are you doing, then? Take it to Shelburne Hall — get it identified."

"Harrison's on his way."

"Can't you at least find out how the bloody man got in?"

"I think so," Monk said levelly. "There was a visitor for one of the other residents, a Mr. Yeats. He came in at nine forty-five and left at roughly ten thirty. He was a biggish man, dark, well muffled. He's the only person unaccounted for; the others were women. I don't want to leap to conclusions too soon, but it looks as if he could be the murderer. Otherwise I don't know any way a stranger could have got in. Grimwade locks up at midnight, or earlier if all the residents are in, and after that even they have to ring the bell and get him up."

Runcorn put the letter carefully on Monk's desk.

"And what time did he lock up that night?" he asked.

"Eleven," Monk replied. "No one was out."

"What did Lamb say about this man who visited Yeats?" Runcorn screwed up his face.

"Not much. Apparently he only spoke to Yeats once, and then he spent most of the time trying to find out something about Grey. Maybe he didn't realize the importance of the visitor at that time. Grimwade said he took him up to Yeats's door and Yeats met him. Lamb was still looking for a thief off the street then —"

"Then!" Runcorn leapt on the word, sharp, eager. "So what are you looking for now?"

Monk realized what he had said, and that he meant it. He frowned, and answered as carefully as he could.

"I think I'm looking for someone who knew him, and hated him; someone who intended to kill him."

"Well for God's sake don't say so to the Dowager Lady Shelburne!" Runcorn said dangerously.

"I'm hardly likely to be speaking to her," Monk answered with more than a trace of sarcasm.

"Oh yes you are!" There was a ring of triumph in Runcorn's voice and his big face was glowing with color. "You are going down to Shelburne today to assure Her Ladyship that we are doing everything humanly possible to apprehend the murderer, and that after intensive effort and brilliant work, we at last have a lead to discovering this monster." His lip curled very faintly. "You're generally so blunt, damn near rude, in spite of your fancy airs, she won't take you for a liar." Suddenly his tone altered again and became soft. "Anyway, why do you think it was someone who knew him? Maniacs can kill with a hell of a mess; madmen strike over and over again, hate for no reason."

"Possibly." Monk stared back at him, matching dislike for dislike. "But they don't scout out the names of other residents, call upon them, and then go and kill someone else. If he was merely a homicidal lunatic, why didn't he kill Yeats? Why go and look for Grey?"

Runcorn's eyes were wide; he resented it,

but he took the point.

"Find out everything you can about this Yeats," he ordered. "Discreetly, mind! I don't want him scared away!"

"What about Lady Shelburne?" Monk affected innocence.

"Go and see her. Try to be civil, Monk — make an effort! Evan can chase after Yeats, and tell you whatever he finds when you get back. Take the train. You'll be in Shelburne a day or two. Her Ladyship won't be surprised to see you, after the rumpus she's raised. She demanded a report on progress, in person. You can put up at the inn. Well, off you go then. Don't stand there like an ornament, man!"

Monk took the train on the Great Northern line from the King's Cross Station. He ran across the platform and jumped in, slamming the carriage door just as the engine belched forth a cloud of steam, gave a piercing shriek and jolted forward. It was an exciting sensation, a surge of power, immense, controlled noise, and then gathering speed as they emerged from the cavern of the station buildings out into the sharp late-afternoon sunlight.

Monk settled himself into a vacant seat opposite a large woman in black bombazine with a fur tippet around her neck (in spite of the season) and a black hat on at a fierce angle. She had a packet of sandwiches, which she opened immediately and began to eat. A little man with large spectacles eyed them hopefully, but said nothing. Another man in striped trousers studiously read his *Times*.

They roared and hissed their way past tenements, houses and factories, hospitals, churches, public halls and offices, gradually thinning, more interspersed with stretches of green, until at last the city fell away and Monk stared with genuine pleasure at the beauty of soft countryside spread wide in the lushness of full summer. Huge boughs clouded green over fields heavy with ripening crops and thick hedgerows starred with late wild roses. Coppices of trees huddled in folds of the slow hills, and villages were easily marked by the tapering spires of churches, or the occasional squarer Norman tower.

Shelburne came too quickly, while he was still drinking in the loveliness of it. He grabbed his valise off the rack and opened the door hastily, excusing himself past the fat woman in the bombazine and incurring her silent displeasure. On the platform he inquired of the lone attendant where Shelburne Hall lay, and was told it was less than a mile. The man waved his arm to indicate the direction, then sniffed and added, "But the village be two mile in t'opposite way, and doubtless that be w'ere you're a-goin'."

"No thank you," Monk replied. "I have business at the hall."

The man shrugged. "If'n you say so, sir. Then you'd best take the road left an' keep walking."

Monk thanked him again and set out.

It took him only fifteen minutes to walk from the station entrance to the drive gates. It was a truly magnificent estate, an early Georgian mansion three stories high, with a handsome frontage, now covered in places by vines and creepers, and approached by a sweeping carriageway under beech trees and cedars that dotted a parkland which seemed to stretch towards distant fields, and presumably the home farm.

Monk stood in the gateway and looked for several minutes. The grace of proportion, the way it ornamented rather than intruded upon the landscape, were all not only extremely pleasing but also perhaps indicative of something in the nature of the people who had been born here and grown up in such a place.

Finally he began walking up the considerable distance to the house itself, a further third of a mile, and went around past the outhouses and stables to the servants' entrance. He was received by a rather impatient footman.

"We don't buy at the door," he said coldly, looking at Monk's case.

"I don't sell," Monk replied with more tartness than he had intended. "I am from the Metropolitan Police. Lady Shelburne wished a report on the progress we have made in investigating the death of Major Grey. I have come to give that report."

The footman's eyebrows went up.

"Indeed? That would be the Dowager Lady Shelburne. Is she expecting you?"

"Not that I know of. Perhaps you would tell her I am here."

"I suppose you'd better come in." He opened the door somewhat reluctantly. Monk stepped in, then without further explanation the man disappeared, leaving Monk in the back hallway. It was a smaller, barer and more utilitarian version of the front hall, only without pictures, having only the functional furniture necessary for servants' use. Presumably he had gone to consult some higher authority, perhaps even that autocrat of belowstairs — and sometimes above — the butler. It was several minutes before he returned, and motioned Monk to go with him.

"Lady Shelburne will see you in half an hour." He left Monk in a small parlor adjacent to the housekeeper's room, a suitable place for such persons as policemen; not precisely servants or tradesmen, and most certainly not to be considered as of quality.

Monk walked slowly around the room after the footman had gone, looking at the worn furniture, brown upholstered chairs with bow legs and an oak sideboard and table. The walls were papered and fading, the pictures anonymous and rather puritan reminders of rank and the virtues of duty. He preferred the wet grass and heavy trees sloping down to ornamental water beyond the window.

He wondered what manner of woman she was who could control her curiosity for thirty long minutes rather than let her dignity falter in front of a social inferior. Lamb had said nothing about her. Was it likely he had not even seen her? The more he considered it, the more certain he became. Lady Shelburne would not direct her inquiries through a mere employee, and there had been no cause to question her in anything.

But Monk wanted to question her; if Grey had been killed by a man who hated him, not a maniac in the sense of someone without reason, only insofar as he had allowed a passion to outgrow control until it had finally exploded in murder, then it was imperative Monk learn to know Grey better. Intentionally or not, Grey's mother would surely betray something of him, some honesty through the memories and the grief, that would give color to the outline.

He had had time to think a lot about Grey and formulate questions in his mind by the time the footman returned and conducted him through the green baize door and across the corridor to Lady Fabia's sitting room. It was decorated discreetly with deep pink velvet and rosewood furniture. Lady Fabia herself was seated on a Louis Quinze sofa and when Monk saw her all his preconceptions fled his tongue. She was not very big, but as hard and fragile as porcelain, her coloring perfect, not a blemish on her skin, not a soft, fair hair out of place. Her features were regular, her blue eyes wide, only a slightly jutting chin spoiled the delicacy of her face. And she was perhaps too thin; slenderness had given way to angularity. She was dressed in violet and black, as became someone in mourning, although on her it looked more like something to be observed for one's own dignity than any sign of distress. There was nothing frail in her manner.

"Good morning," she said briskly, dismissing the footman with a wave of her hand. She did not regard Monk with any particular interest and her eyes barely glanced at his face. "You may sit if you wish. I am told you have come to report to me the progress you have made in discovering and apprehending the murderer of my son. Pray proceed."

Opposite him Lady Fabia sat, her back ramrod-straight from years of obedience to governesses, walking as a child with a book on her head for deportment, and riding upright in a sidesaddle in the park or to hounds. There was little Monk could do but obey, sitting reluctantly on one of the ornate chairs and feeling self-conscious.

"Well?" she demanded when he remained silent. "The watch your constable brought was not my son's."

Monk was stung by her tone, by her almost unthinking assumption of superiority. In the past he must have been used to this, but he could not remember; and now it stung with the shallow sharpness of gravel rash, not a wound but a blistering abrasion. A memory of Beth's gentleness came to his mind. She would not have resented this. Why was the difference between them? Why did he not have her soft Northumbrian accent? Had he eradicated it intentionally, washing out his origins in an attempt to appear some kind of gentleman? The thought made him blush for its stupidity.

Lady Shelburne was staring at him.

"We have established the only time a man could have gained entry to the buildings," he replied, still stiff with his own sense of pride.

"And we have a description of the only man who did so." He looked straight into her chilly and rather surprised blue eyes. "He was roughly six feet tall, of solid build, as far as can be judged under a greatcoat. He was dark-complexioned and clean-shaven. He went ostensibly to visit a Mr. Yeats, who also lives in the building. We have not yet spoken to Mr. Yeats —"

"Why not?"

"Because you required that I come and report our progress to you, ma'am."

Her eyebrows rose in incredulity, touched with contempt. The sarcasm passed her by entirely.

"Surely you cannot be the only man directed to conduct such an important case? My son was a brave and distinguished soldier who risked his life for his country. Is this the best with which you can repay him?"

"London is full of crimes, ma'am; and every man or woman murdered is a loss to someone."

"You can hardly equate the death of a marquis's son with that of some thief or indigent in the street!" she snapped back.

"Nobody has more than one life to lose, ma'am; and all are equal before the law, or they should be."

"Nonsense! Some men are leaders, and contribute to society; most do not. My son was one of those who did."

"Some have nothing to —" he began.

"Then that is their own fault!" she interrupted. "But I do not wish to hear your philosophies. I am sorry for those in the gutter, for whatever reason, but they really do not interest me. What are you doing about apprehending this madman who killed my son? Who is he?"

"We don't know —"

"Then what are you doing to find out?" If she had any feelings under her exquisite exterior, like generations of her kind she had been bred to conceal them, never to indulge herself in weakness or vulgarity. Courage and good taste were her household gods and no sacrifice to them was questioned, nor too great, made daily and without fuss.

Monk ignored Runcorn's admonition, and wondered in passing how often he had done so in the past. There had been a certain asperity in Runcorn's tone this morning which surpassed simply frustration with the case, or Lady Shelburne's letter.

"We believe it was someone who knew Major Grey," he answered her. "And planned to kill him."

"Nonsense!" Her response was immediate. "Why should anyone who knew my son have wished to kill him? He was a man of the greatest charm; everyone liked him, even those who barely knew him." She stood up and walked over towards the window, her back half to him. "Perhaps that is difficult for you to understand; but you never met him. Lovel, my eldest son, has the sobriety, the sense of responsibility, and something of a gift to manage men; Menard is excellent with facts and figures. He can make anything profitable; but it was Joscelin who had the charm, Joscelin who could make one laugh." There was a catch in her voice now, the sound of real grief. "Menard cannot sing as Joscelin could; and Lovel has no imagination. He will make an excellent master of Shelburne. He will govern it well and be just to everyone, as just as it is wise to be — but my God" — there was sudden heat in her voice, almost passion — "compared with Joscelin, he is such a bore!"

Suddenly Monk was touched by the sense of loss that came through her words, the loneliness, the feeling that something irrecoverably pleasing had gone from her life and part of her could only look backwards from now on.

"I'm sorry," he said, and he meant it deeply. "I know it cannot bring him back, but we will find the man, and he will be punished."

"Hanged," she said tonelessly. "Taken out

one morning and his neck broken on the rope."

"Yes."

"That is of little use to me." She turned back to him. "But it is better than nothing. See to it that it is done."

It was dismissal, but he was not yet ready to go. There were things he needed to know. He stood up.

"I mean to, ma'am; but I still need your help —"

"Mine?" Her voice expressed surprise, and disapproval.

"Yes ma'am. If I am to learn who hated Major Grey enough to kill him" — he caught her expression — "for whatever reason. The finest people, ma'am, can inspire envy, or greed, jealousy over a woman, a debt of honor that cannot be paid —"

"Yes, you make your point." She blinked and the muscles in her thin neck tightened. "What is your name?"

"William Monk."

"Indeed. And what is it you wish to know about my son, Mr. Monk?"

"To start with, I would like to meet the rest of the family."

Her eyebrows rose in faint, dry amusement.

"You think I am biased, Mr. Monk, that I have told you something less than the truth?"

"We frequently show only our most flattering sides to those we care for most, and who care for us," he replied quietly.

"How perceptive of you." Her voice was stinging. He tried to guess what well-covered pain was behind those words.

"When may I speak to Lord Shelburne?" he asked. "And anyone else who knew Major Grey well?"

"If you consider it necessary, I suppose you had better." She went back to the door. "Wait here, and I shall ask him to see you, when it is convenient." She pulled the door open and walked through without looking back at him.

He sat down, half facing the window. Outside a woman in a plain stuff dress walked past, a basket on her arm. For a wild moment memory surged back to him. He saw in his mind a child as well, a girl with dark hair, and he knew the cobbled street beyond the trees, going down to the water. There was something missing; he struggled for it, and then knew it was wind, and the scream of gulls. It was a memory of happiness, of complete safety. Childhood — perhaps his mother, and Beth?

Then it was gone. He fought to add to it, focus it more sharply and see the details again, but nothing else came. He was an adult back in Shelburne, with the murder of Joscelin Grey.

He waited for another quarter of an hour before the door opened again and Lord Shelburne came in. He was about thirty-eight or forty, heavier of build than Joscelin Grey, to judge by the description and the clothes; but Monk wondered if Joscelin had also had that air of confidence and slight, even unintentional superiority. He was darker than his mother and the balance of his face was different, sensible, without a jot of humor in the mouth.

Monk rose to his feet as a matter of courtesy — and hated himself for doing it.

"You're the police fellow?" Shelburne said with a slight frown. He remained standing, so Monk was obliged to also. "Well, what is it you want? I really can't imagine how anything I can tell you about my brother could help you find the lunatic who broke in and killed him, poor devil."

"No one broke in, sir," Monk corrected him. "Whoever it was, Major Grey gave entrance to him himself."

"Really?" The level brows rose a fraction. "I find that very unlikely."

"Then you are not acquainted with the facts, sir." Monk was irked by the condescension and the arrogance of a man who presumed to know Monk's job better than he did, simply because he was a gentleman. Had he always found it so hard to bear? Had he been quick-tempered? Runcorn had said something about lack of diplomacy, but he could not remember what it was now. His mind flew back to the church the day before, to the woman who had hesitated as she passed him down the aisle. He could see her face as sharply here at Shelburne as he had then; the rustle of taffeta, the faint, almost imaginary perfume, the widening of her eyes. It was a memory that made his heart beat faster and excitement catch in his throat.

"I know my brother was beaten to death by a lunatic." Shelburne's voice cut across him, scattering his thoughts. "And you haven't caught him yet. Those are facts!"

Monk forced his attention to the present.

"With respect, sir." He tried to choose his words with tact. "We know that he was beaten to death. We do not know by whom, or why; but there were no marks of forced entry, and the only person unaccounted for who could possibly have entered the building appears to have visited someone else. Whoever attacked Major Grey took great care about the way he did it, and so far as we know, did not steal anything."

"And you deduce from that that it was

someone he knew?" Shelburne was skeptical.

"That, and the violence of the crime," Monk agreed, standing across the room from him so he could see Shelburne's face in the light. "A simple burglar does not go on hitting his victim long after he is quite obviously dead."

Shelburne winced. "Unless he is a madman! Which was rather my point. You are dealing with a madman, Mr. — er." He could not recall Monk's name and did not wait for it to be offered. It was unimportant. "I think there's scant chance of your catching him now. You would probably be better employed stopping muggings, or pickpockets, or whatever it is you usually do."

Monk swallowed his temper with difficulty. "Lady Shelburne seems to disagree with you."

Lovel Grey was unaware of having been rude; one could not be rude to a policeman.

"Mama?" His face flickered for an instant with unaccustomed emotion, which quickly vanished and left his features smooth again. "Oh, well; women feel these things. I am afraid she has taken Joscelin's death very hard, worse than if he'd been killed in the Crimea." It appeared to surprise him slightly.

"It's natural," Monk persisted, trying a different approach. "I believe he was a very charming person — and well liked?"

Shelburne was leaning against the mantelpiece and his boots shone in the sun falling wide through the French window. Irritably he kicked them against the brass fender.

"Joscelin? Yes, I suppose he was. Cheerful sort of fellow, always smiling. Gifted with music, and telling stories, that kind of thing. I know my wife was very fond of him. Great pity, and so pointless, just some bloody madman." He shook his head. "Hard on Mother."

"Did he come down here often?" Monk sensed a vein more promising.

"Oh, every couple of months or so. Why?" He looked up. "Surely you don't think someone followed him from here?"

"Every possibility is worth looking into, sir." Monk leaned his weight a little against the sideboard. "Was he here shortly before he was killed?"

"Yes, as a matter of fact he was; couple of weeks, or less. But I think you are mistaken. Everyone here had known him for years, and they all liked him." A shadow crossed his face. "Matter of fact, I think he was pretty well the servants' favorite. Always had a pleasant word, you know; remembered people's names, even though he hadn't lived here for years."

Monk imagined it: the solid, plodding older

brother, worthy but boring; the middle brother still an outline only; and the youngest, trying hard and finding that charm could bring him what birth did not, making people laugh, unbending the formality, affecting an interest in the servants' lives and families, winning small treats for himself that his brothers did not — and his mother's love.

"People can hide hatred, sir," Monk said aloud. "And they usually do, if they have murder in mind."

"I suppose they must," Lovel conceded, straightening up and standing with his back to the empty fireplace. "Still, I think you're on the wrong path. Look for some lunatic in London, some violent burglar; there must be loads of them. Don't you have contacts, people who inform to the police? Why don't you try them?"

"We have, sir — exhaustively. Mr. Lamb, my predecessor, spent weeks combing every possibility in that direction. It was the first place to look." He changed the subject suddenly, hoping to catch him less guarded. "How did Major Grey finance himself, sir? We haven't uncovered any business interest yet."

"What on earth do you want to know that for?" Lovel was startled. "You cannot imagine he had the sort of business rivals who would beat him to death with a stick! That's ludicrous!"

"Someone did."

He wrinkled his face with distaste. "I had not forgotten that! I really don't know what his business interests were. He had a small allowance from the estate, naturally."

"How much, sir?"

"I hardly think that needs to concern you." Now the irritation was back; his affairs had been trespassed upon by a policeman. Again his boot kicked absently at the fender behind him.

"Of course it concerns me, sir." Monk had command of his temper now. He was in control of the conversation, and he had a direction to pursue. "Your brother was murdered, probably by someone who knew him. Money may well come into it; it is one of the commonest motives for murder."

Lovel looked at him without replying.

Monk waited.

"Yes, I suppose it is," Lovel said at last. "Four hundred pounds á year — and of course there was his army pension."

To Monk it sounded a generous amount; one could run a very good establishment and keep a wife and family, with two maids, for less than a thousand pounds. But possibly Joscelin Grey's tastes had been a good deal

135

more extravagant: clothes, clubs, horses, gambling, perhaps women, or at least presents for women. They had not so far explored his social circle, still believing it to have been an intruder from the streets, and Grey a victim of ill fortune rather than someone of his own acquaintance.

"Thank you," he replied to Lord Shelburne. "You know of no other?"

"My brother did not discuss his financial affairs with me."

"You say your wife was fond of him? Would it be possible for me to speak to Lady Shelburne, please? He may have said something to her the last time he was here that could help us."

"Hardly, or she would have told me; and naturally I should have told you, or whoever is in authority."

"Something that meant nothing to Lady Shelburne might have meaning for me," Monk pointed out. "Anyway, it is worth trying."

Lovel moved to the center of the room as if somehow he would crowd Monk to the door. "I don't think so. And she has already suffered a severe shock; I don't see any purpose in distressing her any further with sordid details."

"I was going to ask her about Major Grey's personality, sir," Monk said with the shadow of irony in his voice. "His friends and his interests, nothing further. Or was she so attached to him that would distress her too much?"

"I don't care for your impertinence!" Lovel said sharply. "Of course she wasn't. I just don't want to rake the thing over any further. It is not very pleasant to have a member of one's family beaten to death!"

Monk faced him squarely. There was not more than a yard between them.

"Of course not, but that surely is all the more reason why we must find the man."

"If you insist." With ill humor he ordered Monk to follow him, and led him out of the very feminine sitting room along a short corridor into the main hall. Monk glanced around as much as was possible in the brief time as Shelburne paced ahead of him towards one of the several fine doorways. The walls were paneled to shoulder height in wood, the floor parqueted and scattered with Chinese carpets of cut pile and beautiful pastel shades, and the whole was dominated by a magnificent staircase dividing halfway up and sweeping to left and right at either end of a railed landing. There were pictures in ornate gold frames on all sides, but he had no time to look at them.

Shelburne opened the withdrawing room door and waited impatiently while Monk followed him in, then closed it. The room was long and faced south, with French windows looking onto a lawn bordered with herbaceous flowers in brilliant bloom. Rosamond Shelburne was sitting on a brocaded chaise longue, embroidery hoop in her hand. She looked up when they came in. She was at first glance not unlike her mother-in-law: she had the same fair hair and good brow, the same shape of eye, although hers were dark brown, and there was a different balance to her features, the resolution was not yet hard, there was humor, a width of imagination waiting to be given flight. She was dressed soberly, as befitted one who had recently lost a brother-in-law, but the wide skirt was the color of wine in shadow, and only her beads were black.

"I am sorry, my dear." Shelburne glanced pointedly at Monk. "But this man is from the police, and he thinks you may be able to tell him something about Joscelin that will help." He strode past her and stopped by the first window, glancing at the sun across the grass.

Rosamond's fair skin colored very slightly and she avoided Monk's eyes.

"Indeed?" she said politely. "I know very little of Joscelin's London life, Mr. —?"

"Monk, ma'am," he answered. "But I understand Major Grey had an affection for you,

138

and perhaps he may have spoken of some friend, or an acquaintance who might lead us to another, and so on?"

"Oh." She put her needle and frame down; it was a tracery of roses around a text. "I see. I am afraid I cannot think of anything. But please be seated, and I will do my best to help."

Monk accepted and questioned her gently, not because he expected to learn a great deal from her directly, but because indirectly he watched her, listening to the intonations of her voice, and the fingers turning in her lap.

Slowly he discovered a picture of Joscelin Grey.

"He seemed very young when I came here after my marriage," Rosamond said with a smile, looking beyond Monk and out of the window. "Of course that was before he went to the Crimea. He was an officer then; he had just bought his commission and he was so" — she searched for just the right word — "so jaunty! I remember that day he came in his uniform, scarlet tunic and gold braid, boots gleaming. One could not help feeling happy for him." Her voice dropped. "It all seemed like an adventure then."

"And after?" Monk prompted, watching the delicate shadows in her face, the search for something glimpsed but not understood except by a leap of instinct.

"He was wounded, you know?" She looked at him, frowning.

"Yes," he said.

"Twice — and ill too." She searched his eyes to see if he knew more than she, and there was nothing in his memory to draw on. "He suffered very much," she continued. "He was thrown from his horse in the charge at Balaclava and sustained a sword wound in his leg at Sebastopol. He refused to speak much to us about being in hospital at Scutari; he said it was too terrible to relate and would distress us beyond bearing." The embroidery slipped on the smooth nap of her skirt and rolled away on the floor. She made no effort to pick it up.

"He was changed?" Monk prompted.

She smiled slowly. She had a lovely mouth, sweeter and more sensitive than her mother-in-law's. "Yes — but he did not lose his humor, he could still laugh and enjoy beautiful things. He gave me a musical box for my birthday." Her smile widened at the thought of it. "It had an enamel top with a rose painted on it. It played 'Fur Elise' — Beethoven, you know —"

"Really, my dear!" Lovel's voice cut across her as he turned from where he had been standing by the window. "The man is here on police business. He doesn't know or care about Beethoven and Joscelin's music box. Please try to concentrate on something relevant — in the remote likelihood there is anything. He wants to know if Joscelin offended someone — owed them money — God knows what!"

Her face altered so slightly it could have been a change in the light, had not the sky beyond the windows been a steady cloudless blue. Suddenly she looked tired.

"I know Joscelin found finances a little difficult from time to time," she answered quietly. "But I do not know of any particulars, or whom he owed."

"He would hardly have discussed such a thing with my wife." Lovel swung around sharply. "If he wanted to borrow he would come to me — but he had more sense than to try. He had a very generous allowance as it was."

Monk glanced frantically at the splendid room, the swagged velvet curtains, and the garden and parkland beyond, and forbore from making any remark as to generosity. He looked back at Rosamond.

"You never assisted him, ma'am?"

Rosamond hesitated.

"With what?" Lovel asked, raising his eyebrows.

"A gift?" Monk suggested, struggling to be tactful. "Perhaps a small loan to meet a sudden embarrassment?"

"I can only assume you are trying to cause mischief," Lovel said acidly. "Which is despicable, and if you persist I shall have you removed from the case."

Monk was taken aback; he had not deliberately intended offense, simply to uncover a truth. Such sensibilities were peripheral, and he thought a rather silly indulgence now.

Lovel saw his irritation and mistook it for a failure to understand. "Mr. Monk, a married woman does not own anything to dispose of — to a brother-in-law or anyone else."

Monk blushed for making a fool of himself, and for the patronage in Lovel's manner. When reminded, of course he knew the law. Even Rosamond's personal jewelry was not hers in law. If Lovel said she was not to give it away, then she could not. Not that he had any doubt, from the catch in her speech and the flicker of her eyes, that she had done so.

He had no desire to betray her; the knowledge was all he wanted. He bit back the reply he wished to make.

"I did not intend to suggest anything done without your permission, my lord, simply a gesture of kindness on Lady Shelburne's part."

Lovel opened his mouth to retort, then changed his mind and looked out of the window again, his face tight, his shoulders broad and stiff.

"Did the war affect Major Grey deeply?" Monk turned back to Rosamond.

"Oh yes!" For a moment there was intense feeling in her, then she recalled the circumstances and struggled to control herself. Had she not been as schooled in the privileges and the duties of a lady she would have wept. "Yes," she said again. "Yes, although he mastered it with great courage. It was not many months before he began to be his old self — most of the time. He would play the piano, and sing for us sometimes." Her eyes looked beyond Monk to some past place in her own mind. "And he still told us funny stories and made us laugh. But there were occasions when he would think of the men who died, and I suppose his own suffering as well."

Monk was gathering an increasingly sharp picture of Joscelin Grey: a dashing young officer, easy mannered, perhaps a trifle callow; then through experience of war with its blood and pain, and for him an entirely new kind of responsibility, returning home determined to resume as much of the old life as possible; a youngest son with little money but great charm, and a degree of courage.

He had not seemed like a man to make en-emies through wronging anyone — but it did not need a leap of imagination to conceive that he might have earned a jealousy powerful enough to have ended in murder. All that was needed for that might lie within this lovely room with its tapestries and its view of the parkland.

"Thank you, Lady Shelburne," he said for-mally. "You have given me a much clearer picture of him than I had. I am most grateful." He turned to Lovel. "Thank you, my lord. If I might speak with Mr. Menard Grey —"

"He is out," Lovel replied flatly. "He went to see one of the tenant farmers, and I don't know which so there is no point in your traips-ing around looking. Anyway, you are looking for who murdered Joscelin, not writing an obituary!"

"I don't think the obituary is finished until it contains the answer," Monk replied, meeting his eyes with a straight, challenging stare.

"Then get on with it!" Lovel snapped. "Don't stand here in the sun — get out and do something useful."

Monk left without speaking and closed the withdrawing room door behind him. In the hall a footman was awaiting discreetly to show him out — or perhaps to make sure that he left without pocketing the silver card tray on the hall table, or the ivory-handled letter opener.

The weather had changed dramatically; from nowhere a swift overcast had brought a squall, the first heavy drops beginning even as he left.

He was outside, walking towards the main drive through the clearing rain, when quite by chance he met the last member of the family. He saw her coming towards him briskly, whisking her skirts out of the way of a stray bramble trailing onto the narrower path. She was reminiscent of Fabia Shelburne in age and dress, but without the brittle glamour. This woman's nose was longer, her hair wilder, and she could never have been a beauty, even forty years ago.

"Good afternoon." He lifted his hat in a small gesture of politeness.

She stopped in her stride and looked at him curiously. "Good afternoon. You are a stranger. What are you doing here? Are you lost?"

"No, thank you ma'am. I am from the Metropolitan Police. I came to report our progress on the murder of Major Grey."

Her eyes narrowed and he was not sure whether it was amusement or something else.

"You look a well-set-up young man to be

carrying messages. I suppose you came to see Fabia?"

He had no idea who she was, and for a moment he was at a loss for a civil reply.

She understood instantly.

"I'm Callandra Daviot; the late Lord Shelburne was my brother."

"Then Major Grey was your nephew, Lady Callandra?" He spoke her correct title without thinking, and only realized it afterwards, and wondered what experience or interest had taught him. Now he was only concerned for another opinion of Joscelin Grey.

"Naturally," she agreed. "How can that help you?"

"You must have known him."

Her rather wild eyebrows rose slightly.

"Of course. Possibly a little better than Fabia. Why?"

"You were very close to him?" he said quickly.

"On the contrary, I was some distance removed." Now he was quite certain there was a dry humor in her eyes.

"And saw the clearer for it?" He finished her implication.

"I believe so. Do you require to stand here under the trees, young man? I am being steadily dripped on."

He shook his head, and turned to accompany her back along the way he had come.

"It is unfortunate that Joscelin was murdered," she continued. "It would have been much better if he could have died at Sebastopol — better for Fabia anyway. What do you want of me? I was not especially fond of Joscelin, nor he of me. I knew none of his business, and have no useful ideas as to who might have wished him such intense harm."

"You were not fond of him yourself?" Monk said curiously. "Everyone says he was charming."

"So he was," she agreed, walking with large strides not towards the main entrance of the house but along a graveled path in the direction of the stables, and he had no choice but to go also or be left behind. "I do not care a great deal for charm." She looked directly at him, and he found himself warming to her dry honesty. "Perhaps because I never possessed it," she continued. "But it always seems chameleon to me, and I cannot be sure what color the animal underneath might be really. Now will you please either return to the house, or go wherever it is you are going. I have no inclination to get any wetter than I already am, and it is going to rain again. I do not intend to stand in the stable yard talking polite nonsense that cannot possibly assist you."

He smiled broadly and bowed his head in a small salute. Lady Callandra was the only person in Shelburne he liked instinctively.

"Of course, ma'am; thank you for your . . ." He hesitated, not wanting to be so obvious as to say "honesty." ". . . time. I wish you a good day."

She looked at him wryly and with a little nod and strode past and into the harness room calling loudly for the head groom.

Monk walked back along the driveway again — as she had surmised, through a considerable shower — and out past the gates. He followed the road for the three miles to the village. Newly washed by rain, in the brilliant bursts of sun it was so lovely it caught a longing in him as if once it was out of his sight he would never recall it clearly enough. Here and there a coppice showed dark green, billowing over the sweep of grass and mounded against the sky, and beyond the distant stone walls wheat fields shone dark gold with the wind rippling like waves through their heavy heads.

It took him a little short of an hour and he found the peace of it turning his mind from the temporary matter of who murdered Joscelin Grey to the deeper question as to what manner of man he himself was. Here no one knew him; at least for tonight he would be able to start anew, no previous act could mar it, or help. Perhaps he would learn something of the inner man, unfiltered by expectations. What did he believe, what did he truly value? What drove him from day to day — except ambition, and personal vanity?

He stayed overnight in the village public hostelry, and asked some discreet questions of certain locals in the morning, without significantly adding to his picture of Joscelin Grey, but he found a very considerable respect for both Grey's brothers, in their different ways. They were not liked — that was too close a relationship with men whose lives and stations were so different — but they were trusted. They fitted into expectations of their kind, small courtesies were observed, a mutual code was kept.

Of Joscelin it was different. Affection was possible. Everyone had found him more than civil, remembering as many of the generosities as were consistent with his position as a son of the house. If some had thought or felt otherwise they were not saying so to an outsider like Monk. And he had been a soldier; a certain honor was due the dead.

Monk enjoyed being polite, even gracious. No one was afraid of him — guarded certainly, he was still a Peeler — but there was no personal awe, and they were as keen as he to find who had murdered their hero.

He took luncheon in the taproom with several local worthies and contrived to fall into conversation. By the door with the sunlight streaming in, with cider, apple pie and cheese, opinions began to flow fast and free. Monk became involved, and before long his tongue got the better of him, clear, sarcastic and funny. It was only afterwards as he was walking away that he realized that it was also at times unkind.

He left in the early afternoon for the small, silent station, and took a clattering, steambelching journey back to London.

He arrived a little after four, and went by hansom straight to the police station.

"Well?" Runcorn inquired with lifted eyebrows. "Did you manage to mollify Her Ladyship? I'm sure you conducted yourself like a gentleman?"

Monk heard that slight edge to Runcorn's voice again, and the flavor of resentment. What for? He struggled desperately to recall any wisp of memory, even a guess as to what he might have done to occasion it. Surely not mere abrasiveness of manner? He had not been so stupid as to be positively rude to a superior? But nothing came. It mattered — it mattered acutely: Runcorn held the key to his employment, the only sure thing in his life now, in fact the very means of it. Without work he was not only completely anonymous, but within a few weeks he would be a pauper. Then there would be only the same bitter choice for him as for every other pauper: beggary, with its threat of starvation or imprisonment as a vagrant; or the workhouse. And God knew, there were those who thought the workhouse the greater evil.

"I believe Her Ladyship understood that we are doing all we can," he answered. "And that we had to exhaust the more likely-seeming possibilities first, like a thief off the streets. She understands that now we must consider that it may have been someone who knew him."

Runcorn grunted. "Asked her about him, did you? What sort of feller he was?"

"Yes sir. Naturally she was biased —"

"Naturally," Runcorn agreed tartly, shooting his eyebrows up. "But you ought to be bright enough to see past that."

Monk ignored the implication. "He seems to have been her favorite son," he replied. "Considerably the most likable. Everyone else gave the same opinion, even in the village. Discount some of that as speaking no ill of the dead." He smiled twistedly. "Or of the son of the big house. Even so, you're still left with a man of unusual charm, a good war record, and no especial vices or weaknesses, except that he found it hard to manage on his allowance, bit of a temper now and then, and a mocking wit when he chose; but generous, remembered birthdays and servants' names — knew how to amuse. It begins to look as if jealousy could have been a motive."

Runcorn sighed.

"Messy," he said decidedly, his left eye narrowing again. "Never like having to dig into family relationships, and the higher you go the nastier you get." He pulled his coat a little straighter without thinking, but it still did not sit elegantly. "That's your society for you; cover their tracks better than any of your average criminals, when they really try. Don't often make a mistake, that lot, but oh my grandfather, when they do!" He poked his finger in the air towards Monk. "Take my word for it, if there's something nasty there, it'll get a lot worse before it gets any better. You may fancy the higher classes, my boy, but they play very dirty when they protect their own; you believe it!"

Monk could think of no answer. He wished he could remember the things he had said and done to prompt Runcorn to these flavors, nuances of disapproval. Was he a brazen social climber? The thought was repugnant, even pathetic in a way, trying to appear something you are not, in order to impress people who don't care for you in the slightest, and can most certainly detect your origins even before you open your mouth!

But did not most men seek to improve themselves, given opportunity? But had he been overambitious, and foolish enough to show it?

The thing lying at the back of his mind, troubling him all the time, was why he had not been back to see Beth in eight years. She seemed the only family he had, and yet he had virtually ignored her. Why?

Runcorn was staring at him.

"Well?" he demanded.

"Yes sir." He snapped to attention. "I agree, sir. I think there may be something very unpleasant indeed. One has to hate very much to beat a man to death as Grey was beaten. I imagine if it is something to do with the family, they will do everything they can to hush it up. In fact the eldest son, the present Lord Shelburne, didn't seem very eager for me to probe it. He tried to guide me back to the idea that it was a casual thief, or a lunatic."

"And Her Ladyship?"

"She wants us to continue."

"Then she's fortunate, isn't she?" Runcorn nodded his head with his lips twisted. "Because that is precisely what you are going to do!"

Monk recognized a dismissal.

"Yes sir; I'll start with Yeats." He excused himself and went to his own room.

Evan was sitting at the table, busy writing. He looked up with a quick smile when Monk came in. Monk found himself overwhelmingly glad to see him. He realized he had already begun to think of Evan as a friend as much as a colleague.

"How was Shelburne?" Evan asked.

"Very splendid," he replied. "And very formal. What about Mr. Yeats?"

"Very respectable." Evan's mouth twitched in a brief and suppressed amusement. "And very ordinary. No one is saying anything to his discredit. In fact no one is saying anything much at all; they have trouble in recalling precisely who he is."

Monk dismissed Yeats from his mind, and spoke of the thing which was more pressing to him.

"Runcorn seems to think it will become unpleasant, and he's expecting rather a lot from us —"

"Naturally." Evan looked at him, his eyes perfectly clear. "That's why he rushed you into it, even though you're hardly back from being ill. It's always sticky when we have to deal with the aristocracy; and let's face it, a policeman is usually treated pretty much as

154

the social equal of a parlor maid and about as desirable to be close to as the drains; necessary in an imperfect society, but not fit to have in the withdrawing room."

At another time Monk would have laughed, but now it was too painful, and too urgent.

"Why me?" he pressed.

Evan was frankly puzzled. He hid what looked like embarrassment with formality.

"Sir?"

"Why me?" Monk repeated a little more harshly. He could hear the rising pitch in his own voice, and could not govern it.

Evan lowered his eyes awkwardly.

"Do you want an honest answer to that, sir; although you must know it as well as I do?"

"Yes I do! Please?"

Evan faced him, his eyes hot and troubled. "Because you are the best detective in the station, and the most ambitious. Because you know how to dress and to speak; you'll be equal to the Shelburnes, if anyone is." He hesitated, biting his lip, then plunged on. "And — and if you come unstuck either by making a mess of it and failing to find the murderer, or rubbing up against Her Ladyship and she complains about you, there are a good few who won't mind if you're demoted. And of course worse still, if it turns out to be one of the family —

and you have to arrest him —"

Monk stared at him, but Evan did not look away. Monk felt the heat of shock ripple through him.

"Including Runcorn?" he said very quietly.

"I think so."

"And you?"

Evan was transparently surprised. "No, not me," he said simply. He made no protestations, and Monk believed him.

"Good." He drew a deep breath. "Well, we'll go and see Mr. Yeats tomorrow."

"Yes sir." Evan was smiling, the shadow gone. "I'll be here at eight."

Monk winced inwardly at the time, but he had to agree. He said good-night and turned to go home.

But out in the street he started walking the other way, not consciously thinking until he realized he was moving in the general direction of St. Marylebone Church. It was over two miles away, and he was tired. He had already walked a long way in Shelburne, and his legs were aching, his feet sore. He hailed a cab and when the driver asked him, he gave the address of the church.

It was very quiet inside with only the dimmest of light through the fast-graying windows. Candelabra shed little yellow arcs.

Why the church? He had all the peace and

silence he needed in his own rooms, and he certainly had no conscious thought of God. He sat down in one of the pews.

Why had he come here? No matter how much he had dedicated himself to his job, his ambition, he must know someone, have a friend, or even an enemy. His life must have impinged on someone else's — beside Runcorn.

He had been sitting in the dark without count of time, struggling to remember anything at all — a face, a name, even a feeling, something of childhood, like the momentary glimpse at Shelburne — when he saw the girl in black again, standing a few feet away.

He was startled. She seemed so vivid, familiar. Or was it only that she seemed to him to be lovely, evocative of something he wanted to feel, wanted to remember?

But she was not beautiful, not really. Her mouth was too big, her eyes too deep. She was looking at him.

Suddenly he was frightened. Ought he to know her? Was he being unbearably rude in not speaking? But he could know any number of people, of any walk of life! She could be a bishop's daughter, or a prostitute!

No, never with that face.

Don't be ridiculous, harlots could have faces with just that warmth, those luminous eyes;

at least they could while they were still young, and nature had not yet written itself on the outside.

Without realizing it, he was still looking at her.

"Good evening, Mr. Monk," she said slowly, a faint embarrassment making her blink.

He rose to his feet. "Good evening, ma'am." He had no idea of her name, and now he was terrified, wishing he had never come. What should he say? How well did she know him? He could feel the sweat prickly on his body, his tongue dry, his thoughts in a stultified, wordless mass.

"You have not spoken for such a long time," she went on. "I had begun to fear you had discovered something you did not dare to tell me."

Discovered! Was she connected with some case? It must be old; he had been working on Joscelin Grey since he came back, and before that the accident. He fished for something that would not commit him and yet still make sense.

"No, I'm afraid I haven't discovered anything else." His voice was dry, artificial to his own ears. Please God he did not sound so foolish to her!

"Oh." She looked down. It seemed for a

158

moment as if she could not think of anything else to say, then she lifted her head again and met his eyes very squarely. He could only think how dark they were — not brown, but a multitude of shadows. "You may tell me the truth, Mr. Monk, whatever it is. Even if he killed himself, and for whatever reason, I would rather know."

"It is the truth," he said simply. "I had an accident about seven weeks ago. I was in a cab that overturned and I broke my arm and ribs and cracked my head. I can't even re- member it. I was in hospital for nearly a month, and then went north to my sister's to regain my strength. I'm afraid I haven't done anything about it since then."

"Oh dear." Her face was tight with concern. "I am sorry. Are you all right now? Are you sure you are better?"

She sounded as if it mattered to her. He found himself warmed ridiculously by it. He forced from his mind the idea that she was merely compassionate, or well-mannered.

"Yes, yes thank you; although there are blanks in my memory." Why had he told her that? To explain his behavior — in case it hurt her? He was taking too much upon him- self. Why should she care, more than courtesy required? He remembered Sunday now; she had worn black then too, but expensive black, silk and fashionable. The man accompanying her had been dressed as Monk could not afford to be. Her husband? The thought was acutely depressing, even painful. He did not even think of the other woman.

"Oh." Again she was lost for words.

He was fumbling, trying to find a clue, sharply conscious of her presence; even faintly, although she was several feet away, of her perfume. Or was it imagination?

"What was the last thing I told you?" he asked. "I mean —" He did not know what he meant.

But she answered with only the merest hesitation.

"Not a great deal. You said Papa had certainly discovered that the business was fraudulent but you did not know yet whether he had faced the other partners with it or not. You had seen someone, although you did not name him, but a certain Mr. Robinson disappeared every time you went after him." Her face tightened. "You did not know whether Papa could have been murdered by them, to keep his silence, or if he took his own life, for shame. Perhaps I was wrong to ask you to discover. It just seemed so dreadful that he should choose that way rather than fight them, show them for what they are. It's no crime to be deceived!" There was a spark of anger in her now, as though she were fighting to keep control of herself. "I wanted to believe he would have stayed alive, and fought them, faced his friends, even those who lost money, rather than —" She stopped, otherwise she would have wept. She stood quite still, swallowing hard.

"I'm sorry," he said very quietly. He wanted to touch her, but he was hurtfully aware of the difference between them. It would be a familiarity and would break the moment's trust, the illusion of closeness.

She waited a moment longer, as if for something which did not come; then she abandoned it.

"Thank you. I am sure you have done everything you could. Perhaps I saw what I wished to see."

There was a movement up the aisle, towards the door of the church, and the vicar came down, looking vague, and behind him the same woman with the highly individual face whom Monk had seen on the first occasion in the church. She also was dressed in dark, plain clothes, and her thick hair with a very slight wave was pulled back in a manner that owed more to expediency than fashion.

"Mrs. Latterly, is that you?" the vicar asked uncertainly, peering forward. "Why my dear, what are you doing here all by yourself? You mustn't brood, you know. Oh!" He saw Monk. "I beg your pardon. I did not realize you had company."

"This is Mr. Monk," she said, explaining him. "From the police. He was kind enough to help us when Papa . . . died."

The vicar looked at Monk with disapproval. "Indeed. I do think, my dear child, that it would be wiser for all of us if you were to let the matter rest. Observe mourning, of course, but let your poor father-in-law rest in peace." He crossed the air absently. "Yes — in peace."

Monk stood up. Mrs. Latterly; so she was married — or a widow? He was being absurd.

"If I learn anything more, Mrs. Latterly" — his voice was tight, almost choking — "do you wish me to inform you?" He did not want to lose her, to have her disappear into the past with everything else. He might not discover anything, but he must know where she was, have a reason to see her.

She looked at him for a long moment, undecided, fighting with herself. Then she spoke carefully.

"Yes please, if you will be so kind, but please remember your promise! Good night." She swiveled around, her skirts brushing Monk's feet. "Good night, Vicar. Come, Hester, it is time we returned home; Charles will be expecting us for dinner." And she walked slowly up towards the door. Monk watched her go arm in arm with the other woman as if she had taken the light away with her.

Outside in the sharper evening air Hester Latterly turned to her sister-in-law.

"I think it is past time you explained yourself, Imogen," she said quietly, but with an edge of urgency in her voice. "Just who is that man?"

"He is with the police," Imogen replied, walking briskly towards their carriage, which was waiting at the curbside. The coachman climbed down, opened the door and handed them in, Imogen first, then Hester. Both took his courtesy for granted and Hester arranged her skirts merely sufficiently to be comfortable, Imogen to avoid crushing the fabric.

"What do you mean, 'with'?" Hester demanded as the carriage moved forward. "One does not accompany the police; you make it sound like a social event! 'Miss Smith is with Mr. Jones this evening.' "

"Don't be pedantic," Imogen criticized. "Actually you can say it of a maid as well — 'Tilly is with the Robinsons at present'!"

Hester's eyebrows shot up. "Indeed! And is that man presently playing footman to the police?"

Imogen remained silent.

"I'm sorry," Hester said at length. "But I know there is something distressing you, and I feel so helpless because I don't know what it is."

Imogen put out her hand and held Hester's tightly.

"Nothing," she said in a voice so low it could only just be heard above the rattle of the carriage and the dull thud of hooves and the noises of the street. "It is only Papa's death, and all that followed. None of us are over the shock of it yet, and I do appreciate your leaving everything and coming home as you did."

"I never thought of doing less," Hester said honestly, although her work in the Crimean hospitals had changed her beyond anything Imogen or Charles could begin to understand. It had been a hard duty to leave the nursing service and the white-hot spirit to improve, reform and heal that had moved not only Miss Nightingale but so many other women as well. But the death of first her father, then within a few short weeks her mother also, had made it an undeniable duty that she should return home and be there to mourn, and to assist her brother and his wife in all the affairs that there were to be attended to. Naturally Charles had seen to all the business and the finances, but there had been the house to close up, servants to dismiss, endless letters to write, clothes to dispose of to the poor, bequests of a personal nature to be remembered, and the endless social facade to be kept up. It would have been desperately unfair to expect Imogen to bear the burden and that responsibility alone. Hester had given no second thought as to whether she should come, simply excused herself, packed her few belongings and embarked.

It had been an extraordinary contrast after the desperate years in the Crimea with the unspeakable suffering she had seen, the agony of wounds, bodies torn by shot and sword; and to her even more harrowing, those wasted by disease, the racking pain and nausea of cholera, typhus and dysentery, the cold and the starvation; and driving her almost beyond herself with fury, the staggering incompetence.

She, like the other handful of women, had worked herself close to exhaustion, cleaning up human waste where there were no sanitary facilities, excrement from the helpless running on the floor and dripping through to the packed and wretched huddled in the cellars below. She had nursed men delirious with fever, gangrenous from amputations of limbs lost to everything from musket shot, cannon shot, sword thrust, even frostbite on the exposed and fearful bivouacs of the winter encampments where men and horses had perished by the thousands. She had delivered babies of the hungry and neglected army wives, buried many of them, then comforted the bereaved.

And when she could bear the pity no longer she had expended her last energy in fury, fighting the endless, idiotic inadequacy of the command, who seemed to her not to have the faintest grasp of ordinary sense, let alone management ability.

She had lost a brother, and many friends, chief among them Alan Russell, a brilliant war correspondent who had written home to the newspapers some of the unpalatable truths about one of the bravest and foolhardiest campaigns ever fought. He had shared many of them with her, allowing her to read them before they were posted.

Indeed in the weakness of fever he had dictated his last letter to her and she had sent it. When he died in the hospital at Scutari she had in a rash moment of deep emotion written a dispatch herself, and signed his name to it as if he were still alive.

It had been accepted and printed. From knowledge gleaned from other injured and feverish men she had learned their accounts of battle, siege and trench warfare, crazy charges and long weeks of boredom, and other dispatches had followed, all with Alan's name on them. In the general confusion no one realized.

Now she was home in the orderly, dignified, very sober grief of her brother's household mourning both her parents, wearing black as if this were the only loss and there were nothing else to do but conduct a gentle life of embroidery, letter writing and discreet good works with local charities. And of course obey Charles's continuous and rather pompous orders as to what must be done, and how, and when. It was almost beyond bearing. It was as if she were in suspended animation. She had grown used to having authority, making decisions and being in the heart of emotion, even if overtired, bitterly frustrated, full of anger and pity, desperately needed.

Now Charles was driven frantic because he could not understand her or comprehend the change in her from the brooding, intellectual girl he knew before, nor could he foresee any respectable man offering for her in marriage. He found the thought of having her living under his roof for the rest of her life well nigh insufferable.

The prospect did not please Hester either, but then she had no intention of allowing it to come to pass. As long as Imogen needed her she would remain, then she would consider her future and its possibilities.

However, as she sat in the carriage beside Imogen while they rattled through the dusk streets she had a powerful conviction that there was much troubling her sister-in-law and it was something that, for whatever reasons, Imogen was keeping secret, telling neither Charles nor Hester, and bearing the weight of it alone. It was more than grief, it was something that lay not only in the past but in the future also.

CHAPTER
FIVE

Monk and Evan saw Grimwade only briefly, then went straight up to visit Yeats. It was a little after eight in the morning and they hoped to catch him at breakfast, or possibly even before.

Yeats opened the door himself; he was a small man of about forty, a trifle plump, with a mild face and thinning hair which fell forward over his brow. He was startled and there was still a piece of toast and orange preserve in his hand. He stared at Monk with some alarm.

"Good morning, Mr. Yeats," Monk said firmly. "We are from the police; we would like to speak to you about the murder of Major Joscelin Grey. May we come in please?" He did not step forward, but his height seemed to press over Yeats and vaguely threaten him, and he used it deliberately.

"Y-yes, y-yes of course," Yeats stuttered, backing away, still clutching the toast. "But

169

I assure you I d-don't know anything I haven't already t-told you. Not you — at least — a Mr. Lamb who was — a —"

"Yes I know." Monk followed him in. He knew he was being oppressive, but he could not afford to be gentle. Yeats must have seen the murderer face-to-face, possibly even been in collusion with him, willingly or unwillingly. "But we have learned quite a few new facts," he went on, "since Mr. Lamb was taken ill and I have been put on the case."

"Oh?" Yeats dropped the toast and bent to pick it up, ignoring the preserve on the carpet. It was a smaller room than Joscelin Grey's and overpoweringly furnished in heavy oak covered in photographs and embroidered linen. There were anti-macassars on both the chairs.

"Have you —" Yeats said nervously. "Have you? I still don't think I can — er — could —"

"Perhaps if you were to allow a few questions, Mr. Yeats." Monk did not want him so frightened as to be incapable of thought or memory.

"Well — if you think so. Yes — yes, if . . ." He backed away and sat down sharply on the chair closest to the table.

Monk sat also and was conscious of Evan behind him doing the same on a ladder-back chair by the wall. He wondered fleetingly what Evan was thinking, if he found him harsh, overconscious of his own ambition, his need to succeed. Yeats could so easily be no more than he seemed, a frightened little man whom mischance had placed at the pivot of a murder.

Monk began quietly, thinking with an instant's self-mockery that he might be moderating his tone not to reassure Yeats but to earn Evan's approval. What had led him to such isolation that Evan's opinion mattered so much to him? Had he been too absorbed in learning, climbing, polishing himself, to afford friendship, much less love? Indeed, had anything at all engaged his higher emotions?

Yeats was watching him like a rabbit seeing a stoat, and too horrified to move.

"You yourself had a visitor that night," Monk told him quite gently. "Who was he?"

"I don't know!" Yeats's voice was high, almost a squeak. "I don't know who he was! I told Mr. Lamb that! He came here by mistake; he didn't even really want me!"

Monk found himself holding up his hand, trying to calm him as one would with an overexcited child, or an animal.

"But you saw him, Mr. Yeats." He kept his voice low. "No doubt you have some memory of his appearance, perhaps his voice? He must have spoken to you?" Whether Yeats was lying or not, he would achieve nothing by attacking his statement now; Yeats would only entrench himself more and more deeply into his ignorance.

Yeats blinked.

"I-I really can hardly say, Mr. — Mr. —"

"Monk — I'm sorry," he said, apologizing for not having introduced himself. "And my colleague is Mr. Evans. Was he a large man, or small?"

"Oh large, very large," Yeats said instantly. "Big as you are, and looked heavy; of course he had a thick coat on, it was a very bad night — wet — terribly."

"Yes, yes I remember. Was he taller than I am, do you think?" Monk stood up helpfully.

Yeats stared up at him. "No, no, I don't think so. About the same, as well as I can recall. But it was some time ago now." He shook his head unhappily.

Monk seated himself again, aware of Evan discreetly taking notes.

"He really was here only a moment or two," Yeats protested, still holding the toast, now beginning to break and drop crumbs on his trousers. "He just saw me, asked a question as to my business, then realized I was not the person he sought, and left again. That is really all there was." He brushed ineffectively at his trousers. "You must believe me, if I could help, I would. Poor Major Grey, such an appalling death." He shivered. "Such a charming young man. Life plays some dreadful tricks, does it not?"

Monk felt a quick flicker of excitement inside himself.

"You knew Major Grey?" He kept his voice almost casual.

"Oh not very well, no, no!" Yeats protested, shunning any thought of social arrogance — or involvement. "Only to pass the time of day, you understand? But he was very civil, always had a pleasant word, not like some of these young men of fashion. And he didn't affect to have forgotten one's name."

"And what is your business, Mr. Yeats? I don't think you said."

"Oh perhaps not." The toast shed more pieces in his hand, but now he was oblivious of it. "I deal in rare stamps and coins."

"And this visitor, was he also a dealer?"

Yeats looked surprised.

"He did not say, but I should imagine not. It is a small business, you know; one gets to meet most of those who are interested, at one time or another."

"He was English then?"

"I beg your pardon?"

"He was not a foreigner, whom you would not expect to have known, even had he been in the business?"

"Oh, I see." Yeats's brow cleared. "Yes, yes he was English."

"And who was he looking for, if not for you, Mr. Yeats?"

"I-I-really cannot say." He waved his hand in the air. "He asked if I were a collector of maps; I told him I was not. He said he had been misinformed, and he left immediately."

"I think not, Mr. Yeats. I think he then went to call on Major Grey, and within the next three quarters of an hour, beat him to death."

"Oh my dear God!" Yeats's bones buckled inside him and he slid backwards and down into his chair. Behind Monk, Evan moved as if to help, then changed his mind and sat down again.

"That surprises you?" Monk inquired.

Yeats was gasping, beyond speech.

"Are you sure this man was not known to you?" Monk persisted, giving him no time to regather his thoughts. This was the time to press.

"Yes, yes I am. Quite unknown." He covered his face with his hands. "Oh my dear heaven!"

Monk stared at Yeats. The man was useless now, either reduced to abject horror, or else very skillfully affecting to be. He turned and looked at Evan. Evan's face was stiff with embarrassment, possibly for their presence and their part in the man's wretchedness, possibly merely at being witness to it.

Monk stood up and heard his own voice far away. He knew he was risking a mistake, and that he was doing it because of Evan.

"Thank you, Mr. Yeats. I'm sorry for distressing you. Just one more thing: was this man carrying a stick?"

Yeats looked up, his face sickly pale; his voice was no more than a whisper.

"Yes, quite a handsome one; I noticed it."

"Heavy or light?"

"Oh heavy, quite heavy. Oh no!" He shut his eyes, screwing them up to hide even his imagination.

"There is no need for you to be frightened, Mr. Yeats," Evan said from behind. "We believe he was someone who knew Major Grey personally, not a chance lunatic. There is no reason to suppose he would have harmed you. I daresay he was looking for Major Grey in the first place and found the wrong door."

It was not until they were outside that Monk realized Evan must have said it purely to comfort the little man. It could not have been true. The visitor had asked for Yeats by name. He looked sideways at Evan, now walking silently

175

beside him in the drizzling rain. He made no remark on it.

Grimwade had proved no further help. He had not seen the man come down after leaving Yeats's door, nor seen him go to Joscelin Grey's. He had taken the opportunity to attend the call of nature, and then had seen the man leave at a quarter past ten, three quarters of an hour later.

"There's only one conclusion," Evan said unhappily, striding along with his head down. "He must have left Yeats's door and gone straight along the hallway to Grey, spent half an hour or so with him, then killed him, and left when Grimwade saw him go."

"Which doesn't tell us who he was," Monk said, stepping across a puddle and passing a cripple selling bootlaces. A rag and bone cart trundled by, its driver calling out almost unintelligibly in a singsong voice. "I keep coming back to the one thing," Monk resumed. "Why did anyone hate Joscelin Grey so much? There was a passion of hate in that room. Someone hated him so uncontrollably he couldn't stop beating him even after he was dead."

Evan shivered and the rain ran off his nose and chin. He pulled his collar up closer around his ears and his face was pale.

"Mr. Runcorn was right," he said miserably. "It's going to be extremely nasty. You

176

have to know someone very well to hate them as much as that."

"Or have been mortally wronged," Monk added. "But you're probably right; it'll be in the family, these things usually are. Either that, or a lover somewhere."

Evan looked shocked. "You mean Grey was —?"

"No." Monk smiled with a sharp downward twist. "That wasn't what I meant, although I suppose it's possible; in fact it's distinctly possible. But I was thinking of a woman, with a husband perhaps."

Evan's faced relaxed a fraction.

"I suppose it's too violent for a simple debt, gambling or something?" he said without much hope.

Monk thought for a moment.

"Could be blackmail," he suggested with genuine belief. The idea had only just occurred to him seriously, but he liked it.

Evan frowned. They were walking south along Grey's Inn Road.

"Do you think so?" He looked sideways at Monk. "Doesn't ring right to me. And we haven't found any unaccounted income yet. Of course, we haven't really looked. And blackmail victims can be driven to a very deep hatred indeed, for which I cannot entirely blame them. When a man has been tormented, stripped of all he has, and then is still threatened with ruin, there comes a point when reason breaks."

"We'll have to check on the social company he kept," Monk replied. "Who might have made mistakes damaging enough to be blackmailed over, to the degree that ended in murder."

"Perhaps if he was homosexual?" Evan suggested it with returning distaste, and Monk knew he did not believe his own word. "He might have had a lover who would pay to keep him quiet — and if pushed too far, kill him?"

"Very nasty." Monk stared at the wet pavement. "Runcorn was right." And thought of Runcorn set his mind on a different track.

He sent Evan to question all the local tradesmen, people at the club Grey had been at the evening he was killed, anything to learn about his associates.

Evan began at the wine merchant's whose name they had found on a bill head in Grey's apartments. He was a fat man with a drooping mustache and an unctuous manner. He expressed desolation over the loss of Major Grey. What a terrible misfortune. What an ironic stroke of fate that such a fine officer should survive the war, only to be struck down by a madman in his own home. What a tragedy.

He did not know what to say — and he said it at considerable length while Evan struggled to get a word in and ask some useful question.

When at last he did, the answer was what he had guessed it would be. Major Grey — the Honorable Joscelin Grey — was a most valued customer. He had excellent taste — but what else would you expect from such a gentleman? He knew French wine, and he knew German wine. He liked the best. He was provided with it from this establishment. His accounts? No, not always up to date — but paid in due course. The nobility were that way with money — one had to learn to accommodate it. He could add nothing — but nothing at all. Was Mr. Evan interested in wine? He could recommend an excellent Bordeaux.

No, Mr. Evan, reluctantly, was not interested in wine; he was a country parson's son, well educated in the gentilities of life, but with a pocket too short to indulge in more than the necessities, and a few good clothes, which would stand him in better stead than even the best of wines. None of which he explained to the merchant.

Next he tried the local eating establishments, beginning with the chophouse and working down to the public alehouse, which also served an excellent stew with spotted dick

179

pudding, full of currants, as Evan could attest.

"Major Grey?" the landlord said ruminatively. "Yer mean 'im as was murdered? 'Course I knowed 'im. Come in 'ere reg'lar, 'e did."

Evan did not know whether to believe him or not. It could well be true; the food was cheap and filling and the atmosphere not unpleasant to a man who had served in the army, two years of it in the battlefields of the Crimea. On the other hand it could be a boost to his business — already healthy — to say that a famous victim of murder had dined here. There was a grisly curiosity in many people which would give the place an added interest to them.

"What did he look like?" Evan asked.

" 'Ere!" The landlord looked at him suspiciously. "You on the case — or not, then? Doncher know?"

"I never met him alive," Evan replied reasonably. "It makes a lot of difference, you know."

The landlord sucked his teeth. " 'Course it do — sorry, guv, a daft question. 'E were tall, an' not far from your build, kind o' slight — but 'e were real natty wiv it! Looked like a gennelman, even afore 'e opened 'is mouf. Yer can tell. Fair 'air, 'e 'ad; an' a smile as was summat luv'ly."

"Charming," Evan said, more as an observation than a question.

"Not 'alf," the landlord agreed.

"Popular?" Evan pursued.

"Yeah. Used ter tell a lot o' stories. People like that — passes the time."

"Generous?" Evan asked.

"Gen'rous?" The landlord's eyebrows rose. "No — not gen'rous. More like 'e took more'n 'e gave. Reckon as 'e din't 'ave that much. An' folk liked ter treat 'im — like I said, 'e were right entertainin'. Flash sometimes. Come in 'ere of an occasion an' treat everyone 'andsome — but not often, like — mebbe once a monf."

"Regularly?"

"Wotcher mean?"

"At a set time in the month?"

"Oh no — could be any time, twice a monf, or not fer two monfs."

Gambler, Evan thought to himself. "Thank you," he said aloud. "Thank you very much." And he finished the cider and placed sixpence on the table and left, going out reluctantly into the fading drizzle.

He spent the rest of the afternoon going to bootmakers, hatters, shirtmakers and tailors, from whom he learned precisely what he expected — nothing that his common sense had not already told him.

He bought a fresh eel pie from a vendor on Guilford Street outside the Foundling Hospital, then took a hansom all the way to St. James's, and got out at Boodles, where Joscelin Grey had been a member.

Here his questions had to be a lot more discreet. It was one of the foremost gentlemen's clubs in London, and servants did not gossip about members if they wished to retain their very agreeable and lucrative positions. All he acquired in an hour and a half of roundabout questions was confirmation that Major Grey was indeed a member, that he came quite regularly when he was in town, that of course, like other gentlemen, he gambled, and it was possible his debts were settled over a period of time, but most assuredly they were settled. No gentleman welshed on his debts of honor — tradesmen possibly, but never other gentlemen. Such a question did not arise.

Might Mr. Evan speak with any of Major Grey's associates?

Unless Mr. Evan had a warrant such a thing was out of the question. Did Mr. Evan have such a warrant?

No Mr. Evan did not.

He returned little wiser, but with several thoughts running through his head.

When Evan had gone, Monk walked briskly

182

back to the police station and went to his own room. He pulled out the records of all his old cases, and read. It gave him little cause for comfort.

If his fears for this case proved to be real — a society scandal, sexual perversion, blackmail and murder — then his own path as detective in charge lay between the perils of a very conspicuous and well-publicized failure and the even more dangerous task of probing to uncover the tragedies that had precipitated the final explosion. And a man who would beat to death a lover, turned blackmailer, to keep his secret, would hardly hesitate to ruin a mere policeman. "Nasty" was an understatement.

Had Runcorn done this on purpose? As he looked through the record of his own career, one success after another, he wondered what the price had been; who else had paid it, apart from himself? He had obviously devoted everything to work, to improving his skill, his knowledge, his manners, his dress and his speech. Looking at it as a stranger might, his ambition was painfully obvious: the long hours, the meticulous attention to detail, the flashes of sheer intuitive brilliance, the judgment of other men and their abilities — and weaknesses, always using the right man for any task, then when it was completed, choosing another. His only loyalty seemed to be the pursuit of justice. Could he have imagined it had all gone unnoticed by Runcorn, who lay in its path?

His rise from country boy from a Northumbrian fishing village to inspector in the Metropolitan Police had been little short of meteoric. In twelve years he had achieved more than most men in twenty. He was treading hard on Runcorn's heels; at this present rate of progress he could shortly hope for another promotion, to Runcorn's place — or better.

Perhaps it all depended on the Grey case?

He could not have risen so far, and so fast, without treading on a good many people as he passed. There was a growing fear in him that he might not even have cared. He had read through the cases, very briefly. He had made a god of truth, and — where the law was equivocal, or silent — of what he had believed to be justice. But if there was anything of compassion and genuine feeling for the victims, he had so far failed to find it. His anger was impersonal: against the forces of society that produced poverty and bred helplessness and crime; against the monstrosity of the rookery slums, the sweatshops, extortion, violence, prostitution and infant mortality.

He admired the man he saw reflected in the records, admired his skill and his brain, his energy and tenacity, even his courage; but he could not like him. There was no warmth, no vulnerability, nothing of human hopes or fears, none of the idiosyncrasies that betray the dreams of the heart. The nearest he saw to passion was the ruthlessness with which he pursued injustice; but from the bare written words, it seemed to him that it was wrong itself he hated, and the wronged were not people but the by-products of the crime.

Why was Evan so keen to work with him? To learn? He felt a quick stab of shame at the thought of what he might teach him; and he did not want Evan turned into a copy of himself. People change, all the time; every day one is a little different from yesterday, a little added, a little forgotten. Could he learn something of Evan's feeling instead and teach him excellence without his accompanying ambition?

It was easy to believe Runcorn's feelings for him were ambivalent, at best. What had he done to him, over the years of climbing; what comparisons presented to superiors? What small slights made without sensitivity — had he ever even thought of Runcorn as a man rather than an obstacle between him and the next step up the ladder?

He could hardly blame Runcorn if now he took this perfect opportunity to present him with a case he had to lose; either in failure to solve, or in too much solving, and the uncovering of scandals for which society, and therefore the commissioner of police, would never excuse him.

Monk stared at the paper files. The man in them was a stranger to him, as one-dimensional as Joscelin Grey; in fact more so, because he had spoken to people who cared for Grey, had found charm in him, with whom he had shared laughter and common memories, who missed him with a hollowness of pain.

His own memories were gone, even of Beth, except for the one brief snatch of childhood that had flickered for a moment at Shelburne. But surely more would return, if he did not try to force them and simply let them come?

And the woman in the church, Mrs. Latterly; why had he not remembered her? He had only seen her twice since the accident, and yet her face seemed always at the back of his mind with a sweetness that never quite let him go. Had he spent much time on the case, perhaps questioned her often? It would be ridiculous to have imagined anything personal — the gulf between them was impassable, and if he had entertained ideas, then his ambition was indeed overweening, and indefensible. He blushed hot at the imagination of what he might have betrayed to her in his speech, or his manner. And the vicar had addressed her as "Mrs."— was she wearing black for her father-in-law, or was she a widow? When he saw her again he must correct it, make it plain he dreamed no such effrontery.

But before then he had to discover what on earth the case was about, beyond that her father-in-law had died recently.

He searched all his papers, all the files and everything in his desk, and found nothing with the name Latterly on it. A wretched thought occurred to him, and now an obvious one — the case had been handed on to someone else. Of course it would be, when he had been ill. Runcorn would hardly abandon it, especially if there really was a question of suspicious death involved.

Then why had the new person in charge not spoken to Mrs. Latterly — or more likely her husband, if he were alive? Perhaps he was not. Maybe that was the reason it was she who had asked? He put the files away and went to Runcorn's office. He was startled in passing an outside window to notice that it was now nearly dusk.

Runcorn was still in his office, but on the point of leaving. He did not seem in the least surprised to see Monk.

"Back to your usual hours again?" he said dryly. "No wonder you never married; you've taken a job to wife. Well, cold comfort it'll get you on a winter night," he added with satisfaction. "What is it?"

"Latterly." Monk was irritated by the reminder of what he could now see of himself. Before the accident it must have been there, all his characteristics, habits, but then he was too close to see them. Now he observed them dispassionately, as if they belonged to someone else.

"What?" Runcorn was staring at him, his brow furrowed into lines of incomprehension, his nervous gesture of the left eye more pronounced.

"Latterly," Monk repeated. "I presume you gave the case to someone else when I was ill?"

"Never heard of it," Runcorn said sharply.

"I was working on the case of a man called Latterly. He either committed suicide, or was murdered —"

Runcorn stood up and went to the coat stand and took his serviceable, unimaginative coat off the hook.

"Oh, that case. You said it was suicide and closed it, weeks before the accident. What's the matter with you? Are you losing your memory?"

"No I am not losing my memory!" Monk snapped, feeling a tide of heat rising up inside him. Please heaven it did not show in his face. "But the papers are gone from my files. I presumed something must have occurred to re-open the case and you had given it to someone."

"Oh." Runcorn scowled, proceeding to put on his coat and gloves. "Well, nothing has occurred, and the file is closed. I haven't given it to anyone else. Perhaps you didn't write up anything more? Now will you forget about Latterly, who presumably killed himself, poor devil, and get back to Grey, who most assuredly did not. Have you got anything further? Come on, Monk — you're usually better than this! Anything from this fellow Yeats?"

"No sir, nothing helpful." Monk was stung and his voice betrayed it.

Runcorn turned from the hat stand and smiled fully at him, his eyes bright.

"Then you'd better abandon that and step up your inquiries into Grey's family and friends, hadn't you?" he said with ill-concealed satisfaction. "Especially women friends. There may be a jealous husband somewhere. Looks like that kind of hatred to me. Take my word there's something very nasty at the bottom of this." He tilted his hat slightly on his head, but it simply looked askew rather than rakish. "And you, Monk, are just the man to uncover it. You'd better go and try Shelburne again!" And with that parting shot, ringing with jubilation, he swung his scarf around his neck and went out.

Monk did not go to Shelburne the next day, or even that week. He knew he would have to, but he intended when he went to be as well armed as possible, both for the best chance of success in discovering the murderer of Joscelin Grey, whom he wanted with an intense and driving sense of justice, and — fast becoming almost as important — to avoid all he could of offense in probing the very private lives of the Shelburnes, or whoever else might have been aroused to such a rage, over whatever jealousies, passions or perversions. Monk knew that the powerful were no less frail than the rest of men, but they were usually far fiercer in covering those frailties from the mockery and the delight of the vulgar. It was not a matter of memory so much as instinct, the same way he knew how to shave, or to tie his cravat.

Instead he set out with Evan the following morning to go back to Mecklenburg Square, this time not to find traces of an intruder but to learn anything he could about Grey himself. Although they walked with scant conversation, each deep in his own thought, he was glad not to be alone. Grey's flat oppressed him and he could never free his mind from the violence that had happened there. It was not the blood, or even the death that clung to him, but the hate. He must have seen death before, dozens, if not scores of times, and he could not possibly have been troubled by it like this each time. It must usually have been casual death, pathetic or brainless murder, the utter selfishness of the mugger who wants and takes, or murder by the thief who finds his escape blocked. But in the death of Grey there was a quite different passion, something intimate, a bond of hatred between the killer and the killed.

He was cold in the room, even though the rest of the building was warm. The light through the high windows was colorless as if it would drain rather than illuminate. The furniture seemed oppressive and shabby, too big for the place, although in truth it was exactly like any other. He looked at Evan to see if he felt it also, but Evan's sensitive face was puckered over with the distaste of searching another man's letters, as he opened the desk and began to go through the drawers.

Monk walked past him into the bedroom, a little stale smelling from closed windows. There was a faint film of dust, as last time.

He searched cupboards and clothes drawers, dressers, the tallboy. Grey had an excellent wardrobe; not very extensive, but a beautiful cut and quality. He had certainly possessed good taste, if not the purse to indulge it to the full. There were several sets of cuff links, all gold backed, one with his family crest engraved, two with his own initials. There were three stickpins, one with a fair-sized pearl, and a set of silver-backed brushes, a pigskin toilet kit. Certainly no burglar had come this far. There were many fine pocket handkerchiefs, monogrammed, silk and linen shirts, cravats, socks, clean underwear. He was surprised and somewhat disconcerted to find he knew to within a few shillings the price one would pay for each article, and wondered what aspirations had led him to such knowledge.

He had hoped to find letters in the top drawers, perhaps those too personal to mix with bills and casual correspondence in the desk, but there was nothing, and eventually he went back to the main room. Evan was still at the desk, standing motionless. The place was totally silent, as though both of them were aware that it was a dead man's room, and felt intrusive.

Far down in the street there was a rumble of wheels, the sharper sound of hooves, and a street seller's cry which sounded like "Ole clo' — ole clo'!"

"Well?" He found his voice sunk to a near whisper.

Evan looked up, startled. His face was tight.

"Rather a lot of letters here, sir. I'm not sure really what to make of them. There are several from his sister-in-law, Rosamond Grey; a rather sharp one from his brother Lovel — that's Lord Shelburne, isn't it? A very recent note from his mother, but only one, so it looks as if he didn't keep hers. There are several from a Dawlish family, just prior to his death; among them an invitation to stay at their home for a week. They seem to have been friendly." He puckered his mouth slightly. "One is from Miss Amanda Dawlish, sounds quite eager. In fact there are a number of invitations, all for dates after his death. Apparently he didn't keep old ones. And I'm afraid there's no diary. Funny." He looked up at Monk. "You'd think a man like that would have a social diary, wouldn't you?"

"Yes you would!" Monk moved forward. "Perhaps the murderer took it. You're quite sure?"

"Not in the desk." Evan shook his head. "And I've checked for hidden drawers. But why would anyone hide a social diary anyway?"

"No idea," Monk said honestly, taking a

193

step nearer to the desk and peering at it. "Unless it was the murderer who took it. Perhaps his name figures heavily. We'll have to try these Dawlishes. Is there an address on the letters?"

"Oh yes, I've made a note of it."

"Good. What else?"

"Several bills. He wasn't very prompt in paying up, but I knew that already from talking to the tradesmen. Three from his tailor, four or five from a shirtmaker, the one I visited, two from the wine merchant, rather terse letter from the family solicitor in reply to a request for an increased allowance.

"In the negative, I take it?"

"Very much so."

"Anything from clubs, gambling and so on?"

"No, but then one doesn't usually commit gambling debts to paper, even at Boodles, unless you are the one who is collecting, of course." Then he smiled suddenly. "Not that I can afford to know — except by hearsay!"

Monk relaxed a little. "Quite," he agreed. "Any other letters?"

"One pretty cool one from a Charles Latterly, doesn't say much —"

"Latterly?" Monk froze.

"Yes. You know him?" Evan was watching him.

194

Monk took a deep breath and controlled himself with an effort. Mrs. Latterly at St. Marylebone had said "Charles," and he had feared it might have been her husband.

"I was working on a Latterly case some time ago," he said, struggling to keep his voice level. "It's probably coincidence. I was looking for the file on Latterly yesterday and I couldn't find it."

"Was he someone who could have been connected with Grey, some scandal to hush up, or —"

"No!" He spoke more harshly than he had intended to, betraying his feelings. He moderated his tone. "No, not at all. Poor man is dead anyway. Died before Grey did."

"Oh." Evan turned back to the desk. "That's about all, I'm afraid. Still, we should be able to find a lot of people who knew him from these, and they'll lead us to more."

"Yes, yes quite. I'll take Latterly's address, all the same."

"Oh, right." Evan fished among the letters and passed him one.

Monk read it. It was very cool, as Evan had said, but not impolite, and there was nothing in it to suggest positive dislike, only a relationship which was not now to be continued. Monk read it three times, but could see nothing further in it. He copied down the address, and returned the letter to Evan.

They finished searching the apartment, and then with careful notes went outside again, passing Grimwade in the hall.

"Lunch," Monk said briskly, wanting to be among people, hear laughter and speech and see men who knew nothing about murder and violent, obscene secrets, men engrossed in the trivial pleasures and irritations of daily life.

"Right." Evan fell in step beside him. "There's a good public house about half a mile from here where they serve the most excellent dumplings. That is —" he stopped suddenly. "It's very ordinary — don't know if you —"

"Fine," Monk agreed. "Sounds just what we need. I'm frozen after being in that place. I don't know why, but it seems cold, even inside."

Evan hunched his shoulders and smiled a little sheepishly. "It might be imagination, but it always chills me. I'm not used to murder yet. I suppose you're above that kind of emotionalism, but I haven't got that far —"

"Don't!" Monk spoke more violently than he had meant to. "Don't get used to it!" He was betraying his own rawness, his sudden sensitivity, but did not care. "I mean," he said more softly, aware that he had startled Evan by his vehemence, "keep your brain clear, by all means, but don't let it cease to shock you.

Don't be a detective before you're a man."
Now that he had said it it sounded sententious
and extremely trite. He was embarrassed.

Evan did not seem to notice.

"I've a long way to go before I'm efficient
enough to do that, sir. I confess, even that
room up there makes me feel a little sick. This
is the first murder like this I've been on."
He sounded self-conscious and very young.
"Of course I've seen bodies before, but usually
accidents, or paupers who died in the street.
There are quite a few of them in the winter.
That's why I'm so pleased to be on this case
with you. I couldn't learn from anyone better."

Monk felt himself color with pleasure —
and shame, because he did not deserve it. He
could not think of anything at all to say, and
he strode ahead through the thickening rain
searching for words, and not finding them.
Evan walked beside him, apparently not needing an answer.

The following Monday Monk and Evan got
off the train at Shelburne and set out towards
Shelburne Hall. It was one of the summer days
when the wind is fresh from the east, sharp
as a slap in the face, and the sky is clear and
cloudless. The trees were huge green billows
resting on the bosom of the earth, gently, in-

cessantly moving, whispering. There had been rain overnight, and under the shadows the smell of damp earth was sweet where their feet disturbed it.

They walked in silence, each enjoying it in his own way. Monk was not aware of any particular thoughts, except perhaps a sense of pleasure in the sheer distance of the sky, the width across the fields. Suddenly memory flooded back vividly, and he saw Northumberland again: broad, bleak hills, north wind shivering in the grass. The milky sky was mackerel shredded out to sea, and white gulls floated on the currents, screaming.

He could remember his mother, dark like Beth, standing in the kitchen, and the smell of yeast and flour. She had been proud of him, proud that he could read and write. He must have been very young then. He remembered a room with sun in it, the vicar's wife teaching him letters, Beth in a smock staring at him in awe. She could not read. He could almost feel himself teaching her, years after, slowly, outline by outline. Her writing still carried echoes of those hours, careful, conscious of the skill and its long learning. She had loved him so much, admired him without question. Then the memory disappeared and it was as if someone had drenched him in cold water, leaving him startled and shivering. It was the most acute and powerful memory he had recaptured and its sharpness left him stunned. He did not notice Evan's eyes on him, or the quick glance away as he strove to avoid what he realized would be intrusion.

Shelburne Hall was in sight across the smooth earth, less than a thousand yards away, framed in trees.

"Do you want me to say anything, or just listen?" Evan asked. "It might be better if I listened."

Monk realized with a start that Evan was nervous. Perhaps he had never spoken to a woman of title before, much less questioned her on personal and painful matters. He might not even have seen such a place, except from the distance. He wondered where his own assurance came from, and why he had not ever thought of it before. Runcorn was right, he was ambitious, even arrogant — and insensitive.

"Perhaps if you try the servants," he replied. "Servants notice a lot of things. Sometimes they see a side of their masters that their lordships manage to hide from their equals."

"I'll try the valet," Evan suggested. "I should imagine you are peculiarly vulnerable in the bath, or in your underwear." He grinned suddenly at the thought, and perhaps in some amusement at the physical helplessness of his social superiors to need assistance in such common matters. It offset his own fear of proving inadequate to the situation.

Lady Fabia Shelburne was somewhat surprised to see Monk again, and kept him waiting nearly half an hour, this time in the butler's pantry with the silver polish, a locked desk for the wine book and the cellar keys, and a comfortable armchair by a small grate. Apparently the housekeeper's sitting room was already in use. He was annoyed at the casual insolence of it, and yet part of him was obliged to admire her self-control. She had no idea why he had come. He might even have been able to tell her who had murdered her son, and why.

When he was sent for and conducted to the rosewood sitting room, which seemed to be peculiarly hers, she was cool and gracious, as if he had only just arrived and she had no more than a courteous interest in what he might say.

At her invitation he sat down opposite her on the same deep rose-pink chair as before.

"Well, Mr. Monk?" she inquired with slightly raised eyebrows. "Is there something further you want to say to me?"

"Yes ma'am, if you please. We are even more of the opinion that whoever killed Major Grey did so for some personal reason, and that he was not a chance victim. Therefore we need to know everything further we can about him, his social connections —"

Her eyes widened. "If you imagine his social connections are of a type to indulge in murder, Mr. Monk, then you are extraordinarily ignorant of society."

"I am afraid, ma'am, that most people are capable of murder, if they are hard-pressed enough, and threatened in what they most value —"

"I think not." Her voice indicated the close of the subject and she turned her head a little away from him.

"Let us hope they are rare, ma'am." He controlled his impulse to anger with difficulty. "But it would appear there is at least one, and I am sure you wish to find him, possibly even more than I do."

"You are very slick with words, young man." It was grudgingly given, even something of a criticism. "What is it you imagine I can tell you?"

"A list of his closest friends," he answered. "Family friends, any invitations you may know of that he accepted in the last few months, especially for weeks or weekends away. Perhaps any lady in whom he may have been interested." He saw a slight twitch of distaste cross her immaculate features. "I believe he was extremely charming." He added the flattery in which he felt was her only weakness.

"He was." There was a small movement in her lips, a change in her eyes as for a moment grief overtook her. It was several seconds till she smoothed it out again and was as perfect as before.

Monk waited in silence, for the first time aware of the force of her pain.

"Then possibly some lady was more attracted to him than was acceptable to her other admirers, or even her husband?" he suggested at last, and in a considerably softer tone, although his resolve to find the murderer of Joscelin Grey was if anything hardened even further, and it allowed of no exceptions, no omissions for hurt.

She considered this thought for a moment before deciding to accept it. He imagined she was seeing her son again as he had been in life, elegant, laughing, direct of gaze.

"It might have been," she conceded. "It could be that some young person was indiscreet, and provoked jealousy."

"Perhaps someone who had a little too much to drink?" He pursued it with a tact that did not come to him naturally. "And saw in it more than there was?"

"A gentleman knows how to conduct himself." She looked at Monk with a slight turn downwards at the corners of her mouth. The word *gentleman* was not lost on him. "Even when he has had too much to drink. But unfortunately some people are not as discriminating in their choice of guests as they should be."

"If you would give me some names and addresses, ma'am; I shall conduct my inquiries as cautiously as I can, and naturally shall not mention your name. I imagine all persons of good conscience will be as keen to discover who murdered Major Grey as you are yourself."

It was a well-placed argument, and she acknowledged it with a momentary glance directly into his eyes.

"Quite," she agreed. "If you have a notebook I shall oblige you." She reached across to the rosewood table almost at her side and opened a drawer. She took out a leather-bound and gold-tooled address book.

He made ready and was well started when Lovel Grey came in, again dressed in casual clothes — this time breeches and a Norfolk jacket of well-worn tweed. His face darkened when he saw Monk.

"I really think, Mr. Monk, that if you have something to report, you may do so to me!" he said with extreme irritation. "If you have not, then your presence here serves no purpose, and you are distressing my mother. I am surprised you should come again."

Monk stood up instinctively, annoyed with himself for the necessity.

"I came, my lord, because I needed some further information, which Lady Shelburne has been kind enough to give me." He could feel the color hot in his face.

"There is nothing we can tell you that could be of the least relevance," Lovel snapped. "For heaven's sake, man, can't you do your job without rushing out here every few days?" He moved restlessly, fidgeting with the crop in his hand. "We cannot help you! If you are beaten, admit it! Some crimes are never solved, especially where madmen are concerned."

Monk was trying to compose a civil reply when Lady Shelburne herself intervened in a small, tight voice.

"That may be so, Lovel, but not in this case. Joscelin was killed by someone who knew him, however distasteful that may be to us. Naturally it is also possible it was someone known here. It is far more discreet of Mr. Monk to ask us than to go around inquiring of the whole neighborhood."

"Good God!" Lovel's face fell. "You cannot be serious. To allow him to do that would be monstrous. We'd be ruined."

"Nonsense!" She closed her address book with a snap and replaced it in the drawer. "We do not ruin so easily. There have been Shelburnes on the land for five hundred years, and will continue to be. However I have no intention of allowing Mr. Monk to do any such thing." She looked at Monk coldly. "That is why I am providing him with a list myself, and suitable questions to ask — and to avoid."

"There is no need to do either." Lovel turned furiously from his mother to Monk and back again, his color high. "Whoever killed Joscelin must have been one of his London acquaintances — if indeed it really was someone he knew at all, which I still doubt. In spite of what you say, I believe it was purely chance he was the victim, and not someone else. I daresay he was seen at a club, or some such place, by someone who saw he had money and hoped to rob him."

"It was not robbery, sir," Monk said firmly. "There were all sorts of valuable items quite visible and untouched in his rooms, even the money in his wallet was still there."

"And how do you know how much he had in his wallet?" Lovel demanded. "He may have had hundreds!"

"Thieves do not usually count out change and return it to you," Monk replied, moderating the natural sarcasm in his voice only slightly.

Lovel was too angry to stop. "And have you some reason to suppose this was a 'usual' thief? I did not know you had proceeded so far. In fact I did not know you had proceeded at all."

"Most unusual, thank heaven." Monk ignored the jibe. "Thieves seldom kill. Did Major Grey often walk about with hundreds of pounds in his pocket?"

Lovel's face was scarlet. He threw the crop across the room, intending it to land on the sofa, but it fell beyond and rattled to the floor. He ignored it. "No of course not!" he shouted. "But then this was a unique occasion. He was not simply robbed and left lying, he was beaten to death, if you remember."

Lady Fabia's face pinched with misery and disgust.

"Really, Lovel, the man is doing his best, for whatever that is worth. There is no need to be offensive."

Suddenly his tone changed. "You are upset, Mama; and it's quite natural that you should be. Please leave this to me. If I think there is anything to tell Mr. Monk, I shall do so. Why don't you go into the withdrawing room and have tea with Rosamond?"

"Don't patronize me, Lovel!" she snapped,

rising to her feet. "I am not too upset to conduct myself properly, and to help the police find the man who murdered my son."

"There is nothing whatsoever we can do, Mama!" He was fast losing his temper again. "Least of all assist them to pester half the country for personal information about poor Joscelin's life and friends."

"It was one of poor Joscelin's 'friends' who beat him to death!" Her cheeks were ashen white and a lesser woman might well have fainted before now, but she stood ramrod stiff, her white hands clenched.

"Rubbish!" Lovel dismissed it instantly. "It was probably someone he played at cards and who simply couldn't take losing. Joscelin gambled a damned sight more than he led you to believe. Some people play for stakes they can't afford, and then when they're beaten, they lose control of themselves and go temporarily off their heads." He breathed in and out hard. "Gaming clubs are not always as discriminating as they should be as to whom they allow in. That is quite probably what happened to Joscelin. Do you seriously imagine anyone at Shelburne would know anything about it?"

"It is also possible it was someone who was jealous over a woman," she answered icily. "Joscelin was very charming, you know."

Lovel flushed and the whole skin of his face appeared to tighten.

"So I have frequently been reminded," he said in a soft, dangerous little voice. "But not everyone was as susceptible to it as you, Mama. It is a very superficial quality."

She stared at him with something that bordered on contempt.

"You never understood charm, Lovel, which is your great misfortune. Perhaps you would be good enough to order extra tea in the withdrawing room." Deliberately she ignored her son and contravened propriety, as if to annoy him. "Will you join us, Mr. Monk? Perhaps my daughter-in-law may be able to suggest something. She was accustomed to attend many of the same functions as Joscelin, and women are frequently more observant of other women, especially where" — she hesitated — "affairs of the emotions are concerned."

Without waiting for his reply she assumed his compliance and, still ignoring Lovel, turned to the door and stopped. Lovel wavered for only the barest second, then he came forward obediently and opened the door for her. She swept through without looking again at either of them.

In the withdrawing room the atmosphere was stiff. Rosamond had difficulty hiding her amazement at being expected to take tea with a policeman as if he were a gentleman; and even the maid with the extra cups and muffins seemed uncomfortable. Apparently the below-stairs gossip had already told her who Monk was. Monk silently thought of Evan, and wondered if he had made any progress.

When the maid had handed everyone their cups and plates and was gone Lady Fabia began in a level, quiet voice, avoiding Lovel's eyes.

"Rosamond, my dear, the police require to know everything they can about Joscelin's social activities in the last few months before he died. You attended most of the same functions, and are thus more aware of any relationships than I. For example, who might have shown more interest in him than was prudent?"

"I?" Rosamond was either profoundly surprised or a better actress than Monk had judged her to be on their earlier meeting.

"Yes you, my dear." Lady Fabia passed her the muffins, which she ignored. "I am talking to you. I shall, of course, also ask Ursula."

"Who is Ursula?" Monk interrupted.

"Miss Ursula Wadham; she is betrothed to my second son, Menard. You may safely leave it to me to glean from her any information that would be of use." She dismissed Monk and turned back to Rosamond. "Well?"

"I don't recall Joscelin having any . . . relationship in — in particular." Rosamond sounded rather awkward, as if the subject disturbed her. Watching her, Monk wondered for a moment if she had been in love with Joscelin herself, if perhaps that was why Lovel was so reluctant to have the matter pursued.

Could it even have gone further than a mere attraction?

"That is not what I asked," Lady Fabia said with thin patience. "I asked you if anyone else had shown any interest in Joscelin, albeit a one-sided one?"

Rosamond's head came up. For a moment Monk thought she was about to resist her mother-in-law, then the moment died.

"Norah Partridge was very fond of him," she replied slowly, measuring her words. "But that is hardly new; and I cannot see Sir John taking it badly enough to go all the way up to London and commit murder. I do believe he is fond of Norah, but not enough for that."

"Then you are more observant than I thought," Lady Fabia said with acid surprise. "But without much understanding of men, my dear. It is not necessary to want something yourself in order profoundly to resent some-one else's having the ability to take it away from you; especially if they have the tactlessness to do it publicly." She swiveled to Monk. He was not offered the muffins. "There is somewhere for you to begin. I doubt John Partridge would be moved to murder — or that he would use a stick if he were." Her face flickered with pain again. "But Norah had other admirers. She is a somewhat extravagant creature, and not possessed of much judgment."

"Thank you, ma'am. If you think of anything further?"

For another hour they raked over past romances, affairs and supposed affairs, and Monk half listened. He was not interested in the facts so much as the nuances behind their expression. Joscelin had obviously been his mother's favorite, and if the absent Menard was like his elder brother, it was easy to understand why. But whatever her feelings, the laws of primogeniture ruled that not only the title and the lands, but also the money to support them and the way of life that went with them, must pass to Lovel, the firstborn.

Lovel himself contributed nothing, and Rosamond only enough to satisfy her mother-in-law, of whom she seemed in awe far more than of her husband.

Monk did not see Lady Callandra Daviot,

rather to his disappointment. He would have liked her candor on the subject, although he was not sure she would have expressed herself as freely in front of the grieving family as she had in the garden in the rain.

He thanked them and excused himself in time to find Evan and walk down to the village for a pint of cider before the train back to London.

"Well?" Monk asked as soon as they were out of sight of the house.

"Ah." Evan could scarcely suppress his enthusiasm; his stride was surprisingly long, his lean body taut with energy, and he splashed through puddles on the road with complete disregard for his soaking boots. "It's fascinating. I've never been inside a really big house before, I mean inside to know it. My father was a clergyman, you know, and I went along to the manor house sometimes when I was a child — but it was nothing like this. Good Lord, those servants see things that would paralyze me with shame — I mean the family treat them as if they were deaf and blind."

"They don't think of them as people," Monk replied. "At least not people in the same sense as themselves. They are two different worlds, and they don't impinge, except physically. Therefore their opinions don't matter.

Did you learn anything else?" He smiled slightly at Evan's innocence.

Evan grinned. "I'll say, although of course they wouldn't intentionally tell a policeman, or anyone else, anything they thought confidential about the family. It would be more than their livelihood was worth. Very close-mouthed, they thought they were."

"So how did you learn?" Monk asked curiously, looking at Evan's innocent, imaginative features.

Evan blushed very slightly. "Threw myself on Cook's mercy." He looked down at the ground, but did not decrease his pace in the slightest. "Slandered my landlady appallingly, I'm afraid. Spoke very unkindly about her cooking — oh, and I stood outside for some time before going in, so my hands were cold —" He glanced up at Monk, then away again. "Very motherly sort, Lady Shelburne's cook." He smiled rather smugly. "Daresay I did a lot better than you did."

"I didn't eat at all," Monk said tartly.

"I'm sorry." Evan did not sound it.

"And what did your dramatic debut earn you, apart from luncheon?" Monk asked. "I presume you overheard a good deal — while you were busy being pathetic and eating them out of house and home?"

"Oh yes — did you know that Rosamond

213

comes from a well-to-do family, but a bit come-lately? And she fell for Joscelin first, but her mother insisted she marry the eldest brother, who also offered for her. And she was a good, obedient girl and did as she was told. At least that is what I read between the lines of what the tweeny was saying to the laundry maid — before the parlor maid came in and stopped them gossiping and they were packed off to their duties."

Monk whistled through his teeth.

"And," Evan went on before he could speak, "they had no children for the first few years, then one son, heir to the title, about a year and a half ago. Someone particularly spiteful is said to have observed that he has the typical Shelburne looks, but more like Joscelin than Lovel — so the second footman heard said in the public house. Blue eyes — you see, Lord Shelburne is dark — so is she — at least her eyes are —"

Monk stopped in the road, staring at him.
"Are you sure?"

"I'm sure that's what they say, and Lord Shelburne must have heard it — at last —" He looked appalled. "Oh God! That's what Runcorn meant, isn't it? Very nasty, very nasty indeed." He was comical in his dismay, suddenly the enthusiasm gone out of him. "What on earth are we going to do? I can imagine how Lady Fabia will react if you try opening that one up!"

"So can I," Monk said grimly. "And I don't know what we are going to do."

CHAPTER SIX

Hester Latterly stood in the small withdrawing room of her brother's house in Thanet Street, a little off the Marylebone Road, and stared out of the window at the carriages passing. It was a smaller house, far less attractive than the family home on Regent Square. But after her father's death that house had had to be sold. She had always imagined that Charles and Imogen would move out of this house and back to Regent Square in such an event, but apparently the funds were needed to settle affairs, and there was nothing above that for any inheritance for any of them. Hence she was now residing with Charles and Imogen, and would be obliged to do so until she should make some arrangements of her own. What they might be now occupied her thoughts.

Her choice was narrow. Disposal of her parents' possessions had been completed, all the necessary letters written and servants given excellent references. Most had fortunately found new positions. It remained for Hester herself to make a decision. Of course Charles had said she was more than welcome to remain as long as she wished — indefinitely, if she chose. The thought was appalling. A permanent guest, neither use nor ornament, intruding on what should be a private house for husband and wife, and in time their children. Aunts were all very well, but not for breakfast, luncheon and dinner every day of the week.

Life had to offer more than that.

Naturally Charles had spoken of marriage, but to be frank, as the situation surely warranted, Hester was very few people's idea of a good match. She was pleasing enough in feature, if a little tall — she looked over the heads of rather too many men for her own comfort, or theirs. But she had no dowry and no expectations at all. Her family was well-bred, but of no connection to any of the great houses; in fact genteel enough to have aspirations, and to have taught its daughters no useful arts, but not privileged enough for birth alone to be sufficient attraction.

All of which might have been overcome if her personality were as charming as Imogen's — but it was not. Where Imogen was gentle, gracious, full of tact and discretion, Hester was abrasive, contemptuous of hypocrisy and impatient of dithering or incompetence and disinclined to suffer foolishness with any grace at all. She was also fonder of reading and study than was attractive in a woman, and not free of the intellectual arrogance of one to whom thought comes easily.

It was not entirely her fault, which mitigated blame but did not improve her chances of gaining or keeping an admirer. She had been among the first to leave England and sail, in appalling conditions, to the Crimea and offer her help to Florence Nightingale in the troop hospital in Scutari.

She could remember quite clearly her first sight of the city, which she had expected to be ravaged by war, and how her breath had caught in her throat with delight at the vividness of the white walls and the copper domes green against the blue sky.

Of course afterwards it had been totally different. She had witnessed such wretchedness and waste there, exacerbated by incompetence that beggared the imagination, and her courage had sustained her, her selflessness never looked for reward, her patience for the truly afflicted never flagged. And at the same time the sight of such terrible suffering had made her rougher to lesser pain than was just. Each person's pain is severe to him at the time, and the thought that there might be vastly worse occurs to very few. Hester did not stop to consider this, except when it was forced upon her, and such was most people's abhorrence of candor on unpleasant subjects that very few did.

She was highly intelligent, with a gift for logical thought which many people found disturbing — especially men, who did not expect it or like it in a woman. That gift had enabled her to be invaluable in the administration of hospitals for the critically injured or desperately ill — but there was no place for it in the domestic homes of gentlemen in England. She could have run an entire castle and marshaled the forces to defend it, and had time to spare. Unfortunately no one desired a castle run — and no one attacked them anymore.

And she was approaching thirty.

The realistic choices lay between nursing at a practical level, at which she was now skilled, although more with injury than the diseases that occur most commonly in a temperate climate like that of England, and, on the other hand, a post in the administration of hospitals, junior as that was likely to be; women were not doctors, and not generally considered for more senior posts. But much had changed in the war, and the work to be done, the reforms that might be achieved, excited her more than she cared to admit, since the possibilities of participating were so slight.

And there was also the call of journalism, although it would hardly bring her the income necessary to provide a living. But it need not be entirely abandoned —?

She really wished for advice. Charles would disapprove of the whole idea, as he had of her going to the Crimea in the first place. He would be concerned for her safety, her reputation, her honor — and anything else general and unspecified that might cause her harm. Poor Charles, he was a very conventional soul. How they could ever be siblings she had no idea.

And there was little use asking Imogen. She had no knowledge from which to speak; and lately she seemed to have half her mind on some turmoil of her own. Hester had tried to discover without prying offensively, and succeeded in learning nothing at all, except close to a certainty that whatever it was Charles knew even less of it than she.

As she stared out through the window into the street her thoughts turned to her mentor and friend of pre-Crimean days, Lady Callandra Daviot. She would give sound advice both as to knowledge of what might be achieved and how to go about it, and what might be dared and, if reached, would make her happy. Callandra had never given a fig for doing what was told her was suitable, and she did not assume a person wanted what society said they ought to want.

She had always said that Hester was welcome to visit her either in her London house or at Shelburne Hall at any time she wished. She had her own rooms there and was free to entertain as pleased her. Hester had already written to both addresses and asked if she might come. Today she had received a reply most decidedly in the affirmative.

The door opened behind her and she heard Charles's step. She turned, the letter still in her hand.

"Charles, I have decided to go and spend a few days, perhaps a week or so, with Lady Callandra Daviot."

"Do I know her?" he said immediately, his eyes widening a fraction.

"I should think it unlikely," she replied. "She is in her late fifties, and does not mix a great deal socially."

"Are you considering becoming her companion?" His eye was to the practical. "I don't think you are suited to the position, Hester. With all the kindness in the world, I have to say you are not a congenial person for an elderly lady of a retiring nature. You are extremely bossy — and you have very little sympathy with the ordinary pains of day-to-day life. And you have never yet succeeded in keeping even your silliest opinions to yourself."

"I have never tried!" she said tartly, a little stung by his wording, even though she knew he meant it for her well-being.

He smiled with a slightly twisted humor. "I am aware of that, my dear. Had you tried, even you must have done better!"

"I have no intention of becoming a companion to anyone," she pointed out. It was on the tip of her tongue to add that, had she such a thing in mind, Lady Callandra would be her first choice; but perhaps if she did that, Charles would question Callandra's suitability as a person to visit. "She is the widow of Colonel Daviot, who was a surgeon in the army. I thought I should see her advice as to what position I might be best suited for."

He was surprised. "Do you really think she would have any useful idea? It seems to me unlikely. However do go, by all means, if you wish. You have certainly been a most marvelous help to us here, and we are deeply grateful. You came at a moment's notice, leaving all your friends behind, and gave your time and your affections to us when we were sorely in need."

"It was a family tragedy." For once her candor was also gracious. "I should not have wished to be anywhere else. But yes, Lady Callandra has considerable experience and I should value her opinion. If it is agreeable to you, I shall leave tomorrow early."

"Certainly —" He hesitated, looking a trifle uncomfortable. "Er —"

"What is it?"

"Do you — er — have sufficient means?"

She smiled. "Yes, thank you — for the time being."

He looked relieved. She knew he was not naturally generous, but neither was he grudging with his own family. His reluctance was another reinforcement of the observations she had made that there had been a considerable tightening of circumstances in the last four or five months. There had been other small things: the household had not the complement of servants she remembered prior to her leaving for the Crimea; now there were only the cook, one kitchen maid, one scullery maid, one housemaid and a parlor maid who doubled as lady's maid for Imogen. The butler was the only male indoor servant; no footman, not even a bootboy. The scullery maid did the shoes.

Imogen had not refurbished her summer wardrobe with the usual generosity, and at least one pair of Charles's boots had been repaired. The silver tray in the hall for receiving calling cards was no longer there.

It was most assuredly time she considered her own position, and the necessity of earning her own way. Some academic pursuit had been a suggestion; she found study absorbing, but the tutorial positions open to women were few, and the restrictions of the life did not appeal to her. She read for pleasure.

When Charles had gone she went upstairs and found Imogen in the linen room inspecting pillow covers and sheets. Caring for them was a large task, even for so modest a household, especially without the services of a laundry maid.

"Excuse me." She began immediately to assist, looking at embroidered edges for tears or where the stitching was coming away. "I have decided to go and visit Lady Callandra Daviot, in the country, for a short while. I think she can advise me on what I should do next —" She saw Imogen's look of surprise, and clarified her statement. "At least she will know the possibilities open to me better than I."

"Oh." Imogen's face showed a mixture of pleasure and disappointment and it was not necessary for her to explain. She understood that Hester must come to a decision, but also she would miss her company. Since their first meeting they had become close friends and their differences in nature had been complementary rather than irritating. "Then you had better take Gwen. You can't stay with the aristocracy without a lady's maid."

"Certainly I can," Hester contradicted decisively. "I don't have one, so I shall be obliged to. It will do me no harm whatsoever, and Lady Callandra will be the last one to mind."

Imogen looked dubious. "And how will you dress for dinner?"

"For goodness sake! I can dress myself!"

Imogen's face twitched very slightly. "Yes my dear, I have seen! And I am sure it is admirable for nursing the sick, and fighting stubborn authorities in the army —"

"Imogen!"

"And what about your hair?" Imogen pressed. "You are likely to arrive at table looking as if you had come sideways through a high wind to get there!"

"Imogen!" Hester threw a bundle of towels at her, one knocking a front lock of her hair askew and the rest scattering on the floor.

Imogen threw a sheet back, achieving the same result. They looked at each other's wild appearance and began to laugh. Within moments both were gasping for breath and sitting on the floor in mounds of skirts with previously crisp laundry lying around them in heaps.

The door opened and Charles stood on the threshold looking bemused and a trifle alarmed.

"What on earth is wrong?" he demanded, at first taking their sobs for distress. "Are you ill? What has happened?" Then he saw it was amusement and looked even more confounded, and as neither of them stopped or took any sensible notice of him, he became annoyed.

"Imogen! Control yourself!" he said sharply. "What is the matter with you?"

Imogen still laughed helplessly.

"Hester!" Charles was growing pink in the face. "Hester, stop it! Stop it at once!"

Hester looked at him and found it funnier still.

Charles sniffed, dismissed it as women's weakness and therefore inexplicable, and left, shutting the door hard so none of the servants should witness such a ridiculous scene.

Hester was perfectly accustomed to travel, and the journey from London to Shelburne was barely worth comment compared with the fearful passage by sea across the Bay of Biscay and through the Mediterranean to the Bosporus and up the Black Sea to Sebastopol. Troopships replete with terrified horses, overcrowded, and with the merest of accommodations, were things beyond the imagination of most Englishmen, let alone women. A simple train journey through the summer countryside was a positive pleasure, and the warm, quiet and sweet-scented mile in the dog cart at the far end before she reached the hall was a glory to the senses.

She arrived at the magnificent front entrance with its Doric columns and portico. The driver had no time to hand her down because she had grown unaccustomed to such courtesies and scrambled to the ground herself while he was still tying the reins. With a frown he unloaded her box and at the same moment a footman opened the door and held it for her to pass through. Another footman carried in the box and disappeared somewhere upstairs with it.

Fabia Shelburne was in the withdrawing room where Hester was shown. It was a room of considerable beauty, and at this height of the year, with the French windows open onto the garden and the scent of roses drifting on a warm breeze, the soft green of the rolling parkland beyond, the marble-surrounded fireplace seemed unnecessary, and the paintings keyholes to another and unnecessary world.

Lady Fabia did not rise, but smiled as Hester was shown in.

"Welcome to Shelburne Hall, Miss Latterly.

I hope your journey was not too fatiguing. Why my dear, you seem very blown about! I am afraid it is very windy beyond the garden. I trust it has not distressed you. When you have composed yourself and taken off your traveling clothes, perhaps you would care to join us for afternoon tea? Cook is particularly adept at making crumpets." She smiled, a cool, well-practiced gesture. "I expect you are hungry, and it will be an excellent opportunity for us to become acquainted with each other. Lady Callandra will be down, no doubt, and my daughter-in-law, Lady Shelburne. I do not believe you have met?"

"No, Lady Fabia, but it is a pleasure I look forward to." She had observed Fabia's deep violet gown, less somber than black but still frequently associated with mourning. Apart from that Callandra had told her of Joscelin Grey's death, although not in detail. "May I express my deepest sympathy for the loss of your son. I have a little understanding of how you feel."

Fabia's eyebrows rose. "Have you!" she said with disbelief.

Hester was stung. Did this woman imagine she was the only person who had been bereaved? How self-absorbed grief could be.

"Yes," she replied perfectly levelly. "I lost my eldest brother in the Crimea, and a few months ago my father and mother within three weeks of each other."

"Oh —" For once Fabia was at a loss for words. She had supposed Hester's sober dress merely a traveling convenience. Her own mourning consumed her to the exclusion of anyone else's. "I am sorry."

Hester smiled; when she truly meant it it had great warmth.

"Thank you," she accepted. "Now if you permit I will accept your excellent idea and change into something suitable before joining you for tea. You are quite right; the very thought of crumpets makes me realize I am very hungry."

The bedroom they had given her was in the west wing, where Callandra had had a bedroom and sitting room of her own since she had moved out of the nursery. She and her elder brothers had grown up at Shelburne Hall. She had left it to marry thirty years ago, but still visited frequently, and in her widowhood had been extended the courtesy of retaining the accommodation and the hospitality that went with it.

Hester's room was large and a little somber, being hung with muted tapestries on one entire wall and papered in a shade that was undecided between green and gray. The only relief was a delightful painting of two dogs, framed in gold leaf which caught the light. The windows faced westward, and on so fine a day the evening sky was a glory between the great beech trees close to the house, and beyond was a view of an immaculately set-out walled herb garden with fruit trees carefully lined against it. On the far side the heavy boughs of the orchard hid the parkland beyond.

There was hot water ready in a large blue-and-white china jug, and a matching basin beside it, with fresh towels, and she wasted no time in taking off her heavy, dusty skirts, washing her face and neck, and then putting the basin on the floor and easing her hot, aching feet into it.

She was thus employed, indulging in the pure physical pleasure of it, when there was a knock on the door.

"Who is it?" she said in alarm. She was wearing only a camisole and pantaloons and was at a considerable disadvantage. And since she already had water and towels she was not expecting a maid.

"Callandra," came the reply.

"Oh —" Perhaps it was foolish to try to impress Callandra Daviot with something she could not maintain. "Come in!"

Callandra opened the door and stood with a smile of delight in her face.

"My dear Hester! How truly pleased I am to see you. You look as if you have not changed in the slightest — at the core at least." She closed the door behind her and came in, sitting down on one of the upholstered bedroom chairs. She was not and never had been a beautiful woman; she was too broad in the hip, too long in the nose, and her eyes were not exactly the same color. But there was humor and intelligence in her face, and a remarkable strength of will. Hester had never known anyone she had liked better, and the mere sight of her was enough to lift the spirits and fill the heart with confidence.

"Perhaps not." She wriggled her toes in the now cool water. The sensation was delicious. "But a great deal has happened: my circumstances have altered."

"So you wrote to me. I am extremely sorry about your parents — please know that I feel for you deeply."

Hester did not want to talk of it; the pain was still very sharp. Imogen had written and told her of her father's death, although not a great deal of the circumstances, except that he had been shot in what might have been an accident with a pair of dueling pistols he kept, or that he might have surprised an intruder, although since it had happened in the late afternoon it was unlikely, and the police

231

had implied but not insisted that suicide was probable. In consideration to the family, the verdict had been left open. Suicide was not only a crime against the law but a sin against the Church which would exclude him from being buried in hallowed ground and be a burden of shame the family would carry indefinitely.

Nothing appeared to have been taken, and no robber was ever apprehended. The police did not pursue the case.

Within a week another letter had arrived, actually posted two weeks later, to say that her mother had died also. No one had said that it was of heartbreak, but such words were not needed.

"Thank you," Hester acknowledged with a small smile.

Callandra looked at her for a moment, then was sensitive enough to see the hurt in her and understand that probing would only injure further, discussion was no longer any part of the healing. Instead she changed the subject to the practical.

"What are you considering doing now? For heaven's sake don't rush into a marriage!"

Hester was a trifle surprised at such unorthodox advice, but she replied with self-deprecatory frankness.

"I have no opportunity to do such a thing.

I am nearly thirty, of an uncompromising disposition, too tall, and have no money and no connections. Any man wishing to marry me would be highly suspect as to his motives or his judgment."

"The world is not short of men with either shortcoming," Callandra replied with an answering smile. "As you yourself have frequently written me. The army at least abounds with men whose motives you suspect and whose judgment you abhor."

Hester pulled a face. "Touché," she conceded. "But all the same they have enough wits where their personal interest is concerned." Her memory flickered briefly to an army surgeon in the hospital. She saw again his weary face, his sudden smile, and the beauty of his hands as he worked. One dreadful morning during the siege she had accompanied him to the redan. She could smell the gunpowder and the corpses and feel the bitter cold again as if it were only a moment ago. The closeness had been so intense it had made up for everything else — and then the sick feeling in her stomach when he had spoken for the first time of his wife. She should have known — she should have thought of it — but she had not.

"I should have to be either beautiful or unusually helpless, or preferably both, in order to have them flocking to my door. And as you know, I am neither."

Callandra looked at her closely. "Do I detect a note of self-pity, Hester?"

Hester felt the color hot up her cheeks, betraying her so no answer was necessary.

"You will have to learn to conquer that," Callandra observed, settling herself a little deeper in the chair. Her voice was quite gentle; there was no criticism in it, simply a statement of fact. "Too many women waste their lives grieving because they do not have something other people tell them they should want. Nearly all married women will tell you it is a blessed state, and you are to be pitied for not being in it. That is arrant nonsense. Whether you are happy or not depends to some degree upon outward circumstances, but mostly it depends how you choose to look at things yourself, whether you measure what you have or what you have not."

Hester frowned, uncertain as to how much she understood, or believed, what Callandra was saying.

Callandra was a trifle impatient. She jerked forward, frowning. "My dear girl, do you really imagine every woman with a smile on her face is really happy? No person of a healthy mentality desires to be pitied, and the simplest way to avoid it is to keep your troubles to yourself and wear a complacent expression. Most of the world will then assume that you are as self-satisfied as you seem. Before you pity yourself, take a great deal closer look at others, and then decide with whom you would, or could, change places, and what sacrifice of your nature you would be prepared to make in order to do so. Knowing you as I do, I think precious little."

Hester absorbed this thought in silence, turning it over in her mind. Absently she pulled her feet out of the basin at last and began to dry them on the towel.

Callandra stood up. "You will join us in the withdrawing room for tea? It is usually very good as I remember; there is nothing wrong with your appetite. Then later we shall discuss what possibilities there are for you to exercise your talents. There is so much to be done; great reforms are long overdue in all manner of things, and your experience and your emotion should not go to waste."

"Thank you." Hester suddenly felt much better. Her feet were refreshed and clean, she was extremely hungry, and although the future was a mist with no form to it as yet, it had in half an hour grown from gray to a new brightness. "I most certainly shall."

Callandra looked at Hester's hair. "I shall send my maid. Her name is Effie, and she is better than my appearance would lead you to believe." And with that she went cheerfully out of the door, humming to herself in a rich contralto voice, and Hester could hear her rather firm tread along the landing.

Afternoon tea was taken by the ladies alone. Rosamond appeared from the boudoir, a sitting room especially for female members of the household, where she had been writing letters. Fabia presided, although of course there was the parlor maid to pass the cups and the sandwiches of cucumber, hothouse grown, and later the crumpets and cakes.

The conversation was extremely civilized to the point of being almost meaningless for any exchange of opinion or emotion. They spoke of fashion, what color and what line flattered whom, what might be the season's special feature, would it be a lower waist, or perhaps a greater use of lace, or indeed more or different buttons? Would hats be larger or smaller? Was it good taste to wear green, and did it really become anyone; was it not inclined to make one sallow? A good complexion was so important!

What soap was best for retaining the blush of youth? Were Dr. So-and-so's pills really helpful for female complaints? Mrs. Wellings had it that they were little less than miraculous! But then Mrs. Wellings was much given to exaggeration. She would do anything short of standing on her head in order to attract attention.

Frequently Hester caught Callandra's eyes, and had to look away in case she should giggle and betray an unseemly and very discourteous levity. She might be taken for mocking her hostess, which would be unforgivable — and true.

Dinner was a quite different affair. Effie turned out to be a very agreeable country girl with a cloud of naturally wavy auburn hair many a mistress would have swapped her dowry for and a quick and garrulous tongue. She had hardly been in the room five minutes, whisking through clothes, pinning here, flouncing there, rearranging everything with a skill that left Hester breathless, before she had recounted the amazing news that the police had been at the hall, about the poor major's death up in London, twice now. They had sent two men, one a very grim creature, with a dark visage and manner grand enough to frighten the children, who had spoken with the mistress and taken tea in the withdrawing room as if he thought himself quite the gentleman.

The other, however, was as charming as you could wish, and so terribly elegant — although what a clergyman's son was doing in such an occupation no one could imagine! Such a personable young man should have done something decent, like taking the cloth himself, or tutoring boys of good family, or any other respectable calling.

"But there you are!" she said, seizing the hairbrush and beginning on Hester's hair with determination. "Some of the nicest people do the oddest things, I always say. But Cook took a proper fancy to him. Oh dear!" She looked at the back of Hester's head critically. "You really shouldn't wear your hair like that, ma'am; if you don't mind me saying." She brushed swiftly, piled, stuck pins and looked again. "There now — very fine hair you have, when it's done right. You should have a word with your maid at home, miss — she's not doing right by you — if you'll excuse me saying so. I hope that gives satisfaction?"

"Oh indeed!" Hester assured her with amazement. "You are quite excellent."

Effie colored with pleasure. "Lady Callandra says I talk too much," she essayed modestly.

Hester smiled. "Definitely," she agreed. "So do I. Thank you for your help — please tell Lady Callandra I am very grateful."

"Yes ma'am." And with a half-curtsy Effie grabbed her pincushion and flew out of the door, forgetting to close it behind her, and Hester heard her feet along the passage.

She really looked very striking; the rather severe style she had worn for convenience since embarking on her nursing career had been dramatically softened and filled out. Her gown had been masterfully adapted to be less modest and considerably fuller over a borrowed petticoat, unknown to its owner, and thus height was turned from a disadvantage into a considerable asset. Now that it was time she swept down the main staircase feeling very pleased with herself indeed.

Both Lovel and Menard Grey were at home for the evening, and she was introduced to them in the withdrawing room before going in to the dining room and being seated at the long, highly polished table, which was set for six but could easily have accommodated twelve. There were two joins in it where additional leaves could be inserted so it might have sat twenty-four.

Hester's eye swept over it quickly and noticed the crisp linen napkins, all embroidered with the family crest, the gleaming silver similarly adorned, the cruet sets, the crystal goblets reflecting the myriad lights of the chandelier, a tower of glass like a miniature iceberg alight. There were flowers from the conservatory and from the garden, skillfully arranged in three flat vases up the center of the table, and the whole glittered and gleamed like a display of art.

This time the conversation was centered on the estate, and matters of more political interest. Apparently Lovel had been in the nearest market town all day discussing some matter of land, and Menard had been to one of the tenant farms regarding the sale of a breeding ram, and of course the beginning of harvest.

The meal was served efficiently by the footmen and parlor maid and no one paid them the slightest attention.

They were halfway through the remove, a roast saddle of mutton, when Menard, a handsome man in his early thirties, finally addressed Hester directly. He had similar dark brown hair to his elder brother, and a ruddy complexion from much time spent in the open. He rode to hounds with great pleasure, and considerable daring, and shot pheasant in season. He smiled from enjoyment, but seldom from perception of wit.

"How agreeable of you to come and visit Aunt Callandra, Miss Latterly. I hope you will be able to stay with us for a while?"

"Thank you, Mr. Grey," she said graciously. "That is very kind of you. It is a quite beautiful place, and I am sure I shall enjoy myself."

"Have you known Aunt Callandra long?" He was making polite conversation and she knew precisely the pattern it would take.

"Some five or six years. She has given me excellent advice from time to time."

Lady Fabia frowned. The pairing of Callandra and good advice was obviously foreign to her. "Indeed?" she murmured disbelievingly. "With regard to what, pray?"

"What I should do with my time and abilities," Hester replied.

Rosamond looked puzzled. "Do?" she said quietly. "I don't think I understand." She looked at Lovel, then at her mother-in-law. Her fair face and remarkable brown eyes were full of interest and confusion.

"It is necessary that I provide for myself, Lady Shelburne," Hester explained with a smile. Suddenly Callandra's words about happiness came back to her with a force of meaning.

"I'm sorry," Rosamond murmured, and looked down at her plate, obviously feeling she had said something indelicate.

"Not at all," Hester assured her quickly. "I have already had some truly inspiring experiences, and hope to have more." She was about to add that it is a marvelous feeling to be of use, then realized how cruel it would be, and swallowed the words somewhat awkwardly over a mouthful of mutton and sauce.

"Inspiring?" Lovel frowned. "Are you a religious, Miss Latterly?"

Callandra coughed profusely into her napkin; apparently she had swallowed something awry. Fabia passed her a glass of water. Hester averted her eyes.

"No, Lord Shelburne," she said with as much composure as she could. "I have been nursing in the Crimea."

There was a stunned silence all around, not even the clink of silver on porcelain.

"My brother-in-law, Major Joscelin Grey, served in the Crimea," Rosamond said into the void. Her voice was soft and sad. "He died shortly after he returned home."

"That is something of a euphemism," Lovel added, his face hardening. "He was murdered in his flat in London, as no doubt you will hear. The police have been inquiring into it, even out here! But they have not arrested anyone yet."

"I am terribly sorry!" Hester meant it with genuine shock. She had nursed a Joscelin Grey in the hospital in Scutari, only briefly; his injury was serious enough, but not compared with the worst, and those who also suffered from disease. She recalled him: he had been young and fair-haired with a wide, easy smile and a natural grace. "I remember him —"

Now Effie's words came back to her with clarity.

Rosamond dropped her fork, the color rushing to her cheeks, then ebbing away again leaving her ash-white. Fabia closed her eyes and took in a very long, deep breath and let it go soundlessly.

Lovel stared at his plate. Only Menard was looking at her, and rather than surprise or grief there was an expression in his face which appeared to be wariness, and a kind of closed, careful pain.

"How remarkable," he said slowly. "Still, I suppose you saw hundreds of soldiers, if not thousands. Our losses were staggering, so I am told."

"They were," she agreed grimly. "Far more than is generally understood, over eighteen thousand, and many of them needlessly — eight-ninths died not in battle but of wounds or disease afterwards."

"Do you remember Joscelin?" Rosamond said eagerly, totally ignoring the horrific figures. "He was injured in the leg. Even afterwards he was compelled to walk with a limp — indeed he often used a stick to support himself."

"He only used it when he was tired!" Fabia said sharply.

"He used it when he wanted sympathy,"

Menard said half under his breath.

"That is unworthy!" Fabia's voice was dangerously soft, laden with warning, and her blue eyes rested on her second son with chill disfavor. "I shall consider that you did not say it."

"We observe the convention that we speak no ill of the dead," Menard said with irony unusual in him. "Which limits conversation considerably."

Rosamond stared at her plate. "I never understand your humor, Menard," she complained.

"That is because he is very seldom intentionally funny," Fabia snapped.

"Whereas Joscelin was always amusing." Menard was angry and no longer made any pretense at hiding it. "It is marvelous what a little laughter can do — entertain you enough and you will turn a blind eye on anything!"

"I loved Joscelin." Fabia met his eyes with a stony glare. "I enjoyed his company. So did a great many others. I love you also, but you bore me to tears."

"You are happy enough to enjoy the profits of my work!" His face was burning and his eyes bright with fury. "I preserve the estate's finances and see that it is properly managed, while Lovel keeps up the family name, sits in the House of Lords or does whatever else peers of the realm do — and Joscelin never did a damn thing but lounge around in clubs and drawing rooms gambling it away!"

The blood drained from Fabia's skin leaving her grasping her knife and fork as if they were lifelines.

"And you still resent that?" Her voice was little more than a whisper. "He fought in the war, risked his life serving his Queen and country in terrible conditions, saw blood and slaughter. And when he came home wounded, you grudged him a little entertainment with his friends?"

Menard drew in his breath to retort, then saw the pain in his mother's face, deeper than her anger and underlying everything else, and held his tongue.

"I was embarrassed by some of his losses," he said softly. "That is all."

Hester glanced at Callandra, and saw a mixture of anger, pity and respect in her highly expressive features, although which emotion was for whom she did not know. She thought perhaps the respect was for Menard.

Lovel smiled very bleakly. "I am afraid you may find the police are still around here, Miss Latterly. They have sent a very ill-mannered fellow, something of an upstart, although I daresay he is better bred than most policemen. But he does not seem to have much idea of what he is doing, and asks some very impertinent questions. If he should return during your stay and give you the slightest trouble, tell him to be off, and let me know."

"By all means," Hester agreed. To the best of her knowledge she had never conversed with a policeman, and she had no interest in doing so now. "It must all be most distressing for you."

"Indeed," Fabia agreed. "But an unpleasantness we have no alternative but to endure. It appears more than possible poor Joscelin was murdered by someone he knew."

Hester could think of no appropriate reply, nothing that was not either wounding or completely senseless.

"Thank you for your counsel," she said to Menard, then lowered her eyes and continued with her meal.

After the fruit had been passed the women withdrew and Lovel and Menard drank port for half an hour or so, then Lovel put on his smoking jacket and retired to the smoking room to indulge, and Menard went to the library. No one remained up beyond ten o'clock, each making some excuse why they had found the day tiring and wished to sleep.

Breakfast was the usual generous meal: porridge, bacon, eggs, deviled kidneys, chops, kedgeree, smoked haddock, toast, butter, sweet preserves, apricot compote, marmalade, honey, tea and coffee. Hester ate lightly; the very thought of partaking of all of it made her feel bloated. Both Rosamond and Fabia ate in their rooms, Menard had already dined and left and Callandra had not arisen. Lovel was her only companion.

"Good morning, Miss Latterly. I hope you slept well?"

"Excellently, thank you, Lord Shelburne." She helped herself from the heated dishes on the sideboard and sat down. "I hope you are well also?"

"What? Oh — yes thank you. Always well." He proceeded with his heaped meal and it was several minutes before he looked up at her again. "By the way, I hope you will be generous enough to disregard a great deal of what Menard said at dinner yesterday? We all take grief in different ways. Menard lost his closest friend also — fellow he was at school and Cambridge with. Took it terribly hard. But he was really very fond of Joscelin, you know, just that as immediately elder brother he had — er — " He searched for the right words to explain his thoughts, and failed to find them. "He — er — had —"

"Responsibilities to care for him?" she suggested.

Gratitude shone in his face. "Exactly. Sometimes I daresay Joscelin gambled more than he should, and it was Menard who — er . . ."

"I understand," she said, more to put him out of his embarrassment and end the painful conversation than because she believed him.

Later in a fine, blustery morning, walking under the trees with Callandra, she learned a good deal more.

"Stuff and nonsense," Callandra said sharply. "Joscelin was a cheat. Always was, even in the nursery. I shouldn't be at all surprised if he never grew out of it, and Menard had to pick up after him to avoid a scandal. Very sensitive to the family name, Menard."

"Is Lord Shelburne not also?" Hester was surprised.

"I don't think Lovel has the imagination to realize that a Grey could cheat," Callandra answered frankly. "I think the whole thing would be beyond him to conceive. Gentlemen do not cheat; Joscelin was his brother — and so of course a gentleman — therefore he could not cheat. All very simple."

"You were not especially fond of Joscelin?" Hester searched her face.

Callandra smiled. "Not especially, although I admit he was very witty at times, and we can forgive a great deal of one who makes us laugh. And he played beautifully, and we can also overlook a lot in one who creates glorious sound — or perhaps I should say recreates it. He did not compose, so far as I know."

They walked a hundred yards in silence except for the roar and rustle of the wind in giant oaks. It sounded like the torrent of a stream falling, or an incessant sea breaking on rocks. It was one of the pleasantest sounds Hester had ever heard, and the bright, sweet air was a sort of cleansing of her whole spirit.

"Well?" Callandra said at last. "What are your choices, Hester? I am quite sure you can find an excellent position if you wish to continue nursing, either in an army hospital or in one of the London hospitals that may be persuaded to accept women." There was no lift in her voice, no enthusiasm.

"But?" Hester said for her.

Callandra's wide mouth twitched in the ghost of a smile. "But I think you would be wasted in it. You have a gift for administration, and a fighting spirit. You should find some cause and battle to win it. You have learned a great deal about better standards of nursing in the Crimea. Teach them here in England, force people to listen — get rid of cross-infection, insanitary conditions, ignorant nurses, incompetent treatments that any good housekeeper would abhor. You will save more lives, and be a happier woman."

Hester did not mention the dispatches she had sent in Alan Russell's name, but a truth in Callandra's words rested with an unusual warmth in her, a kind of resolution as if discord had been melted into harmony.

"How do I do it?" The writing of articles could wait, find its own avenue. The more she knew, the more she would be able to speak with power and intelligence. Of course she already knew that Miss Nightingale would continue to campaign with every ounce of the passion which all but consumed her nervous strength and physical health for a reformation of the entire Army Medical Corps, but she could not do it alone, or even with all the adulation the country offered her or the friends she had in the seats of power. Vested interests were spread through the corridors of authority like the roots of a tree through the earth. The bonds of habit and security of position were steellike in endurance. Too many people would have to change, and in doing so admit they had been ill-advised, unwise, even incompetent.

"How can I obtain a position?"

"I have friends," Callandra said with quiet confidence. "I shall begin to write letters, very discreetly, either to beg favors, prompt a sense of duty, prick consciences, or else threaten disfavor both public and private, if someone does not help!" There was a light of humor in her eyes, but also a complete intention to do exactly what she had said.

"Thank you," Hester accepted. "I shall endeavor to use my opportunities so as to justify your effort."

"Certainly," Callandra agreed. "If I did not believe so, I should not exert them." And she matched her stride to Hester's and together they walked in the wood under the branches and out across the park.

Two days later General Wadham came to dinner with his daughter Ursula, who had been betrothed for several months to Menard Grey. They arrived early enough to join the family in the withdrawing room for conversation before the meal was announced, and Hester found herself immediately tested in her tact. Ursula was a handsome girl whose mane of hair had a touch of red in its fairness and whose skin had the glow of someone who spends a certain amount of time in the open. Indeed, conversation had not proceeded far before her interest in riding to hounds became apparent. This evening she was dressed in a rich blue which in Hester's opinion was too powerful for her; something more subdued would have flattered her and permitted her natural vitality to show through. As it was she appeared a trifle conspicuous between Fabia's lavender silk and her light hair faded to gray at the front, Rosamond in a blue so dull and dark it made her flawless cheeks like alabaster, and Hester herself in a somber grape color rich and yet not out of keeping with her own recent state of mourning. Actually she thought privately she had never worn a color which flattered her more!

Callandra wore black with touches of white, a striking dress, but somehow not quite the right note of fashion. But then whatever Callandra wore was not going to have panache, only distinction; it was not in her nature to be glamorous.

General Wadham was tall and stout with bristling side whiskers and very pale blue eyes which were either farsighted or nearsighted, Hester was unsure which, but they certainly did not seem to focus upon her when he addressed her.

"Visiting, Miss — er — Miss —"

"Latterly," she supplied.

"Ah yes — of course — Latterly." He reminded her almost ludicrously of a dozen or so middle-aged soldiers she had seen whom she and Fanny Bolsover had lampooned when they were tired and frightened and had sat up all night with the wounded, then afterwards lain together on a single straw pallet, huddled close for warmth and telling each other silly stories, laughing because it was better than weeping, and making fun of the officers because loyalty and pity and hate were too big to deal with, and they had not the energy or spirit left.

"Friend of Lady Shelburne's, are you?" General Wadham said automatically. "Charming — charming."

Hester felt her irritation rise already.

"No," she contradicted. "I am a friend of Lady Callandra Daviot's. I was fortunate enough to know her some time ago."

"Indeed." He obviously could think of nothing to add to that, and moved on to Rosamond, who was more prepared to make light conversation and fall in with whatever mood he wished.

When dinner was announced there was no gentleman to escort her into the dining room, so she was obliged to go in with Callandra, and at table found herself seated opposite the general.

The first course was served and everyone began to eat, the ladies delicately, the men with appetite. At first conversation was slight, then when the initial hunger had been assuaged and the soup and fish eaten, Ursula began to speak about the hunt, and the relative merits of one horse over another.

Hester did not join in. The only riding she had done had been in the Crimea, and the sight of the horses there injured, diseased and starving had so distressed her she put it from her mind. Indeed so much did she close her attention from their speech that Fabia had addressed her three times before she was startled into realizing it.

"I beg your pardon!" she apologized in some embarrassment.

"I believe you said, Miss Latterly, that you were briefly acquainted with my late son, Major Joscelin Grey?"

"Yes. I regret it was very slight — there were so many wounded." She said it politely, as if she were discussing some ordinary commodity, but her mind went back to the reality of the hospitals when the wounded, the frost-bitten and those wasted with cholera, dysentery and starvation were lying so close there was barely room for more, and the rats scuttled, huddled and clung everywhere.

And worse than that she remembered the earthworks in the siege of Sebastopol, the bitter cold, the light of lamps in the mud, her body shaking as she held one high for the surgeon to work, its gleam on the saw blade, the dim shapes of men crowding together for a fraction of body's warmth. She remembered the first time she saw the great figure of Rebecca Box striding forward over the battlefield beyond the trenches to ground lately occupied by Russian troops, and lifting the bodies of the fallen and hoisting them over her shoulder to carry them back. Her strength was surpassed only by her sublime courage. No man fell injured so far forward she would not go out for him and carry him back to hospital hut or tent.

They were staring at her, waiting for her to say something more, some word of praise for him. After all, he had been a soldier — a major in the cavalry.

"I remember he was charming." She refused to lie, even for his family. "He had the most delightful smile."

Fabia relaxed and sat back. "That was Joscelin," she agreed with a misty look in her blue eyes. "Courage and a kind of gaiety, even in the most dreadful circumstances. I can still hardly believe he is gone — I half think he will throw the door open and stride in, apologizing for being late and telling us how hungry he is."

Hester looked at the table piled high with food that would have done half a regiment at the height of the siege. They used the word *hunger* so easily.

General Wadham sat back and wiped his napkin over his lips.

"A fine man," he said quietly. "You must have been very proud of him, my dear. A soldier's life is all too often short, but he carries honor with him, and he will not be forgotten."

The table was silent but for the clink of silver on porcelain. No one could think of any immediate reply. Fabia's face was full of a bleak and terrible grief, an almost devastating loneliness. Rosamond stared into space, and Lovel looked quietly wretched, whether for their pain or his own was impossible to know. Was it memory or the present which robbed him?

Menard chewed his food over and over, as if his throat were too tight and his mouth too dry to swallow it.

"Glorious campaign," the general went on presently. "Live in the annals of history. Never be surpassed for courage. Thin Red Line, and all that."

Hester found herself suddenly choked with tears, anger and grief boiling up inside her, and intolerable frustration. She could see the hills beyond the Alma River more sharply than the figures around the table and the winking crystal. She could see the breastwork on the forward ridges as it had been that morning, bristling with enemy guns, the Greater and Lesser Redoubts, the wicker barricades filled with stones. Behind them were Prince Menshikoff's fifty thousand men. She remembered the smell of the breeze off the sea. She had stood with the women who had followed the army and watched Lord Raglan sitting in frock coat and white shirt, his back ramrod stiff in the saddle.

At one o'clock the bugle had sounded and the infantry advanced shoulder to shoulder into the mouths of the Russian guns and were cut down like corn. For ninety minutes they were massacred, then at last the order was given and the Hussars, Lancers and Fusiliers joined in, each in perfect order.

"Look well at that," a major had said to one of the wives, "for the Queen of England would give her eyes to see it."

Everywhere men were falling. The colors carried high were ragged with shot. As one bearer fell another took his place, and in his turn fell and was succeeded. Orders were conflicting, men advanced and retreated over each other. The Grenadiers advanced, a moving wall of bearskins, then the Black Watch of the Highland Brigade.

The Dragoons were held back, never used. Why? When asked, Lord Raglan had replied that he had been thinking of Agnes!

Hester remembered going over the battle-field afterwards, the ground soaked with blood, seeing mangled bodies, some so terrible the limbs lay yards away. She had done all she could to relieve the suffering, working till exhaustion numbed her beyond feeling and she was dizzy with the sights and sounds of pain. Wounded were piled on carts and trundled to field hospital tents. She had worked all night and all day, exhausted, dry-mouthed with thirst, aching and drenched with horror. Orderlies had tried to stop the bleeding; there was little to do for shock but a few precious drops of brandy. What she would have given then for the contents of Shelburne's cellars.

The dinner table conversation buzzed on around her, cheerful, courteous, and ignorant. The flowers swam in her vision, summer blooms grown by careful gardeners, orchids tended in the glass conservatory. She thought of herself walking in the grass one hot afternoon with letters from home in her pocket, amid the dwarf roses and the blue larkspur that grew again in the field of Balaclava the year after the Charge of the Light Brigade, that idiotic piece of insane bungling and suicidal heroism. She had gone back to the hospital and tried to write and tell them what it was really like, what she was doing and how if felt, the sharing and the good things, the friendships, Fanny Bolsover, laughter, courage. The dry resignation of the men when they were issued green coffee beans, and no means to roast or grind them, had evoked her admiration so deeply it made her throat ache with sudden pride. She could hear the scratching of the quill over the paper now — and the sound as she tore it up.

"Fine man," General Wadham was saying, staring into his claret glass. "One of England's heroes. Lucan and Cardigan are related — I suppose you know? Lucan married one of Lord Cardigan's sisters — what a family." He shook his head in wonder. "What duty!"

"Inspires us all," Ursula agreed with shining eyes.

"They hated each other on sight," Hester said before she had time for discretion to guard her tongue.

"I beg your pardon!" The general stared at her coldly, his rather wispy eyebrows raised. His look centered all his incredulity at her impertinence and disapproval of women who spoke when it was not required of them.

Hester was stung by it. He was exactly the sort of blind, arrogant fool who had caused such immeasurable loss on the battlefield through refusal to be informed, rigidity of thought, panic when they found they were wrong, and personal emotion which overrode truth.

"I said that Lord Lucan and Lord Cardigan hated each other from the moment they met," she repeated clearly in the total silence.

"I think you are hardly in a position to judge such a thing, madame." He regarded her with total contempt. She was less than a subaltern, less than a private, for heaven's sake — she was a woman! And she had contradicted him, at least by implication, and at the dinner table.

"I was on the battlefield at the Alma, at Inkermann and at Balaclava, and at the siege of Sebastopol, sir," she answered without dropping her gaze. "Where were you?"

His face flushed scarlet. "Good manners, and regard for our hosts, forbid me from giving you the answer you deserve, madame," he said very stiffly. "Since the meal is finished, perhaps it is time the ladies wished to retire to the withdrawing room?"

Rosamond made as if to rise in obedience, and Ursula laid her napkin beside her plate, although there was still half a pear unfinished on it.

Fabia sat where she was, two spots of color in her cheeks, and very carefully and deliberately Callandra reached for a peach and began to peel it with her fruit knife and fork, a small smile on her face.

No one moved. The silence deepened.

"I believe it is going to be a hard winter," Lovel said at last. "Old Beckinsale was saying he expects to lose half his crop."

"He says that every year," Menard grunted and finished the remnant of his wine, throwing it back without savor, merely as if he would not waste it.

"A lot of people say things every year." Callandra cut away a squashy piece of fruit carefully and pushed it to the side of her plate. "It is forty years since we beat Napoleon at Waterloo, and most of us still think we have the same invincible army and we expect to win with the same tactics and the same discipline and courage that defeated half Europe and ended an empire."

"And by God, we shall, madame!" The general slammed down his palm, making the cutlery jump. "The British soldier is the superior of any man alive!"

"I don't doubt it," Callandra agreed. "It is the British general in the field who is a hidebound and incompetent ass."

"Callandra! For God's sake!" Fabia was appalled.

Menard put his hands over his face.

"Perhaps we should have done better had you been there, General Wadham," Callandra continued unabashed, looking at him frankly.

"You at least have a very considerable imagination!"

Rosamond shut her eyes and slid down in her seat. Lovel groaned.

Hester choked with laughter, a trifle hysterically, and stuffed her napkin over her mouth to stifle it.

General Wadham made a surprisingly graceful strategic retreat. He decided to accept the remark as a compliment.

"Thank you, madame," he said stiffly. "Perhaps I might have prevented the slaughter of the Light Brigade."

And with that it was left. Fabia, with a little help from Lovel, rose from her seat and excused the ladies, leading them to the withdrawing room, where they discussed such matters as music, fashion, society, forthcoming weddings, both planned and speculated, and were excessively polite to one another.

When the visitors finally took their leave, Fabia turned upon her sister-in-law with a look that should have shriveled her.

"Callandra — I shall never forgive you!"

"Since you have never forgiven me for wearing the exact shade of gown as you when we first met forty years ago," Callandra replied, "I shall just have to bear it with the same fortitude I have shown over all the other episodes since."

"You are impossible. Dear heaven, how I miss Joscelin." She stood up slowly and Hester rose as a matter of courtesy. Fabia walked towards the double doors. "I am going to bed. I shall see you tomorrow." And she went out, leaving them also.

"You are impossible, Aunt Callandra," Rosamond agreed, standing in the middle of the floor and looking confused and unhappy. "I don't know why you say such things."

"I know you don't," Callandra said gently. "That is because you have never been anywhere but Middleton, Shelburne Hall or London society. Hester would say the same, if she were not a guest here — indeed perhaps more. Our military imagination has ossified since Waterloo." She stood up and straightened her skirts. "Victory — albeit one of the greatest in history and turning the tide of nations — has still gone to our heads and we think all we have to do to win is to turn up in our scarlet coats and obey the rules. And only God can measure the suffering and the death that pigheadedness has caused. And we women and politicians sit here safely at home and cheer them on without the slightest idea what the reality of it is."

"Joscelin is dead," Rosamond said bleakly, staring at the closed curtains.

"I know that, my dear," Callandra said from

close behind her. "But he did not die in the Crimea."

"He may have died because of it!"

"Indeed he may," Callandra conceded, her face suddenly touched with gentleness. "And I know you were extremely fond of him. He had a capacity for pleasure, both to give and to receive, which unfortunately neither Lovel nor Menard seem to share. I think we have exhausted both ourselves and the subject. Good night, my dear. Weep if you wish; tears too long held in do us no good. Composure is all very well, but there is a time to acknowledge pain also." She slipped her arm around the slender shoulders and hugged her briefly, then knowing the gesture would release the hurt as well as comfort, she took Hester by the elbow and conducted her out to leave Rosamond alone.

The following morning Hester overslept and rose with a headache. She did not feel like early breakfast, and still less like facing any of the family across the table. She felt passionately about the vanity and the incompetence she had seen in the army, and the horror at the suffering would never leave her; probably the anger would not either. But she had not behaved very well at dinner; and the memory of it churned around in her mind, trying to fall into a happier picture with less fault attached to herself, and did not improve either her headache or her temper.

She decided to take a brisk walk in the park for as long as her energy lasted. She wrapped up appropriately, and by nine o'clock was striding rapidly over the grass getting her boots wet.

She first saw the figure of the man with considerable irritation, simply because she wished to be alone. He was probably inoffensive, and presumably had as much right to be here as herself — perhaps more? He no doubt served some function. However she felt he intruded, he was another human being in a world of wind and great trees and vast, cloud-racked skies and shivering, singing grass.

When he drew level he stopped and spoke to her. He was dark, with an arrogant face, all lean, smooth bones and clear eyes.

"Good morning, ma'am. I see you are from Shelburne Hall —"

"How observant," she said tartly, gazing around at the totally empty parkland. There was no other place she could conceivably have come from, unless she had emerged from a hole in the ground.

His face tightened, aware of her sarcasm. "Are you a member of the family?" He was staring at her with some intensity and she found it disconcerting, and bordering on the offensive.

"How is that your concern?" she asked coldly.

The concentration deepened in his eyes, and then suddenly there was a flash of recognition, although for the life of her she could not think of any occasion on which she had seen him before. Curiously he did not refer to it.

"I am inquiring into the murder of Joscelin Grey. I wonder if you had known him."

"Good heavens!" she said involuntarily. Then she collected herself. "I have been accused of tactlessness in my time, but you are certainly in a class of your own." A total lie — Callandra would have left him standing! "It would be quite in your deserving if I told you I had been his fiancée — and fainted on the spot!"

"Then it was a secret engagement," he retorted. "And if you go in for clandestine romance you must expect to have your feelings bruised a few times."

"Which you are obviously well equipped to do!" She stood still with the wind whipping her skirts, still wondering why he had seemed to recognize her.

"Did you know him?" he repeated irritably.

"Yes!"

"For how long?"

266

"As well as I remember it, about three weeks."

"That's an odd time to know anyone!"

"What would you consider a usual time to know someone?" she demanded.

"It was very brief," he explained with careful condescension. "You can hardly have been a friend of the family. Did you meet him just before he died?"

"No. I met him in Scutari."

"You what?"

"Are you hard of hearing? I met him in Scutari!" She remembered the general's patronizing manner and all her memories of condescension flooded back, the army officers who considered women out of place, ornaments to be used for recreation or comfort but not creatures of any sense. Gentlewomen were for cossetting, dominating and protecting from everything, including adventure or decision or freedom of any kind. Common women were whores or drudges and to be used like any other livestock.

"Oh yes," he agreed with a frown. "He was injured. Were you out there with your husband?"

"No I was not!" Why should that question be faintly hurtful? "I went to nurse the injured, to assist Miss Nightingale, and those like her."

His face did not show the admiration and profound sense of respect close to awe that the name usually brought. She was thrown off balance by it He seemed to be single-minded in his interest in Joscelin Grey.

"You nursed Major Grey?"

"Among others. Do you mind if we proceed to walk? I am getting cold standing here."

"Of course." He turned and fell into step with her and they began along the faint track in the grass towards a copse of oaks. "What were your impressions of him?"

She tried hard to distinguish her memory from the picture she had gathered from his family's words, Rosamond's weeping, Fabia's pride and love, the void he had left in her happiness, perhaps Rosamond's also, his brothers' mixture of exasperation and — what — envy?

"I can recall his leg rather better than his face," she said frankly.

He stared at her with temper rising sharply in his face.

"I am not interested in your female fantasies, madame, or your peculiar sense of humor! This is an investigation into an unusually brutal murder!"

She lost her temper completely.

"You incompetent idiot!" she shouted into the wind. "You grubby-minded, fatuous nincompoop. I was nursing him. I dressed and cleaned his wound — which, in case you have forgotten, was in his leg. His face was uninjured, therefore I did not regard it any more than the faces of the other ten thousand injured and dead I saw. I would not know him again if he came up and spoke to me."

His face was bleak and furious. "It would be a memorable occasion, madame. He is eight weeks dead — and beaten to a pulp."

If he had hoped to shock her he failed.

She swallowed hard and held his eyes. "Sounds like the battlefield after Inkermann," she said levelly. "Only there at least we knew what had happened to them — even if no one had any idea why."

"We know what happened to Joscelin Grey — we do not know who did it. Fortunately I am not responsible for explaining the Crimean War — only Joscelin Grey's death."

"Which seems to be beyond you," she said unkindly. "And I can be of no assistance. All I can remember is that he was unusually agreeable, that he bore his injury with as much fortitude as most, and that when he was recovering he spent quite a lot of his time moving from bed to bed encouraging and cheering other men, particularly those closest to death. In fact when I think of it, he was a most admirable man. I had forgotten that until now.

He comforted many who were dying, and wrote letters home for them, told their families of their deaths and probably gave them much ease in their distress. It is very hard that he should survive that, and come home to be murdered here."

"He was killed very violently — there was a passion of hatred in the way he was beaten." He was looking at her closely and she was startled by the intelligence in his face; it was uncomfortably intense, and unexpected. "I believe it was someone who knew him. One does not hate a stranger as he was hated."

She shivered. Horrific as was the battlefield, there was still a world of difference between its mindless carnage and the acutely personal malevolence of Joscelin Grey's death.

"I am sorry," she said more gently, but still with the stiffness he engendered in her. "I know nothing of him that would help you find such a relationship. If I did I should tell you. The hospital kept records; you would be able to find out who else was there at the same time, but no doubt you have already done that —" She saw instantly from the shadow in his face that he had not. Her patience broke. "Then for heaven's sake, what have you been doing for eight weeks?"

"For five of them I was lying injured myself," he snapped back. "Or recovering. You make far too many assumptions, madame. You are arrogant, domineering, ill-tempered and condescending. And you leap to conclusions for which you have no foundation. God! I hate clever women!"

She froze for an instant before the reply was on her lips.

"I love clever men!" Her eyes raked him up and down. "It seems we are both to be disappointed." And with that she picked up her skirts and strode past him and along the path towards the copse, tripping over a bramble across her way. "Drat," she swore furiously. "Hellfire."

CHAPTER SEVEN

"Good morning, Miss Latterly," Fabia said coolly when she came into the sitting room at about quarter past ten the following day. She looked smart and fragile and was already dressed as if to go out. She eyed Hester very briefly, noting her extremely plain muslin gown, and then turned to Rosamond, who was sitting poking apologetically at an embroidery frame. "Good morning, Rosamond. I hope you are well? It is a most pleasant day, and I believe we should take the opportunity to visit some of the less fortunate in the village. We have not been lately, and it is your duty, my dear, even more than it is mine."

The color deepened a trifle in Rosamond's cheeks as she accepted the rebuke. From the quick lift in her chin Hester thought there might be far more behind the motion than was apparent. The family was in mourning, and Fabia had quite obviously felt the loss most keenly, at least to the outward eye. Had

Rosamond tried to resume life too quickly for her, and this was Fabia's way of choosing the time?

"Of course, Mama-in-law," Rosamond said without looking up.

"And no doubt Miss Latterly will come with us," Fabia added without consulting her. "We shall leave at eleven. That will allow you time to dress appropriately. The day is most warm — do not be tempted to forget your position." And with that admonition, delivered with a frozen smile, she turned and left them, stopping by the door for a moment to add, "and we might take luncheon with General Wadham, and Ursula." And then she went out.

Rosamond threw the hoop at her workbasket and it went beyond and skittered across the floor. "Drat," she said quietly under her breath. Then she met Hester's eyes and apologized.

Hester smiled at her. "Please don't," she said candidly. "Playing Lady Bountiful 'round the estates is enough to make anyone resort to language better for the stable, or even the barracks, than the drawing room. A simple 'drat' is very mild."

"Do you miss the Crimea, now you are home?" Rosamond said suddenly, her eyes intent and almost frightened of the answer. "I mean —" She looked away, embarrassed and now finding it hard to speak the words which only a moment before had been so ready.

Hester saw a vision of endless days being polite to Fabia, attending to the trivial household management that she was allowed, never feeling it was her house until Fabia was dead; and perhaps even afterwards Fabia's spirit would haunt the house, her belongings, her choices of furniture, of design, marking it indelibly. There would be morning calls, luncheon with suitable people of like breeding and position, visits to the poor — and in season there would be balls, the races at Ascot, the regatta at Henley, and of course in winter the hunt. None of it would be more than pleasant at best, tedious at worst — but without meaning.

But Rosamond did not deserve a lie, even in her loneliness — nor did she deserve the pain of Hester's view of the truth. It was only her view; for Rosamond it might be different.

"Oh yes, sometimes I do," she said with a small smile. "But we cannot fight wars like that for long. It is very dreadful as well as vivid and real. It is not fun being cold and dirty and so tired you feel as if you've been beaten — nor is it pleasant to eat army rations. It is one of the finest things in life to be truly useful — but there are less distressing places to do it, and I am sure I shall find many here in England."

"You are very kind," Rosamond said gently, meeting her eyes again. "I admit I had not imagined you would be so thoughtful." She rose to her feet. "Now I suppose we had better change into suitable clothes for calling — have you something modest and dowdy, but very dignified?" She stifled a giggle and turned it into a sneeze. "I'm sorry — what a fearful thing to ask!"

"Yes — most of my wardrobe is like that," Hester replied with an amusing smile. "All dark greens and very tired-looking blues — like faded ink. Will they do?"

"Perfectly — come!"

Menard drove the three of them in the open trap, bowling along the carriageway through the park towards the edge of the home estate and across heavy cornfields towards the village and the church spire beyond the slow swell of the hill. He obviously enjoyed managing the horse and did it with the skill of one who is long practiced. He did not even try to make conversation, supposing the loveliness of the land, the sky and the trees would be enough for them, as it was for him.

Hester sat watching him, leaving Rosamond and Fabia to converse. She looked at his powerful hands holding the reins lightly, at the ease of his balance and the obvious reticence in his expression. The daily round of duties in the estate was no imprisonment to him; she had seen a brooding in his face occasionally in the time she had been at Shelburne, sometimes anger, sometimes a stiffness and a jumpiness of the muscles which made her think of officers she had seen the night before battle, but it was when they were all at table, with Fabia's conversation betraying the ache of loneliness underneath as if Joscelin had been the only person she had totally and completely loved.

The first house they called at was that of a farm laborer on the edge of the village, a tiny cottage, one room downstairs crowded with a sunburned, shabby woman and seven children all sharing a loaf of bread spread with pork drippings. Their thin, dusty legs, barefooted, splayed out beneath simple smocks and they were obviously in from working in the garden or fields. Even the youngest, who looked no more than three or four, had fruit stains on her fingers where she had been harvesting.

Fabia asked questions and passed out practical advice on financial management and how to treat croup which the woman received in polite silence. Hester blushed for the condescension of it, and then realized it had been a way of life with little substantial variation for over a thousand years, and both parties were comfortable with its familiarity; and she had nothing more certain to put in its place.

Rosamond spoke with the eldest girl, and took the wide pink ribbon off her own hat and gave it to her, tying it around the child's hair to her shy delight.

Menard stood patiently by the horse, talking to it in a low voice for a few moments, then falling into a comfortable silence. The sunlight on his face showed the fine lines of anxiety around his eyes and mouth, and the deeper marks of pain. Here in the rich land with its great trees, the wind and the fertile earth he was relaxed, and Hester saw a glimpse of a quite different man from the stolid, resentful second son he appeared at Shelburne Hall. She wondered if Fabia had ever allowed herself to see it. Or was the laughing charm of Joscelin always in its light?

The second call was similar in essence, although the family was composed of an elderly woman with no teeth and an old man who was either drunk or had suffered some seizure which impaired both his speech and his movement.

Fabia spoke to him briskly with words of impersonal encouragement, which he ignored, making a face at her when her back was turned, and the old woman bobbed a curtsy, accepted two jars of lemon curd, and once again they climbed into the trap and were on their way.

Menard left them to go out into the fields, high with ripe corn, the reapers already digging the sickles deep, the sun hot on their backs, arms burned, sweat running freely. There was much talk of weather, time, the quarter of the wind, and when the rain would break. The smell of the grain and the broken straw in the heat was one of the sweetest things Hester had ever known. She stood in the brilliant light with her face lifted to the sky, the heat tingling on her skin, and gazed across the dark gold of the land — and thought of those who had been willing to die for it — and prayed that the heirs to so much treasured it deeply enough, to see it with the body and with the heart as well.

Luncheon was another matter altogether. They were received courteously enough until General Wadham saw Hester, then his florid face stiffened and his manner became exaggeratedly formal.

"Good morning, Miss Latterly. How good of you to call. Ursula will be delighted that you are able to join us for luncheon."

"Thank you, sir," she replied equally

gravely. "You are very generous."

Ursula did not look particularly delighted to see them at all, and was unable to hide her chagrin that Menard had seen fit to be out with the harvesters instead of here at the dining room table.

Luncheon was a light meal: poached river fish with caper sauce, cold game pie and vegetables, then a sorbet and a selection of fruit, followed by an excellent Stilton cheese.

General Wadham had obviously neither forgotten nor forgiven his rout by Hester on their previous meeting. His chill, rather glassy eye met hers over the cruet sets a number of times before he actually joined battle in a lull between Fabia's comments on the roses and Ursula's speculations as to whether Mr. Danbury would marry Miss Fothergill or Miss Ames.

"Miss Ames is a fine young woman," the general remarked, looking at Hester. "Most accomplished horsewoman, rides to hounds like a man. Courage. And handsome too, dashed handsome." He looked at Hester's dark green dress sourly. "Grandfather died in the Peninsular War — at Corunna — 1810. Don't suppose you were there too, were you, Miss Latterly? Bit before your time, eh?" He smiled, as if he had intended it to be goodnatured.

"1809," Hester corrected him. "It was before Talavera and after Vimiero and the Convention of Cintra. Otherwise you are perfectly correct — I was not there."

The general's face was scarlet. He swallowed a fish bone and choked into his napkin.

Fabia, white with fury, passed him a glass of water.

Hester, knowing better, removed it instantly and replaced it with bread.

The general took the bread and the bone was satisfactorily coated with it and passed down his throat.

"Thank you," he said freezingly, and then took the water also.

"I am happy to be of assistance," Hester replied sweetly. "It is most unpleasant to swallow a bone, and so easily done, even in the best of fish — and this is delicious."

Fabia muttered something blasphemous and inaudible under her breath and Rosamond launched into a sudden and overenthusiastic recollection of the Vicar's midsummer garden party.

Afterwards, when Fabia had elected to remain with Ursula and the general, and Rosamond hurried Hester out to the trap to resume their visiting of the poor, she whispered to her rapidly and with a little self-consciousness.

"That was awful. Sometimes you remind me of Joscelin. He used to make me laugh like that."

"I didn't notice you laughing," Hester said honestly, climbing up into the trap after her and forgetting to arrange her skirts.

"Of course not." Rosamond took the reins and slapped the horse forward. "It would never do to be seen. You will come again some time, won't you?"

"I am not at all sure I shall be asked," Hester said ruefully.

"Yes you will — Aunt Callandra will ask you. She likes you very much — and I think sometimes she gets bored with us here. Did you know Colonel Daviot?"

"No." For the first time Hester regretted that she had not. She had seen his portrait, but that was all; he had been a stocky, upright man with a strong-featured face, full of wit and temper. "No, I didn't."

Rosamond urged the horse faster and they careered along the track, the wheels bouncing over the ridges.

"He was very charming," she said, watching ahead. "Sometimes. He had a great laugh when he was happy — he also had a filthy temper and was terribly bossy — even with Aunt Callandra. He was always interfering, telling her how she ought to do everything

— when he got the whim for it. Then he would forget about whatever it was, and leave her to clear up the mess."

She reined in the horse a little, getting it under better control.

"But he was very generous," she added. "He never betrayed a friend's confidence. And the best horseman I ever saw — far better than either Menard or Lovel — and far better than General Wadham." Her hair was coming undone in the wind, and she ignored it. She giggled happily. "They couldn't bear each other."

It opened up an understanding of Callandra that Hester had never imagined before — a loneliness, and a freedom which explained why she had never entertained the idea of remarriage. Who could follow such a highly individual man? And perhaps also her independence had become more precious as she became more used to its pleasures. And perhaps also there had been more unhappiness there than Hester had imagined in her swift and rather shallow judgments?

She smiled and made some acknowledgment of having heard Rosamond's remark, then changed the subject. They arrived at the small hamlet where their further visiting was to be conducted, and it was late in the afternoon, hot and vividly blue and gold as they returned through the heavy fields past the reapers, whose backs were still bent, arms bare. Hester was glad of the breeze of their movement and passing beneath the huge shade trees that leaned over the narrow road was a pleasure. There was no sound but the thud of the horse's hooves, the hiss of the wheels and the occasional bird song. The light gleamed pale on the straw stalks where the laborers had already passed, and darker on the ungathered heads. A few faint clouds, frail as spun floss, drifted across the horizon.

Hester looked at Rosamond's hands on the reins and her quiet, tense face, and wondered if she saw the timeless beauty of it, or only the unceasing sameness, but it was a question she could not ask.

Hester spent the evening with Callandra in her rooms and did not dine with the family, but she took breakfast in the main dining room the following morning and Rosamond greeted her with evident pleasure.

"Would you like to see my son?" she invited with a faint blush for her assumption, and her vulnerability.

"Of course I would," Hester answered immediately; it was the only possible thing to say. "I cannot think of anything nicer." Indeed that was probably true. She was not looking forward to her next encounter with Fabia and she certainly did not wish to do any more visiting with General Wadham, any more "good works" among those whom Fabia considered "the deserving poor," nor to walk in the park again where she might meet that peculiarly offensive policeman. His remarks had been impertinent, and really very unjust. "It will make a beautiful beginning to the day," she added.

The nursery was a bright south-facing room full of sunlight and chintz, with a low nursing chair by the window, a rocking chair next to the large, well-railed and guarded fireplace, and at present, since the child was so young, a day crib. The nursery maid, a young girl with a handsome face and skin like cream, was busy feeding the baby, about a year and a half old, with fingers of bread and butter dipped in a chopped and buttered boiled egg. Hester and Rosamond did not interrupt but stood watching.

The baby, a quiff of blond hair along the crown of his head like a little bird's comb, was obviously enjoying himself immensely. He accepted every mouthful with perfect obedience and his cheeks grew fatter and fatter. Then with shining eyes he took a deep breath and blew it all out, to the nursery maid's utter consternation. He laughed so hard his face was bright pink and he fell over sideways in his chair, helpless with delight.

Rosamond was filled with embarrassment, but all Hester could do was laugh with the baby, while the maid dabbed at her once spotless apron with a damp cloth.

"Master Harry, you shouldn't do that!" the maid said as fiercely as she dared, but there was no real anger in her voice, more simple exasperation at having been caught yet again.

"Oh you dreadful child." Rosamond went and picked him up, holding him close to her and laying the pale head with its wave of hair close to her cheek. He was still crowing with joy, and looked over his mother's shoulder at Hester with total confidence that she would love him.

They spent a happy hour in gentle conversation, then left the maid to continue with her duties, and Rosamond showed Hester the main nursery where Lovel, Menard and Joscelin had played as children: the rocking horse, the toy soldiers, the wooden swords, the musical boxes, and the kaleidoscope; and the dolls' houses left by an earlier generation of girls — perhaps Callandra herself?

Next they looked at the schoolroom with its tables and shelves of books. Hester found her hands picking at first idly over old exercises of copperplate writing, a child's early, careful attempts. Then as she progressed to adolescent years and essays she found herself absorbed in reading the maturing hand. It was an essay in light, fluent style, surprisingly sharp for one so young and with a penetrating, often unkind wit. The subject was a family picnic, and she found herself smiling as she read, but there was pain in it, an awareness under the humor of cruelty. She did not need to look at the spine of the book to know it was Joscelin's.

She found one of Lovel's and turned the pages till she discovered an essay of similar length. Rosamond was searching a small desk for a copy of some verses, and there was time to read it carefully. It was utterly unlike, diffident, romantic, seeing beyond the simple woodland of Shelburne a forest where great deeds could be done, an ideal woman wooed and loved with a clean and untroubled emotion so far from the realities of human need and difficulty Hester found her eyes prickling for the disillusion that must come to such a youth.

She closed the pages with their faded ink and looked across at Rosamond, the sunlight on her bent head as she fingered through duty books looking for some special poem that caught her own high dream. Did either she or Lovel see beyond the princesses and the knights in armor the fallible, sometimes weak, sometimes frightened, often foolish people beneath — who needed immeasurably more courage, generosity and power to forgive than the creatures of youth's dreams — and were so much more precious?

She wanted to find the third essay, Menard's — and it took her several minutes to locate a book of his and read it. It was stiff, far less comfortable with words, and all through it there was a passionate love of honor, a loyalty to friendship and a sense of history as an unending cavalcade of the proud and the good, with sudden images borrowed from the tales of King Arthur. It was derivative and stilted, but the sincerity still shone through, and she doubted the man had lost the values of the boy who had written so intensely — and awkwardly.

Rosamond had found her poem at last, and was so absorbed in it that she was unaware of Hester's movement towards her, or that Hester glanced over her shoulder and saw that it was an anonymous love poem, very small and very tender.

Hester looked away and walked to the door. It was not something upon which to intrude.

Rosamond closed the book and followed a moment after, recapturing her previous gaiety with an effort which Hester pretended not to notice.

"Thank you for coming up," she said as they came back into the main landing with its huge jardinieres of flowers. "It was kind of you to be so interested."

"It is not kindness at all," Hester denied quickly. "I think it is a privilege to see into the past as one does in nurseries and old schoolrooms. I thank you for allowing me to come. And of course Harry is delightful! Who could fail to be happy in his presence?"

Rosamond laughed and made a small gesture of denial with her hand, but she was obviously pleased. They made their way downstairs together and into the dining room, where luncheon was already served and Lovel was waiting for them. He stood up as they came in, and took a step towards Rosamond. For a moment he seemed about to speak, then the impulse died.

She waited a moment, her eyes full of hope. Hester hated herself for being there, but to leave now would be absurd; the meal was set and the footman waiting to serve it. She knew Callandra had gone to visit an old acquaintance, because it was on Hester's behalf that she had made the journey, but Fabia was also absent and her place was not set.

Lovel saw her glance.

"Mama is not well," he said with a faint chill. "She has remained in her room."

"I am sorry," Hester said automatically. "I hope it is nothing serious?"

"I hope not," he agreed, and as soon as they were seated, resumed his own seat and indicated that the footman might begin to serve them.

Rosamond nudged Hester under the table with her foot, and Hester gathered that the situation was delicate, and wisely did not pursue it.

The meal was conducted with stilted and trivial conversation, layered with meanings, and Hester thought of the boy's essay, the old poem, and all the levels of dreams and realities where so much fell through between one set of meanings and another, and was lost.

Afterwards she excused herself and went to do what she realized was her duty. She must call on Fabia and apologize for having been rude to General Wadham. He had deserved it, but she was Fabia's guest, and she should not have embarrassed her, regardless of the provocation.

It was best done immediately; the longer she thought about it the harder it would be. She had little patience with minor ailments; she had seen too much desperate disease, and her own health was good enough she did not know from experience how debilitating even a minor pain can be when stretched over time.

She knocked on Fabia's door and waited until she heard the command to enter, then she turned the handle and went in.

It was a less feminine room than she had expected. It was plain light Wedgwood blue and sparsely furnished compared with the usual cluttered style. A single silver vase held summer roses in full bloom on the table by the window; the bed was canopied in white muslin, like the inner curtains. On the farthest wall, where the sun was diffused, hung a fine portrait of a young man in the uniform of a cavalry officer. He was slender and straight, his fair hair falling over a broad brow, pale, intelligent eyes and a mobile mouth, humorous, articulate, and she thought in that fleeting instant, a little weak.

Fabia was sitting up in her bed, a blue satin bedjacket covering her shoulders and her hair brushed and knotted loosely so it fell in a faded coil over her breast. She looked thin and much older than Hester was prepared for. Suddenly the apology was not difficult. She could see all the loneliness of years in the pale face, the loss which would never be repaired.

"Yes?" Fabia said with distinct chill.

"I came to apologize, Lady Fabia," Hester replied quietly. "I was very rude to General Wadham yesterday, and as your guest it was inexcusable. I am truly sorry."

Fabia's eyebrows rose in surprise, then she smiled very slightly.

"I accept your apology. I am surprised you had the grace to come — I had not expected it of you. It is not often I misjudge a young woman." Her smile lifted the corners of her mouth fractionally, giving her face a sudden life, echoing the girl she must once have been. "It was most embarrassing for me that General Wadham should be so — so deflated. But it was not entirely without its satisfactions. He is a condescending old fool — and I sometimes get very weary of being patronized."

Hester was too surprised to say anything at all. For the first time since arriving at Shelburne Hall she actually liked Fabia.

"You may sit down," Fabia offered with a gleam of humor in her eyes.

"Thank you." Hester sat on the dressing chair covered with blue velvet, and looked around the room at the other, lesser paintings and the few photographs, stiff and very posed for the long time that the camera required to set the image. There was a picture of Rosamond and Lovel, probably at their wedding. She looked fragile and very happy; he was facing the lens squarely, full of hope.

On the other chest there was an early daguerreotype of a middle-aged man with handsome side-whiskers, black hair and a vain, whimsical face. From the resemblance to Joscelin, Hester assumed it to be the late Lord Shelburne. There was also a pencil sketch of all three brothers as boys, sentimental, features a little idealized, the way one remembers summers of the past.

"I'm sorry you are feeling unwell," Hester said quietly. "Is there anything I can do for you?"

"I should think it highly unlikely; I am not a casualty of war — at least not in the sense that you are accustomed to," Fabia replied.

Hester did not argue. It rose to the tip of her tongue to say she was accustomed to all sorts of hurt, but then she knew it would be trite — she had not lost a son, and that was the only grief Fabia was concerned with.

"My eldest brother was killed in the Crimea." Hester still found the words hard to say. She could see George in her mind's eye, the way he walked, hear his laughter, then it dissolved and a sharper memory returned of herself and Charles and George as children, and the tears ached in her throat beyond bearing. "And both my parents died shortly after," she said quickly. "Shall we speak of something else?"

For a moment Fabia looked startled. She had forgotten, and now she was faced with a loss as huge as her own.

"My dear — I'm so very sorry. Of course — you did say so. Forgive me. What have you done this morning? Would you care to take the trap out later? It would be no difficulty to arrange it."

"I went to the nursery and met Harry." Hester smiled and blinked. "He's beautiful —" And she proceeded to tell the story.

She remained at Shelburne Hall for several more days, sometimes taking long walks alone in the wind and brilliant air. The parkland had a beauty which pleased her immensely and she felt at peace with it as she had in few other places. She was able to consider the future much more clearly, and Callandra's advice, repeated several times more in their many conversations, seemed increasingly wise the more she thought of it. The tension among the members of the household changed after the dinner with General Wadham. Surface anger was covered with the customary good manners, but she became aware through a multitude of small observations that the unhappiness was a deep and abiding part of the fabric of their lives.

Fabia had a personal courage which might have been at least half the habitual discipline of her upbringing and the pride that would not allow others to see her vulnerability. She was autocratic, to some extent selfish, although she would have been the last to think it of herself. But Hester saw the loneliness in her face in moments when she believed herself unobserved, and at times beneath the old woman so immaculately dressed, a bewilderment which laid bare the child she had once been. Undoubtedly she loved her two surviving sons, but she did not especially like them, and no one could charm her or make her laugh as Joscelin had. They were courteous, but they did not flatter her, they did not bring back with small attentions the great days of her beauty when dozens had courted her and she had been the center of so much. With Joscelin's death her own hunger for living had gone.

Hester spent many hours with Rosamond and became fond of her in a distant, non-confiding sort of way. Callandra's words about a brave, protective smile came to her sharply on several occasions, most particularly one late afternoon as they sat by the fire and made light, trivial conversation. Ursula Wadham was visiting, full of excitement and plans for the time when she would be married to Menard. She babbled on, facing Rosamond but apparently not seeing anything deeper than the perfect complexion, the carefully dressed hair and the rich afternoon gown. To her

Rosamond had everything a woman could desire, a wealthy and titled husband, a strong child, beauty, good health and sufficient talent in the arts of pleasing. What else was there to desire?

Hester listened to Rosamond agreeing to all the plans, how exciting it would be and how happy the future looked, and she saw behind the dark eyes no gleam of confidence and hope, only a sense of loss, a loneliness and a kind of desperate courage that keeps going because it knows no way to stop. She smiled because it brought her peace, it prevented question and it preserved a shred of pride.

Lovel was busy. At least he had purpose and as long as he was fulfilling it any darker emotion was held at bay. Only at the dinner table when they were all together did the occasional remark betray the underlying knowledge that something had eluded him, some precious element that seemed to be his was not really. He could not have called it fear — he would have hated the word and rejected it with horror — but staring at him across the snow-white linen and the glittering crystal, Hester thought that was what it was. She had seen it so often before, in totally different guises, when the danger was physical, violent and immediate. At first because the threat was so different she thought only of anger, then as it nagged persistently at the back of her mind, unclassified, suddenly she saw its other face, domestic, personal, emotional pain, and she knew it was a jar of familiarity.

With Menard it was also anger, but a sharp awareness too of something he saw as injustice; past now in act, but the residue still affecting him. Had he tidied up too often after Joscelin, his mother's favorite, protecting her from the truth that he was a cheat? Or was it himself he protected, and the family name?

Only with Callandra did she feel relaxed, but it did on one occasion cross her mind to wonder whether Callandra's comfort with herself was the result of many years' happiness or the resolution within her nature of its warring elements, not a gift but an art. It was one evening when they had taken a light supper in Callandra's sitting room instead of dinner in the main wing, and Callandra had made some remark about her husband, now long dead. Hester had always assumed the marriage to have been happy, not from anything she knew of it, or of Callandra Daviot, but from the peace within Callandra.

Now she realized how blindly she had leaped to such a short-sighted conclusion.

Callandra must have seen the idea waken in her eyes. She smiled with a touch of wryness, and a gentle humor in her face.

"You have a great deal of courage, Hester, and a hunger for life which is a far richer blessing than you think now — but, my dear, you are sometimes very naive. There are many kinds of misery, and many kinds of fortitude, and you should not allow your awareness of one to build to the value of another. You have an intense desire, a passion, to make people's lives better. Be aware that you can truly help people only by aiding them to become what they are, not what you are. I have heard you say 'If I were you, I would do this — or that.' 'I' am never 'you' — and my solutions may not be yours."

Hester remembered the wretched policeman who had told her she was domineering, overbearing and several other unpleasant things.

Callandra smiled. "Remember, my dear, you are dealing with the world as it is, not as you believe, maybe rightly, that it ought to be. There will be a great many things you can achieve not by attacking them but with a little patience and a modicum of flattery. Stop to consider what it is you really want, rather than pursuing your anger or your vanity to charge in. So often we leap to passionate judgments — when if we but knew the one thing more, they would be so different."

Hester was tempted to laugh, in spite of

having heard very clearly what Callandra had said, and perceiving the truth of it.

"I know," Callandra agreed quickly. "I preach much better than I practice. But believe me, when I want something enough, I have the patience to bide my time and think how I can bring it about."

"I'll try," Hester promised, and she did mean it. "That miserable policeman will not be right — I shall not allow him to be right."

"I beg your pardon?"

"I met him when I was out walking," Hester explained. "He said I was overbearing and opinionated, or something like that."

Callandra's eyebrows shot up and she did not even attempt to keep a straight face.

"Did he really? What temerity! And what perception, on such a short acquaintance. And what did you think of him, may I ask?"

"An incompetent and insufferable nincompoop!"

"Which of course you told him?"

Hester glared back at her. "Certainly!"

"Quite so. I think he had more of the right of it than you did. I don't think he is incompetent. He has been given an extremely difficult task. There were a great many people who might have hated Joscelin, and it will be exceedingly difficult for a policeman, with all his disadvantages, to discover which one it was

— and even harder, I imagine, to prove it."

"You mean, you think —" Hester left it unsaid, hanging in the air.

"I do," Callandra replied. "Now come, we must settle what you are to do with yourself. I shall write to certain friends I have, and I have little doubt, if you hold a civil tongue in your head, refrain from expressing your opinion of men in general and of Her Majesty's Army's generals in particular, we may obtain for you a position in hospital administration which will not only be satisfying to you but also to those who are unfortunate enough to be ill."

"Thank you." Hester smiled. "I am very grateful." She looked down in her lap for a moment, then up at Callandra and her eyes sparkled. "I really do not mind walking two paces behind a man, you know — if only I can find one who can walk two paces faster than I! It is being tied at the knees by convention I hate — and having to pretend I am lame to suit someone else's vanity."

Callandra shook her head very slowly, amusement and sadness sharp in her face. "I know. Perhaps you will have to fall a few times, and have someone else pick you up, before you will learn a more equable pace. But do not walk slowly simply for company — ever. Not even God would wish you to be unequally yoked and result in destroying both of you — in fact God least of all."

Hester sat back and smiled, lifting up her knees and hugging them in a most unladylike fashion. "I daresay I shall fall many times — and look excessively foolish — and give rise to a good deal of hilarity among those who dislike me — but that is still better than not trying."

"Indeed it is," Callandra agreed. "But you would do it anyway."

CHAPTER
EIGHT

The most productive of Joscelin Grey's acquaintances was one of the last that Monk and Evan visited, and not from Lady Fabia's list, but from the letters in the flat. They had spent over a week in the area near Shelburne, discreetly questioning on the pretense of tracing a jewel thief who specialized in country houses. They had learned something of Joscelin Grey, of the kind of life he led, at least while home from London. And Monk had had the unnerving and extremely irritating experience one day while walking across the Shelburne parkland of coming upon the woman who had been with Mrs. Latterly in St. Marylebone Church. Perhaps he should not have been startled — after all, society was very small — but it had taken him aback completely. The whole episode in the church with its powerful emotion had returned in the windy, rain-spattered land with its huge trees, and Shelburne Hall in the distance.

There was no reason why she should not have visited the family, precisely as he later discovered. She was a Miss Hester Latterly, who had nursed in the Crimea, and was a friend of Lady Callandra Daviot. As she had told him, she had known Joscelin Grey briefly at the time of his injury. It was most natural that once she was home she should give her condolences in person. And also certainly within her nature that she should be outstandingly rude to a policeman.

And give the devil her due, he had been rude back — and gained considerable satisfaction from it. It would all have been of no possible consequence were she not obviously related to the woman in the church whose face so haunted him.

What had they learned? Joscelin Grey was liked, even envied for his ease of manner, his quick smile and a gift for making people laugh; and perhaps even more rather than less, because the amusement had frequently an underlying caustic quality. What had surprised Monk was that he was also, if not pitied, then sympathized with because he was a younger son. The usual careers open to younger sons such as the church and the army were either totally unsuitable to him or else denied him now because of his injury, gained in the service of his country. The heiress he had courted had married his elder brother, and he had not yet found another to replace her, at least not one whose family considered him a suitable match. He was, after all, invalided out of the army, without a merchandisable skill and without financial expectations.

Evan had acquired a rapid education in the manners and morals of his financial betters, and now was feeling both bemused and disillusioned. He sat in the train staring out of the window, and Monk regarded him with a compassion not unmixed with humor. He knew the feeling, although he could not recall experiencing it himself. Was it possible he had never been so young? It was an unpleasant thought that he might always have been cynical, without that particular kind of innocence, even as a child.

Discovering himself step by step, as one might a stranger, was stretching his nerves further than he had been aware of until now. Sometimes he woke in the night, afraid of knowledge, feeling himself full of unknown shames and disappointments. The shapelessness of his doubt was worse than certainty would have been; even certainty of arrogance, indifference, or of having overridden justice for the sake of ambition.

But the more he pulled and struggled with it, the more stubbornly it resisted; it would come only thread by thread, without cohesion, a fragment at a time. Where had he learned his careful, precise diction? Who had taught him to move and to dress like a gentleman, to be so easy in his manners? Had he merely aped his betters over the years? Something very vague stirred in his mind, a feeling rather than a thought, that there had been someone he admired, someone who had taken time and trouble, a mentor — but no voice, nothing but an impression of working, practicing — and an ideal.

The people from whom they learned more about Joscelin Grey were the Dawlishes. Their house was in Primrose Hill, not far from the Zoological Gardens, and Monk and Evan went to visit them the day after returning from Shelburne. They were admitted by a butler too well trained to show surprise, even at the sight of policemen on the front doorstep. Mrs. Dawlish received them in the morning room. She was a small, mild-featured woman with faded hazel eyes and brown hair which escaped its pins.

"Mr. Monk?" She queried his name because it obviously meant nothing to her.

Monk bowed very slightly.

"Yes ma'am; and Mr. Evan. If Mr. Evan might have your permission to speak to the servants and see if they can be of assistance?"

"I think it unlikely, Mr. Monk." The idea was obviously futile in her estimation. "But as long as he does not distract them from their duties, of course he may."

"Thank you, ma'am." Evan departed with alacrity, leaving Monk still standing.

"About poor Joscelin Grey?" Mrs. Dawlish was puzzled and a little nervous, but apparently not unwilling to help. "What can we tell you? It was a most terrible tragedy. We had not known him very long, you know."

"How long, Mrs. Dawlish?"

"About five weeks before he . . . died." She sat down and he was glad to follow suit. "I believe it cannot have been more."

"But you invited him to stay with you? Do you often do that, on such short acquaintance?"

She shook her head, another strand of hair came undone and she ignored it.

"No, no hardly ever. But of course he was Menard Grey's brother —" Her face was suddenly hurt, as if something had betrayed her inexplicably and without warning, wounding where she had believed herself safe. "And Joscelin was so charming, so very natural," she went on. "And of course he also knew Edward, my eldest son, who was killed at Inkermann."

"I'm sorry."

Her face was very stiff, and for a moment he was afraid she would not be able to control herself. He spoke to cover the silence and her embarrassment.

"You said 'also.' Did Menard Grey know your son?"

"Oh yes," she said quietly. "They were close friends — for years." Her eyes filled with tears. "Since school."

"So you invited Joscelin Grey to stay with you?" He did not wait for her to reply; she was beyond speech. "That's very natural." Then quite a new idea occurred to him with sudden, violent hope. Perhaps the murder was nothing to do with any current scandal, but a legacy from the war, something that had happened on the battlefield? It was possible. He should have thought of it before — they all should.

"Yes," she said very quietly, mastering herself again. "If he knew Edward in the war, we wanted to talk with him, listen to him. You see — here at home, we know so little of what really happened." She took a deep breath. "I am not sure if it helps, indeed in some ways it is harder, but we feel . . . less cut off. I know Edward is dead and it cannot matter to him anymore; it isn't reasonable, but I feel closer to him, however it hurts."

She looked at him with a curious need to

be understood. Perhaps she had explained precisely this to other people, and they had tried to dissuade her, not realizing that for her, being excluded from her son's suffering was not a kindness but an added loss.

"Of course," he agreed quietly. His own situation was utterly different, yet any knowledge would surely be better than this uncertainty. "The imagination conjures so many things, and one feels the pain of them all, until one knows."

Her eyes widened in surprise. "You understand? So many friends have tried to persuade me into acceptance, but it gnaws away at the back of my mind, a sort of dreadful doubt. I read the newspapers sometimes" — she blushed — "when my husband is out of the house. But I don't know what to believe of them. Their accounts are —" She sighed, crumpling her handkerchief in her lap, her fingers clinging around it. "Well, they are sometimes a little softened so as not to distress us, or make us feel critical of those in command. And they are sometimes at variance with each other."

"I don't doubt it." He felt an unreasonable anger for the confusion of this woman, and all the silent multitude like her, grieving for their dead and being told that the truth was too harsh for them. Perhaps it was, perhaps many could not have borne it, but they had not been consulted, simply told; as their sons had been told to fight. For what? He had no idea. He had looked at many newspapers in the last few weeks, trying to learn, and he still had only the dimmest notion — something to do with the Turkish Empire and the balance of power.

"Joscelin used to speak to us so — so carefully," she went on softly, watching his face. "He told us a great deal about how he felt, and Edward must have felt the same. I had had no idea it was so very dreadful. One just doesn't know, sitting here in England —" She stared at him anxiously. "It wasn't very glorious, you know — not really. So many men dead, not because the enemy killed them, but from the cold and the disease. He told us about the hospital at Scutari. He was there, you know; with a wound in his leg. He suffered quite appallingly. He told us about seeing men freezing to death in the winter. I had not known the Crimea was cold like that. I suppose it was because it was east from here, and I always think of the East as being hot. He said it was hot in the summer, and dry. Then with winter there was endless rain and snow, and winds that all but cut the flesh. And the disease." Her face pinched. "I thanked God that if

Edward had to die, at least it was quickly, of a bullet, or a sword, not cholera. Yes, Joscelin was a great comfort to me, even though I wept as I hadn't done before; not only for Edward, but for all the others, and for the women like me, who lost sons and husbands. Do you understand, Mr. Monk?"

"Yes," he said quickly. "Yes I do. I'm very sorry I have to distress you now by speaking of Major Grey's death. But we must find whoever killed him."

She shuddered.

"How could anyone be so vile? What evil gets into a man that he could beat another to death like that? A fight I deplore, but I can understand it; but to go on, to mutilate a man after he is dead! The newspapers say it was dreadful. Of course my husband does not know I read them — having known the poor man, I felt I had to. Do you understand it, Mr. Monk?"

"No, I don't. In all the crimes I have investigated, I have not seen one like this." He did not know if it was true, but he felt it. "He must have been hated with a passion hard to conceive."

"I cannot imagine it, such a violence of feeling." She closed her eyes and shook her head fractionally. "Such a wish to destroy, to — to disfigure. Poor Joscelin, to have been the victim of such a — a creature. It would frighten me even to think someone could feel such an intensity of hatred for me, even if I were quite sure they could not touch me, and I were innocent of its cause. I wonder if poor Joscelin knew?"

It was a thought that had not occurred to Monk before — had Joscelin Grey had any idea that his killer hated him? Had he known, but merely thought him impotent to act?

"He cannot have feared him," he said aloud. "Or he would hardly have allowed him into his rooms while he was alone."

"Poor man." She hunched her shoulders involuntarily, as if chilled. "It is very frightening to think that someone with that madness in their hearts could walk around, looking like you or me. I wonder if anyone dislikes me intensely and I have no idea of it. I had never entertained such a thought before, but now I cannot help it. I shall be unable to look at people as I used to. Are people often killed by those they know quite well?"

"Yes ma'am, I am afraid so; most often of all by relatives."

"How appalling." Her voice was very soft, her eyes staring at some spot beyond him. "And how very tragic."

"Yes it is." He did not want to seem crass, nor indifferent to her horror, but he had to pursue the business of it. "Did Major Grey ever say anything about threats, or anyone who might be afraid of him —"

She lifted her eyes to look at him; her brow was puckered and another strand of hair escaped the inadequate pins. "Afraid of him? But it was he who was killed!"

"People are like other animals," he replied. "They most often kill when they are afraid themselves."

"I suppose so. I had not thought of that." She shook her head a little, still puzzled. "But Joscelin was the most harmless of people! I never heard him speak as if he bore real ill will towards anyone. Of course he had a sharp wit, but one does not kill over a joke, even if it is a trifle barbed, and possibly even not in the kindest of taste."

"Even so," he pressed, "against whom were these remarks directed?"

She hesitated, not only in an effort to remember, but it seemed the memory was disturbing her.

He waited.

"Mostly against his own family," she said slowly. "At least that was how it sounded to me — and I think to others. His comments on Menard were not always kind, although my husband knows more of that than I — I always liked Menard — but then that was

311

no doubt because he and Edward were so close. Edward loved him dearly. They shared so much —" She blinked and screwed up her mild face even more. "But then Joscelin often spoke harshly of himself also — it is hard to understand."

"Of himself?" Monk was surprised. "I've been to his family, naturally, and I can understand a certain resentment. But in what way of himself?"

"Oh, because he had no property, being a third son; and after his being wounded he limped, you know. So of course there was no career for him in the army. He appeared to feel he was of little — little standing — that no one accounted him much. Which was quite untrue, of course. He was a hero — and much liked by all manner of people!"

"I see." Monk was thinking of Rosamond Shelburne, obliged by her mother to marry the son with the title and the prospects. Had Joscelin loved her, or was it more an insult than a wound, a reminder that he was third best? Had he cared, it could only have hurt him that she had not the courage to follow her heart and marry as she wished. Or was the status more important to her, and she had used Joscelin to reach Lovel? That would perhaps have hurt differently, with a bitterness that would remain.

Perhaps they would never know the answer to that.

He changed the subject. "Did he at any time mention what his business interests were? He must have had some income beyond the allowance from his family."

"Oh yes," she agreed. "He did discuss it with my husband, and he mentioned it to me, although not in any great detail."

"And what was it, Mrs. Dawlish?"

"I believe it was some investment, quite a sizable one, in a company to trade with Egypt." The memory of it was bright in her face for a moment, the enthusiasm and expectation of that time coming back.

"Was Mr. Dawlish involved in this investment?"

"He was considering it; he spoke highly of its possibilities."

"I see. May I call again later when Mr. Dawlish is at home, and learn more details of this company from him?"

"Oh dear." The lightness vanished. "I am afraid I have expressed myself badly. The company is not yet formed. I gathered it was merely a prospect that Joscelin intended to pursue."

Monk considered for a moment. If Grey were only forming a company, and perhaps persuading Dawlish to invest, then what had been his source of income up to that time?

"Thank you." He stood up slowly. "I understand. All the same, I should like to speak to Mr. Dawlish. He may well know something about Mr. Grey's finances. If he were contemplating entering business with him, it would be natural he should inquire."

"Yes, yes of course." She poked ineffectually at her hair. "Perhaps about six o'clock."

Evan's questioning of the half-dozen or so domestic servants yielded nothing except the picture of a very ordinary household, well run by a quiet, sad woman stricken with a grief she bore as bravely as she could, but of which they were all only too aware and each in their own way shared. The butler had a nephew who served as a foot soldier and had returned a cripple. Evan was suddenly sobered by the remembrance of so many other losses, so many people who had to struggle on without the notoriety, or the sympathy, of Joscelin Grey's family.

The sixteen-year-old between-stairs maid had lost an elder brother at Inkermann. They all recalled Major Grey, how charming he was, and that Miss Amanda was very taken with him. They had hoped he would return, and were horrified that he could be so terribly murdered right here in his home. They had an obvious duality of thought that confounded Evan — it shocked them that a gentleman should be so killed, and yet they viewed their own losses as things merely to be borne with quiet dignity.

He came away with an admiration for their stoicism, and an anger that they should accept the difference so easily. Then as he came through the green baize door back into the main hallway, the thought occurred to him that perhaps that was the only way of bearing it — anything else would be too destructive, and in the end only futile.

And he had learned little of Joscelin Grey that he had not already deduced from the other calls.

Dawlish was a stout, expensively dressed man with a high forehead and dark, clever eyes, but at present he was displeased at the prospect of speaking with the police, and appeared distinctly ill at ease. There was no reason to assume it was an unquiet conscience; to have the police at one's house, for any reason, was socially highly undesirable, and judging from the newness of the furniture and the rather formal photographs of the family — Mrs. Dawlish seated in imitation of the Queen — Mr. Dawlish was an ambitious man.

It transpired that he knew remarkably little

about the business he had half committed himself to support. His involvement was with Joscelin Grey personally, and it was this which had caused him to promise funds, and the use of his good name. "Charming fellow," he said, half facing Monk as he stood by the parlor fire. "Hard when you're brought up in a family, part of it and all that, then the eldest brother marries and suddenly you're nobody." He shook his head grimly. "Dashed hard to make your way if you're not suited to the church, and invalided out of the army. Only thing really is to marry decently." He looked at Monk to see if he understood. "Don't know why young Joscelin didn't, certainly a handsome enough chap, and pleasing with women. Had all the charm, right words to say, and so on. Amanda thought the world of him." He coughed. "My daughter, you know. Poor girl was very distressed over his death. Dreadful thing! Quite appalling." He stared down at the embers and a sharp sadness filled his eyes and softened the lines around his mouth. "Such a decent man. Expect it in the Crimea, die for your country, and so on; but not this. Lost her first suitor at Sebastopol, poor girl; and of course her brother at Balaclava. That's where he met young Grey." He swallowed hard and looked up at Monk, as if to defy his emotions. "Damned good to him." He took a deep breath and fought to control a conflict of emotions that were obviously acutely painful. "Actually spoke to each other night before the battle. Like to think of that, someone we've met, with Edward the night before he was killed. Been a great source of —" He coughed again and was forced to look away, his eyes brimming. "Comfort to us, my wife and I. Taken it hard, poor woman; only son, you know. Five daughters. And now this."

"I understand Menard Grey was also a close friend of your son's," Monk said, as much to fill the silence as that it might have mattered.

Dawlish stared at the coals. "Prefer not to speak of it," he replied with difficulty, his voice husky. "Thought a lot of him — but he led Edward into bad ways — no doubt about it. It was Joscelin who paid his debts — so he did not die with dishonor."

He swallowed convulsively. "We became fond of Joscelin, even on the few weekends he stayed with us." He lifted the poker out of its rest and jabbed at the fire fiercely. "I hope to heaven you catch the madman who did it."

"We'll do everything we can, sir." Monk wanted to say all sorts of other things to express the pity he felt for so much loss. Thousands of men and horses had died, frozen, starved, or been massacred or wasted by disease on the bitter hillsides of a country they neither knew nor loved. If he had ever known the purpose of the war in the Crimea he had forgotten it now. It could hardly have been a war of defense. Crimea was a thousand miles from England. Presumably from the newspapers it was something to do with the political ramifications of Turkey and its disintegrating empire. It hardly seemed a reason for the wretched, pitiful deaths of so many, and the grief they left behind.

Dawlish was staring at him, waiting for him to say something, expecting a platitude.

"I am sorry your son had to die in such a way." Monk held out his hand automatically. "And so young. But at least Joscelin Grey was able to assure you it was with courage and dignity, and that his suffering was brief."

Dawlish took his hand before he had time to think.

"Thank you." There was a faint flush on his skin and he was obviously moved. He did not even realize until after Monk had gone that he had shaken hands with a policeman as frankly as if he had been a gentleman.

That evening Monk found himself for the first time caring about Grey personally. He sat in his own quiet room with nothing but the faint noises from the street in the distance below. In the small kindnesses to the Dawlishes, in paying a dead man's debts, Grey had developed a solidity far more than in the grief of his mother or the pleasant but rather insubstantial memories of his neighbors. He had become a man with a past of something more than a resentment that his talent was wasted while the lesser gifts of his elder brother were overrewarded, more than the rejected suitor of a weak young woman who preferred the ease of doing as she was told and the comfort of status to the relative struggle of following her own desires. Or perhaps she had not really wanted anything enough to fight for it?

Shelburne was comfortable, physically everything was provided; one did not have to work, morally there were no decisions — if something was unpleasant one did not have to look at it. If there were beggars in the street, mutilated or diseased, one could pass to the other side. There was the government to make the social decisions, and the church to make the moral ones.

Of course society demanded a certain, very rigid code of conduct, of taste, and a very small circle of friends and suitable ways to pass one's time, but for those who had been brought up from childhood to observe it, it was little extra effort.

Small wonder if Joscelin Grey was angry with it, even contemptuous after he had seen the frozen bodies on the heights before Sebastopol, the carnage at Balaclava, the filth, the disease and the agony of Scutari.

In the street below a carriage clattered by and someone shouted and there was a roar of laughter.

Suddenly Monk found himself feeling this same strange, almost impersonal disgust Grey must have suffered coming back to England afterwards, to a family who were strangers insofar as their petty, artificial little world was concerned; who knew only the patriotic placebos they read in the newspapers, and had no wish to look behind them for uglier truths.

He had felt the same himself after visiting the "rookeries," the hell-like, rotting tenements crawling with vermin and disease, sometimes only a few dozen yards from the lighted streets where gentlemen rode in carriages from one sumptuous house to another. He had seen fifteen or twenty people in one room, all ages and sexes together, without heating or sanitation. He had seen child prostitutes of eight or ten years old with eyes tired and old as sin, and bodies riddled with venereal disease; children of five or even less frozen to death in the gutters because they could not beg a night's shelter. Small wonder they stole, or sold for a few pence the only things they possessed, their own bodies.

How did he remember that, when his own father's face was still a blank to him? He must have cared very much, been so shocked by it that it left a scar he could not forget, even now. Was that, at least in part, the fire behind his ambition, the fire behind his relentless drive to improve himself, to copy the mentor whose features he could not recall, whose name, whose station, eluded him? Please God that was so. It made a more tolerable man of him, even one he could begin to accept.

Had Joscelin Grey cared?

Monk intended to avenge him; he would not be merely another unsolved mystery, a man remembered for his death rather than his life.

And he must pursue the Latterly case. He could hardly go back to Mrs. Latterly without knowing at least the outline of the matter he had promised her to solve, however painful the truth. And he did intend to go back to her. Now that he thought about it, he realized he had always intended to visit her again, speak with her, see her face, listen to her voice, watch the way she moved; command her attention, even for so short a time.

There was no use looking among his files again; he had already done that almost page by page. Instead he went directly to Runcorn.

"Morning, Monk." Runcorn was not at his desk but over by the window, and he sounded positively cheerful; his rather sallow face was touched with color as if he had walked briskly in the sun, and his eyes were bright. "How's the Grey case coming along? Got something to tell the newspapers yet? They're still pressing, you know." He sniffed faintly and reached in his pocket for a cigar. "They'll be calling for our blood soon; resignations, and that sort of thing!"

Monk could see his satisfaction in the way he stood, shoulders a little high, chin up, the shine on his shoes gleaming in the light.

"Yes sir, I imagine they will," he conceded. "But as you said over a week ago, it's one of those investigations that is bound to rake up something extremely unpleasant, possibly several things. It would be very rash to say anything before we can prove it."

"Have you got anything at all, Monk?" Runcorn's face hardened, but his sense of anticipation was still there, his scent of blood. "Or are you as lost as Lamb was?"

"It looks at the moment as if it could be in the family, sir," Monk replied as levelly as he could. He had a sickening awareness that Runcorn was controlling this, and enjoying it. "There was considerable feeling between the brothers," he went on. "The present Lady Shelburne was courted by Joscelin before she married Lord Shelburne —"

"Hardly a reason to murder him," Runcorn said with contempt. "Would only make sense if it had been Shelburne who was murdered. Doesn't sound as if you have anything there!"

Monk kept his temper. He felt Runcorn trying to irritate him, provoke him into betraying all the pent-up past that lay between them; victory would be sweeter if it were acknowledged, and could be savored in the other's presence. Monk wondered how he could have been so insensitive, so stupid as not to have known it before. Why had he not forestalled it, even avoided it altogether? How had he been so blind then when now it was so glaring? Was it really no more than that he was rediscovering himself, fact by fact, from the outside?

"Not that in itself." He went back to the question, keeping his voice light and calm. "But I think the lady still preferred Joscelin, and her one child, conceived just before Joscelin went to the Crimea, looks a good deal more like him than like his lordship."

Runcorn's face fell, then slowly widened

again in a smile, showing all his teeth; the cigar was still unlit in his hand.

"Indeed. Yes. Well, I warned you it would be nasty, didn't I? You'll have to be careful, Monk; make any allegations you can't prove, and the Shelburnes will have you dismissed before you've time to get back to London."

Which is just what you want, Monk thought.

"Precisely sir," he said aloud. "That is why as far as the newspapers are concerned, we are still in the dark. I came because I wanted to ask you about the Latterly case —"

"Latterly! What the hell does that matter? Some poor devil committed suicide." He walked around and sat down at his desk and began fishing for matches. "It's a crime for the church, not for us. Have you got any matches, Monk? We wouldn't have taken any notice of it at all if that wretched woman hadn't raised it. Ah — don't bother, here they are. Let them bury their own dead quietly, no fuss." He struck a light and held it to his cigar, puffing gently. "Man got in over his head with a business deal that went sour. All his friends invested in it on his recommendation, and he couldn't take the shame of it. Took that way out; some say coward's way, some say it's the honorable way." He blew out smoke and stared up at Monk. "Damn silly, I call it. But that class is very jealous of what it thinks is its good name. Some of them will keep servants they can't afford for the sake of appearance, serve six-course meals to guests, and live on bread and dripping the rest of the time. Light a fire when there's company, and perish with cold the rest of the time. Pride is a wicked master, most especially social pride." His eyes flickered with malicious pleasure. "Remember that, Monk."

He looked down at the papers in front of him. "Why on earth are you bothering with Latterly? Get on with Grey; we need to solve it, however painful it may prove. The public won't wait much longer; they're even asking questions in the House of Lords. Did you know that?"

"No sir, but considering how Lady Shelburne feels, I'm not surprised. Do you have a file on the Latterly case, sir?"

"You are a stubborn man, Monk. It's a very dubious quality. I've got your written report that it was a suicide, and nothing to concern us. You don't want that again, do you?"

"Yes sir, I do." Monk took it without looking at it and walked out.

He had to visit the Latterlys' house in the evening, in his own time, since he was not officially working on any case that involved them. He must have been here before; he could not have met with Mrs. Latterly casually, nor expected her to report to the police station. He looked up and down the street, but there was nothing familiar in it.

The only streets he could remember were the cold cobbles of Northumberland, small houses whipped clean by the wind, gray seas and the harbor below and the high moors rising to the sky. He could remember vaguely, once, a visit to Newcastle in the train, the enormous furnaces towering over the rooftops, the plumes of smoke, the excitement running through him in their immense, thrumming power, the knowledge of coal-fired blast furnaces inside; steel hammered and beaten into engines to draw trains over the mountains and plains of the whole Empire. He could still capture just an echo of the thrill that had been high in his throat then, tingling his arms and legs, the awe, the beginning of adventure. He must have been very young.

It had been quite different when he had first come to London. He had been so much older, more than the ten or so years the calendar had turned. His mother was dead; Beth was with an aunt. His father had been lost at sea when Beth was still in arms. Coming to London had been the beginning of something new, and the end of all that belonged to childhood.

Beth had seen him off at the station, crying, screwing up her pinafore in her hand, refusing to be comforted. She could not have been more than nine, and he about fifteen. But he could read and write, and the world was his for the labor.

But that was a long time ago. He was well over thirty now, probably over thirty-five. What had he done in more than twenty years? Why had he not returned? That was something else he had yet to learn. His police record was there in his office, and in Runcorn's hate. What about himself, his personal life? Or had he no one, was he only a public man?

And what before the police? His files here went back only twelve years, so there must have been more than eight years before that. Had he spent them all learning, climbing, improving himself with his faceless mentor, his eyes always on the goal? He was appalled at his own ambition, and the strength of his will. It was a little frightening, such single-mindedness.

He was at the Latterlys' door, ridiculously nervous. Would she be in? He had thought about her so often; he realized only now and with a sense of having been foolish, vulnerable, that she had probably not thought of him at all. He might even have to explain who he was. He would seem clumsy, gauche, when he said he had no further news.

He hesitated, unsure whether to knock at all, or to leave, and come again when he had a better excuse. A maid came out into the areaway below him, and in order not to appear a loiterer, he raised his hand and knocked.

The parlor maid came almost immediately. Her eyebrows rose in the very slightest of surprise.

"Good evening, Mr. Monk; will you come in, sir?" It was sufficiently courteous not to be in obvious haste to get him off the doorstep. "The family have dined and are in the withdrawing room, sir. Do you wish me to ask if they will receive you?"

"Yes please. Thank you." Monk gave her his coat and followed her through to a small morning room. After she had gone he paced up and down because he could not bear to be still. He hardly noticed anything about the furniture or the pleasant, rather ordinary paintings and the worn carpet. What was he going to say? He had charged into a world where he did not belong, because of something he dreamed in a woman's face. She probably found him distasteful, and would not have suffered him if she were not so concerned about her father-in-law, hoping he could use his skills to discover something that would ease her grief. Suicide was a terrible shame, and in the eyes of the church financial disgrace would not excuse it. He could still be buried in unconsecrated ground if the conclusion were inevitable.

It was too late to back away now, but it crossed his mind. He even considered concocting an excuse, another reason for calling, something to do with Grey and the letter in his flat, when the parlor maid returned and there was no time.

"Mrs. Latterly will see you, sir, if you come this way."

Obediently, heart thumping and mouth dry, he followed the maid.

The withdrawing room was medium sized, comfortable, and originally furnished with the disregard for money of those who have always possessed it, but the ease, the unostentation of those for whom it has no novelty. Now it was still elegant, but the curtains were a little faded in portions where the sun fell on them, and the fringing on the swags with which they were tied was missing a bobble here and there. The carpet was not of equal quality with the piecrust tables or the chaise longue. He felt pleasure in the room immediately, and wondered where in his merciless self-improvement he had learned such taste.

His eyes went to Mrs. Latterly beside the

fire. She was no longer in black, but dark wine, and it brought a faint flush to her skin. Her throat and shoulders were as delicate and slender as a child's, but there was nothing of the child in her face. She was staring at him with luminous eyes, wide now, and too shadowed to read their expression.

Monk turned quickly to the others. The man, fairer than she and with less generous mouth, must be her husband, and the other woman sitting opposite with the proud face with so much anger and imagination in it he knew immediately; they had met and quarreled at Shelburne Hall — Miss Hester Latterly.

"Good evening, Monk." Charles Latterly did not stand. "You remember my wife?" He gestured vaguely towards Imogen. "And my sister, Miss Hester Latterly. She was in the Crimea when our father died." There was a strong accent of disapproval in his voice and it was apparent that he resented Monk's involvement in the affair.

Monk was assailed by an awful thought — had he somehow disgraced himself, been too brash, too insensitive to their pain and added not only to their loss but the manner of it? Had he said something appallingly thoughtless, or been too familiar? The blood burned up his face and he stumbled into speech to cover the hot silence.

"Good evening, sir." Then he bowed very slightly to Imogen and then to Hester. "Good evening, ma'am; Miss Latterly." He would not mention that they had already met. It was not a fortunate episode.

"What can we do for you?" Charles asked, nodding towards a seat, indicating that Monk might make himself comfortable.

Monk accepted, and another extraordinary thought occurred to him. Imogen had been very discreet, almost furtive in speaking to him in St. Marylebone Church. Was it conceivable neither her husband nor her sister-in-law knew that she had pursued the matter beyond the first, formal acknowledgment of the tragedy and the necessary formalities? If that were so he must not betray her now.

He drew a deep breath, hoping he could make sense, wishing to God he could remember anything at all of what Charles had told him, and what he had learned from Imogen alone. He would have to bluff, pretend there was something new, a connection with the murder of Grey; it was the only other case he was working on, or could remember anything at all about. These people had known him, however slightly. He had been working for them shortly before the accident; surely they could tell him something about himself?

But that was less than half a truth. Why lie to himself? He was here because of Imogen Latterly. It was purposeless, but her face haunted his mind, like a memory from the past of which the precise nature is lost, or a ghost from the imagination, from the realm of daydreams so often repeated it seems they must surely have been real.

They were all looking at him, still waiting.

"It is possible . . ." His voice was rough at first. He cleared his throat. "I have discovered something quite new. But before I tell you I must be perfectly sure, more especially since it concerns other people." That should prevent them, as a matter of good taste, from pressing him. He coughed again. "It is some time since I spoke to you last, and I made no notes, as a point of discretion —"

"Thank you," Charles said slowly. "That was considerate of you." He seemed to find it hard to say the words, as if it irritated him to acknowledge that policemen might possess such delicate virtues.

Hester was staring at him with frank disbelief.

"If I could go over the details we know again?" Monk asked, hoping desperately they would fill in the gaping blanks in his mind; he knew only what Runcorn had told him, and that was in turn only what he had told

Runcorn. Heaven knew, that was barely enough to justify spending time on the case.

"Yes, yes of course." Again it was Charles who spoke, but Monk felt the eyes of the women on him also: Imogen anxious, her hands clenched beneath the ample folds of her skirt, her dark eyes wide; Hester was thoughtful, ready to criticize. He must dismiss them both from his mind, concentrate on making sense, picking up the threads from Charles, or he would make a complete fool of himself, and he could not bear that in front of them.

"Your father died in his study," he began. "In his home in Highgate on June fourteenth." That much Runcorn had said.

"Yes." Charles agreed. "It was early evening, before dinner. My wife and I were staying with them at the time. Most of us were upstairs changing."

"Most of you?"

"Perhaps I should say 'both of us.' My mother and I were. My wife was late coming in. She had been over to see Mrs. Standing, the vicar's wife, and as it transpired my father was in his study."

The means of death had been a gunshot. The next question was easy.

"And how many of you heard the report?"

"Well, I suppose we all heard it, but my wife was the only one to realize what it was.

She was coming in from the back garden entrance and was in the conservatory."

Monk turned to Imogen.

She was looking at him, a slight frown on her face as if she wanted to say something, but dared not. Her eyes were troubled, full of dark hurt.

"Mrs. Latterly?" He forgot what he had intended to ask her. He was conscious of his hands clenched painfully by his sides and had to ease the fingers out deliberately. They were sticky with sweat.

"Yes, Mr. Monk?" she said quietly.

He scrambled for something sensible to say. His brain was blank. What had he said to her the first time? She had come to him; surely she would have told him everything she knew? He must ask her something quickly. They were all waiting, watching him. Charles Latterly cool, disliking the effrontery, Hester exasperated at his incompetence. He already knew what she thought of his abilities. Attack was the only defense his mind could think of.

"Why do you think, Mrs. Latterly, that you suspected a shot, when no one else did?" His voice was loud in the silence, like the sudden chimes of a clock in an empty room. "Were you afraid even then that your father-in-law contemplated taking his life, or that he was in some danger?"

The color came to her face quickly and there was anger in her eyes.

"Of course not, Mr. Monk; or I should not have left him alone." She swallowed, and her next words were softer. "I knew he was distressed, we all knew that; but I did not imagine it was serious enough to think of shooting himself — nor that he was sufficiently out of control of his feelings or his concentration that he would be in danger of having an accident." It was a brave attempt.

"I think if you have discovered something, Mr. Monk," Hester interrupted stiffly, "you had better ascertain what it is, and then come back and tell us. Your present fumbling around is pointless and unnecessarily distressing. And your suggestion that my sister-in-law knew something that she did not report at the time is offensive." She looked him up and down with some disgust. "Really, is this the best you can do? I don't know how you catch anyone, unless you positively fall over them!"

"Hester!" Imogen spoke quite sharply, although she kept her eyes averted. "It is a question Mr. Monk must ask. It is possible I may have seen or heard something to make me anxious — and only realize it now in retrospect."

Monk felt a quick, foolish surge of pleasure. He had not deserved defending.

"Thank you, ma'am." He tried to smile at

her, and felt his lips grimacing. "Did you at that time know the full extent of your father-in-law's financial misfortune?"

"It was not the money that killed him," Imogen replied before Charles could get his own words formed and while Hester was still standing in resigned silence — at least temporarily. "It was the disgrace." She bit her lip on all the distress returned to her. Her voice dropped to little more than a whisper, tight with pity. "You see, he had advised so many of his friends to invest. He had lent his name to it, and they had put in money because they trusted him."

Monk could think of nothing to say, and platitudes offended him in the face of real grief. He longed to be able to comfort her, and knew it was impossible. Was this the emotion that surged through him so intensely — pity? And the desire to protect?

"The whole venture has brought nothing but tragedy," Imogen went on very softly, staring at the ground. "Papa-in-law, then poor Mama, and now Joscelin as well."

For an instant everything seemed suspended, an age between the time she spoke and the moment overwhelming realization of what she had said came to Monk.

"You knew Joscelin Grey?" It was as if another person spoke for him and he was still distant, watching strangers, removed from him, on the other side of a glass.

Imogen frowned a little, confused by his apparent unreason; there was a deep color in her face and she lowered her eyes the moment after she had spoken, avoiding everyone else's, especially her husband's.

"For the love of heaven!" Charles's temper snapped. "Are you completely incompetent, man?"

Monk had no idea what to say. What on earth had Grey to do with it? Had he known him?

What were they thinking of him? How could he possibly make sense of it now? They could only conclude he was mad, or was playing some disgusting joke. It was the worst possible taste — life was not sacred to them, but death most certainly was. He could feel the embarrassment burning in his face, and was as conscious of Imogen as if she were touching him, and of Hester's eyes filled with unutterable contempt.

Again it was Imogen who rescued him.

"Mr. Monk never met Joscelin, Charles," she said quietly. "It is very easy to forget a name when you do not know the person to whom it belongs."

Hester stared from one to the other of them, her clear, intelligent eyes filled with a growing perception that something was profoundly wrong.

"Of course," Imogen said more briskly, covering her feelings. "Mr. Monk did not come until after Papa was dead; there was no occasion." She did not look at her husband, but she was obviously speaking to him. "And if you recall, Joscelin did not return after that."

"You can hardly blame him." Charles's voice contained a sharpening of criticism, an implication that Imogen was somehow being unfair. "He was as distressed as we were. He wrote me a very civil letter, expressing his condolences." He put his hands in his pocket, hard, and hunched his shoulders. "Naturally, he felt it unsuitable to call, in the circumstances. He quite understood our association must end; very delicate of him, I thought." He looked at Imogen with impatience, and ignored Hester altogether.

"That was like him, so very sensitive." Imogen was looking far away. "I do miss him."

Charles swiveled to look at her beside him. He seemed about to say something, and then changed his mind and bit it off. Instead he took his hand out of his pocket and put it around her arm. "So you didn't meet him?" he said to Monk.

Monk was still floundering.

"No." It was the only answer he had left himself room to make. "He was out of town." Surely that at least could have been true?

"Poor Joscelin." Imogen appeared unaware of her husband, or his fingers tightening on her shoulder. "He must have felt dreadful," she went on. "Of course he was not responsible, he was as deceived as any of us, but he was the sort of person who would take it on himself." Her voice was sad, gentle and utterly without criticism.

Monk could only guess, he dared not ask: Grey must somehow have been involved in the business venture in which Latterly Senior lost money, and so ill advised his friends. And it would seem Joscelin had lost money himself, which he could hardly afford; hence perhaps the request to the family estate for an increased allowance? The date on the letter from the solicitor was about right, shortly after Latterly's death. Possibly it was that financial disaster that had prompted Joscelin Grey to gamble rashly, or to descend to blackmail. If he had lost enough in the business he might have been desperate, with creditors pressing, social disgrace imminent. Charm was his only stock in trade; his entertainment value was his passport to hospitality in other people's houses the year round, and his only path to the heiress who might ultimately make him independent, no longer begging from his mother and the brother he scarcely loved.

But who? Who among his acquaintances was vulnerable enough to pay for silence; and desperate, murderous enough to kill for it?

Whose houses had he stayed in? All sorts of indiscretions were committed on long weekends away from the city. Scandal was not a matter of what was done but of what was known to have been done. Had Joscelin stumbled on some well-kept secret adultery?

But adultery was hardly worth killing over, unless there was a child to inherit, or some other domestic crisis, a suit for divorce with all its scandal, and the complete social ostracism that followed. To kill would need a secret far worse, like incest, perversion or impotence. The shame of impotence was mortal, God knew why, but it was the most abhorred of afflictions, something not even whispered of.

Runcorn was right, even to speak of such a possibility would be enough to have him reported to the highest authorities, his career blocked forever, if he were not dismissed out of hand. He could never be forgiven for exposing a man to the ruin which must follow such an abominable scandal.

They were all staring at him. Charles was making no secret of his impatience. Hester was exasperated almost beyond endurance; her fingers were fiddling with the plain cambric handkerchief and her foot tapped rapidly and silently on the floor. Her opinion was in every line of her remarkable face.

"What is it you think you may know, Mr. Monk?" Charles said sharply. "If there is nothing, I would ask that you do not distress us again by raking over what can only be to us a tragedy. Whether my father took his own life or it was an accident while his mind was distracted with distress cannot be proved, and we should be obliged if you allowed those who are charitable enough to allow that it might have been an accident to prevail! My mother died of a broken heart. One of our past friends has been brutally murdered. If we cannot be of assistance to you, I would prefer that you permit us to come to terms with our grief in our own way, and do our best to resume the pattern of our lives again. My wife was quite wrong to have persisted in her hope for some more pleasant alternative, but women are tender-hearted by nature, and she finds it hard to accept a bitter truth."

"All she wished of me was to ascertain that it was indeed the truth," Monk said quickly, instinctively angry that Imogen should be criticized. "I cannot believe that mistaken." He stared with chill, level eyes at Charles.

"That is courteous of you, Mr. Monk." Charles glanced at Imogen condescendingly, to imply that Monk had been humoring her. "But I have no doubt she will come to the same conclusion, in time. Thank you for calling; I am sure you have done what you believed to be your duty."

Monk accepted the dismissal and was in the hall before he realized what he had done. He had been thinking of Imogen, and of Hester's scalding disdain, and he had allowed himself to be awed by the house, by Charles Latterly's self-assurance, his arrogance, and his very natural attempts to conceal a family tragedy and mask it in something less shameful.

He turned on his heel and faced the closed door again. He wanted to ask them about Grey, and he had the excuse for it, indeed he had no excuse not to. He took a step forward, and then felt foolish. He could hardly go back and knock like a servant asking entry. But he could not walk out of the house, knowing they had had a relationship with Joscelin Grey, that Imogen at least had cared for him, and not ask more. He stretched out his hand, then withdrew it again.

The door opened and Imogen came out. She stopped in surprise, a foot from him, her back against the panels. The color came up her face.

"I'm sorry." She took a breath. "I — I did not realize you were still here."

He did not know what to say either; he was idiotically speechless. Seconds ticked by. Eventually it was she who spoke.

"Was there something else, Mr. Monk? Have you found something?" Her voice lifted, all eagerness, hope in her eyes; and he felt sure now that she had come to him alone, trusted him with something she had not confided to her husband or Hester.

"I'm working on the Joscelin Grey case." It was the only thing he could think of to say. He was floundering in a morass of ignorance. If only he could remember!

Her eyes dropped. "Indeed. So that is why you came to see us. I'm sorry, I misunderstood. You — you wish to know something about Major Grey?"

It was far from the truth.

"I —" He drew a deep breath. "I dislike having to disturb you, so soon after —"

Her head came up, her eyes angry. He had no idea why. She was so lovely, so gentle; she woke yearnings in him for something his memory could not grasp: some old sweetness, a time of laughter and trust. How could he be stupid enough to feel this torrent of emotion for a woman who had simply come to him for help because of family tragedy, and almost certainly regarded him in the same light as she would the plumber or the fireman?

"Sorrows do not wait for one another." She was talking to him in a stiff little voice. "I know what the newspapers are saying. What do you wish to know about Major Grey? If we knew anything that was likely to be of help, we should have told you ourselves."

"Yes." He was withered by her anger, confusingly and painfully hurt by it. "Of course you would. I — I was just wondering if there was anything else I should have asked. I don't think there is. Good night, Mrs. Latterly."

"Good night, Mr. Monk." She lifted her head a little higher and he was not quite sure whether he saw her blink to disguise tears. But that was ridiculous — why should she weep now? Disappointment? Frustration? Disillusion in him, because she had hoped and expected better? If only he could remember!

"Parkin, will you show Mr. Monk to the door." And without looking at him again, or waiting for the maid, she walked away, leaving him alone.

CHAPTER NINE

Monk was obliged to go back to the Grey case, although both Imogen Latterly, with her haunting eyes, and Hester, with her anger and intelligence, intruded into his thoughts. Concentration was almost beyond him, and he had to drive himself even to think of its details and try to make patterns from the amorphous mass of facts and suppositions they had so far.

He sat in his office with Evan, reviewing the growing amount of it, but it was all inconclusive of any fact, negative and not positive. No one had broken in, therefore Grey had admitted his murderer himself; and if he had admitted him, then he had been unaware of any reason to fear him. It was not likely he would invite in a stranger at that time in the evening, so it was more probably someone he knew, and who hated him with an intense but secret violence.

Or did Grey know of the hatred, but feel himself safe from it? Did he believe that person powerless to injure, either for an emotional reason, or a physical? Even that answer was still beyond him.

The description both Yeats and Grimwade had given of the only visitor unaccounted for did not fit Lovel Grey, but it was so indistinct that it hardly mattered. If Rosamond Grey's child was Joscelin's, and not Lovel's, that could be reason enough for murder; especially if Joscelin himself knew it and perhaps had not been averse to keeping Lovel reminded. It would not be the first time a cruel tongue, the mockery at pain or impotence had ended in an uncontrolled rage.

Evan broke into his thoughts, almost as if he had read them.

"Do you suppose Shelburne killed Joscelin himself?" He was frowning, his face anxious, his wide eyes clouded. He had no need to fear for his own career — the establishment, even the Shelburnes, would not blame him for a scandal. Was he afraid for Monk? It was a warm thought.

Monk looked up at him.

"Perhaps not. But if he paid someone else, they would have been cleaner and more efficient about it, and less violent. Professionals don't beat a man to death; they usually either stab him or garrote him, and not in his own house."

Evan's delicate mouth turned down at the corners. "You mean an attack in the street, follow him to a quiet spot — and all over in a moment?"

"Probably; and leave the body in an alley where it won't be found too soon, preferably out of his own area. That way there would be less to connect them with the victim, and less of a risk of their being recognized."

"Perhaps he was in a hurry?" Evan suggested. "Couldn't wait for the right time and place?" He leaned back a little in his chair and tilted the legs.

"What hurry?" Monk shrugged. "No hurry if it was Shelburne, not if it were over Rosamond anyway. Couldn't matter a few days, or even a few weeks."

"No." Evan looked gloomy. He allowed the front legs of the chair to settle again. "I don't know how we begin to prove anything, or even where to look."

"Find out where Shelburne was at the time Grey was killed," Monk answered. "I should have done that before."

"Oh, I asked the servants, in a roundabout way." Evan's face was surprised, and there was a touch of satisfaction in it he could not conceal.

"And?" Monk asked quickly. He would not spoil Evan's pleasure.

"He was away from Shelburne; they were told he came to town for dinner. I followed it up. He was at the dinner all right, and spent the night at his club, off Tavistock Place. It would have been difficult for him to have been in Mecklenburg Square at the right time, because he might easily have been missed, but not at all impossible. If he'd gone along Compton Street, right down Hunter Street, 'round Brunswick Square and Lansdowne Place, past the Foundling Hospital, up Caroline Place — and he was there. Ten minutes at the outside, probably less. He'd have been gone at least three quarters of an hour, counting the fight with Grey — and returning. But he could have done it on foot — easily."

Monk smiled; Evan deserved praise and he was glad to give it.

"Thank you. I ought to have done that myself. It might even have been less time, if the quarrel was an old one — say ten minutes each way, and five minutes for the fight. That's not long for a man to be out of sight at a club."

Evan looked down, a faint color in his face. He was smiling.

"It doesn't get us any further," he pointed out ruefully. "It could have been Shelburne, or it could have been anyone else. I suppose we shall have to investigate every other family he could have blackmailed? That should make us rather less popular than the ratman. Do you think it was Shelburne, sir, and we'll just never prove it?"

Monk stood up.

"I don't know but I'm damned if it'll be for lack of trying." He was thinking of Joscelin Grey in the Crimea, seeing the horror of slow death by starvation, cold and disease, the blinding incompetence of commanders sending men to be blown to bits by enemy guns, the sheer stultifying of it all; feeling fear and physical pain, exhaustion, certainly pity, shown by his brief ministrations to the dying in Scutari — all while Lovel stayed at home in his great hall, marrying Rosamond, adding money to money, comfort to comfort.

Monk strode to the door. Injustice ached in him like a gathering boil, angry and festering. He pulled the handle sharply and jerked it open.

"Sir!" Evan half rose to his feet.

Monk turned.

Evan did not know the words, how to phrase the warning urgent inside him. Monk could see it in his face, the wide hazel eyes, the sensitive mouth.

"Don't look so alarmed," he said quietly, pushing the door to again. "I'm going back to Grey's flat. I remember a photograph of his family there. Shelburne was in it, and Menard Grey. I want to see if Grimwade or Yeats recognize either of them. Do you want to come?"

Evan's face ironed out almost comically with relief. He smiled in spite of himself.

"Yes sir. Yes I would." He reached for his coat and scarf. "Can you do that without letting them know who they are? If they know they were his brothers — I mean — Lord Shelburne —"

Monk looked at him sideways and Evan pulled a small face of apology.

"Yes of course," he muttered, following Monk outside. "Although the Shelburnes will deny it, of course, and they'll still ride us to hell and back if we press a charge!"

Monk knew that, and he had no plan even if anyone in the photograph were recognized, but it was a step forward, and he had to take it.

Grimwade was in his cubbyhole as usual and he greeted them cheerfully.

"Lovely mild day, sir." He squinted towards the street. "Looks as if it could clear up."

"Yes," Monk agreed without thinking. "Very pleasant." He was unaware of being wet. "We're going up to Mr. Grey's rooms again, want to pick up one or two things."

"Well with all of you on the case, I 'spec' you'll get somewhere one of these days." Grimwade nodded, a faint trace of sarcasm in his rather lugubrious face. "You certainly are a busy lot, I'll give yer that."

Monk was halfway up the stairs with the key before the significance of Grimwade's remark came to him. He stopped sharply and Evan trod on his heel.

"Sorry," Evan apologized.

"What did he mean?" Monk turned, frowning. "All of us? There's only you and me — isn't there?"

Evan's eyes shadowed. "So far as I know! Do you think Runcorn has been here?"

Monk stood stiffly to the spot. "Why should he? He doesn't want to be the one to solve this, especially if it is Shelburne. He doesn't want to have anything to do with it."

"Curiosity?" There were other thoughts mirrored in Evan's face, but he did not speak them.

Monk thought the same thing — perhaps Runcorn wanted some proof it was Shelburne, then he would force Monk to find it, and then to make the charge. For a moment they stared at each other, the knowledge silent and complete between them.

"I'll go and find out." Evan turned around and went slowly down again.

It was several minutes before he came back, and Monk stood on the stair waiting, his mind at first searching for a way out, a way to avoid accusing Shelburne himself. Then he was drawn to wonder more about Runcorn. How old was the enmity between them? Was it simply an older man fearing a rival on the ladder of success, a younger, cleverer rival?

Only younger and cleverer? Or also harder, more ruthless in his ambitions, one who took credit for other people's work, who cared more for acclaim than for justice, who sought the public, colorful cases, the ones well reported; even a man who managed to shelve his failures onto other people, a thief of other men's work?

If that were so, then Runcorn's hatred was well earned, and his revenge had a justice to it.

Monk stared up at the old, carefully plastered ceiling. Above it was the room where Grey had been beaten to death. He did not feel ruthless now — only confused, oppressed by the void where memory should be, afraid of what he might find out about his own nature, anxious that he would fail in his job. Surely the crack on the head, however hard, could not have changed him so much? But even if the injury could not, maybe the fear had? He had woken up lost and alone, knowing nothing, having to find himself clue by clue, in what others could tell him, what they thought of him, but never why. He knew nothing of the motives for his acts, the nice rationalizations and excuses he had made to himself at the time. All the emotions that had driven him and blocked out judgment were in that empty region that yawned before the hospital bed and Runcorn's face.

But he had no time to pursue it further. Evan was back, his features screwed up in anxiety.

"It was Runcorn!" Monk leaped to the conclusion, suddenly frightened, like a man faced with physical violence.

Evan shook his head.

"No. It was two men I don't recognize at all from Grimwade's description. But he said they were from the police, and he saw their papers before he let them in."

"Papers?" Monk repeated. There was no point in asking what the men had looked like; he could not remember the men of his own division, let alone those from any other.

"Yes." Evan was obviously still anxious. "He said they had police identification papers, like ours."

"Did he see if they were from our station?"

"Yes sir, they were." His face puckered. "But I can't think who they could be. Anyway,

353

why on earth would Runcorn send anyone else? What for?"

"I suppose it would be too much to ask that they gave names?"

"I'm afraid Grimwade didn't notice."

Monk turned around and went back up the stairs, more worried than he wished Evan to see. On the landing he put the key Grimwade had given him into the lock and swung Grey's door open. The small hallway was just as before, and it gave him an unpleasant jar of familiarity, a sense of foreboding for what was beyond.

Evan was immediately behind him. His face was pale and his eyes shadowed, but Monk knew that his oppression stemmed from Runcorn, and the two men who had been here before them, not any sensitivity to the violence still lingering in the air.

There was no purpose in hesitating anymore. He opened the second door.

There was a long sigh from behind him almost at his shoulder as Evan let out his breath in amazement.

The room was in wild disorder; the desk had been tipped over and all its contents flung into the far corner — by the look of them, the papers a sheet at a time. The chairs were on their sides, one upside down, the seats had been taken out, the stuffed sofa ripped open with a knife. All the pictures lay on the floor, backs levered out.

"Oh my God." Evan was stupefied.

"Not the police, I think," Monk said quietly.

"But they had papers," Evan protested. "Grimwade actually read them."

"Have you never heard of a good screever?"

"Forged?" Evan said wearily. "I suppose Grimwade wouldn't have known the difference."

"If the screever were good enough, I daresay we wouldn't either." Monk pulled a sour expression. Some forgeries of testimonials, letters, bills of sale were good enough to deceive even those they were purported to come from. At the upper end, it was a highly skilled and lucrative trade, at the lower no more than a makeshift way of buying a little time, or fooling the hasty or illiterate.

"Who were they?" Evan went past Monk and stared around the wreckage. "And what on earth did they want here?"

Monk's eyes went to the shelves where the ornaments had been.

"There was a silver sugar scuttle up there," he said as he pointed. "See if it's on the floor under any of that paper." He turned slowly. "And there were a couple of pieces of jade on that table. There were two snuffboxes in that alcove; one of them had an inlaid lid. And try the sideboard; there should be silver in the second drawer."

"What an incredible memory you have; I never noticed them." Evan was impressed and his admiration was obvious in his luminous eyes before he knelt down and began carefully to look under the mess, not moving it except to raise it sufficiently to explore beneath.

Monk was startled himself. He could not remember having looked in such detail at trivialities. Surely he had gone straight to the marks of the struggle, the bloodstains, the disarranged furniture, the bruised paint and the crooked pictures on the walls? He had no recollection now of even noticing the sideboard drawer, and yet his mind's eye could see silver, laid out neatly in green-baize-lined fittings.

Had it been in some other place? Was he confusing this room with another, an elegant sideboard somewhere in his past, belonging to someone else? Perhaps Imogen Latterly?

But he must dismiss Imogen from his mind — however easily, with whatever bitter fragrance, she returned. She was a dream, a creation of his own memories and hungers. He could never have known her well enough to feel anything but a charm, a sense of her distress, her courage in fighting it, the strength of her loyalty.

He forced himself to think of the present; Evan searching in the sideboard, the remark on his memory.

"Training," he replied laconically, although he didn't understand it himself. "You'll develop it. It might not be the second drawer, better look in all of them."

Evan obeyed, and Monk turned back to the pile on the floor and began to pick his way through the mess, looking for something to tell him its purpose, or give any clue as to who could have caused it.

"There's nothing here." Evan closed the drawer, his mouth turned down in a grimace of disgust. "But this is the right place; it's all slotted for them to fit in, and lined with cloth. They went to a lot of trouble for a dozen settings of silver. I suppose they expected to get more. Where did you say the jade was?"

"There." Monk stepped over a pile of papers and cushions to an empty shelf, then wondered with a sense of unease how he knew, when he could have noticed it.

He bent and searched the floor carefully, replacing everything as he found it. Evan was watching him.

"No jade?" he asked.

"No, it's gone." Monk straightened up, his back stiff. "But I find it hard to believe ordinary thieves would go to the trouble, and the expense, of forging police identification papers just for a few pieces of silver and a jade ornament, and I think a couple of snuffboxes." He looked around. "They couldn't take much more without being noticed. Grimwade would certainly have been suspicious if they had taken anything like furniture or pictures."

"Well, I suppose the silver and the jade are worth something?"

"Not much, after the fence has taken his cut." Monk looked at the heap of wreckage on the floor and imagined the frenzy and the noise of such a search. "Hardly worth the risk," he said thoughtfully. "Much easier to have burgled a place in which the police have no interest. No, they wanted something else; the silver and the jade were a bonus. Anyway, what professional thief leaves a chaos like this behind him?"

"You mean it was Shelburne?" Evan's voice was half an octave higher with sheer disbelief.

Monk did not know what he meant.

"I can't think what Shelburne could want," he said, staring around the room again, his mind's eye seeing it as it had been before. "Even if he left something here that belonged to him, there are a dozen reasons he could invent if we'd asked him, with Joscelin dead and not able to argue. He could have left it here, whatever it was, any time, or lent it to Joscelin; or Joscelin could simply have taken it." He stared around the ceiling at the elaborate plaster work of acanthus leaves. "And I can't imagine him employing a couple of men to forge police papers and come here to ransack the place. No, it can't have been Shelburne."

"Then who?"

Monk was frightened because suddenly there was no rationality in it at all. Everything that had seemed to fit ten minutes ago was now senseless, like puzzle parts of two quite different pictures. At the same time he was almost elated — if it were not Shelburne, if it were someone who knew forgers and thieves, then perhaps there was no society scandal or blackmail at all.

"I don't know," he answered Evan with sudden new firmness. "But there's no need to tiptoe in this one to find out. Nobody will lose us our jobs if we ask embarrassing questions of a few screevers, or bribe a nose, or even press a fence a little hard."

Evan's face relaxed into a slow smile and his eyes lit up. Monk guessed that perhaps he had had little taste so far of the color of the underworld, and as yet it still held the glamour of mystery. He would find its tones dark; gray of misery, black of long-used pain and habitual fear; its humor quick and bitter, gallows laughter.

He looked at Evan's keen face, its soft, sensitive lines. He could not explain to him; words are only names for what you already know — and what could Evan know that would prepare him for the hive of human waste that teemed in the shadows of Whitechapel, St. Giles, Bluegate Fields, Seven Dials, or the Devil's Acre? Monk had known hardship himself in childhood; he could remember hunger now — it was coming back to him — and cold, shoes that leaked, clothes that let through the bitter northeast wind, plenty of meals of bread and gravy. He remembered faintly the pain of chilblains, angry itching fire when at last you warmed a little; Beth with chapped lips and white, numb fingers.

But they were not unhappy memories; behind all the small pains there had always been a sense of well-being, a knowledge of eventual safety. They were always clean: clean clothes, however few and however old, clean table, smell of flour and fish, salt wind in the spring and summer when the windows were open.

It was sharper in his mind now; he could recall whole scenes, taste and touch, and always the whine of the wind and the cry of gulls. They had all gone to church on Sundays;

he could not bring back everything that had been said, but he could think of snatches of music, solemn and full of the satisfaction of people who believe what they sing, and know they sing it well.

His mother had taught him all his values: honesty, labor and learning. He knew even without her words that she believed it. It was a good memory, and he was more grateful for its return than for any other. It brought with it identity. He could not clearly picture his mother's face; each time he tried it blurred and melted into Beth's, as he had seen her only a few weeks ago, smiling, confident of herself. Perhaps they were not unalike.

Evan was waiting for him, eyes still bright with anticipation of seeing at last the real skill of detection, delving into the heartland of crime.

"Yes." Monk recalled himself. "We shall be free there to pursue as we wish." And no satisfaction for Runcorn, he thought, but he did not add it aloud.

He went back to the door and Evan followed him. There was no point in tidying anything; better to leave it as it was — even that mess might yield a clue, some time.

He was in the hallway, next to the small table, when he noticed the sticks in the stand. He had seen them before, but he had been too preoccupied with the acts of violence in the room beyond to look closely. Anyway, they already had the stick that had been the weapon. Now he saw that there were still four there. Perhaps since Grey had used a stick to walk with, he had become something of a collector. It would not be unnatural; he had been a man to whom appearance mattered: everything about him said as much. Probably he had a stick for morning, another for evening, a casual one, and a rougher one for the country.

Monk's eye was caught by a dark, straight stick, the color of mahogany and with a fine brass band on it embossed like the links of a chain. It was an extraordinary sensation, hot, almost like a dizziness; it prickled in his skin — he knew with total clarity that he had seen that stick before, and seen it several times.

Evan was beside him, waiting, wondering why he had stopped. Monk tried to clear his head, to broaden the image till it included where and when, till he saw the man who held it. But nothing came, only the vivid tingle of familiarity — and fear.

"Sir?" Evan's voice was doubtful. He could see no reason for the sudden paralysis. They were both standing in the hallway, frozen, and the only reason was in Monk's mind. And try as he might, bending all the force of his will on it, still he could see nothing but the stick, no man, not even a hand holding it.

"Have you thought of something, sir?" Evan's voice intruded into the intensity of his thought.

"No." Monk moved at last. "No." He must think of something sensible to say, to explain himself, a reason for his behavior. He found the words with difficulty. "I was just wondering where to start. You say Grimwade didn't get any names from those papers?"

"No; but then they wouldn't use their own names anyway, would they?"

"No, of course not, but it would have helped to know what name the screever used for them." It was a foolish question to have asked, but he must make sense of it. Evan was listening to his every word, as to a teacher. "There are a vast number of screevers in London." He made his voice go on with authority, as if he knew what he was saying, and it mattered. "And I daresay more than one who has forged police papers in the last few weeks."

"Oh — yes, of course," Evan was instantly satisfied. "No, I did ask, before I knew they were burglars, but he didn't notice. He was more interested in the authorization part."

"Oh well." Monk had control of himself again. He opened the door and went out. "I daresay the name of the station will be enough anyway." Evan came out also and he turned and closed the door behind him, locking it.

But when they reached the street Monk changed his mind. He wanted to see Runcorn's face when he heard of the robbery and realized Monk would not be forced to ferret for scandals as the only way to Grey's murderer. There was suddenly and beautifully a new way open to him, where the worst possibility was simple failure; and there was even a chance now of real success, unqualified.

He sent Evan off on a trivial errand, with instructions to meet him again in an hour, and caught a hansom through sunny, noisy streets back to the station. Runcorn was in, and there was a glow of satisfaction on his face when Monk came into his office.

"Morning, Monk," he said cheerfully. "No further, I see?"

Monk let the pleasure sink a little deeper into him, as one hesitates exquisitely in a hot bath, inching into it to savor each additional moment.

"It is a most surprising case," he answered meaninglessly, his eyes meeting Runcorn's, affecting concern.

Runcorn's face clouded, but Monk could feel the pleasure in him as if it were an odor in the room.

"Unfortunately the public does not give us

credit for amazement," Runcorn replied, stretching out the anticipation. "Just because they are puzzled that does not, in their view, allow us the same privilege. You're not pressing hard enough, Monk." He frowned very slightly and leaned farther back in his chair, the sunlight in a bar through the window falling in on the side of his head. His voice changed to one of unctuous sympathy. "Are you sure you are fully recovered? You don't seem like your old self. You used not to be so —" He smiled as the word pleased him. "So hesitant. Justice was your first aim, indeed your only aim; I've never known you to balk before, even at the most unpleasant inquiries." There was doubt at the very back of his eyes, and dislike. He was balancing between courage and experience, like a man beginning to ride a bicycle. "You believe that very quality was what raised you so far, and so fast." He stopped, waiting; and Monk had a brief vision of spiders resting in the hearts of their webs, knowing flies would come, sooner or later: the time was a matter of delicacy, but they would come.

He decided to play it out a little longer; he wanted to watch Runcorn himself, let him bring his own feelings into the open, and betray his vulnerability.

"This case is different," he answered hesitantly, still putting the anxiety into his manner. He sat down on the chair opposite the desk. "I can't remember any other like it. One cannot make comparison."

"Murder is murder." Runcorn shook his head a trifle pompously. "Justice does not differentiate; and let me be frank, neither does the public — in fact if anything, they care more about this. It has all the elements the public likes, all the journalists need to whip up passions and make people frightened — and indignant."

Monk decided to split hairs.

"Not really," he demurred. "There is no love story, and the public likes romance above all things. There is no woman."

"No love story?" Runcorn's eyebrows went up. "I never suspected you of cowardice, Monk; and never, ever of stupidity!" His face twitched with an impossible blend of satisfaction and affected concern. "Are you sure you are quite well?" He leaned forward over the desk again to reinforce the effect. "You don't get headaches, by any chance, do you? It was a very severe blow you received, you know. In fact, I daresay you don't recall it now, but when I first saw you in the hospital you didn't even recognize me."

Monk refused to acknowledge the appalling thought that had come to the edge of his mind.

"Romance?" he asked blankly, as if he had heard nothing after that.

"Joscelin Grey and his sister-in-law!" Runcorn was watching him closely, pretending to be hazy, his eyes a little veiled, but Monk saw the sharp pinpoints under his heavy lids.

"Do the public know of that?" Monk equally easily pretended innocence. "I have not had time to look at newspapers." He pushed out his lip in doubt. "Do you think it was wise to tell them? Lord Shelburne will hardly be pleased!"

The skin across Runcorn's face tightened.

"No of course I didn't tell them yet!" He barely controlled his voice. "But it can only be a matter of time. You cannot put it off forever." There was a hard gleam in his face, almost an appetite. "You have most assuredly changed, Monk. You used to be such a fighter. It is almost as if you were a different person, a stranger to yourself. Have you forgotten how you used to be?"

For a moment Monk was unable to answer, unable to do anything but absorb the shock. He should have guessed it. He had been over-confident, stupidly blind to the obvious. Of course Runcorn knew he had lost his memory. If he had not known from the beginning, then he had surely guessed it in Monk's careful maneuvering, his unawareness of their relationship. Runcorn was a professional; he spent his life telling truth from lies, divining motives, uncovering the hidden. What an arrogant fool Monk must have been to imagine he had deceived him. His own stupidity made him flush hot at the embarrassment of it.

Runcorn was watching him, seeing the tide of color in his face. He must control it, find a shield; or better, a weapon. He straightened his body a little more and met Runcorn's eyes.

"A stranger to you perhaps, sir, but not to myself. But then we are few of us as plain as we seem to others. I think I am only less rash than you supposed. And it is as well." He savored the moment, although it had not the sweetness he had expected.

He looked at Runcorn's face squarely. "I came to tell you that Joscelin Grey's flat has been robbed, at least it has been thoroughly searched, even ransacked, by two men posing as police. They seemed to have had quite competently forged papers which they showed to the porter."

Runcorn's face was stiff and there was a mottle of red on his skin. Monk could not resist adding to it.

"Puts a different light on it, doesn't it?" he went on cheerfully, pretending they were both pleased. "I don't see Lord Shelburne hiring an accomplice and posing as a Peeler to search his brother's flat."

A few seconds had given Runcorn time to think.

"Then he must have hired a couple of men. Simple enough!"

But Monk was ready. "If it was something worth such a terrible risk," he countered, "why didn't they get it before? It must have been there two months by now."

"What terrible risk?" Runcorn's voice dropped a little in mockery of the idea. "They passed it off beautifully. And it would have been easy enough to do: just watch the building a little while to make sure the real police were not there, then go in with their false papers, get what they went for, and leave. I daresay they had a crow out in the street."

"I wasn't referring to the risk of their being caught in the act," Monk said scornfully. "I was thinking of the much greater risk, from his point of view, of placing himself in the hands of possible blackmailers."

He felt a surge of pleasure as Runcorn's face betrayed that he hadn't thought of that.

"Do it anonymously." Runcorn dismissed the idea.

Monk smiled at him. "If it was worth paying thieves, and a first-class screever, in order to get it back, it wouldn't take a very bright thief to work out it would be worth raising the price a little before handing it over. Everyone in London knows there was murder done in that room. If whatever he wanted was worth paying thieves and forgers to get back, it must be damning."

Runcorn glared at the table top, and Monk waited.

"So what are you suggesting then?" Runcorn said at last. "Somebody wanted it. Or do you say it was just a casual thief, trying his luck?" His contempt for the idea was heavy in his voice and it curled his lip.

Monk avoided the question.

"I intend to find out what it is," he replied, pushing back his chair and rising. "It may be something we haven't even thought of."

"You'll have to be a damn good detective to do that!" The triumph came back into Runcorn's eyes.

Monk straightened and looked levelly back at him.

"I am," he said without a flicker. "Did you think that had changed?"

When he left Runcorn's office Monk had had no idea even how to begin. He had forgotten all his contacts; now a fence or an informer could pass him in the street and he would not recognize him. He could not ask any of his colleagues. If Runcorn hated him, it was more than likely many of them did too and he had no idea which; and to show such vulnerability would invite a coup de grace. Runcorn knew he had lost his memory, of that he was perfectly sure now, although nothing had been said completely beyond ambiguity. There was a chance, a good chance he could fend off one man until he regained at least enough mixture of memory and skill to do his job well enough to defy them all. If he solved the Grey case he would be unassailable; then let Runcorn say what he pleased.

But it was unpleasant knowledge that he was so deeply and consistently hated, and with what he increasingly realized was good reason.

And was he fighting for survival? Or was there also an instinct in him to attack Runcorn; not only to find the truth, to be right, but also to be there before Runcorn was and make sure he knew it? Perhaps if he had been an onlooker at this, watching two other men, at least some of his sympathy would have been with Runcorn. There was a cruelty in himself he was seeing for the first time, a pleasure in winning that he did not admire.

Had he always been like this — or was it born of his fear?

How to start finding the thieves? Much as he liked Evan — and he did like him increasingly every day; the man had enthusiasm and gentleness, humor, and a purity of intention Monk envied — even so, he dare not place himself in Evan's hands by telling him the truth. And if he were honest (there was a little vanity in it also), Evan was the only person, apart from Beth, who seemed unaffectedly to think well of him, even to like him. He could not bear to forfeit that.

So he could not ask Evan to tell him the names of informers and fences. He would just have to find them for himself. But if he had been as good a detective as everything indicated, he must know many. They would recognize him.

He was late and Evan had been waiting for him. He apologized, somewhat to Evan's surprise, and only afterward realized that as a superior it was not expected of him. He must be more careful, especially if he were to conceal his purpose, and his inability, from Evan. He wanted to go to an underworld eating house for luncheon, and hoped that if he left word with the potman someone would approach him. He would have to do it in several places, but within three or four days at most he should find a beginning.

He could not bring back to memory any names or faces, but the smell of the back taverns was sharply familiar. Without thinking, he knew how to behave; to alter color like a chameleon, to drop his shoulders, loosen his gait, keep his eyes down and wary. It is not clothes that make the man; a cardsharp, a dragsman, a superior pickpocket or a thief from the Swell Mob could dress as well as most — indeed the nurse at the hospital had taken him for one of the Swell Mob himself.

Evan, with his fair face and wide, humorous eyes, looked too clean to be dishonest. There was none of the wiliness of a survivor in him; yet some of the best survivors of all were those most skilled in deception and the most innocent of face. The underworld was big enough for any variation of lie and fraud, and no weakness was left unexploited.

They began a little to the west of Mecklenburg Square, going to the King's Cross Road. When the first tavern produced nothing immediate, they moved north to the Pentonville Road, then south and east again into Clerkenwell.

In spite of all that logic could tell him, by the following day Monk was beginning to feel as if he were on a fool's errand, and Runcorn would have the last laugh. Then, in a congested public house by the name of the Grinning Rat, a scruffy little man, smiling, showing yellow teeth, slid into the seat beside them, looking warily at Evan. The room was full of noise, the strong smell of ale, sweat, the dirt of clothes and bodies long unwashed, and the heavy steam of food. The floor was covered with sawdust and there was a constant chink of glass.

" 'Ello, Mr. Monk; I hain't seen you for a long time. W'ere yer bin?"

Monk felt a leap of excitement and studied hard to hide it.

"Had an accident," he answered, keeping his voice level.

The man looked him up and down critically and grunted, dismissing it.

"I 'ears as yer after som'un as'll blow a little?"

"That's right," Monk agreed. He must not be too precipitate, or the price would be high, and he could not afford the time to bargain; he must be right first time, or he would appear green. He knew from the air, the smell of it, that haggling was part of the game.

"Worf anyfink?" the man asked.

"Could be."

"Well," the man said, thinking it over. "Yer always bin fair, that's why I comes to yer stead o' some 'o them other jacks. Proper mean, some o' them; yer'd be right ashamed if yer knew." He shook his head and sniffed hard, pulling a face of disgust.

Monk smiled.

"Wotcher want, then?" the man asked.

"Several things." Monk lowered his voice even further, still looking across the table and not at the man. "Some stolen goods — a fence, and a good screever."

The man also looked at the table, studying the stain ring marks of mugs.

"Plenty o' fences, guv; and a fair few screevers. Special goods, these?"

"Not very."

"W'y yer want 'em ven? Som'one done over bad?"

"Yes."

"O'right, so wot are vey ven?"

Monk began to describe them as well as he could; he had only memory to go on.

"Table silver —"

The man looked at him witheringly.

Monk abandoned the silver. "A jade ornament," he continued. "About six inches high, of a dancing lady with her arms up in front of her, bent at the elbows. It was pinky-colored jade —"

"Aw, nar vat's better." The man's voice lifted; Monk avoided looking at his face. "Hain't a lot o' pink jade abaht," he went on. "Anyfink else?"

"A silver scuttle, about four or five inches, I think, and a couple of inlaid snuffboxes."

"Wot kind o' snuffboxes, guv: siller, gold,

enamel? Yer gotta give me mor'n vat!"

"I can't remember."

"Yer wot? Don't ve geezer wot lorst 'em know?" His face darkened with suspicion and for the first time he looked at Monk. " 'Ere! 'E croaked, or suffink?"

"Yes," Monk said levelly, still staring at the wall. "But no reason to suppose the thief did it. He was dead long before the robbery."

"Yer sure o' vat? 'Ow d'yer know 'e were gorn afore?"

"He was dead two months before." Monk smiled acidly. "Even I couldn't mistake that. His empty house was robbed."

The man thought this over for several minutes before delivering his opinion.

Somewhere over near the bar there was a roar of laughter.

"Robbin' a deadlurk?" he said with heavy condescension. "Bit chancy to find anyfink, in' it? Wot did yer say abaht a screever? Wot yer want a screever fer ven?"

"Because the thieves used forged police papers to get in," Monk replied.

The man's face lit up with delight and he chuckled richly.

"A proper downy geezer, vat one. I like it!" He wiped the back of his hand across his mouth and laughed again. "It'd be a sin ter shop a feller wiv vat kind o' class."

Monk took a gold half sovereign out of his pocket and put it on the table. The man's eyes fastened onto it as if it mesmerized him.

"I want the screever who made those fakements for them," Monk repeated. He put out his hand and took the gold coin back again. He put it into his inside pocket. The man's eyes followed it. "And no sly faking," Monk warned. "I'll feel your hands in my pockets, and you remember that, unless you fancy picking oakum for a while. Not do your sensitive fingers any good, picking oakum!" He winced inwardly as a flash of memory returned of men's fingers bleeding from the endless unraveling of rope ends, day in, day out, while years of their lives slid by.

The man flinched. "Now vat ain't nice, Mr. Monk. I never took nuffink from yer in me life." He crossed himself hastily and Monk was not sure whether it was a surety of truth or a penance for the lie. "I s'pose yer tried all ve jollyshops?" the man continued, screwing up his face. "Couldn't christen that jade lady."

Evan looked vaguely confused, although Monk was not sure by what.

"Pawnshops," he translated for him. "Naturally thieves remove any identification from most articles, but nothing much you can do to jade without spoiling its value." He took five shillings out of his pocket and gave them to the man. "Come back in two days, and if you've got anything, you'll have earned the half sovereign."

"Right, guv, but not 'ere; vere's a slap bang called ve Purple Duck dahn on Plumber's Row — orf ve Whitechapel Road. Yer go vere." He looked Monk up and down with distaste. "An' come out o' twig, eh; not all square rigged like a prater! And bring the gold, 'cos I'll 'ave suffink. Yer 'ealf, guv, an' yers." He glanced sideways at Evan, then slid off the seat and disappeared into the crowd. Monk felt elated, suddenly singing inside. Even the fast-cooling plum duff was bearable. He smiled broadly across at Evan.

"Come in disguise," he explained. "Not soberly dressed like a fake preacher."

"Oh." Evan relaxed and began to enjoy himself also. "I see." He stared around at the throng of faces, seeing mystery behind the dirt, his imagination painting them with nameless color.

Two days later Monk obediently dressed himself in suitable secondhand clothes; "translators" the informer would have called them. He wished he could remember the man's name, but for all his efforts it remained completely beyond recall, hidden like almost everything else after the age of about seventeen. He had had glimpses of the years up to then, even including his first year or two in London, but although he lay awake, staring into the darkness, letting his mind wander, going over and over all he knew in the hope his brain would jerk into life again and continue forward, nothing more returned.

Now he and Evan were sitting in the saloon in the Purple Duck, Evan's delicate face registering both his distaste and his efforts to conceal it. Looking at him, Monk wondered how often he himself must have been here to be so unoffended by it. It must have become habit, the noise, the smell, the uninhibited closeness, things his subconscious remembered even if his mind did not.

They had to wait nearly an hour before the informer turned up, but he was grinning again, and slid into the seat beside Monk without a word.

Monk was not going to jeopardize the price by seeming too eager.

"Drink?" he offered.

"Nah, just ve guinea," the man replied. "Don' want ter draw attention to meself drinkin' wiv ve likes o' you, if yer'll pardon me. But potmen 'as sharp mem'ries an' loose tongues."

"Quite," Monk agreed. "But you'll earn the

guinea before you get it."

"Aw, nah Mr. Monk." He pulled a face of deep offense. " 'Ave I ever shorted yer? Now 'ave I?"

Monk had no idea.

"Did you find my screever?" he asked instead.

"I carsn't find yer jade, nor fer sure, like."

"Did you find the screever?"

"You know Tommy, the shofulman?"

For a moment Monk felt a touch of panic. Evan was watching him, fascinated by the bargaining. Ought he to know Tommy? He knew what a shofulman was, someone who passed forged money.

"Tommy?" he blinked.

"Yeah!" the man said impatiently. "Blind Tommy, least 'e pretends 'e's blind. I reckon as 'e 'alf is."

"Where do I find him?" If he could avoid admitting anything, perhaps he could bluff his way through. He must not either show an ignorance of something he would be expected to know or on the other hand collect so little information as to be left helpless.

"You find 'im?" The man smiled condescendingly at the idea. "Yer'll never find 'im on yer own; wouldn't be safe anyhow. 'E's in ve rookeries, an' yer'd get a shiv in yer gizzard sure as 'ell's on fire if yer went in vere on yer tod. I'll take yer."

"Tommy taken up screeving?" Monk concealed his relief by making a general and he hoped meaningless remark.

The little man looked at him with amazement.

" 'Course not! 'E can't even write 'is name, let alone a fakement fer some'un else! But 'e knows a right downy geezer wot does. Reckon 'e's the one as writ yer police papers for yer. 'E's known to do vat kind o' fing."

"Good. Now what about the jade — anything at all?"

The man twisted his rubberlike features into the expression of an affronted rodent.

"Bit 'ard, vat, guv. Know one feller wot got a piece, but 'e swears blind it were a snoozer wot brought it — an' you din't say nuffink abaht no snoozer."

"This was no hotel thief," Monk agreed. "That the only one?"

"Only one as I knows fer sure."

Monk knew the man was lying, although he could not have said how — an accumulation of impressions too subtle to be analyzed.

"I don't believe you, Jake; but you've done well with the screever." He fished in his pocket and brought out the promised gold. "And if it leads to the man I want, there'll be another for you. Now take me

381

to Blind Tommy the shofulman."

They all stood up and wormed their way out through the crowd into the street. It was not until they were two hundred yards away that Monk realized, with a shudder of excitement he could not control, that he had called the man by name. It was coming back, more than merely his memory for his own sake, but his skill was returning. He quickened his step and found himself smiling broadly at Evan.

The rookery was monstrous, a rotting pile of tenements crammed one beside the other, piled precariously, timbers awry as the damp warped them and floors and walls were patched and repatched. It was dark even in the late summer afternoon and the humid air was clammy to the skin. It smelled of human waste and the gutters down the overhung alleys ran with filth. The squeaking and slithering of rats was a constant background. Everywhere there were people, huddled in doorways, lying on stones, sometimes six or eight together, some of them alive, some already dead from hunger or disease. Typhoid and pneumonia were endemic in such places and venereal diseases passed from one to another, as did the flies and lice.

Monk looked at a child in the gutter as he passed, perhaps five or six years old, its face gray in the half-light, pinched sharp; it was impossible to tell whether it was male or female. Monk thought with a dull rage that bestial as it was to beat a man to death as Grey had been beaten, it was still a better murder than this child's abject death.

He noticed Evan's face, white in the gloom, eyes like holes in his head. There was nothing he could think of to say — no words that served any purpose. Instead he put out his hand and touched him briefly, an intimacy that came quite naturally in that awful place.

They followed Jake through another alley and then another, up a flight of stairs that threatened to give way beneath them with each step, and at the top at last Jake stopped, his voice hushed as if the despair had reached even him. He spoke as one does in the presence of death.

"One more lot o' steps, Mr. Monk, from 'ere, an' Blind Tommy's be'ind ver door on yer right."

"Thank you. I'll give you your guinea when I've seen him, if he can help."

Jake's face split in a grin.

"I already got it, Mr. Monk." He held up a bright coin. "Fink I fergot 'ow ter do it, did yer? I used ter be a fine wirer, I did, w'en I were younger." He laughed and slipped it into his pocket. "I were taught by the best kidsman in ve business. I'll be seein' yer, Mr.

Monk; yer owes me anuvver, if yer gets vem fieves."

Monk smiled in spite of himself. The man was a pickpocket, but he had been taught by one of those who make their own living by teaching children to steal for them, and taking the profits in return for the child's keep. It was an apprenticeship in survival. Perhaps his only alternative had been starvation, like the child they had passed. Only the quick-fingered, the strong and the lucky reached adulthood. Monk could not afford to indulge in judgment, and he was too torn with pity and anger to try.

"It's yours, Jake, if I get them," he promised, then started up the last flight and Evan followed. At the top he opened the door without knocking.

Blind Tommy must have been expecting him. He was a dapper little man, about five feet tall with a sharp, ugly face, and dressed in a manner he himself would have described as "flash." He was apparently no more than shortsighted because he saw Monk immediately and knew who he was.

" 'Evenin', Mr. Monk. I 'ears as yer lookin' fer a screever, a partic'lar one, like?"

"That's right, Tommy. I want one who made some fakements for two rampsmen who robbed a house in Mecklenburg Square. Went in pretending to be Peelers."

Tommy's face lit up with amusement.

"I like that," he admitted. "It's a smart lay, vat is."

"Providing you don't get caught."

"Wot's it worf?" Tommy's eyes narrowed.

"It's murder, Tommy. Whoever did it'll be topped, and whoever helps them stands a good chance of getting the boat."

"Oh Gawd!" Tommy's face paled visibly. "I 'an't no fancy for Horstralia. Boats don't suit me at all, vey don't. Men wasn't meant ter go orf all over like vat! In't nat'ral. An' 'orrible stories I've 'eard about vem parts." He shivered dramatically. "Full o' savages an' creatures wot weren't never made by no Christian Gawd. Fings wif dozens 'o legs, an' fings wi' no legs at all. Ugh!" He rolled his eyes. "Right 'eathen place, it is."

"Then don't run any risk of being sent there," Monk advised without any sympathy. "Find me this screever."

"Are yer sure it's murder?" Tommy was still not entirely convinced. Monk wondered how much it was a matter of loyalties, and how much simply a weighing of one advantage against another.

"Of course I'm sure!" he said with a low, level voice. He knew the threat was implicit in it. "Murder and robbery. Silver and jade stolen. Know anything about a jade dancing lady, pink jade, about six inches high?"

Tommy was defensive, a thin, nasal quality of fear in his tone.

"Fencin's not my life, guv. Don't do none o' vat — don't yer try an' hike vat on me."

"The screever?" Monk said flatly.

"Yeah, well I'll take yer. Anyfink in it fer me?" Hope seldom died. If the fearful reality of the rookery did not kill it, Monk certainly could not.

"If it's the right man," he grunted.

Tommy took them through another labyrinth of alleys and stairways, but Monk wondered how much distance they had actually covered. He had a strong feeling it was more to lose their sense of direction than to travel above a few hundred yards. Eventually they stopped at another large door, and after a sharp knock, Blind Tommy disappeared and the door swung open in front of them.

The room inside was bright and smelled of burning. Monk stepped in, then looked up involuntarily and saw glass skylights. He saw down the walls where there were large windows as well. Of course — light for a forger's careful pen.

The man inside turned to look at the intruders. He was squat, with powerful shoulders and large spatulate hands. His face was pale-skinned but ingrained with the dirt of years, and his colorless hair stuck to his head in thin spikes.

"Well?" he demanded irritably. When he spoke Monk saw his teeth were short and black; Monk fancied he could smell the stale odor of them, even from where he stood.

"You wrote police identification papers for two men, purporting to come from the Lye Street station." He made a statement, not a question. "I don't want you for it; I want the men. It's a case of murder, so you'd do well to stay on the right side of it."

The man leered, his thin lips stretching wide in some private amusement. "You Monk?"

"And if I am?" He was surprised the man had heard of him. Was his reputation so wide? Apparently it was.

"Your case they walked inter, was it?" The man's mirth bubbled over in a silent chuckle, shaking his mass of flesh.

"It's my case now," Monk replied. He did not want to tell the man the robbery and the murder were separate; the threat of hanging was too useful.

"Wotcher want?" the man asked. His voice was hoarse, as if from too much shouting or laughter, yet it was hard imagining him doing either.

"Who are they?" Monk pressed.

"Now Mr. Monk, 'ow should I know?" His massive shoulders were still twitching. "Do I ask people's names?"

"Probably not, but you know who they are. Don't pretend to be stupid; it doesn't suit you."

"I know some people," he conceded in little more than a whisper. " 'Course I do; but not every muck snipe 'oo tries 'is 'and at thievin'."

"Muck snipe?" Monk looked at him with derision. "Since when did you hand out fakements for nothing? You don't do favors for down-and-outs. They paid you, or someone did. If they didn't pay you themselves, tell me who did; that'll do."

The man's narrow eyes widened a fraction. "Oh clever, Mr. Monk, very clever." He clapped his broad, powerful hands together in soundless applause.

"So who paid you?"

"My business is confidential, Mr. Monk. Lose it all if I starts putting the down on people wot comes ter me. It was a moneylender, that's all I'll tell yer."

"Not much call for a screever in Australia." Monk looked at the man's subtle, sensitive fingers. "Hard labor — bad climate."

"Put me on the boat, would yer?" The man's lip curled. "Yer'd 'ave ter catch me first, and yer know as well as I do yer'd never find me." The smile on his face did not alter even a fraction. "An' yer'd be a fool ter look; 'orrible fings 'appen ter a Peeler as gets caught in ver rookeries, if ve word goes aht."

"And horrible things happen to a screever who informs on his clients — if the word goes out," Monk added immediately. "Horrible things — like broken fingers. And what use is a screever without his fingers?"

The man stared at him, suddenly hatred undisguised in his heavy eyes.

"An' w'y should the word go out, Mr. Monk, seein' as 'ow I aven't told yer nuffink?"

In the doorway Evan moved uncomfortably. Monk ignored him.

"Because I shall put it out," he replied, "that you have."

"But you ain't got no one fer yer robbery." The hoarse whisper was level again, the amusement creeping back.

"I'll find someone."

"Takes time, Mr. Monk; and 'ow are yer goin' ter do it if I don't tell yer?"

"You are leaping to conclusions, screever," Monk said ruthlessly. "It doesn't have to be the right ones; anyone will do. By the time the word gets back I have the wrong people, it'll be too late to save your fingers. Broken fingers heal hard, and they ache for years, so I'm told."

The man called him something obscene.

"Quite." Monk looked at him with disgust. "So who paid you?"

The man glared at him, hate hot in his face.

"Who paid you?" Monk leaned forward a little.

"Josiah Wigtight, moneylender," the man spat out. "Find 'im in Gun Lane, White-chapel. Now get out!"

"Moneylender. What sort of people does he lend money to?"

"The sort o' people wot can pay 'im back, o' course, fool!"

"Thank you." Monk smiled and straight-ened up. "Thank you, screever; your business is secure. You have told us nothing."

The screever swore at him again, but Monk was out of the door and hurrying down the rickety stairs, Evan, anxious and doubtful, at his heel, but Monk offered him no explana-tion, and did not meet his questioning look.

It was too late to try the moneylender that day, and all he could think of was to get out of the rookeries in one piece before someone stabbed one of them for his clothes, poor as they were, or merely because they were strangers.

He said good-night briefly and watched Evan hesitate, then reply in his quiet voice and turn away in the darkness, an elegant figure, oddly young in the gaslight.

Back at Mrs. Worley's, he ate a hot meal, grateful for it, at once savoring each mouthful and hating it because he could not dismiss from his mind all those who would count it victory merely to have survived the day and eaten enough to sustain life.

None of it was strange to him, as it obviously had been to Evan. He must have been to such places many times before. He had behaved instinctively, altering his stance, knowing how to melt into the background, not to look like a stranger, least of all a figure of authority. The beggars, the sick, the hopeless moved him to excruciating pity, and a deep, abiding anger — but no surprise.

And his mercilessness with the screever had come without calculation, his natural reaction. He knew the rookeries and their denizens. He might even have survived in them himself.

Only afterwards, when the plate was empty, did he lean back in the chair and think of the case.

A moneylender made sense. Joscelin Grey might well have borrowed money when he lost his small possessions in the affair with Latterly, and his family would not help. Had the moneylender meant to injure him a little, to frighten repayment from him, and warn other tardy borrowers, and when Grey had

391

fought back it had gone too far? It was possible. And Yeats's visitor had been a moneylender's ruffian. Yeats and Grimwade had both said he was a big man, lean and strong, as far as they could tell under his clothes.

What a baptism for Evan. He had said nothing about it afterwards. He had not even asked if Monk would really have arrested people he knew to be innocent and then spread the word the screever had betrayed them.

Monk flinched as he remembered what he had said; but it had simply been what instinct directed. It was a streak of ruthlessness in himself he had been unaware of; and it would have shocked him in anyone else. Was that really what he was like? Surely it was only a threat, and he would never have carried it out? Or would he? He remembered the anger that had welled up inside him at the mention of moneylenders, parasites of the desperate poor who clung to respectability, to a few precious standards. Sometimes a man's honesty was his only real possession, his only source of pride and identity in the anonymous, wretched, teeming multitude.

What had Evan thought of him? He cared; it was a miserable thought that Evan would be disillusioned, finding his methods as ugly as the crime he fought, not understanding he was using words, only words.

Or did Evan know him better than he knew himself? Evan would know his past. Perhaps in the past the words had been a warning, and reality had followed.

And what would Imogen Latterly have felt? It was a preposterous dream. The rookeries were as foreign to her as the planets in the sky. She would be sick, disgusted even to see them, let alone to have passed through them and dealt with their occupants. If she had seen him threaten the screever, standing in the filthy room, she would not permit him to enter her house again.

He sat staring up at the ceiling, full of anger and pain. It was cold comfort to him that tomorrow he would find the usurer who might have killed Joscelin Grey. He hated the world he had to deal with; he wanted to belong to the clean, gracious world where he could speak as an equal with people like the Latterlys; Charles would not patronize him, he could converse with Imogen Latterly as a friend, and quarrel with Hester without the hindrance of social inferiority. That would be a delicate pleasure. He would dearly like to put that opinionated young woman in her place.

But purely because he hated the rookeries so fiercely, he could not ignore them. He had seen them, known their squalor and their desperation, and they would not go away.

Well at least he could turn his anger to some purpose; he would find the violent, greedy man who had paid to have Joscelin Grey beaten to death. Then he could face Grey in peace in his imagination — and Runcorn would be defeated.

CHAPTER TEN

Monk sent Evan to try pawnshops for the pink jade, and then himself went to look for Josiah Wigtight. He had no trouble finding the address. It was half a mile east of Whitechapel off the Mile End Road. The building was narrow and almost lost between a seedy lawyer's office and a sweatshop where in dim light and heavy, breathless air women worked eighteen hours a day sewing shirts for a handful of pence. Some felt driven to walk the street at night also, for the extra dreadfully and easily earned silver coins that meant food and rent. A few were wives or daughters of the poor, the drunken or the inadequate; many were women who had in the past been in domestic service, and had lost their "character" one way or another — for impertinence, dishonesty, loose morals, or because a mistress found them "uppity," or a master had taken advantage of them and been discovered, and in a number of cases they had become with child, and thus not only unemployable but a disgrace and an affront.

Inside, the office was dim behind drawn blinds and smelled of polish, dust and ancient leather. A black-dressed clerk sat at a high stool in the first room. He looked up as Monk came in.

"Good morning, sir; may we be of assistance to you?" His voice was soft, like mud. "Perhaps you have a little problem?" He rubbed his hands together as though the cold bothered him, although it was summer. "A temporary problem, of course?" He smiled at his own hypocrisy.

"I hope so." Monk smiled back.

The man was skilled at his job. He regarded Monk with caution. His expression had not the nervousness he was accustomed to; if anything it was a little wolfish. Monk realized he had been clumsy. Surely in the past he must have been more skilled, more attuned to the nuances of judgment?

"That rather depends on you," he added to encourage the man, and allay any suspicion he might unwittingly have aroused.

"Indeed," the clerk agreed. "That's what we're in business for: to help gentlemen with a temporary embarrassment of funds. Of course there are conditions, you understand?" He fished out a clean sheet of paper and held his pen ready. "If I could just have the details, sir?"

"My problem is not a shortage of funds," Monk replied with the faintest smile. He hated moneylenders; he hated the relish with which they plied their revolting trade. "At least not pressing enough to come to you. I have a matter of business to discuss with Mr. Wigtight."

"Quite." The man nodded with a smirk of understanding. "Quite so. All matters of business are referred to Mr. Wigtight, ultimately, Mr. — er?" He raised his eyebrows.

"I do not want to borrow any money," Monk said rather more tartly. "Tell Mr. Wigtight it is about something he had mislaid, and very badly wishes to have returned to him."

"Mislaid?" The man screwed up his pallid face. "Mislaid? What are you talking about, sir? Mr. Wigtight does not mislay things." He sniffed in offended disapproval.

Monk leaned forward and put both hands on the counter, and the man was obliged to face him.

"Are you going to show me to Mr. Wigtight?" Monk said very clearly. "Or do I take my information elsewhere?" He did not want to tell the man who he was, or Wigtight would be forewarned, and he needed the slight advantage of surprise.

"Ah —" The man made up his mind rapidly. "Ah — yes; yes sir. I'll take you to Mr. Wigtight, sir. If you'll come this way." He closed his ledger with a snap and slid it into a drawer. With one eye still on Monk he took a key from his waistcoat pocket and locked the drawer, then straightened up. "Yes sir, this way."

The inner office of Josiah Wigtight was quite a different affair from the drab attempt at anonymous respectability of the entrance. It was frankly lush, everything chosen for comfort, almost hedonism. The big armchairs were covered in velvet and the cushions were deep in both color and texture; the carpet muffled sound and the gas lamps hissing softly on the walls were mantled in rose-colored glass which shed a glow over the room, obscuring outlines and dulling glare. The curtains were heavy and drawn in folds to keep out the intrusion and the reality of daylight. It was not a matter of taste, not even of vulgarity, but purely the uses of pleasure. After a moment or two the effect was curiously soporific. Immediately Monk's respect for Wigtight rose. It was clever.

"Ah." Wigtight breathed out deeply. He was a portly man, swelling out like a giant toad behind his desk, wide mouth split into a smile that died long before it reached his bulbous eyes. "Ah," he repeated. "A matter of business somewhat delicate, Mr. — er?"

"Somewhat," Monk agreed. He decided not to sit down in the soft, dark chair; he was almost afraid it would swallow him, like a mire, smother his judgment. He felt he would be at a disadvantage in it and not able to move if he should need to.

"Sit down, sit down!" Wigtight waved. "Let us talk about it. I'm sure some accommodation can be arrived at."

"I hope so." Monk perched on the arm of the chair. It was uncomfortable, but in this room he preferred to be uncomfortable.

"You are temporarily embarrassed?" Wigtight began. "You wish to take advantage of an excellent investment? You have expectations of a relative, in poor health, who favors you —"

"Thank you, I have employment which is quite sufficient for my needs."

"You are a fortunate man." There was no belief in his smooth, expressionless voice; he had heard every lie and excuse human ingenuity could come up with.

"More fortunate than Joscelin Grey!" Monk said baldly.

Wigtight's face changed in only the minutest of ways — a shadow, no more. Had Monk

399

not been watching for it he would have missed it altogether.

"Joscelin Grey?" Wigtight repeated. Monk could see in his face the indecision whether to deny knowing him or admit it as a matter of common knowledge. He decided the wrong way.

"I know no such person, sir."

"You've never heard of him?" Monk tried not to press too hard. He hated moneylenders with far more anger than reason could tell him of. He meant to trap this soft, fat man in his own words, trap him and watch the bloated body struggle.

But Wigtight sensed a pitfall.

"I hear so many names," he added cautiously.

"Then you had better look in your books," Monk suggested. "And see if his is there, since you don't remember."

"I don't keep books, after debts are paid." Wigtight's wide, pale eyes assumed a blandness. "Matter of discretion, you know. People don't like to be reminded of their hard times."

"How civil of you," Monk said sarcastically. "How about looking through the lists of those who didn't repay you?"

"Mr. Grey is not among them."

"So he paid you." Monk allowed only a little of his triumph to creep through.

"I have not said I lent him anything."

"Then if you lent him nothing, why did you hire two men to deceive their way into his flat and ransack it? And incidentally, to steal his silver and small ornaments?" He saw with delight that Wigtight flinched. "Clumsy, that, Mr. Wigtight. You're hiring a very poor class of ruffian these days. A good man would never have helped himself on the side like that. Dangerous; brings another charge into it — and those goods are so easy to trace."

"You're police!" Wigtight's understanding was sudden and venomous.

"That's right."

"I don't hire thieves." Now Wigtight was hedging, trying to gain time to think, and Monk knew it.

"You hire collectors, who turned out to be thieves as well," Monk said immediately. "The law doesn't see any difference."

"I hire people to do my collecting, of course," Wigtight agreed. "Can't go out into the streets after everybody myself."

"How many do you call on with forged police papers, two months after you've murdered them?"

Every vestige of color drained out of Wigtight's face, leaving it gray, like a cold fish skin. Monk thought for a moment he was

401

having some kind of a fit, and he felt no concern at all.

It was long seconds before Wigtight could speak, and Monk merely waited.

"Murdered!" The word when it came was hollow. "I swear on my mother's grave, I never had anything to do with that. Why should I? Why should I do that? It's insane. You're crazed."

"Because you're a usurer," Monk said bitterly, a well of anger and scalding contempt opening up inside him. "And usurers don't allow people not to pay their debts, with all the interest when they're due." He leaned forward toward the man, threatening by his movement when Wigtight was motionless in the chair. "Bad for business if you let them get away with it," he said almost between his teeth. "Encourages other people to do the same. Where would you be if everyone refused to pay you back? Bleed themselves white to satisfy your interest. Better one goose dead than the whole wretched flock running around free and fat, eh?"

"I never killed him!" Wigtight was frightened, not only by the facts, but by Monk's hatred. He knew unreason when he saw it; and Monk enjoyed his fear.

"But you sent someone — it comes to the same thing," Monk pursued.

"No! It wouldn't make sense!" Wigtight's voice was growing higher, a new, sharp note on it. The panic was sweet to Monk's ear. "All right." Wigtight raised his hands, soft and fat. "I sent them to see if Grey had kept any record of borrowing from me. I knew he'd been murdered and I thought he might have kept the canceled IOU. I didn't want to have anything to do with him. That's all, I swear!" There was sweat on his face now, glistening in the gaslight. "He paid me back. Mother of God, it was only fifty pounds anyway! Do you think I'd send out men to murder a debtor for fifty pounds? It would be mad, insane. They'd have a hold over me for the rest of my life. They'd bleed me dry — or see me to the gibbet."

Monk stared at him. Painfully the truth of it conquered him. Wigtight was a parasite, but he was not a fool. He would not have hired such clumsy chance help to murder a man for a debt, of whatever size. If he had intended murder he would have been cleverer, more discreet about it. A little violence might well have been fruitful, but not this, and not in Grey's own house.

But he might well have wanted to be sure there was no trace of the association left, purely to avoid inconvenience.

"Why did you leave it so long?" Monk

403

asked, his voice flat again, without the hunting edge. "Why didn't you go and look for the IOU straightaway?"

Wigtight knew he had won. It was there gleaming in his pallid, globular face, like pond slime on a frog.

"At first there were too many real police about," he answered. "Always going in and out." He spread his hands in reasonableness. Monk would have liked to call him a liar, but he could not, not yet. "Couldn't get anyone prepared to take the risk," Wigtight went on. "Pay a man too much for a job, and immediately he begins to wonder if there's more to it than you've told him. Might start thinking I had something to be afraid of. Your lot was looking for thieves, in the beginning. Now it's different; you're asking about business, money —"

"How do you know?" Monk believed him, he was forced to, but he wanted every last ounce of discomfort he could drag out.

"Word gets about; you asked his tailor, his wine merchant, looking into the paying of his bills —"

Monk remembered he had sent Evan to do these things. It would seem the usurer had eyes and ears everywhere. He realized now it was to be expected: that was how he found his customers, he learned weaknesses, sought

404

out vulnerability. God, how he loathed this man and his kind.

"Oh." In spite of himself his face betrayed his defeat. "I shall have to be more discreet with my inquiries."

Wigtight smiled coldly.

"I shouldn't trouble yourself. It will make no difference." He knew his success; it was a taste he was used to, like a ripe Stilton cheese and port after dinner.

There was nothing more to say, and Monk could not stomach more of Wigtight's satisfaction. He left, going out past the oily clerk in the front office; but he was determined to take the first opportunity to charge Josiah Wigtight with something, preferably something earning a good long spell on the prison treadmill. Perhaps it was hate of usury and all its cancerous agonies eating away the hearts of people, or hate for Wigtight particularly, for his fat belly and cold eyes; but more probably it was the bitterness of disappointment because he knew it was not the moneylender who had killed Joscelin Grey.

All of which brought him back again to facing the only other avenue of investigation. Joscelin Grey's friends, the people whose secrets he might have known. He was back to Shelburne again — and Runcorn's triumph.

But before he began on that course to one

of its inevitable conclusions — either the arrest of Shelburne, and his own ruin after it; or else the admission that he could not prove his case and must accept failure; and Runcorn could not lose — Monk would follow all the other leads, however faint, beginning with Charles Latterly.

He called in the late afternoon, when he felt it most likely Imogen would be at home, and he could reasonably ask to see Charles.

He was greeted civilly, but no more than that. The parlor maid was too well trained to show surprise. He was kept waiting only a few minutes before being shown into the withdrawing room and its discreet comfort washed over him again.

Charles was standing next to a small table in the window bay.

"Good afternoon, Mr. — er — Monk," he said with distinct chill. "To what do we owe this further attention?"

Monk felt his stomach sink. It was as if the smell of the rookeries still clung to him. Perhaps it was obvious what manner of man he was, where he worked, what he dealt with; and it had been all the time. He had been too busy with his own feelings to be aware of theirs.

"I am still inquiring into the murder of Joscelin Grey," he replied a little stiltedly. He

406

knew both Imogen and Hester were in the room but he refused to look at them. He bowed very slightly, without raising his eyes. He made a similar acknowledgment in their direction.

"Then it's about time you reached some conclusion, isn't it?" Charles raised his eyebrows. "We are very sorry, naturally, since we knew him; but we do not require a day-by-day account of your progress, or lack of it."

"It's as well," Monk answered, stirred to tartness in his hurt, and the consciousness that he did not, and would never, belong in this faded and gracious room with its padded furniture and gleaming walnut. "Because I could not afford it. It is because you knew Major Grey that I wish to speak to you again." He swallowed. "We naturally first considered the possibility of his having been attacked by some chance thief, then of its being over a matter of debt, perhaps gambling, or borrowing. We have exhausted these avenues now, and are driven back to what has always, regrettably, seemed the most probable —"

"I thought I had explained it to you, Mr. Monk." Charles's voice was sharper. "We do not wish to know! And quite frankly, I will not have my wife or my sister distressed by hearing of it. Perhaps the women of your —"

He searched for the least offensive word. "Your background — are less sensitive to such things: unfortunately they may be more used to violence and the sordid aspects of life. But my sister and my wife are gentlewomen, and do not even know of such things. I must ask you to respect their feelings."

Monk could sense the color burning up his face. He ached to be equally rude in return, but his awareness of Imogen, only a few feet from him, was overwhelming. He did not care in the slightest what Hester thought; in fact it would be a positive pleasure to quarrel with her, like the sting in the face of clean, icy water — invigorating.

"I had no intention of distressing anyone unnecessarily, sir." He forced the words out, muffled between his teeth. "And I have not come for your information, but to ask you some further questions. I was merely trying to give you the reason for them, that you might feel freer to answer."

Charles blinked at him. He was half leaning against the mantel shelf, and he stiffened.

"I know nothing whatsoever about the affair, and naturally neither do my family."

"I am sure we should have helped you if we could," Imogen added. For an instant Monk thought she looked abashed by Charles's so open condescension.

Hester stood up and walked across the room opposite Monk.

"We have not been asked any questions yet," she pointed out to Charles reasonably. "How do we know whether we could answer them or not? And I cannot speak for Imogen, of course, but I am not in the least offended by being asked; indeed if you are capable of considering the murder, then so am I. We surely have a duty."

"My dear Hester, you don't know what you are speaking of." Charles's face was sharp and he put his hand out towards her, but she avoided it. "What unpleasant things may be involved, quite beyond your experience!"

"Balderdash!" she said instantly. "My experience has included a multitude of things you wouldn't have in your nightmares. I've seen men hacked to death by sabers, shot by cannon, frozen, starved, wasted by disease —"

"Hester!" Charles exploded. "For the love of heaven!"

"So don't tell me I cannot survive the drawing room discussion of one wretched murder," she finished.

Charles's face was very pink and he ignored Monk. "Has it not crossed your very unfeminine mind that Imogen has feelings, and has led a considerably more decorous life than you have chosen for yourself?" he demanded. "Really, sometimes you are beyond enduring!"

"Imogen is not nearly as helpless as you seem to imagine," Hester retorted, but there was a faint blush to her cheeks. "Nor, I think, does she wish to conceal truth because it may be unpleasant to discuss. You do her courage little credit."

Monk looked at Charles and was perfectly sure that had they been alone he would have disciplined his sister in whatever manner was open to him — which was probably not a great deal. Personally Monk was very glad it was not his problem.

Imogen took the matter into her own hands. She turned towards Monk.

"You were saying that you were driven to an inevitable conclusion, Mr. Monk. Pray tell us what it is." She stared at him and her eyes were angry, almost defensive. She seemed more inwardly alive and sensitive to hurt than anyone else he had ever seen. For seconds he could not think of words to answer her. The moments hung in the air. Her chin came a little higher, but she did not look away.

"I —" he began, and failed. He tried again. "That — that it was someone he knew who killed him." Then his voice came mechanically. "Someone well known to him, of his own position and social circle."

"Nonsense!" Charles interrupted him

sharply, coming into the center of the room as if to confront him physically. "People of Joscelin Grey's circle do not go around murdering people. If that's the best you can do, then you had better give up the case and hand it over to someone more skilled."

"You are being unnecessarily rude, Charles." Imogen's eyes were bright and there was a touch of color in her face. "We have no reason to suppose that Mr. Monk is not skilled at his job, and quite certainly no call to suggest it."

Charles's whole body tightened; the impertinence was intolerable.

"Imogen," he began icily; then remembering the feminine frailty he had asserted, altered his tone. "The matter is naturally upsetting to you; I understand that. Perhaps it would be better if you were to leave us. Retire to your room and rest for a little while. Return when you have composed yourself. Perhaps a tisane?"

"I am not tired, and I do not wish for a tisane. I am perfectly composed, and the police wish to question me." She swung around. "Don't you, Mr. Monk?"

He wished he could remember what he knew of them, but although he strained till his brain ached, he could recall nothing. All his memories were blurred and colored by the

411

overwhelming emotion she aroused in him, the hunger for something always just out of reach, like a great music that haunts the senses but cannot quite be caught, disturbingly and unforgettably sweet, evocative of a whole life on the brink of remembrance.

But he was behaving like a fool. Her gentleness, something in her face had woken in him the memory of a time when he had loved, of the softer side of himself which he had lost when the carriage had crashed and obliterated the past. There was more in him than the detective, brilliant, ambitious, sharp tongued, solitary. There had been those who loved him, as well as the rivals who hated, the subordinates who feared or admired, the villains who knew his skill, the poor who looked for justice — or vengeance. Imogen reminded him that he had a humanity as well, and it was too precious for him to drown in reason. He had lost his balance, and if he were to survive this nightmare — Runcorn, the murder, his career — he must regain it.

"Since you knew Major Grey," he tried again, "it is possible he may have confided in you any anxieties he may have had for his safety — anyone who disliked him or was harassing him for any reason." He was not being as articulate as he wished, and he cursed himself for it.

"Did he mention any envies or rivalries to you?"

"None at all. Why would anyone he knew kill him?" she asked. "He was very charming; I never knew of him picking a quarrel more serious than a few sharp words. Perhaps his humor was a little unkind, but hardly enough to provoke more than a passing irritation."

"My dear Imogen, they wouldn't!" Charles snapped. "It was robbery; it must have been."

Imogen breathed in and out deeply and ignored her husband, still regarding Monk with solemn eyes, waiting for his reply.

"I believe blackmail," Monk replied. "Or perhaps jealousy over a woman."

"Blackmail!" Charles was horrified and his voice was thick with disbelief. "You mean Grey was blackmailing someone? Over what, may I ask?"

"If we knew that, sir, we should almost certainly know who it was," Monk answered. "And it would solve the case."

"Then you know nothing." There was derision back again in Charles's voice.

"On the contrary, we know a great deal. We have a suspect, but before we charge him we must have eliminated all the other possibilities." That was overstating the case dangerously, but Charles's smug face, his patronizing manner roused Monk's temper beyond the point where he had complete control. He wanted to shake him, to force him out of his complacence and his infuriating superiority.

"Then you are making a mistake." Charles looked at him through narrow eyes. "At least it seems most likely you are."

Monk smiled dryly. "I am trying to avoid that, sir, by exploring every alternative first, and by gaining all the information anyone can give. I'm sure you appreciate that!"

From the periphery of his vision Monk could see Hester smile and was distinctly pleased.

Charles grunted.

"We do really wish to help you," Imogen said in the silence. "My husband is only trying to protect us from unpleasantness, which is most delicate of him. But we were exceedingly fond of Joscelin, and we are quite strong enough to tell you anything we can."

" 'Exceedingly fond' is overstating it, my dear," Charles said uncomfortably. "We liked him, and of course we felt an extra affection for him for George's sake."

"George?" Monk frowned, he had not heard George mentioned before.

"My younger brother," Charles supplied.

"He knew Major Grey?" Monk asked keenly. "Then may I speak with him also?"

"I am afraid not. But yes, he knew Grey

414

quite well. I believe they were very close, for a while."

"For a while? Did they have some disagreement?"

"No, George is dead."

"Oh." Monk hesitated, abashed. "I am sorry."

"Thank you." Charles coughed and cleared his throat. "We were fond of Grey, but to say we were extremely so is too much. My wife is, I think, quite naturally transferring some of our affection for George to George's friend."

"I see." Monk was not sure what to say. Had Imogen seen in Joscelin only her dead brother-in-law's friend, or had Joscelin himself charmed her with his wit and talent to please? There had been a keenness in her face when she had spoken of him. It reminded him of Rosamond Shelburne: there was the same gentleness in it, the same echo of remembered times of happiness, shared laughter and grace. Had Charles been too blind to see it — or too conceited to understand it for what it was?

An ugly, dangerous thought came to his mind and refused to be ignored. Was the woman not Rosamond, but Imogen Latterly? He wanted intensely to disprove it. But how? If Charles had been somewhere else at the time, provably so, then the whole question

415

was over, dismissed forever.

He stared at Charles's smooth face. He looked irritable, but totally unconscious of any guilt. Monk tried frantically to think of an oblique way to ask him. His brain was like glue, heavy and congealing. Why in God's name did Charles have to be Imogen's husband?

Was there another way? If only he could remember what he knew of them. Was this fear unreasonable, the result of an imagination free of the sanity of memory? Or was it memory slowly returning, in bits and pieces, that woke that very fear?

The stick in Joscelin Grey's hall stand. The image of it was so clear in his head. If only he could enlarge it, see the hand and the arm, the man who held it. That was the knowledge that lay like a sickness in his stomach; he knew the owner of the stick, and he knew with certainty that Lovel Grey was a complete stranger to him. When he had been to Shelburne not one member of the household had greeted him with the slightest flicker of recognition. And why should they pretend? In fact to do so would in itself have been suspicious, since they had no idea he had lost his memory. Lovel Grey could not be the owner of that stick with the brass chain embossed around the top.

But it could be Charles Latterly.

"Have you ever been to Major Grey's flat, Mr. Latterly?" The question was out before he realized it. It was like a die cast, and he did not now want to know the answer. Once begun, he would have to pursue it; even if only for himself he would have to know, always hoping he was wrong, seeking the one more fact to prove himself so.

Charles looked slightly surprised.

"No. Why? Surely you have been there yourself? I cannot tell you anything about it!"

"You have never been there?"

"No, I have told you so. I had no occasion."

"Nor, I take it, have any of your family?" He did not look at either of the women. He knew the question would be regarded as indelicate, if not outrightly impertinent.

"Of course not!" Charles controlled his temper with some difficulty. He seemed about to add something when Imogen interrupted.

"Would you care for us to account for our whereabouts on the day Joscelin was killed, Mr. Monk?"

He looked carefully, but he could see no sarcasm in her. She regarded him with deep, steady eyes.

"Don't be ridiculous!" Charles snapped with mounting fury. "If you cannot treat this matter with proper seriousness, Imogen, then you had better leave us and return to your room."

"I am perfectly serious," she replied, turning away from Monk. "If it was one of Joscelin's friends who killed him, then there is no reason why we should not be suspected. Surely, Charles, it would be better to clear ourselves by the simple fact of having been elsewhere at the time than it would be to have Mr. Monk satisfy himself we had no reason to, by investigating our affairs?"

Charles paled visibly and looked at Imogen as if she were some venomous creature that had come out of the carpeting and bitten him. Monk felt the tightness in his stomach grip harder.

"I was at dinner with friends," Charles said thinly.

Considering he had just supplied what seemed to be an alibi, he looked peculiarly wretched. Monk could not avoid it; he had to press. He stared at Charles's pale face.

"Where was that, sir?"

"Doughty Street."

Imogen looked at Monk blandly, innocently, but Hester had turned away.

"What number, sir?"

"Can that matter, Mr. Monk?" Imogen asked innocently.

Hester's head came up, waiting.

Monk found himself explaining to her, guilt surprising him.

"Doughty Street leads into Mecklenburg Square, Mrs. Latterly. It is no more than a two- or three-minute walk from one to the other."

"Oh." Her voice was small and flat. She turned slowly to her husband.

"Twenty-two," he said, teeth clenched. "But I was there all evening, and I had no idea Grey lived anywhere near."

Again Monk spoke before he permitted himself to think, or he would have hesitated.

"I find that hard to believe, sir, since you wrote to him at that address. We found your letter among his effects."

"God damn it — I —" Charles stopped, frozen.

Monk waited. The silence was so intense he imagined he could hear horses' hooves in the next street. He did not look at either of the women.

"I mean —" Charles began, and again stopped.

Monk found himself unable to avoid it any longer. He was embarrassed for them, and desperately sorry. He looked at Imogen, wanting her to know that, even if it meant nothing to her at all.

She was standing very still. Her eyes were

so dark he could see nothing in them, but there did not seem to be the hate he feared. For a wild moment he felt that if only he could have talked to her alone he could have explained, made her understand the necessity for all this, the compulsion.

"My friends will swear I was there all evening." Charles's words cut across them. "I'll give you their names. This is ridiculous; I liked Joscelin, and our misfortunes were as much his. There was no reason whatever to wish him harm, and you will find none!"

"If I could have their names, Mr. Latterly?"

Charles's head came up sharply.

"You're not going to go 'round asking them to account for me at the time of a murder, for God's sake! I'll only give you their names —"

"I shall be discreet, sir."

Charles snorted with derision at the idea of so delicate a virtue as discretion in a policeman.

Monk looked at him patiently.

"It will be easier if you give me their names, sir, than if I have to discover them for myself."

"Damn you!" Charles's face was suffused with blood.

"Their names, please sir?"

Charles strode over to one of the small tables and took out a sheet of paper and a pencil.

He wrote for several moments before folding it and handing it to Monk.

Monk took it without looking and put it in his pocket.

"Thank you, sir."

"Is that all?"

"No, I'm afraid I would still like to ask you anything further you might know about Major Grey's other friends, anyone with whom he stayed, and could have known well enough to be aware, even accidentally, of some secret damaging to them."

"Such as what, for God's sake?" Charles looked at him with extreme distaste.

Monk did not wish to be drawn into speaking of the sort of things his imagination feared, especially in Imogen's hearing. In spite of the irrevocable position he was now in, every vestige of good opinion she might keep of him mattered, like fragments of a broken treasure.

"I don't know, sir; and without strong evidence it would be unseemly to suggest anything."

"Unseemly," Charles said sarcastically, his voice grating with the intensity of his emotion. "You mean that matters to you? I'm surprised you know what the word means."

Imogen turned away in embarrassment, and Hester's face froze. She opened her mouth as if to speak, then realized she would be wiser to keep silent.

Charles colored faintly in the silence that followed, but he was incapable of apology.

"He spoke of some people named Dawlish," he said irritably. "And I believe he stayed with Gerry Fortescue once or twice."

Monk took down such details as they could remember of the Dawlishes, the Fortescues and others, but it sounded useless, and he was aware of Charles's heavy disbelief, as if he were humoring an uncaged animal it might be dangerous to annoy. He stayed only to justify himself, because he had said to them that it was his reason for having come.

When he left he imagined he could hear the sigh of relief behind him, and his mind conjured up their quick looks at each other, then the understanding in their eyes, needing no words, that an intruder had gone at last, an extreme unpleasantness was over. All the way along the street his thoughts were in the bright room behind him and on Imogen. He considered what she was doing, what she thought of him, if she saw him as a man at all, or only the inhabiter of an office that had become suddenly more than usually offensive to her.

And yet she had looked so directly at him. That seemed a timeless moment, recurring again and again — or was it simply that he dwelt in it? What had she asked of him originally? What had they said to one another?

What a powerful and ridiculous thing the imagination was — had he not known it so foolish, he could have believed there must have been deep memories between them.

When Monk had gone, Hester, Imogen and Charles were left standing in the withdrawing room, the sun streaming in from the French windows into the small garden, bright through the leaves in the silence.

Charles drew in his breath as if to speak, looked first at his wife, then at Hester, and let out a sigh. He said nothing. His face was tight and unhappy as he walked to the door, excused himself perfunctorily, and went out.

A torrent of thoughts crowded Hester's mind. She disliked Monk, and he angered her, yet the longer she watched him the less did she think he was as incompetent as he had first seemed. His questions were erratic, and he appeared to be no nearer finding Joscelin Grey's killer than he had been when he began; and yet she was keenly aware both of an intelligence and a tenacity in him. He cared about it, more than simply for vanity or ambition. For justice sake he wanted to know and to do something about it.

She would have smiled, did it not wound

so deep, but she had also seen in him a startling softness towards Imogen, an admiration and a desire to protect — something which he certainly did not feel for Hester. She had seen that look on several men's faces; Imogen had woken precisely the same emotions in Charles when they first met, and in many men since. Hester never knew if Imogen herself was aware of it or not.

Had she stirred Joscelin Grey as well? Had he fallen in love with her, the gentleness, those luminous eyes, the quality of innocence which touched everything she did?

Charles was still in love with her. He was quiet, admittedly a trifle pompous, and he had been anxious and shorter tempered than customarily since his father's death; but he was honorable, at times generous, and sometimes fun — at least he had been. Lately he had become more sober, as though a heavy weight could never be totally forgotten.

Was it conceivable that Imogen had found the witty, charming, gallant Joscelin Grey more interesting, even if only briefly? If that had been so, then Charles, for all his seeming self-possession, would have cared deeply, and the hurt might have been something he could not control.

Imogen was keeping a secret. Hester knew her well enough, and liked her, to be aware of the small tensions, the silences where before she would have confided, the placing of a certain guard on her tongue when they were together. It was not Charles she was afraid might notice and suspect; he was not perceptive enough, he did not expect to understand any woman — it was Hester. She was still as affectionate, as generous with small trinkets, the loan of a kerchief or a silk shawl, a word of praise, gratitude for a courtesy — but she was careful, she hesitated before she spoke, she told the exact truth and the impetuosity was gone.

What was the secret? Something in her attitude, an extra awareness, made Hester believe it had to do with Joscelin Grey, because Imogen both pursued and was afraid of the policeman Monk.

"You did not mention before that Joscelin Grey had known George," she said aloud.

Imogen looked out of the window. "Did I not? Well, it was probably a desire not to hurt you, dear. I did not wish to remind you of George, as well as Mama and Papa."

Hester could not argue with that. She did not believe it, but it was exactly the sort of thing Imogen would have done.

"Thank you," she replied. "It was most thoughtful of you, especially since you were so fond of Major Grey."

Imogen smiled, her far-off gaze seeing beyond the dappled light through the window, but to what Hester thought it unfair to guess.

"He was fun," Imogen said slowly. "He was so different from anyone else I know. It was a very dreadful way to die — but I suppose it was quick, and much less painful than many you have seen."

Again Hester did not know what to say.

When Monk returned to the police station Runcorn was waiting for him, sitting at his desk looking at a sheaf of papers. He put them down and pulled a face as Monk came in.

"So your thief was a moneylender," he said dryly. "And the newspapers are not interested in moneylenders, I assure you."

"Then they should be!" Monk snapped back. "They're a filthy infestation, one of the more revolting symptoms of poverty —"

"Oh for heaven's sake, either run for Parliament or be a policeman," Runcorn said with exasperation. "But if you value your job, stop trying to do both at once. And policemen are employed to solve cases, not make moral commentary."

Monk glared at him.

"If we got rid of some of the poverty, and its parasites, we might prevent the crime before it came to the stage of needing a solution," he said with heat that surprised himself. A

426

memory of passion was coming back, even if he could not know anything of its cause.

"Joscelin Grey," Runcorn said flatly. He was not going to be diverted.

"I'm working," Monk replied.

"Then your success has been embarrassingly limited!"

"Can you prove it was Shelburne?" Monk demanded. He knew what Runcorn was trying to do, and he would fight him to the very last step. If Runcorn forced him to arrest Shelburne before he was ready, he would see to it that it was publicly Runcorn's doing.

But Runcorn was not to be drawn.

"It's your job," he said acidly. "I'm not on the case."

"Perhaps you should be." Monk raised his eyebrows as if he were really considering it. "Perhaps you should take over?"

Runcorn's eyes narrowed. "Are you saying you cannot manage?" he asked very softly, a lift at the end of his words. "That it is too big for you?"

Monk called his bluff.

"If it is Shelburne, then perhaps it is. Maybe you should make the arrest; a senior officer, and all that."

Runcorn's face fell blank, and Monk tasted a certain sweetness; but it was only for a moment.

"It seems you've lost your nerve, as well as your memory," Runcorn answered with a faint sneer. "Are you giving up?"

Monk took a deep breath.

"I haven't lost anything," he said deliberately. "And I certainly haven't lost my head. I don't intend to go charging in to arrest a man against whom I have a damn good suspicion, but nothing else. If you want to, then take this case from me, officially, and do it yourself. And God help you when Lady Fabia hears about it. You'll be beyond anyone else's help, I promise you."

"Coward! By God you've changed, Monk."

"If I would have arrested a man without proof before, then I needed to change. Are you taking the case from me?"

"I'll give you another week. I don't think I can persuade the public to give you any more than that."

"Give *us*," Monk corrected him. "As far as they know, we are all working for the same end. Now have you anything helpful to say, like an idea how to prove it was Shelburne, without a witness? Or would you have gone ahead and done it yourself, if you had?"

The implication was not lost on Runcorn. Surprisingly, his face flushed hotly in anger, perhaps even guilt.

"It's your case," he said angrily. "I shan't

take it from you till you come and admit you've failed or I'm asked to remove you."

"Good. Then I'll get on with it."

"Do that. Do that, Monk; if you can!"

Outside the sky was leaden and it was raining hard. Monk thought grimly as he walked home that the newspapers were right in their criticism; he knew little more now than he had when Evan had first showed him the material evidence. Shelburne was the only one for whom he knew a motive, and yet that wretched walking stick clung in his mind. It was not the murder weapon, but he knew he had seen it before. It could not be Joscelin Grey's because Imogen had said quite distinctly that Grey had not been back to the Latterlys' house since her father-in-law's death, and of course Monk had never been to the house before then.

Then whose was it?

Not Shelburne's.

Without realizing it his feet had taken him not towards his own rooms but to Mecklenburg Square.

Grimwade was in the hallway.

"Evenin', Mr. Monk. Bad night, sir. I dunno wot summer's comin' ter — an' that's the truth. 'Ailstones an' all! Lay like snow, it did, in July. An' now this. Cruel to be out in, sir." He regarded Monk's soaking clothes with sympathy. "Can I 'elp yer wif summink, sir?"

"The man who came to see Mr. Yeats —"

"The murderer?" Grimwade shivered but there was a certain melodramatic savoring in his thin face.

"It would seem so," Monk conceded. "Describe him again, will you?"

Grimwade screwed up his eyes and ran his tongue around his lips.

"Well that's 'ard, sir. It's a fair while ago now, an' the more I tries to remember 'im, the fainter 'e gets. 'E were tallish, I know vat, but not outsize, as you might say. 'Ard ter say w'en somebody's away from yer a bit. W'en 'e came in 'e seemed a good couple o' hinches less than you are, although 'e seemed bigger w'en 'e left. Can be deceivin', sir."

"Well that's something. What sort of coloring had he: fresh, sallow, pale, swarthy?"

"Kind o' fresh, sir. But then that could 'a' bin the cold. Proper wicked night it were, somethin' cruel for July. Shockin' unseasonal. Rainin' 'ard, an' east wind like a knife."

"And you cannot remember whether he had a beard or not?"

"I think as 'e 'adn't, leastways if 'e 'ad, it were one o' vem very small ones wot can be 'idden by a muffler."

"And dark hair? Or could it have been brown, or even fair?"

"No sir, it couldn't 'a' bin fair, not yeller, like; but it could 'a' bin brahn. But I do remember as 'e 'ad very gray eyes. I noticed that as 'e were goin' out, very piercin' eyes 'e 'ad, like one o' vem fellers wot puts people inter a trance."

"Piercing eyes? You're sure?" Monk said dubiously, skeptical of Grimwade's sense of melodrama in hindsight.

"Yes sir, more I fink of it, more I'm sure. Don't remember 'is face, but I do remember 'is eyes w'en 'e looked at me. Not w'en 'e was comin' in, but w'en 'e was a-goin' out. Funny thing, that. Yer'd fink I'd a noticed vem w'en 'e spoke ter me, but sure as I'm standin' 'ere, I didn't." He looked at Monk ingenuously.

"Thank you, Mr. Grimwade. Now I'll see Mr. Yeats, if he's in. If he isn't then I'll wait for him."

"Oh 'e's in, sir. Bin in a little while. Shall I take you up, or do you remember the way?"

"I remember the way, thank you." Monk smiled grimly and started up the stairs. The place was becoming wretchedly familiar to him. He passed Grey's entrance quickly, still conscious of the horror inside, and knocked sharply at Yeats's door, and a moment later

431

it opened and Yeats's worried little face looked up at him.

"Oh!" he said in some alarm. "I — I was going to speak to you. I — I, er — I suppose I should have done it before." He wrung his hands nervously, twisting them in front of him, red knuckled. "But I heard all about the — er — the burglar — from Mr. Grimwade, you know — and I rather thought you'd, er — found the murderer — so —"

"May I come in, Mr. Yeats?" Monk interrupted. It was natural Grimwade should have mentioned the burglar, if only to warn the other tenants, and because one could hardly expect a garrulous and lonely old man to keep to himself such a thrilling and scandalous event, but Monk was irritated by the reminder of its uselessness.

"I'm — I'm sorry," Yeats stammered as Monk moved past him. "I — I do realize I should have said something to you before."

"About what, Mr. Yeats?" Monk exercised his patience with an effort. The poor little man was obviously much upset.

"Why, about my visitor, of course. I was quite sure you knew, when you came to the door." Yeats's voice rose to a squeak in amazement.

"What about him, Mr. Yeats? Have you recalled something further?" Suddenly hope shot up inside him. Could this be the beginning of proof at last?

"Why sir, I discovered who he was."

"What?" Monk did not dare to believe. The room was singing around him, bubbling with excitement. In an instant this funny little man was going to tell him the name of the murderer of Joscelin Grey. It was incredible, dazzling.

"I discovered who he was," Yeats repeated. "I knew I should have told you as soon as I found out, but I thought —"

The moment of paralysis was broken.

"Who?" Monk demanded; he knew his voice was shaking. "Who was it?"

Yeats was startled. He began to stammer again.

"Who was it?" Monk made a desperate effort to control himself, but his own voice was rising to a shout.

"Why — why, sir, it was a man called Bartholomew Stubbs. He is a dealer in old maps, as he said. Is it — is it important, Mr. Monk?"

Monk was stunned.

"Bartholomew Stubbs?" he repeated foolishly.

"Yes sir. I met him again, through a mutual acquaintance. I thought I would ask him." His hands fluttered. "I was quite shockingly nervous, I assure you; but I felt in view of the fate of poor Major Grey that I must approach him. He was most civil. He left here straight after speaking to me at my doorstep. He was at a temperance meeting in Farringdon Road, near the House of Correction, fifteen minutes later. I ascertained that because my friend was there also." He moved from one foot to the other in his agitation. "He distinctly remembers Mr. Stubbs's arrival, because the first speaker just commenced his address."

Monk stared at him. It was incomprehensible. If Stubbs had left immediately, and it seemed he had, then who was the man Grimwade had seen leaving later?

"Did — did he remain at the temperance meeting all evening?" he asked desperately.

"No sir." Yeats shook his head. "He only went there to meet my friend, who is also a collector, a very learned one —"

"He left!" Monk seized on it.

"Yes sir." Yeats danced around in his anxiety, his hands jerking to and fro. "I am trying to tell you! They left together and went to get some supper —"

"Together?"

"Yes sir. I am afraid, Mr. Monk, Mr. Stubbs could not have been the one to have so dreadfully attacked poor Major Grey."

"No." Monk was too shaken, too overwhelmingly disappointed to move. He did not know where to start again.

"Are you quite well, Mr. Monk?" Yeats asked tentatively. "I am so sorry. Perhaps I really should have told you earlier, but I did not think it would be important, since he was not guilty."

"No — no, never mind," Monk said almost under his breath. "I understand."

"Oh, I'm so glad. I thought perhaps I was in error."

Monk muttered something polite, probably meaningless — he did not want to be unkind to the little man — and made his way out onto the landing again. He was hardly aware of going down the stairs, nor did he register the drenching weight of the rain when he passed Grimwade and went outside into the street with its gaslight and swirling gutters.

He began to walk, blindly, and it was not until he was spattered with mud and a cab wheel missed him by less than a foot that he realized he was on Doughty Street.

" 'Ere!" the cabby shouted at him. "Watch w'ere yer goin', guv! Yer want ter get yerself killed?"

Monk stopped, staring up at him. "You occupied?"

"No guv. Yer want ter go somewhere? Mebbe yer'd better, afore yer get someb'dy into a haccident."

435

"Yes," Monk accepted, still without moving.

"Well come on then," the cabby said sharply, leaning forward to peer at him. "Not a night fer man ner beast ter be out in, it ain't. Mate o' mine were killed on a night like this, poor sod. 'Orse bolted and 'is cab turned over. Killed, 'e were. 'It 'is 'ead on the curb an' 'e died, jes' like that. And 'is fare were all smashed abaht too, but they say as 'e were o'right, in the end. Took 'im orf ter 'orspital, o' course. 'Ere, are yer goin' ter stand there all night, guv? Come on now, either get in, or don't; but make up yer mind!"

"This friend of yours." Monk's voice was distorted, as if from far away. "When was he killed, when was this accident, exactly?"

"July it were, terrible weather fer July. Wicked night. 'Ailstorm wot lay like snow. Swear ter Gawd — I don't know wot the wevver's comin' ter."

"What date in July?" Monk's whole body was cold, and idiotically calm.

"Come on now, sir?" the cabby wheedled, as one does a drunk or a recalcitrant animal. "Get in aht o' the rain. It's shockin' wet aht there. Yer'll catch yer death."

"What date?"

"I fink as it were the fourf. Why? We ain't

goin' ter 'ave no haccident ternight, I promises yer. I'll be as careful as if you was me muvver. Jus' make up yer mind, sir!"

"Did you know him well?"

"Yes sir, 'e were a good mate o' mine. Did yer know 'im too, sir? Yer live 'rahnd 'ere, do yer? 'E used ter work this patch all ve time. Picked up 'is last fare 'ere, right in vis street, accordin' ter 'is paper. Saw 'im vat very night meself, I did. Nah is yer comin', sir, or ain't yer? 'Cos I 'aven't got all night. I reckon w'en yer goes a henjoyin' yerself, yer oughter take someone wiv yer. Yer in't safe."

On this street. The cabby had picked him, Monk, up on this street, less than a hundred yards from Mecklenburg Square, on the night Joscelin Grey was murdered. What had he been doing here? Why?

"Yer sick, sir?" The cabby's voice changed; he was suddenly concerned. " 'Ere, yer ain't 'ad one too many?" He climbed down off his box and opened the cab door.

"No, no I'm quite well." Monk stepped up and inside obediently and the cabby muttered something to himself about gentlemen whose families should take better care of them, stepped back up onto the box and slapped the reins over his horse's back.

As soon as they arrived at Grafton Street

Monk paid the cabby and hurried inside.

"Mrs. Worley!"

Silence.

"Mrs. Worley!" His voice was hard, hoarse.

She came out, rubbing her hands dry on her apron.

"Oh my heavens, you are wet. You'd like an 'ot drink. You'll 'ave to change them clothes; you've let yourself get soaked through! What 'ave you bin thinking of?"

"Mrs. Worley."

The tone of his voice stopped her.

"Why, whatever is the matter, Mr. Monk? You look proper poorly."

"I —" The words were slow, distant. "I can't find a stick in my room, Mrs. Worley. Have you seen it?"

"No, Mr. Monk, I 'aven't, although what you're thinking about sticks for on a night like this, I'm sure I don't know. What you need is an umbrella."

"Have you seen it?"

She stood there in front of him, square and motherly. "Not since you 'ad yer haccident, I 'aven't. You mean that dark reddish brown one with the gold chain like 'round the top as yer bought the day afore? Proper 'andsome it were, although wot yer want one like that fer, I'll never know. I do 'ope as you 'aven't gorn and lorst it. If yer did, it must 'a' bin

438

in yer haccident. You 'ad it with yer, 'cos I remember plain as day. Proud of it. Proper dandy, yer was."

There was a roaring in Monk's ears, shapeless and immense. Through the darkness one thought was like a brilliant stab of light, searingly painful. He had been in Grey's flat the night he was killed; he had left his own stick there in the hall stand. He himself was the man with the gray eyes whom Grimwade had seen leaving at half past ten. He must have gone in when Grimwade was showing Bartholomew Stubbs up to Yeats's door.

There was only one conclusion — hideous and senseless — but the only one left. God knew why, but he himself had killed Joscelin Grey.

CHAPTER
ELEVEN

Monk sat in the armchair in his room staring at the ceiling. The rain had stopped and the air was warm and clammy, but he was still chilled to the bone.

Why?

Why? It was as inconceivably senseless as a nightmare, and as entanglingly, recurringly inescapable.

He had been in Grey's flat that night, and something had happened after which he had gone in such haste he had left his stick in the stand behind him. The cabby had picked him up from Doughty Street, and then barely a few miles away, met with an accident which had robbed him of his life, and Monk of all memory.

But why should he have killed Grey? In what connection did he even know him? He had not met him at the Latterlys'; Imogen had said so quite clearly. He could imagine no way in which he could have met him socially. If he were involved in any case, then Runcorn would have known; and his own case notes would have shown it.

So why? Why kill him? One did not follow a complete stranger to his house and then beat him to death for no reason. Unless one were insane?

Could that be it — he was mad? His brain had been damaged even before the accident? He had forgotten what he had done because it was another self which had enacted such a hideousness, and the self he was in now knew nothing of it, was unaware even of its lusts and compulsions, its very existence? And there had been feeling — inescapable, consuming, and appalling feeling — a passion of hate. Was it possible?

He must think. Thought was the only possible way of dealing with this, making some sense, finding an escape back into reason and an understandable world again, following and examining it, piece by piece — but he could not believe it. But then perhaps no clever, ambitious man truly believes he is mad? He turned that over in his mind too.

Minutes turned into hours, dragging through the night. At first he paced restlessly, back and forth, back and forth, till his legs ached, then he threw himself into the chair and sat motionless, his hands and feet so cold he lost all sensation in them, and still the nightmare was just as real, and just as senseless. He tormented his memory, scrambling after tiny fragments, retelling himself everything he could remember from the schoolroom onward, but there was nothing of Joscelin Grey, not even his face. There was no reason to it, no pattern, no vestige of anger left, no jealousy, no hatred, no fear — only the evidence. He had been there; he must have gone up when Grimwade had taken Bartholomew Stubbs up to see Yeats and been absent for a moment on his other errand.

He had been in Joscelin Grey's flat for three quarters of an hour, and Grimwade had seen him going out and presumed he was Stubbs leaving, whereas in truth Stubbs must have passed him on the stair, as Stubbs left and he arrived. Grimwade had said that the man leaving had seemed heavier, a little taller, and he had especially noticed his eyes. Monk remembered the eyes he had seen staring back at him from the bedroom mirror when he had first come from the hospital. They were unusual, as Grimwade had said, level, dark, clear gray; clever, almost hypnotic eyes. But he had been trying to find the mind beyond, a flash of the memory — the shade was irrelevant. He had made no connection of thought between his grave policeman's gaze — and the stare of the man that night — any more than had Grimwade.

He had been there, inside Grey's flat; it was incontrovertible. But he had not followed Grey; he had gone afterwards, independently, knowing where to find him. So he had known Grey, known where he lived. But why? Why in God's name did he hate him enough to have lost all reason, ignored all his adult life's training and beliefs and beaten the man to death, and gone on beating him when even a madman must have seen he was dead?

He must have known fear before, of the sea when he was young. He could dimly remember its monumental power when the bowels of the deep opened to engulf men, ships, even the shore itself. He could still feel its scream like an echo of all childhood.

And later he must have known fear on the dark streets of London, fear in the rookeries; even now his skin crawled at the memory of the anger and the despair in them, the hunger and the disregard for life in the fight to survive. But he was too proud and too ambitious to be a coward. He had grasped what he wanted without flinching.

But how do you face the unknown darkness, the monstrosity inside your own brain, your own soul?

He had discovered many things in himself

he did not like: insensitivity, overpowerful ambition, a ruthlessness. But they were bearable, things for which he could make amends, improve from now on — indeed he had started.

But why should he have murdered Joscelin Grey? The more he struggled with it the less did it make any sense. Why should he have cared enough? There was nothing in his life, no personal relationship that called up such passion.

And he could not believe he was simply mad. Anyway, he had not attacked a stranger in the street, he had deliberately sought out Grey, taken trouble to go to his home; and even madmen have some reason, however distorted.

He must find it, for himself — and he must find the reason before Runcorn found it.

Only it would not be Runcorn, it would be Evan.

The cold inside him grew worse. That was one of the most painful realizations of all, the time when Evan must know that it was he who had killed Grey, he was the murderer who had raised such horror in both of them, such revulsion for the mad appetite, the bestiality. They had looked upon the murderer as being another kind of creature, alien, capable of some darkness beyond their comprehension. To Evan it would still be such a creature, less than quite human — whereas to Monk it was not outward and foreign, where he could sometimes forget it, bar it out, but the deformed and obscene within himself.

Tonight he must sleep; the clock on the mantel said thirteen minutes past four. But tomorrow he would begin a new investigation. To save his own mind, he must discover why he had killed Joscelin Grey; and he must discover it before Evan did.

He was not ready to see Evan when he went into his office in the morning, not prepared; but then he would never be.

"Good morning, sir," Evan said cheerfully.

Monk replied, but kept his face turned away, so Evan could not read his expression. He found lying surprisingly hard; and he must lie all the time, every day in every contact from now on.

"I've been thinking, sir." Evan did not appear to notice anything unusual. "We should look into all these other people before we try to charge Lord Shelburne. You know, Joscelin Grey may well have had affairs with other women. We should try the Dawlishes; they had a daughter. And there's Fortescue's wife, and Charles Latterly may have a wife."

Monk froze. He had forgotten that Evan

had seen Charles's letter in Grey's desk. He had been supposing blithely that Evan knew nothing of the Latterlys.

Evan's voice cut across him, low and quite gentle. It sounded as though there were nothing more than concern in it.

"Sir?"

"Yes," Monk agreed quickly. He must keep control, speak sensibly. "Yes I suppose we had better." What a hypocrite he was, sending Evan off to pry the secret hurts out of people in the search for a murderer. What would Evan think, feel, when he discovered that the murderer was Monk?

"Shall I start with Latterly, sir?" Evan was still talking. "We don't know much about him."

"No!"

Evan looked startled.

Monk mastered himself; when he spoke his voice was quite calm again, but still he kept his face away.

"No, I'll try the people here: I want you to go back to Shelburne Hall." He must get Evan out of the city for a while, give himself time. "See if you can learn anything more from the servants," he elaborated. "Become friendly with the upstairs maids, if you can, and the parlor maid. Parlor maids are on in the morning; they observe all sorts of things when people are off their guard. It may be one of the other families, but Shelburne is still the most likely. It can be harder to forgive a brother for cuckolding you than it would be a stranger — it's not just an offense, it's a betrayal — and he's constantly there to remind you of it."

"You think so, sir?" There was a lift of surprise in Evan's voice.

Oh God. Surely Evan could not know, could not suspect anything so soon? Sweat broke out on Monk's body, and chilled instantly, leaving him shivering.

"Isn't that what Mr. Runcorn thinks?" he asked, his voice husky with the effort of seeming casual. What isolation this was. He felt cut off from every human contact by his fearful knowledge.

"Yes sir." He knew Evan was staring at him, puzzled, even anxious. "It is, but he could be wrong. He wants to see you arrest Lord Shelburne —" That was an understanding he had not committed to words before. It was the first time he had acknowledged that he understood Runcorn's envy, or his intention. Monk was startled into looking up, and instantly regretted it. Evan's eyes were anxious and appallingly direct.

"Well he won't — unless I have evidence," Monk said slowly. "So go out to Shelburne

Hall and see what you can find. But tread softly, listen rather than speak. Above all, don't make any implications."

Evan hesitated.

Monk said nothing. He did not want conversation.

After a moment Evan left and Monk sat down on his own chair, closing his eyes to shut out the room. It was going to be even harder than it had seemed last night. Evan had believed in him, liked him. Disillusionment so often turned to pity, and then to hate.

And what about Beth? Perhaps far up in Northumberland she need never know. Maybe he could find someone to write to her and say simply that he had died. They would not do it for him; but if he explained, told them of her children, then for her?

"Asleep, Monk? Or dare I hope you are merely thinking?" It was Runcorn's voice, dark with sarcasm.

Monk opened his eyes. He had no career left, no future. But one of the few reliefs it brought was that he need no longer be afraid of Runcorn. Nothing Runcorn could do would matter in the least, compared with what he had already done to himself.

"Thinking," Monk replied coldly. "I find it better to think before I face a witness than after I have got there. Either one stands foolishly silent, or rushes, even more foolishly, into saying something inept, merely to fill the chasm."

"Social arts again?" Runcorn raised his eyebrows. "I would not have thought you would have had time for them now." He was standing in front of Monk, rocking a little on his feet, hands behind his back. Now he brought them forward with a sheaf of daily newspapers displayed belligerently. "Have you read the newspapers this morning? There has been a murder in Stepney, a man knifed in the street, and they are saying it is time we did our job, or were replaced by someone who can."

"Why do they presume there is only one person in London capable of knifing a man?" Monk asked bitterly.

"Because they are angry and frightened," Runcorn snapped back. "And they have been let down by the men they trusted to safeguard them. That is why." He slammed the newspapers down on the desk top. "They do not care whether you speak like a gentleman or know which knife and fork to eat with, Mr. Monk; but they care very much whether you are capable of doing your job and catching murderers and taking them off the streets."

"Do you think Lord Shelburne knifed this man in Stepney?" Monk looked straight into Runcorn's eyes. He was pleased to be able to hate someone freely and without feeling any guilt about lying to him.

"Of course I don't." Runcorn's voice was thick with anger. "But I think it past time you stopped giving yourself airs and graces and found enough courage to forget climbing the ladder of your own career for a moment and arrested Shelburne."

"Indeed? Well I don't, because I'm not at all sure that he's guilty," Monk answered him with a straight, hard stare. "If you are sure, then you arrest him!"

"I'll have you for insolence!" Runcorn shouted, leaning forward towards him, fists clenched white. "And I'll make damned sure you never reach senior rank as long as I'm in this station. Do you hear me?"

"Of course I hear you." Monk deliberately kept calm. "Although it was unnecessary for you to say so, your actions have long made it obvious; unless of course you wish to inform the rest of the building? Your voice was certainly loud enough. As for me, I knew your intentions long ago. And now . . . ." He stood up and walked past him to the door. "If you have nothing else to say, sir; I have several witnesses to question."

"I'll give you till the end of the week," Runcorn bellowed behind him, his face purple, but Monk was outside and going down the stairs for his hat and coat. The only advantage of disaster was that all lesser ills are swallowed up in it.

By the time he had reached the Latterlys' house and been shown in by the parlor maid, he had made up his mind to do the only thing that might lead him to the truth. Runcorn had given him a week. And Evan would be back long before that. Time was desperately short.

He asked to see Imogen, alone. The maid hesitated, but it was morning and Charles was quite naturally out; and anyway, as a servant she had not the authority to refuse.

He paced backwards and forwards nervously, counting seconds until he heard light, decisive footsteps outside and the door opened. He swung around. It was not Imogen but Hester Latterly who came in.

He felt an immediate rush of disappointment, then something almost resembling relief. The moment was put off; Hester had not been here at the time. Unless Imogen had confided in her she could not help. He would have to return. He needed the truth, and yet it terrified him.

"Good morning, Mr. Monk," she said curiously. "What may we do for you this time?"

"I am afraid you cannot help me," he replied. He did not like her, but it would be

451

pointless and stupid to be rude. "It is Mrs. Latterly I would like to see, since she was here at the time of Major Grey's death. I believe you were still abroad?"

"Yes I was. But I am sorry, Imogen is out all day and I do not expect her return until late this evening." She frowned very slightly and he was uncomfortably aware of her acute perception, the sensitivity with which she was regarding him. Imogen was kinder, immeasurably less abrasive, but there was an intelligence in Hester which might meet his present need more readily.

"I can see that something very serious troubles you," she said gravely. "Please sit down. If it is to do with Imogen, I would greatly appreciate it if you would confide in me, and I may help the matter to be dealt with with as little pain as possible. She has already suffered a great deal, as has my brother. What have you discovered, Mr. Monk?"

He looked at her levelly, searching the wide, very clear eyes. She was a remarkable woman and her courage must be immense to have defied her family and traveled virtually alone to one of the most dreadful battlefields in the world, and to have risked her own life and health to care for the wounded. She must have very few illusions, and that thought was comforting now. There was an infinity of experience between himself and Imogen: horror, violence, hatred and pain outside her grasp to think of, and which from now on would be his shadow, even his skin. Hester must have seen men in the very extremity of life and death, the nakedness of soul that comes when fear strips everything away and the honesty that loosens the tongue when pretense is futile.

Perhaps after all it was right he should speak to her.

"I have a most profound problem, Miss Latterly," he began. It was easier to talk to her than he had expected. "I have not told you, or anyone else, the entire truth about my investigation of Major Grey's death."

She waited without interruption; surprisingly, she did know when to keep silent.

"I have not lied," he went on. "But I have omitted one of the most important facts."

She was very pale. "About Imogen?"

"No! No. I do not know anything about her, beyond what she told me herself — that she knew and liked Joscelin Grey, and that he called here, as a friend of your brother George. What I did not tell you is about myself."

He saw the flash of concern in her face, but he did not know the reason for it. Was it her nurse's professional training, or some fear for Imogen, something she knew and he did not? But again she did not interrupt.

"The accident I suffered before beginning the Joscelin Grey case is a severe complication which I did not mention." Then for a hideous moment he thought she might imagine he was seeking some kind of sympathy, and he felt the blood burn up his skin. "I lost my memory." He rushed to dispel the idea. "Completely. When I came to my senses in the hospital I could not even think of my own name." How far away that minimal nightmare seemed now! "When I was recovered enough to go back to my rooms they were strange to me, like the rooms of a man I had never met. I knew no one, I could not even think how old I was, or what I looked like. When I saw myself in the mirror I did not recognize myself even then."

There was pity in her face, gentle and quite pure, without a shadow of condescension or setting herself apart. It was far sweeter than anything he had expected.

"I'm deeply sorry," she said quietly. "Now I understand why some of your questions seemed so very odd. You must have had to learn everything over again."

"Miss Latterly — I believe your sister-in-law came to me before, asked me something, confided — perhaps to do with Joscelin Grey — but I cannot remember. If she could tell me everything she knows of me, anything I may have said —"

"How could that help you with Joscelin Grey?" Then suddenly she looked down at the hand in her lap. "You mean you think Imogen may have something to do with his death?" Her head came up sharply, her eyes candid and full of fear. "Do you think Charles may have killed him, Mr. Monk?"

"No — no, I am quite sure he did not." He must lie; the truth was impossible, but he needed her help. "I found old notes of mine, made before the accident, which indicate I knew something important then, but I can't remember it. Please, Miss Latterly — ask her to help me."

Her face was a little bleak, as if she too feared the outcome.

"Of course, Mr. Monk. When she returns I will explain the necessity to her, and when I have something to tell you I shall come and do so. Where may I find you that we can talk discreetly?"

He was right: she was afraid. She did not wish her family to overhear — perhaps especially Charles. He stared at her, smiling with a bitter humor, and saw it answered in her eyes. They were in an absurd conspiracy, she to protect her family as far as was possible, he to discover the truth about himself, before

Evan or Runcorn made it impossible. He must know *why* he had killed Joscelin Grey.

"Send me a message, and I shall meet you in Hyde Park, at the Piccadilly end of the Serpentine. No one will remark two people walking together."

"Very well, Mr. Monk. I shall do what I can."

"Thank you." He rose and took his leave, and she watched his straight, very individual figure as he walked down the steps and out into the street. She would have recognized his stride anywhere; there was an ease in it not unlike a soldier's who was used to the self-discipline of long marches, and yet it was not military.

When he was out of sight she sat down, cold, unhappy, but knowing it was unavoidable she should do exactly as he had asked. Better she should learn the truth first than that it should be dragged out longer, and found by others.

She spent a solitary and miserable evening, dining alone in her room. Until she knew the truth from Imogen she could not bear to risk a long time with Charles, such as at a meal table. It was too likely her thoughts would betray her and end in hurting them both. As a child she had imagined herself to be marvelously subtle and capable of all sorts of deviousness. At about twenty she had mentioned it quite seriously at the dinner table. It was the only occasion she could recall of every member of her family laughing at once. George had begun, his face crinkling into uncontrollable delight and his voice ringing out with hilarity. The very idea was funny. She had the most transparent emotions any of them had seen. Her happiness swept the house in a whirlwind; her misery wrapped it in a purple gloom.

It would be futile, and painful, to try to deceive Charles now.

It was the following afternoon before she had the opportunity to speak alone with Imogen for any length of time. Imogen had been out all morning and came in in a swirl of agitation, swinging her skirts around as she swept into the hallway and deposited a basket full of linen on the settle at the bottom of the stairs and took off her hat.

"Really, I don't know what the vicar's wife is thinking of," she said furiously. "Sometimes I swear that woman believes all the world's ills can be cured with an embroidered homily on good behavior, a clean undershirt and a jar of homemade broth. And Miss Wentworth is the last person on earth to help a young mother with too many children and no maidservant."

"Mrs. Addison?" Hester said immediately.

"Poor creature doesn't know whether she is coming or going," Imogen argued. "Seven children, and she's as thin as a slat and exhausted. I don't think she eats enough to keep a bird alive — giving it all to those hungry little mouths forever asking for more. And what use is Miss Wentworth? She has fits of the vapors every few minutes! I spend half my time picking her up off the floor."

"I'd have fits of the vapors myself if my stays were as tight as hers," Hester said wryly. "Her maid must lace them with one foot on the bedpost. Poor soul. And of course her mother's trying to marry her off to Sydney Abernathy — he has plenty of money and a fancy for wraithlike fragility — it makes him feel masterful."

"I shall have to see if I can find a suitable homily for her on vanity." Imogen ignored the basket and led the way through to the withdrawing room and threw herself into one of the large chairs. "I am hot and tired. Do have Martha bring us some lemonade. Can you reach the bell?"

It was an idle question, since Hester was still standing. Absently she pulled the end. "It isn't vanity," she said, still referring to Miss Wentworth. "It's survival. What is the poor creature to do if she doesn't marry? Her mother and sisters have convinced her the only alternative is shame, poverty and a lonely and pitiful old age."

"That reminds me," Imogen said, pushing her boots off. "Have you heard from Lady Callandra's hospital yet? I mean the one you want to administer."

"I don't aim quite so high; I merely want to assist," Hester corrected.

"Rubbish!" Imogen stretched her feet luxuriously and sank a little further into the chair. "You want to order around the entire staff."

The maid came in and stood waiting respectfully.

"Lemonade, please, Martha," Imogen ordered. "I'm so hot I could expire. This climate really is ridiculous. One day it rains enough to float an ark, the next we are all suffocated with heat."

"Yes ma'am. Would you like some cucumber sandwiches as well, ma'am?"

"Oh yes. Yes I would — thank you."

"Yes ma'am." And with a whisk of skirts she was gone.

Hester filled the few minutes while the maid was absent with trivial conversation. She had always found it easy to talk to Imogen and their friendship was more like that of sisters than of two women related only by marriage, whose patterns of life were so different. When Martha had brought the sandwiches and lemonade and they were alone, she turned at last to the matter which was pressing so urgently on her mind.

"Imogen, that policeman, Monk, was here again yesterday —"

Imogen's hand stopped in the air, the sandwich ignored, but there was curiosity in her face and a shadow of amusement. There was nothing that looked like fear. But then Imogen, unlike Hester, could conceal her feelings perfectly if she chose.

"Monk? What did he want this time?"

"Why are you smiling?"

"At you, my dear. He annoys you so much, and yet I think part of you quite likes him. You are not dissimilar in some ways, full of impatience at stupidity and anger at injustice, and perfectly prepared to be as rude as you can."

"I am nothing like him whatever," Hester said impatiently. "And this is not a laughing matter." She could feel an irritating warmth creep up in her cheeks. Just once in a while she would like to take more naturally to feminine arts, as Imogen did as easily as breathing. Men did not rush to protect her as they did Imogen; they always assumed she was perfectly competent to take care of herself, and it was a compliment she was growing tired of.

Imogen ate her sandwich, a tiny thing about two inches square.

"Are you going to tell me what he came for, or not?"

"Certainly I am." Hester took a sandwich herself and bit into it; it was lacily thin and the cucumber was crisp and cool. "A few weeks ago he had a very serious accident, about the time Joscelin Grey was killed."

"Oh — I'm sorry. Is he ill now? He seemed perfectly recovered."

"I think his body is quite mended," Hester answered, and seeing the sudden gravity and concern in Imogen's face felt a gentleness herself. "But he was struck very severely on the head, and he cannot remember anything before regaining his senses in a London hospital."

"Not anything." A flicker of amazement crossed Imogen's face. "You mean he didn't remember me — I mean us?"

"He didn't remember himself," Hester said starkly. "He did not know his name or his occupation. He did not recognize his own face when he saw it in the glass."

"How extraordinary — and terrible. I do not always like myself completely — but to lose yourself! I cannot imagine having nothing at all left of all your past — all your experiences, and the reason why you love or hate things."

"Why did you go to him, Imogen?"

"What? I mean, I beg your pardon?"

"You heard what I said. When we first saw Monk in St. Marylebone Church you went over to speak to him. You knew him. I assumed at the time that he knew you, but he did not. He did not know anyone."

Imogen looked away, and very carefully took another sandwich.

"I presume it is something Charles does not know about," Hester went on.

"Are you threatening me?" Imogen asked, her enormous eyes quite frank.

"No I am not!" Hester was annoyed, with herself for being clumsy as well as Imogen for thinking such a thing. "I didn't know there was anything to threaten you with. I was going to say that unless it is unavoidable, I shall not tell him. Was it something to do with Joscelin Grey?"

Imogen choked on her sandwich and had to sit forward sharply to avoid suffocating herself altogether.

"No," she said when at last she caught her breath. "No it was not. I can see that perhaps it was foolish, on reflection. But at the time I really hoped —"

"Hoped what? For goodness sake, explain yourself."

Slowly, with a good deal of help, criticism and consolation from Hester, Imogen recounted detail by detail what she had done, what she had told Monk, and why.

Four hours later, in the golden sunlight of early evening, Hester stood in the park by the Serpentine watching the light dimple on the water. A small boy in a blue smock carrying a toy boat under his arm passed by with his nursemaid. She was dressed in a plain stuff dress, had a starched lace cap on her head and walked as uprightly as any soldier on parade. An off-duty bandsman watched her with admiration.

Beyond the grass and trees two ladies of fashion rode along Rotten Row, their horses gleaming, harnesses jingling and hooves falling with a soft thud on the earth. Carriages rattling along Knightsbridge towards Piccadilly seemed in another world, like toys in the distance.

She heard Monk's step before she saw him. She turned when he was almost upon her. He stopped a yard away; their eyes met. Lengthy politeness would be ridiculous between them. There was no outward sign of fear in him — his gaze was level and unflinching — but she

463

knew the void and the imagination that was there.

She was the first to speak.

"Imogen came to you after my father's death, in the rather fragile hope that you might discover some evidence that it was not suicide. The family was devastated. First George had been killed in the war, then Papa had been shot in what the police were kind enough to say might have been an accident, but appeared to everyone to be suicide. He had lost a great deal of money. Imogen was trying to salvage something out of the chaos — for Charles's sake, and for my mother's." She stopped for a moment, trying to keep her composure, but the pain of it was still very deep.

Monk stood perfectly still, not intruding, for which she was grateful. It seemed he understood she must tell it all without interruption in order to be able to tell it at all.

She let out her breath slowly, and resumed.

"It was too late for Mama. Her whole world had collapsed. Her youngest son dead, financial disgrace, and then her husband's suicide — not only his loss but the shame of the manner of it. She died ten days later — she was simply broken —" Again she was obliged to stop for several minutes. Monk said nothing, but stretched out his hand and held hers, hard, firmly, and the pressure of his fingers was like a lifeline to the shore.

In the distance a dog scampered through the grass, and a small boy chased a penny hoop.

"She came to you without Charles's knowing — he would not have approved. That is why she never mentioned it to you again — and of course she did not know you had forgotten. She says you questioned her about everything that had happened prior to Papa's death, and on successive meetings you asked her about Joscelin Grey. I shall tell you what she told me —"

A couple in immaculate riding habits cantered down the Row. Monk still held her hand.

"My family first met Joscelin Grey in March. They had none of them heard of him before and he called on them quite unexpectedly. He came one evening. You never met him, but he was very charming — even I can remember that from his brief stay in the hospital where I was in Scutari. He went out of his way to befriend other wounded men, and often wrote letters for those too ill to do it for themselves. He often smiled, even laughed and made small jokes. It did a great deal for morale. Of course his wound was not as serious as many, nor did he have cholera or dysentery."

Slowly they began to walk, so as not to draw

attention to themselves, close together.

She forced her mind back to that time, the smell, the closeness of pain, the constant tiredness and the pity. She pictured Joscelin Grey as she had last seen him, hobbling away down the steps with a corporal beside him, going down to the harbor to be shipped back to England.

"He was a little above average height," she said aloud. "Slender, fair-haired. I should think he still had quite a limp — I expect he always would have had. He told them his name, and that he was the younger brother of Lord Shelburne, and of course that he had served in the Crimea and been invalided home. He explained his own story, his time in Scutari, and that his injury was the reason he had delayed so long in calling on them."

She looked at Monk's face and saw the unspoken question.

"He said he had known George — before the battle of the Alma, where George was killed. Naturally the whole family made him most welcome, for George's sake, and for his own. Mama was still deeply grieved. One knows with one's mind that if young men go to war there is always a chance they will be killed, but that is nothing like a preparation for the feelings when it happens. Papa had his loss, so Imogen said, but for Mama it was

466

the end of something terribly precious. George was the youngest son and she always had a special feeling for him. He was —" She struggled with memories of childhood like a patch of sunlight in a closed garden. "He looked the most like Papa — he had the same smile, and his hair grew the same way, although it was dark like Mama's. He loved animals. He was an excellent horseman. I suppose it was natural he should join the cavalry.

"Anyway, of course they did not ask Grey a great deal about George the first time he called. It would have been very discourteous, as if they had no regard for his own friendship, so they invited him to return any time he should find himself free to do so, and would wish to —"

"And he did?" Monk spoke for the first time, quietly, just an ordinary question. His face was pinched and there was a darkness in his eyes.

"Yes, several times, and after a while Papa finally thought it acceptable to ask him about George. They had received letters, of course, but George had told them very little of what it was really like." She smiled grimly. "Just as I did not. I wonder now if perhaps we both should have? At least to have told Charles. Now we live in different worlds: And I should be distressing him to no purpose."

She looked beyond Monk to a couple walking arm in arm along the path.

"It hardly matters now. Joscelin Grey came again, and stayed to dinner, and then he began to tell them about the Crimea. Imogen says he was always most delicate; he never used unseemly language, and although Mama was naturally terribly upset, and grieved to hear how wretched the conditions were, he seemed to have a special sense of how much he could say without trespassing beyond sorrow and admiration into genuine horror. He spoke of battles, but he told them nothing of the starvation and the disease. And he always spoke so well of George, it made them all proud to hear.

"Naturally they also asked him about his own exploits. He saw the Charge of the Light Brigade at Balaclava. He said the courage was sublime: never were soldiers braver or more loyal to their duty. But he said the slaughter was the most dreadful thing he had ever seen, because it was so needless. They rode right into the guns; he told them that." She shivered as she remembered the cartloads of dead and wounded, the labor all through the night, the helplessness, all the blood. Had Joscelin Grey felt anything of the overwhelming emotions of anger and pity that she had?

"There was never any chance whatsoever

that they could have survived," she said quietly, her voice so low it was almost carried away by the murmur of the wind. "Imogen said he was very angry about it. He said some terrible things about Lord Cardigan. I think that was the moment I most thought I should have liked him."

Deeply as it hurt, Monk also most liked him for it. He had heard of that suicidal charge, and when the brief thrill of admiration had passed, he was left with a towering rage at the monumental incompetence and the waste, the personal vanity, the idiotic jealousies that had uselessly, senselessly squandered so many lives.

For what, in heaven's name, could he have hated Joscelin Grey?

She was talking and he was not listening. Her face was earnest, pinched for the loss and the pain. He wanted to touch her, to tell her simply, elementally, without words that he felt the same.

What sort of revulsion would she feel if she knew it was he who had beaten Joscelin Grey to death in that dreadful room?

"— as they got to know him," she was saying, "they all came to like him better and better for himself. Mama used to look forward to his visits; she would prepare for them days before. Thank heavens she never

469

knew what happened to him."

He refrained at the last moment, when it was on the tip of his tongue, from asking her when her mother had died. He remembered something about shock, a broken heart.

"Go on," he said instead. "Or is that all about him?"

"No." She shook her head. "No, there is much more. As I said, they were all fond of him; Imogen and Charles also. Imogen used to like to hear about the bravery of the soldiers, and of the hospital in Scutari, I suppose at least in part because of me."

He remembered what he had heard of the military hospital — of Florence Nightingale and her women. The sheer physical labor of it, quite apart from the social stigma. Nurses were traditionally mostly men; the few women were of the strongest, the coarsest, and they did little but clean up the worst of the refuse and waste.

She was speaking again. "It was about four weeks after they first met him that he first mentioned the watch —"

"Watch?" He had heard nothing of a watch, except he recalled they had found no watch on the body. Constable Harrison had found one at a pawnbroker's — which had turned out to be irrelevant.

"It was Joscelin Grey's," she replied. "Apparently it was a gold watch of great personal value to him because he had been given it by his grandfather, who had fought with the Duke of Wellington at Waterloo. It had a dent in it where a ball from a French musket struck it and was deflected, thus saving his grandfather's life. When he had first expressed a desire to be a soldier himself, the old man had given it to him. It was considered something of a talisman. Joscelin Grey said that poor George had been nervous that night, the night before the Battle of the Alma, perhaps something of a premonition, and Joscelin had lent him the watch. Of course George was killed the next day, and so never returned it. Joscelin did not make much of it, but he said that if it had been returned to them with George's effects, he would be most grateful if he might have it again. He described it most minutely, even to the inscription inside."

"And they returned it to him?" he asked.

"No. No, they did not have it. They had no idea what could have happened to it, but it was not among the things that the army sent them from George's body, nor his personal possessions. I can only presume someone must have stolen it. It is the most contemptible of crimes, but it happens. They felt quite dreadful about it, especially Papa."

"And Joscelin Grey?"

"He was distressed, of course, but according to Imogen he did his best to hide it; in fact he hardly mentioned it again."

"And your father?"

Her eyes were staring blindly past him at the wind in the leaves. "Papa could not return the watch, nor could he replace it, since in spite of its monetary value, its personal value was far greater, and it was that which really mattered. So when Joscelin Grey was interested in a certain business venture, Papa felt it was the very least he could do to offer to join him in it. Indeed from what both he and Charles said, it seemed at the time to be, in their judgment, an excellent scheme."

"That was the one in which your father lost his money?"

Her face tightened.

"Yes. He did not lose it all, but a considerable amount. What caused him to take his life, and Imogen has accepted now that he did so, was that he had recommended the scheme to his friends, and some of them had lost far more. That was the shame of it. Of course Joscelin Grey lost much of his own money too, and he was terribly distressed."

"And from that time their friendship ceased?"

"Not immediately. It was a week later, when Papa shot himself. Joscelin Grey sent

472

a letter of condolence, and Charles wrote back, thanking him, and suggesting that they discontinue their acquaintance, in the circumstances."

"Yes, I saw the letter. Grey kept it — I don't know why."

"Mama died a few days after that." She went on very quietly. "She simply collapsed, and never got up again. And of course it was not a time for social acquaintance: they were all in mourning." She hesitated a moment. "We still are."

"And it was after your father's death that Imogen came to see me?" He prompted after a moment.

"Yes, but not straightaway. She came the day after they buried Mama. I cannot think there was ever anything you could have done, but she was too upset to be thinking as deeply as she might, and who can blame her? She just found it too hard then to accept what must have been the truth."

They turned and began walking back again.

"So she came to the police station?" he asked.

"Yes."

"And told me everything that you have told me now?"

"Yes. And you asked her all the details of Papa's death: how he died, precisely when, who was in the house, and so on."

"And I noted it?"

"Yes, you said it might have been murder, or an accident, although you doubted it. You said that you would make some investigation."

"Do you know what I did?"

"I asked Imogen, but she did not know, only that you found no evidence that it was other than it seemed, which was that he took his own life while in deep despair. But you said you would continue to investigate it and let her know if you discovered anything further. But you never did, at least not until after we saw you again in the church, more than two months later."

He was disappointed, and becoming frightened as well. There was still no direct connection between himself and Joscelin Grey, still less any reason why he should have hated him. He tried a last time.

"And she does not know what my investigations were? I told her nothing?"

"No." She shook her head. "But I imagine, from the questions you asked her about Papa and the business, such as she knew it, that you inquired into that."

"Did I meet Joscelin Grey?"

"No. You met a Mr. Marner, who was one of the principals. You spoke of him; but you never met Joscelin Grey so far as she knows.

In fact the last time she saw you you said quite plainly that you had not. He was also a victim of the same misfortune, and you seemed to consider Mr. Marner the author of it, whether intentionally or not."

It was something, however frail; a place to begin.

"Do you know where I can find Mr. Marner now?"

"No, I am afraid not. I asked Imogen, but she had no knowledge."

"Did she know his Christian name?"

Again she shook her head. "No. You mentioned him only very briefly. I'm sorry. I wish I could help."

"You have helped. At least now I know what I was doing before the accident. It is somewhere to begin." That was a lie, but there was nothing to be gained in the truth.

"Do you think Joscelin Grey was killed over something to do with the business? Could he have known something about this Mr. Marner?" Her face was blank and sad with the sharpness of memory, but she did not evade the thought. "Was the business fraudulent, and he discovered it?"

Again he could only lie.

"I don't know. I'll start again, from the beginning. Do you know what manner of business it was, or at least the names of some of the friends of your father who invested in it? They would be able to give me the details."

She told him several names and he wrote them down, with addresses. He thanked her, feeling a little awkward, wanting her to know, without the embarrassment for both of them of his saying it, that he was grateful — for her candor, her understanding without pity, the moment's truce from all argument or social games.

He hesitated, trying to think of words. She put her hand very lightly on his sleeve and met his eyes for an instant. For a wild moment he thought of friendship, a closeness better than romance, cleaner and more honest; then it disappeared. There was the battered corpse of Joscelin Grey between him and everyone else.

"Thank you," he said calmly. "You have been very helpful. I appreciate your time and your frankness." He smiled very slightly, looking straight into her eyes. "Good afternoon, Miss Latterly."

CHAPTER
TWELVE

The name Marner meant nothing to Monk, and the following day, even after he had been to three of the addresses Hester had given him, he still had no more than a name and the nature of the business — importing. It seemed no one else had met the elusive Mr. Marner either. All inquiries and information had come from Latterly, through Joscelin Grey. The business was for the importing of tobacco from the United States of America, and a very profitable retailing of it was promised, in alliance with a certain Turkish house. No one knew more than that; except of course a large quantity of figures which indicated the amount of capital necessary to begin the venture and the projected increase to the fortunes of those who participated.

Monk did not leave the last house until well into the afternoon, but he could not afford time for leisure. He ate briefly, purchasing fresh sandwiches from a street seller, then went to the police station to seek the help of a man he had learned investigated business fraud. He might at least know the name of dealers in tobacco; perhaps he could find the Turkish house in question.

"Marner?" the man repeated agreeably, pushing his fingers through his scant hair. "Can't say as I've ever heard of him. You don't know his first name, you say?"

"No, but he floated a company for importing tobacco from America, mixing it with Turkish, and selling it at a profit."

The man pulled a face.

"Sounds unpleasant — can't stand Turkish myself — but then I prefer snuff anyway. Marner?" He shook his head. "You don't mean old Zebedee Marner, by any chance? I suppose you've tried him, or you wouldn't ask. Very sly old bird, that. But I never knew him mixed up with importing."

"What does he do?"

The man's eyebrows went up in surprise.

"Losing your grip, Monk? What's the matter with you?" He squinted a little. "You must know Zebedee Marner. Never been able to charge him with anything because he always weasels his way out, but we all know he's behind half the pawnbrokers, sweatshops and brothels in the Limehouse area right down to the Isle of Dogs. Personally

I think he takes a percentage from the child prostitutes and the opium as well, although he's far too downy to go anywhere near them himself." He sighed in disgust. "But then, of course, there's a few who wouldn't say as far as that."

Monk hardly dared hope. If this were the same Marner, then here at last was something that could lead to motive. It was back to the underworld, to greed, fraud and vice. Reason why Joscelin Grey should have killed — but why should he have been the victim?

Was there something in all this evidence that could at last convict Zebedee Marner? Was Grey in collusion with Marner? But Grey had lost his own money — or had he?

"Where can I find Marner?" he asked urgently. "I need him, and time is short." There was no time to seek out addresses himself. If this man thought he was peculiar, incompetent at his job, he would just have to think it. Soon it would hardly matter anyway.

The man looked at Monk, interest suddenly sharpening in his face, his body coming upright.

"Do you know something about Marner that I don't, Monk? I've been trying to catch that slimy bastard for years. Let me in on it?" His face was eager, a light in his eyes as if he had seen a sudden glimpse of an elusive happiness. "I don't want any of the credit; I won't say anything. I just want to see his face when he's pinched."

Monk understood. He was sorry not to be able to help.

"I don't have anything on Marner," he answered. "I don't even know if the business I'm investigating is fraudulent or not. Someone committed suicide, and I'd like to know the reasons."

"Why?" He was curious and his puzzlement was obvious. He cocked his head a little to one side. "What do you care about a suicide? I thought you were on the Grey case. Don't tell me Runcorn's let you off it — without an arrest?"

So even this man knew of Runcorn's feelings about him. Did everyone? No wonder Runcorn knew he had lost his memory! He must have laughed at Monk's confusion, his fumbling.

"No." He pulled a wry face. "No, it's all part of the same thing. Grey was involved in the business."

"Importing?" His voice rose an octave. "Don't tell me he was killed over a shipment of tobacco!"

"Not over tobacco; but there was a lot of money invested, and apparently the company failed."

"Oh yes? That's a new departure for Marner —"

"If it's the same man," Monk said cautiously. "I don't know that it is. I don't know anything about him but his name, and only part of that. Where do I find him?"

"Thirteen Gun Lane, Limehouse." He hesitated. "If you get anything, Monk, will you tell me, as long as it isn't the actual murder? Is that what you're after?"

"No. No, I just want some information. If I find evidence of fraud I'll bring it back for you." He smiled bleakly. "You have my word."

The man's face eased into a smile. "Thank you."

Monk went early in the morning and was in Limehouse by nine o'clock. He would have been there sooner had there been any purpose. He had spent much of the time since he woke at six planning what he would say.

It was a long way from Grafton Street and he took a hansom eastward through Clerkenwell, Whitechapel and down towards the cramped and crowded docks and Limehouse. It was a still morning and the sun was gleaming on the river, making white sparkles on the water between the black barges coming up from the Pool of London. Across on the far side were Bermondsey — the Venice of the Drains — and Rotherhithe, and ahead of him the Surrey Docks, and along the shining Reach the Isle of Dogs, and on the far side Deptford and then the beautiful Greenwich with its green park and trees and the exquisite architecture of the naval college.

But his duty lay in the squalid alleys of Limehouse with beggars, usurers and thieves of every degree — and Zebedee Marner.

Gun Lane was a byway off the West India Dock Road, and he found Number 13 without difficulty. He passed an evil-looking idler on the pavement and another lounging in the doorway, but neither troubled him, perhaps considering him unlikely to give to a beggar and too crisp of gait to be wise to rob. There was other, easier prey. He despised them, and understood them at the same time.

Good fortune was with him: Zebedee Marner was in, and after a discreet inquiry, the clerk showed Monk into the upper office.

"Good morning, Mr. — Monk." Marner sat behind a large, important desk, his white hair curled over his ears and his white hands spread on the leather-inlaid surface in front of him. "What can I do for you?"

"You come recommended as a man of many businesses, Mr. Marner," Monk started smoothly, gliding over the hatred in his voice.

"With a knowledge of all kinds of things."

"And so I am, Mr. Monk, so I am. Have you money to invest?"

"What could you offer me?"

"All manner of things. How much money?" Marner was watching him narrowly, but it was well disguised as a casual cheerfulness.

"I am interested also in safety, rather than quick profit," Monk said, ignoring the question. "I wouldn't care to lose what I have."

"Of course not, who would?" Marner spread his hands wide and shrugged expressively, but his eyes were fixed and blinkless as a snake's. "You want your money invested safely?"

"Oh, quite definitely," Monk agreed. "And since I know of many other gentlemen who are also interested in investment, I should wish to be certain that any recommendation I made was secure."

Marner's eyes flickered, then the lids came down to hide his thoughts. "Excellent," he said calmly. "I quite understand, Mr. Monk. Have you considered importing and exporting? Very nourishing trade; never fails."

"So I've heard." Monk nodded. "But is it safe?"

"Some is, some isn't. It is the skill of people like me to know the difference." His eyes were wide again, his hands folded across his paunch.

"That is why you came here, instead of investing it yourself."

"Tobacco?"

Marner's face did not change in the slightest.

"An excellent commodity." He nodded. "Excellent. I cannot see gentlemen giving up their pleasures, whatever the economic turns of life. As long as there are gentlemen, there will be a market for tobacco. And unless our climate changes beyond our wit to imagine" — he grinned and his body rocked with silent mirth at his own humor — "we will be unable to grow it, so must need import it. Have you any special company in mind?"

"Are you familiar with the market?" Monk asked, swallowing hard to contain his loathing of this man sitting here like a fat white spider in his well-furnished office, safe in his gray web of lies and facades. Only the poor flies like Latterly got caught — and perhaps Joscelin Grey.

"Of course," Marner replied complacently. "I know it well."

"You have dealt in it?"

"I have, frequently. I assure you, Mr. Monk, I know very well what I am doing."

"You would not be taken unaware and find yourself faced with a collapse?"

"Most certainly not." Marner looked at him

484

as if he had let fall some vulgarity at the table.

"You are sure?" Monk pressed him.

"I am more than sure, my dear sir." Now he was quite pained. "I am positive."

"Good." Monk at last allowed the venom to flood into his voice. "That is what I thought. Then you will no doubt be able to tell me how the disaster occurred that ruined Major Joscelin Grey's investment in the same commodity. You were connected with it."

Marner's face paled and for a moment he was confused to find words.

"I — er — assure you, you need have no anxiety as to its happening again," he said, avoiding Monk's eyes, then looking very directly at him, to cover the lie of intent.

"That is good," Monk answered him coolly. "But hardly of more than the barest comfort now. It has cost two lives already. Was there much of your own money lost, Mr. Marner?"

"Much of mine?" Marner looked startled.

"I understand Major Grey lost a considerable sum?"

"Oh — no. No, you are misinformed." Marner shook his head and his white hair bounced over his ears. "The company did not precisely fail. Oh dear me no. It simply transferred its operation; it was taken over. If you are not a man of affairs, you could not be expected to understand. Business is highly complicated these days, Mr. Monk."

"It would seem so. And you say Major Grey did not lose a great deal of his own money? Can you substantiate that in any way?"

"I could, of course." The smug veils came over Marner's eyes again. "But Major Grey's affairs are his own, of course, and I should not discuss his affairs with you, any more than I should dream of discussing yours with him. The essence of good business is discretion, sir." He smiled, pleased with himself, his composure at least in part regained.

"Naturally," Monk agreed. "But I am from the police, and am investigating Major Grey's murder, therefore I am in a different category from the merely inquisitive." He lowered his voice and it became peculiarly menacing. He saw Marner's face tighten. "And as a law-abiding man," he continued, "I am sure you will be only too happy to give me every assistance you can. I should like to see your records in the matter. Precisely how much did Major Grey lose, Mr. Marner, to the guinea, if you please?"

Marner's chin came up sharply; his eyes were hot and offended.

"The police? You said you wanted to make an investment."

"No, I did not say that — you assumed it. How much did Joscelin Grey lose, Mr. Marner?"

"Oh, well, to the guinea, Mr. Monk, he — he did not lose any."

"But the company dissolved."

"Yes — yes, that is true; it was most unfortunate. But Major Grey withdrew his own investment at the last moment, just before the — the takeover."

Monk remembered the policeman from whom he had learned Marner's address. If he had been after Marner for years, let him have the satisfaction of taking him now.

"Oh." Monk sat back, altering his whole attitude, almost smiling. "So he was not really concerned in the loss?"

"No, not at all."

Monk stood up.

"Then it hardly constitutes a part of his murder. I'm sorry to have wasted your time, Mr. Marner. And I thank you for your cooperation. You do, of course, have some papers to prove this, just for my superiors?"

"Yes. Yes, I have." Marner relaxed visibly. "If you care to wait for a moment —" He stood up from his desk and went to a large cabinet of files. He pulled a drawer and took out a small notebook ruled in ledger fashion. He put it, open, on the desk in front of Monk.

Monk picked it up, glanced at it, read the entry where Grey had withdrawn his money, and snapped it shut.

"Thank you." He put the book in the inside pocket of his coat and stood up.

Marner's hand came forward for the return of the book. He realized he was not going to get it, debated in his mind whether to demand it or not, and decided it would raise more interest in the subject than he could yet afford. He forced a smile, a sickly thing in his great white face.

"Always happy to be of service, sir. Where should we be without the police? So much crime these days, so much violence."

"Indeed," Monk agreed. "And so much theft that breeds violence. Good day, Mr. Marner."

Outside he walked briskly along Gun Lane and back towards the West India Dock Road, but he was thinking hard. If this evidence was correct, and not fiddled with by Zebedee Marner, then the hitherto relatively honest Joscelin Grey had almost certainly been forewarned in time to escape at the last moment himself, leaving Latterly and his friends to bear the loss. Dishonest, but not precisely illegal. It would be interesting to know who had shares in the company that took over the tobacco importing, and if Grey was one of them.

Had he uncovered this much before? Marner had shown no signs of recognition. He had behaved as if the whole question were entirely new to him. In fact it must be, or Monk would never have been able to deceive him into imagining him an investor.

But even if Zebedee Marner had never seen him before, it was not impossible he had known all this before Grey's death, because then he had had his memory, known his contacts, who to ask, who to bribe, who could be threatened, and with what.

But there was no way yet to find out. On the West India Dock Road he found a hansom and sank back for the long ride, thinking.

At the police station he went to the man who had given him Zebedee Marner's address and told him of his visit, gave him the ledger and showed him what he thought the fraud would be. The man positively bubbled with delight, like someone who contemplates a rich feast only hours away. Monk had a brief, fierce glow of satisfaction.

It did not last.

Runcorn was waiting for him in his own office.

"No arrest yet?" he said with black relish. "No one charged?"

Monk did not bother to reply.

"Monk!" Runcorn slammed his fist on the table.

"Yes sir?"

"You sent John Evan out to Shelburne to question the staff?"

"Yes I did. Isn't that what you wanted?" He raised sarcastic eyebrows. "Evidence against Shelburne?"

"You won't get it out there. We know what his motive was. What we need is evidence of opportunity, someone who saw him here."

"I'll start looking," Monk said with bitter irony. Inside himself he was laughing, and Runcorn knew it, but he had not the faintest idea why, and it infuriated him.

"You should have been looking for the last month!" he shouted. "What in hell is the matter with you, Monk? You were always a hard, arrogant devil, with airs beyond your station, but you were a good policeman. But now you're a fool. This crack on the head seems to have impaired your brain. Perhaps you should have some more sick leave?"

"I am perfectly well." Misery was black inside Monk; he wanted to frighten this man who hated him so much and was going to have the last victory. "But maybe you ought to take over this case? You are right, I am getting nowhere with it." He looked straight back at Runcorn with wide eyes. "The powers that be want a result — you should do the job yourself."

Runcorn's face set. "You must take me for a fool. I've sent for Evan. He'll be back tomorrow." He held up his thick finger, wagging it in Monk's face. "Arrest Shelburne this week, or I will take you off it." He turned and strode out, leaving the door squealing on its hinges.

Monk stared after him. So he had sent for Evan to return. Time was even shorter than he had feared. Before much longer Evan must come to the same conclusion as he had, and that would be the end.

In fact Evan came back the next day, and Monk met him for luncheon. They sat together in a steamy public house. It was heavy and damp with the odor of massed bodies, sawdust, spilled ale and nameless vegetables stewed into soup.

"Anything?" Monk asked as a matter of form. It would have seemed remarkable had he not.

"Lots of indication," Evan replied with a frown. "But I wonder sometimes if I see it only because I'm looking for it."

"You mean invent it for yourself?"

Evan's eyes came up quickly and met Monk's. They were devastatingly clear.

"You don't honestly believe he did it, do you, sir?"

How could he know so quickly? Rapidly Monk flew in his mind through all the possible things he might say. Would Evan know a lie? Had he seen all the lies already? Was he clever enough, subtle enough, to be leading Monk gently into trapping himself? Was it conceivable the whole police department knew, and were simply waiting for him to uncover his own proof, his own condemnation? For a moment fear engulfed him and the cheerful rattle of the alehouse became a din like bedlam — witless, formless and persecutory. They all knew; they were merely waiting for him to know, to betray himself, and then the mystery would end. They would come out in the open, with laughter, handcuffs, questions, congratulations at another murder solved; there would be a trial, a brief imprisonment, and then the tight, strong rope, a quick pain — and nothing.

But why? Why had he killed Joscelin Grey? Surely not because Grey had escaped the crash of the tobacco company — probably even profited from it?

"Sir? Sir, are you all right?" It was Evan's voice cutting across his panic, Evan's face peering at him anxiously. "You look a little pale, sir. Are you sure you are all right?"

Monk forced himself to sit upright and meet Evan's eyes. If he were to be given one wish now, it would be that Evan would not have to know. Imogen Latterly had never really been more than a dream, a reminder of the softer self, the part of him that could be wounded and could care for something better than ambition — but Evan had been a friend. Maybe there had been others, but he could not remember them now.

"Yes," he said carefully. "Yes, thank you. I was just thinking. No, you are right; I am not at all sure it was Shelburne."

Evan leaned forward a little, his face eager.

"I'm glad you say that, sir. Don't let Mr. Runcorn push you." His long fingers were playing with the bread, too excited to eat. "I think it's someone here in London. In fact I have been looking at Mr. Lamb's notes again, and ours, and the more I read them the more I think it could have something to do with money, with business.

"Joscelin Grey seems to have lived fairly comfortably, better than the allowance from his family supported." He put down his spoon and abandoned all pretense of the meal. "So either he was blackmailing someone, or else he gambled very successfully, or, most likely of all, he had some business we know nothing about. And if it were honest, we ought to have

493

found some record of it, and the other people concerned should have come forward. Similarly, if he borrowed money, the lenders would have put in some claim against the estate."

"Unless they were sharks," Monk said automatically, his mind cold with fear, watching Evan draw closer and closer to the thread that must lead him to the truth. Any moment now and his fine, sensitive hands would grasp it.

"But if they were sharks," Evan said quickly, his eyes alight, "they would not have lent to someone like Grey. Sharks are exceedingly careful about their investments. That much I've learned. They don't lend a second sum out before they have the first back, and with interest, or a mortgage on property." A lock of his heavy hair fell forward over his brow and he ignored it. "Which brings us back to the same question: Where did Grey get the repayment, not to mention the interest? He was the third brother, remember, and he had no property of his own. No sir, he had some business, I'm sure of it. And I have some thoughts where to start looking for it."

He was coming closer with every new idea.

Monk said nothing; his mind was racing for a thought, any thought to put Evan off. He could not avoid it forever, the time would come; but before that he must know why.

There was something vital so close, a finger's length out of his reach.

"Do you not agree, sir?" Evan was disappointed; his eyes were shadowed with it. Or was it disappointment that Monk had lied?

Monk jerked himself back, dismissing his pain. He must think clearly just a little longer.

"I was turning it over," he said, trying to keep the desperation out of his voice. "Yes, I think you may very well be right. Dawlish spoke of a business venture. I don't recall how much I told you of it; I gathered it had not yet begun, but there may easily have been others already involved." How he hated lying. Especially to Evan — this betrayal was the worst of all. He could not bear to think what Evan would feel when he knew. "It would be a good thing if we investigated it far more thoroughly."

Evan's face lit up again.

"Excellent. You know I really believe we could yet catch Joscelin Grey's murderer. I think we are near it; it will only take just one or two more clues and it will all fall into place."

Did he know how appallingly near he was to the truth?

"Possibly," Monk agreed, keeping his voice level with an effort. He looked down at the plate in front of him, anything to avoid Evan's

495

eyes. "You will still have to be discreet, though. Dawlish is a man of considerable standing."

"Oh I will, sir, I will. Anyway, I do not especially suspect him. What about the letter we saw from Charles Latterly? That was pretty chilly, I thought. And I found out quite a lot more about him." He took a spoonful of his stew at last. "Did you know his father committed suicide just a few weeks before Grey was killed? Dawlish is a business affair in the future, but Latterly could have been one from the past. Don't you think so, sir?" He was ignoring the taste and texture of the food, almost swallowing it whole in his pre-occupation. "Perhaps there was something not quite right there, and the elder Mr. Latterly took his life when he was implicated, and young Mr. Charles Latterly, the one who sent the letter, was the one who killed Grey in revenge?"

Monk took a deep breath. He must have just a little more time.

"That letter sounded too controlled for a man passionate enough to kill in revenge," he said carefully, beginning to eat his own stew. "But I will look into it. You try Dawlish, and you might try the Fortescues as well. We don't know very much about their connection either." He could not let Evan pursue Charles for his, Monk's, crime; also the truth was too close for Charles to deny it easily. He had no liking for him, but there was something of honor left to cling to — and he was Hester's brother.

"Yes," he added, "try the Fortescues as well."

In the afternoon when Evan set off full of enthusiasm after Dawlish and Fortescue, Monk went back to the police station and again sought out the man who had given him Marner's address. The man's face lit up as soon as Monk came in.

"Ah, Monk, I owe you something. Good old Zebedee at last." He waved a book in the air triumphantly. "Went down to his place on the strength of the ledger you brought, and searched the whole building. The rackets he was running." He positively chortled with delight and hiccupped very slightly. "Swindling left and right, taking a rake-off from half the crime and vice in Limehouse — and the Isle of Dogs. God knows how many thousands of pounds must have gone through his hands, the old blackguard."

Monk was pleased; it was one career other than his own he had helped.

"Good," he said sincerely. "I always like to imagine that particular kind of bloodsucker running his belly off in the treadmills for a few years."

The other man grinned.

"Me too, and that one especially. By the way, the tobacco importing company was a sham. Did you know that?" He hiccupped again and excused himself. "There was a company, but there was never any practical chance it could have done any trading, let alone make a profit. Your fellow Grey took his money out at precisely the right moment. If he wasn't dead I should be wishing I could charge him as well."

Charge Grey? Monk froze. The room vanished except for a little whirling light in front of him, and the man's face.

"Wishing? Why only wishing?" He hardly dared ask. Hope hurt like a physical thing.

"Because there's no proof," the man replied, oblivious of Monk's ecstasy. "He did nothing actually illegal. But I'm as sure as I am that Hell's hot, he was part of it; just too damned clever to step over the law. But he set it up — and brought in the money."

"But he was taken in the fraud," Monk protested, afraid to believe. He wanted to grab the man and shake him; he resisted only with difficulty. "You're sure beyond doubt?"

"Of course I am." The other raised his eyebrows. "I may not be as brilliant a detective as you are, Monk, but I know my job. And I certainly know a fraud when I see one. Your friend Grey was one of the best, and very tidy about it." He hitched himself more comfortably in his seat. "Not much money, not enough to cause suspicion, just a small profit, and no guilt attached to him. If he made a habit of it he must have done quite nicely. Although how he got all those people to trust him with their money I don't know. You should see the names of some of those who invested."

"Yes," Monk said slowly. "I also should like to know how he persuaded them. I think I want to know that almost as much as I want to know anything." His brain was racing, casting for clues, threads anywhere. "Any other names in that ledger, any partners of Marner's?"

"Employees — just the clerk in the outer office."

"No partners; were there no partners? Anyone else who might know the business about Grey? Who got most of the money, if Grey didn't?"

The man hiccupped gently and sighed. "A rather nebulous 'Mr. Robinson,' and a lot of money went on keeping it secret, and tidy, covering tracks. No proof so far that this Robinson actually knew exactly what was going on. We've got a watch on him, but nothing good enough to arrest him yet."

"Where is he?" He had to find out if he had seen this Robinson before, the first time he had investigated Grey. If Marner did not know him, then perhaps Robinson did?

The man wrote an address on a slip of paper and handed it to him.

Monk took it: it was just above the Elephant Stairs in Rotherhithe, across the river. He folded it and put it in his pocket.

"I won't spoil your case," he promised. "I only want to ask him one question, and it's to do with Grey, not the tobacco fraud."

"It's all right," the other man said, sighing happily. "Murder is always more important than fraud, at least it is when it's a lord's son that's been killed." He sighed and hiccupped together. "Of course if he'd been some poor shopkeeper or chambermaid it would be different. Depends who's been robbed, or who's been killed, doesn't it?"

Monk gave a hard little grimace for the injustice of it, then thanked him and left.

Robinson was not at the Elephant Stairs, and it took Monk all afternoon to find him, eventually running him down in a gin mill in Seven Dials, but he learned everything he wanted to know almost before Robinson spoke. The man's face tightened as soon as

Monk came in and a cautious look came into his eyes.

"Good day, Mr. Monk; I didn't expect to see you again. What is it this time?"

Monk felt the excitement shiver through him. He swallowed hard.

"Still the same thing —"

Robinson's voice was low and sibilant, and there was a timber in it that struck Monk with an almost electric familiarity. The sweat tingled on his skin. It was real memory, actual sight and feelings coming back at last. He stared hard at the man.

Robinson's narrow, wedge-shaped face was stiff.

"I've already told you everything I know, Mr. Monk. Anyway, what does it matter now Joscelin Grey is dead?"

"And you told me everything you knew before? You swear it?"

Robinson snorted with a faint contempt.

"Yes I swear it," he said wearily. "Now will you please go away? You're known around 'ere. It don't do me no good to 'ave the police nosing around and asking questions. People think I 'ave something to 'ide."

Monk did not bother to argue with him. The fraud detective would catch up with him soon enough.

"Good," he said simply. "Then I don't need

to trouble you again." He went out into the hot, gray street milling with peddlers and waifs, his feet hardly feeling the pavement beneath. So he had known about Grey before he had been to see him, before he had killed him.

But why was it Grey he had hated so much? Marner was the principal, the brains behind the fraud, and the greatest beneficiary. And it seemed he had made no move against Marner.

He needed to think about it, sort out his ideas, decide where at least to look for the last missing piece.

It was hot and close, the air heavy with the humidity coming up from the river, and his mind was tired, staggering, spinning with the burden of what he had learned. He needed food and something to drink away this terrible thirst, to wash the stench of the rookeries from his mouth.

Without realizing it he had walked to the door of an eating house. He pushed it open and the fresh smell of sawdust and apple cider engulfed him. Automatically he made his way to the counter. He did not want ale, but fresh bread and sharp, homemade pickle. He could smell them, pungent and a little sweet.

The potman smiled at him and fetched the crusty bread, crumbling Wensleydale cheese, and juicy onions. He passed over the plate.

" 'Aven't seen yer for a w'ile, sir," he said cheerfully. "I s'pose you was too late to find that fellow you was looking for?"

Monk took the plate in stiff hands, awkwardly. He could not draw his eyes from the man's face. Memory was coming back; he knew he knew him.

"Fellow?" he said huskily.

"Yes." The potman smiled. "Major Grey; you was looking for 'im last time you was 'ere. It was the same night 'e was murdered, so I don't s'pose you ever found 'im."

Something was just beyond Monk's memory, the last piece, tantalizing, the shape of it almost recognizable at last.

"You knew him?" he said slowly, still holding the plate in his hands.

"Bless you, 'course I knew 'im, sir. I told you that." He frowned. " 'Ere, don't you remember?"

"No." Monk shook his head. It was too late now to lie. "I had an accident that night. I don't remember what you said. I'm sorry. Can you tell me again?"

The man shook his head and continued wiping a glass. "Too late now, sir. Major Grey was murdered that night. You'll not see 'im now. Don't you read the newspapers?"

"But you knew him," Monk repeated.

"Where? In the army? You called him 'Major'!"

"That's right. Served in the army with 'im, I did, till I got invalided out."

"Tell me about him! Tell me everything you told me that night!"

"I'm busy right now, sir. I got to serve or I'll not make me livin'," the man protested. "Come back later, eh?"

Monk fished in his pocket and brought out all the money he had, every last coin. He put it on the counter.

"No, I need it now."

The man looked at the money, shining in the light. He met Monk's eyes, saw the urgency in them, understood something of importance. He slid his hand over the money and put it rapidly in the pocket under his apron before picking up the cloth again.

"You asked me what I knew of Major Grey, sir. I told you when I first met 'im and where — in the army in the Crimea. 'E were a major, and I were just a private o' course. But I served under 'im for a long time. 'E were a good enough officer, not specially good nor specially bad; just like most. 'E were brave enough, as fair as most to 'is men. Good to 'is 'orses, but then most well-bred gents is."

The man blinked. "You didn't seem terribly interested in that," he went on, still absently working on the glass. "You listened, but it didn't seem to weigh much with you. Then you asked me about the Battle o' the Alma, where some Lieutenant Latterly 'ad died; an' I told you as we wasn't at the Battle o' the Alma, so I couldn't tell you about this Lieutenant Latterly —"

"But Major Grey spent the last night before the battle with Lieutenant Latterly." Monk grabbed at his arm. "He lent him his watch. Latterly was afraid; it was a lucky piece, a talisman. It had belonged to his grandfather at Waterloo."

"No sir, I can't say about any Lieutenant Latterly, but Major Grey weren't nowhere near the Battle o' the Alma, and 'e never 'ad no special watch."

"Are you sure?" Monk was gripping the man's wrist, unaware of hurting him.

"O' course I'm sure, sir." The man eased his hand. "I was there. An' 'is watch were an ordinary gold plate one, and as new as 'is uniform. It weren't no more at Waterloo than 'e were."

"And an officer called Dawlish?"

The potman frowned, rubbing his wrist. "Dawlish? I don't remember you asking me about 'im."

"I probably didn't. But do you remember him?"

505 .

"No sir, I don't recall an officer o' that name."

"But you are sure of the Battle of the Alma?"

"Yes sir, I'd swear before God positive. If you'd been in the Crimea, sir, you'd not forget what battle you was at, and what you wasn't. I reckon that's about the worst war there's ever been, for cold and muck and men dyin'."

"Thank you."

"Don't you want your bread an' cheese, sir? That pickle's 'omemade special. You should eat it. You look right peaked, you do."

Monk took it, thanked him automatically, and sat down at one of the tables. He ate without tasting and then walked out into the first spots of rain. He could remember doing this before, remember the slow building anger. It had all been a lie, a brutal and carefully calculated lie to earn first acceptance from the Latterlys, then their friendship, and finally to deceive them into a sufficient sense of obligation, over the lost watch, to repay him by supporting his business scheme. Grey had used his skill to play like an instrument first their grief, then their debt. Perhaps he had even done the same with the Dawlishes.

The rage was gathering up inside him again. It was coming back exactly as it had before. He was walking faster and faster, the rain beating in his face now. He was unaware of it. He splashed through the swimming gutters into the street to hail a cab. He gave the address in Mecklenburg Square, as he knew he had done before.

When he got out he went into the building. Grimwade handed him the key this time; the first time there had been no one there.

He went upstairs. It seemed new, strange, as if he were reliving the first time when it was unknown to him. He got to the top and hesitated at the door. Then he had knocked. Now he slipped the key into the lock. It swung open quite easily and he went in. Before Joscelin Grey had come to the door, dressed in pale dove, his fair face handsome, smiling, just a little surprised. He could see it now as if it had been only a few minutes ago.

Grey had asked him in, quite casually, unperturbed. He had put his stick in the hall stand, his mahogany stick with the brass chain embossed in the handle. It was still there. Then he had followed Grey into the main room. Grey had been very composed, a slight smile on his face. Monk had told him what he had come for: about the tobacco business, the failure, Latterly's death, the fact that Grey had lied, that he had never known George Latterly, and there had been no watch.

He could see Grey now as he had turned

507

from the sideboard, holding out a drink for Monk, taking one himself. He had smiled again, more widely.

"My dear fellow, a harmless little lie." His voice had been light, very easy, very calm. "I told them what an excellent fellow poor George was, how brave, how charming, how well loved. It was what they wanted to hear. What does it matter whether it was true or not?"

"It was a lie," Monk had shouted back. "You didn't even know George Latterly. You did it purely for money."

Grey had grinned.

"So I did, and what's more, I shall do it again, and again. I have an endless stream of gold watches, or whatever; and there's not a thing you can do about it, policeman. I shall go on as long as anyone is left who remembers the Crimea — which will be a hell of a long time — and shall damned well never run out of the dead!"

Monk had stared at him, helpless, anger raging inside him till he could have wept like an impotent child.

"I didn't know Latterly," Grey had gone on. "I got his name from the casualty lists. They're absolutely full of names, you've no idea. Although actually I got some of the better ones from the poor devils themselves — saw

508

them die in Scutari, riddled with disease, bleeding and spewing all over the place. I wrote their last letters for them. Poor George might have been a raving coward, for all I know. But what good does it do to tell his family that? I've no idea what he was like, but it doesn't take much wit to work out what they wanted to hear! Poor little Imogen adored him, and who can blame her? Charles is a hell of a bore; reminds me a bit of my eldest brother, another pompous fool." His fair face had become momentarily ugly with envy. A look of malice and pleasure had slid into it. He looked at Monk up and down knowingly.

"And who wouldn't have told the lovely Imogen whatever she would listen to? I told her all about that extraordinary creature, Florence Nightingale. I painted up the heroism a bit, certainly, gave her all the glory of 'angels of mercy' holding lamps by the dying through the night. You should have seen her face." He had laughed; then seeing something in Monk, a vulnerability, perhaps a memory or a dream, and understanding its depth in a flash: "Ah yes, Imogen." He sighed. "Got to know her very well." His smile was half a leer. "Love the way she walks, all eager, full of promise, and hope." He had looked at Monk and the slow smile spread to his eyes till the light in them was as old as appetite and knowledge itself. He had tittered slightly. "I do believe you're taken with Imogen yourself."

"You clod, she'd no more touch you than carry out her own refuse."

"She's in love with Florence Nightingale and the glory of the Crimea!" His eyes met Monk's, glittering bright. "I could have had her any time, all eager and quivering." His lip curled and he had almost laughed as he looked at Monk. "I'm a soldier; I've seen reality, blood and passion, fought for Queen and country. I've seen the Charge of the Light Brigade, lain in hospital at Scutari among the dying. What do you imagine she thinks of grubby little London policemen who spend their time sniffing about in human filth after the beggars and the degenerate? You're a scavenger, a cleaner up of other people's dirt — one of life's necessities, like the drains." He took a long gulp of his brandy and looked at Monk over the top of the glass.

"Perhaps when they've got over that old idiot getting hysterical and shooting himself, I shall go back and do just that. Can't remember when I've fancied a woman more."

It had been then, with that leer on his mouth, that Monk had taken his own glass and thrown the brandy across Grey's face. He could remember the blinding anger as if it were a dream he had only just woken from. He could still taste the heat and the gall of it on his tongue.

The liquid had hit Grey in his open eyes and burned him, seared his pride beyond bearing. He was a gentleman, one already robbed by birth of fortune, and now this oaf of a policeman, jumped above himself, had insulted him in his own house. His features had altered into a snarl of fury and he had picked up his own heavy stick and struck Monk across the shoulders with it. He had aimed at his head, but Monk had almost felt it before it came, and moved.

They had closed in a struggle. It should have been self-defense, but it was far more than that. Monk had been glad of it — he had wanted to smash that leering face, beat it in, undo all that he had said, wipe from him the thoughts he had had of Imogen, expunge some of the wrong to her family. But above all towering in his head and burning in his soul, he wanted to beat him so hard he would never feed on the gullible and the bereaved again, telling them lies of invented debt and robbing the dead of the only heritage they had left, the truth of memory in those who had loved them.

Grey had fought back; for a man invalided out of the army he had been surprisingly strong. They had been locked together struggling for the stick, crashing into furniture, upsetting chairs. The very violence of it was a catharsis, and all the pent-up fear, the nightmare of rage and the agonizing pity poured forth and he barely felt the pain of blows, even the breaking of his ribs when Grey caught him a tremendous crack on the chest with his stick.

But Monk's weight and strength told, and perhaps his rage was even stronger than Grey's fear and all his held-in anger of years of being slighted and passed over.

Monk could remember quite clearly now the moment when he had wrested the heavy stick out of Grey's hands and struck at him with it, trying to destroy the hideousness, the blasphemy he saw, the obscenity the law was helpless to curb.

Then he had stopped, breathless and terrified by his own violence and the storm of his hatred. Grey was splayed out on the floor, swearing like a trooper.

Monk had turned and gone out, leaving the door swinging behind him, blundering down the stairs, turning his coat collar up and pulling his scarf up to hide the abrasion on his face where Grey had hit him. He had passed Grimwade in the hall. He remembered a bell ringing and Grimwade leaving his position and starting upstairs.

Outside the weather was fearful. As soon as he had opened the door the wind had blown it against him so hard it had knocked him backwards. He had put his head down and plunged out, the rain engulfing him, beating in his face cold and hard. He had his back to the light, going into the darkness between one lamp and the next.

There was a man coming towards him, towards the light and the door still open in the wind — for a moment he saw his face before he turned and went in. It was Menard Grey.

Now it all made obvious and tragic sense — it was not George Latterly's death, or the abuse of it, which had spurred Joscelin Grey's murder, it was Edward Dawlish's — and Joscelin's own betrayal of every ideal his brother believed.

And then the joy vanished just as suddenly as it had come, the relief evaporated, leaving him shivering cold. How could he prove it? It was his word against Menard's. Grimwade had been up the stairs answering the bell, and seen nothing. Menard had gone in the door Monk had left open in the gale. There was nothing material, no evidence — only Monk's memory of Menard's face for a moment in the gaslight.

They would hang him. He could imagine

the trial now, himself standing in the dock, the ridiculousness of trying to explain what manner of man Joscelin Grey had been, and that it was not Monk, but Joscelin's own brother Menard who had killed him. He could see the disbelief in their faces, and the contempt for a man who would try to escape justice by making such a charge.

Despair closed around him like the blackness of the night, eating away strength, crushing with the sheer weight of it. And he began to be afraid. There would be the few short weeks in the stone cell, the stolid warders, at once pitying and contemptuous, then the last meal, the priest, and the short walk to the scaffold, the smell of rope, the pain, the fighting for breath — and oblivion.

He was still drowned and paralyzed by it when he heard the sound on the stairs. The latch turned and Evan stood in the doorway. It was the worst moment of all. There was no point in lying. Evan's face was full of knowledge, and pain. And anyway, he did not want to.

"How did you know?" Monk said quietly.

Evan came in and closed the door. "You sent me after Dawlish. I found an officer who'd served with Edward Dawlish. He didn't gamble, and Joscelin Grey never paid any debts for him. Everything he knew about him he learned from Menard. He took a hell of a chance lying to the family like that — but it worked. They'd have backed him financially, if he hadn't died. They blamed Menard for Edward's fall from honor, and forbade him the house. A nice touch on Joscelin's part."

Monk stared at him. It made perfect sense. And yet it would never even raise a reasonable doubt in a juror's mind.

"I think that is where Grey's money came from — cheating the families of the dead," Evan continued. "You were so concerned about the Latterly case, it wasn't a great leap of the imagination to assume he cheated them too — and that is why Charles Latterly's father shot himself." His eyes were soft and intense with distress. "Did you come this far the first time too — before the accident?"

So he knew about the memory also. Perhaps it was all far more obvious than he believed; the fumbling for words, the unfamiliarity with streets, public houses, old haunts — even Runcorn's hatred of him. It did not matter anymore.

"Yes." Monk spoke very slowly, as if letting the words fall one by one would make them believable. "But I did not kill Joscelin Grey. I fought with him, I probably hurt him — he certainly hurt me — but he was alive and swearing at me when I left." He searched

Evan's countenance feature by feature. "I saw Menard Grey go in as I turned in the street. He was facing the light and I was going away from it. The outer door was still open in the wind."

A desperate, painful relief flooded Evan's face, and he looked bony and young, and very tired. "So it was Menard who killed him." It was a statement.

"Yes." A blossom of gratitude opened wide inside Monk, filling him with sweetness. Even without hope, it was to be treasured immeasurably. "But there is no proof."

"But —" Evan began to argue, then the words died on his lips as he realized the truth of it. In all their searches they had found nothing. Menard had motive, but so had Charles Latterly, or Mr. Dawlish, or any other family Joscelin had cheated, any friend he had dishonored — or Lovel Grey, whom he might have betrayed in the cruelest way of all — or Monk himself. And Monk had been there. Now that they knew it, they also knew how easily provable it was, simply find the shop where he had bought that highly distinctive stick — such a piece of vanity. Mrs. Worley would remember it, and its subsequent absence. Lamb would recall seeing it in Grey's flat the morning after the murder. Imogen Latterly would have to admit Monk had been working on the case of her father's death.

The darkness was growing closer, tighter around them, the light guttering.

"We'll have to get Menard to confess," Evan said at last.

Monk laughed harshly. "And how do you propose we should do that? There's no evidence, and he knows it. No one would take my word against his that I saw him, and kept silent about it till now. It will look like a rather shabby and very stupid attempt to shift the blame from myself."

That was true, and Evan racked his mind in vain for a rebuttal. Monk was still sitting in the big chair, limp and exhausted with emotions from terror through joy and back to fear and despair again.

"Go home," Evan said gently. "You can't stay here. There may be —" Then the idea came to him with a flutter of hope, growing and rising. There was one person who might help. It was a chance, but there was nothing left to lose. "Yes," he repeated. "Go home — I'll be there soon. I've just got an errand. Someone to see — " And he swung on his heel and went out of the door, leaving it ajar behind him.

He ran down the stairs two at a time — he never knew afterwards how he did not break his neck — shot past Grimwade, and plunged out into the rain. He ran all the way along the pavement of Mecklenburg Square along Doughty Street and accosted a hansom as it passed him, driver's coat collar up around his neck and stovepipe hat jammed forward over his brow.

"I ain't on duty, guv!" the driver said crossly. "Finished, I am. Goin' 'ome ter me supper."

Evan ignored him and climbed in, shouting the Latterlys' address in Thanet Street at him.

"I told you, I ain't goin' nowhere!" the cabby repeated, louder this time. " 'Ceptin 'ome fer me supper. You'll 'ave ter get someone else!"

"You're taking me to Thanet Street!" Evan shouted back at him. "Police! Now get on with it, or I'll have your badge!"

"Bleedin' rozzers," the cabby muttered sullenly, but he realized he had a madman in the back, and it would be quicker in the long run to do what he said. He lifted the reins and slapped them on the horse's soaking back, and they set off at a brisk trot.

At Thanet Street Evan scrambled out and commanded the cabby to wait, on pain of his livelihood.

Hester was at home when Evan was shown in by a startled maid. He was streaming water everywhere and his extraordinary, ugly, beautiful face was white. His hair was plastered crazily across his brow and he stared at her with anguished eyes.

She had seen hope and despair too often not to recognize both.

"Can you come with me!" he said urgently. "Please? I'll explain as we go. Miss Latterly — I —"

"Yes." She did not need time to decide. To refuse was an impossibility. And she must leave before Charles or Imogen came from the withdrawing room, impelled by curiosity, and discovered the drenched and frantic policeman in the hall. She could not even go back for her cloak — what use would it be in this downpour anyway? "Yes — I'll come now." She walked past him and out of the front door. The wall of rain hit her in the face and she ignored it, continuing across the pavement, over the bubbling gutter and up into the hansom before either Evan or the driver had time to hand her up.

Evan scrambled behind her and slammed the door, shouting his instructions to drive to Grafton Street. Since the cabby had not yet been paid, he had little alternative.

"What has happened, Mr. Evan?" Hester asked as soon as they were moving. "I can see that it is something very terrible. Have you discovered who murdered Joscelin Grey?"

There was no point in hesitating now; the die was cast.

"Yes, Miss Latterly. Mr. Monk retraced all the steps of his first investigation — with your help." He took a deep breath. He was cold now that the moment came; he was wet to the skin and shaking. "Joscelin Grey made his living by finding the families of men killed in the Crimea, pretending he had known the dead soldier and befriended him — either lending him money, paying the debts he left, or giving him some precious personal belonging, like the watch he claimed to have lent your brother, then when the family could not give it back to him — which they never could, since it did not exist — they felt in his debt, which he used to obtain invitations, influence, financial or social backing. Usually it was only a few hundred guineas, or to be a guest at their expense. In your father's case it was to his ruin and death. Either way Grey did not give a damn what happened to his victims, and he had every intention of continuing."

"What a vile crime," she said quietly. "He was totally despicable. I am glad that he is dead — and perhaps sorry for whoever killed him. You have not said who it was?" Suddenly she was cold also. "Mr. Evan —?"

"Yes ma'am — Mr. Monk went to his flat in Mecklenburg Square and faced him with it. They fought — Mr. Monk beat him, but he was definitely alive and not mortally hurt when Mr. Monk left. But as Monk reached the street he saw someone else arrive, and go towards the door which was still swinging open in the wind."

He saw Hester's face pale in the glare of the streetlamps through the carriage window.

"Who?"

"Menard Grey," he replied, waiting in the dark again to judge from her voice, or her silence, if she believed it. "Probably because Joscelin dishonored the memory of his friend Edward Dawlish, and deceived Edward's father into giving him hospitality, as he did your father — and the money would have followed."

She said nothing for several minutes. They swayed and rattled through the intermittent darkness, the rain battering on the roof and streaming past in torrents, yellow where the gaslight caught it.

"How very sad," she said at last, and her voice was tight with emotion as though the pity caused a physical pain in her throat. "Poor Menard. I suppose you are going to arrest him? Why have you brought me? I can do nothing."

"We can't arrest him," he answered quietly. "There is no proof."

"There —" She swiveled around in her seat; he felt her rather than saw her. "Then what are you going to do? They'll think it was Monk. They'll charge him — they'll —" She swallowed. "They'll hang him."

"I know. We must make Menard confess. I thought you might know how we could do that? You know the Greys far better than we could, from the outside. And Joscelin was responsible for your father's death — and your mother's, indirectly."

Again she sat silent for so long he was afraid he had offended her, or reminded her of grief so deep she was unable to do anything but nurse its pain inside her. They were drawing close to Grafton Street, and soon they must leave the cab and face Monk with some resolution — or admit failure. Then he would be faced with the task he dreaded so much the thought of it made him sick. He must either tell Runcorn the truth, that Monk fought with Joscelin Grey the night of his death — or else deliberately conceal the fact and lay himself open to certain dismissal from the police force — and the possible charge of accessory to murder.

They were in the Tottenham Court Road, lamps gleaming on the wet pavements, gutters awash. There was no time left.

"Miss Latterly."

"Yes. Yes," she said firmly. "I will come with you to Shelburne Hall. I have thought about it, and the only way I can see success is if you tell Lady Fabia the truth about Joscelin. I will corroborate it. My family were his victims as well, and she will have to believe me, because I have no interest in lying. It does not absolve my father's suicide in the eyes of the church." She hesitated only an instant. "Then if you proceed to tell her about Edward Dawlish as well, I think Menard may be persuaded to confess. He may see no other avenue open to him, once his mother realizes that he killed Joscelin — which she will. It will devastate her — it may destroy her." Her voice was very low. "And they may hang Menard. But we cannot permit the law to hang Mr. Monk instead, merely because the truth is a tragedy that will wound perhaps beyond bearing. Joscelin Grey was a man who did much evil. We cannot protect his mother either from her part in it, or from the pain of knowing."

"You'll come to Shelburne tomorrow?" He had to hear her say it again. "You are prepared to tell her your own family's suffering at Joscelin's hands?"

"Yes. And how Joscelin obtained the names of the dying in Scutari, as I now realize, so he could use them to cheat their families. At what time will you depart?"

Again relief swept over him, and an awe for her that she could so commit herself without equivocation. But then to go out to the Crimea to nurse she must be a woman of courage beyond the ordinary imagination, and to remain there, of a strength of purpose that neither danger nor pain could bend.

"I don't know," he said a trifle foolishly. "There was little purpose in going at all unless you were prepared to come. Lady Shelburne would hardly believe us without further substantiation from beyond police testimony. Shall we say the first train after eight o'clock in the morning?" Then he remembered he was asking a lady of some gentility. "Is that too early?"

"Certainly not." Had he been able to see her face there might have been the faintest of smiles on it.

"Thank you. Then do you wish to take this hansom back home again, and I shall alight here and go and tell Mr. Monk?"

"That would be the most practical thing," she agreed. "I shall see you at the railway station in the morning."

He wanted to say something more, but all that came to his mind was either repetitious or vaguely condescending. He simply thanked her again and climbed out into the cold and teeming rain. It was only when the cab had disappeared into the darkness and he was half-way up the stairs to Monk's rooms that he realized with acute embarrassment that he had left her to pay the cabby.

The journey to Shelburne was made at first with heated conversation and then in silence, apart from the small politenesses of travel. Monk was furious that Hester was present. He refrained from ordering her home again only because the train was already moving when she entered the carriage from the corridor, bidding them good-morning and seating herself opposite.

"I asked Miss Latterly to come," Evan explained without a blush, "because her additional testimony will carry great weight with Lady Fabia, who may well not believe us, since we have an obvious interest in claiming Joscelin was a cad. Miss Latterly's experience, and that of her family, is something she cannot so easily deny." He did not make the mistake of claiming that Hester had any moral right to be there because of her own loss, or her part in the solution. Monk wished he had, so he could lose his temper and accuse him of irrelevance. The argument he had presented was extremely reasonable — in fact he was right. Hester's corroboration would be very likely to tip the balance of decision, which otherwise the Greys together might rebut.

"I trust you will speak only when asked?" Monk said to her coldly. "This is a police operation, and a very delicate one." That she of all people should be the one whose assistance he needed at this point was galling in the extreme, and yet it was undeniable. She was in many ways everything he loathed in a woman, the antithesis of the gentleness that still lingered with such sweetness in his memory; and yet she had rare courage, and a force of character which would equal Fabia Grey's any day.

"Certainly, Mr. Monk," she replied with her chin high and her eyes unflinching, and he knew in that instant that she had expected precisely this reception, and come to the carriage late intentionally to circumvent the possibility of being ordered home. Although of course it was highly debatable as to whether she would have gone. And Evan would never countenance leaving her on the station platform at Shelburne. And Monk did care what Evan felt.

He sat and stared across at Hester, wishing he could think of something else crushing to say.

She smiled at him, clear-eyed and agreeable. It was not so much friendliness as triumph.

They continued the rest of the journey with

civility, and gradually each became consumed in private thoughts, and a dread of the task ahead.

When they arrived at Shelburne they alighted onto the platform. The weather was heavy and dark with the presage of winter. It had stopped raining, but a cold wind stirred in gusts and chilled the skin even through heavy coats.

They were obliged to wait some fifteen minutes before a trap arrived, which they hired to take them to the hall. This journey too they made huddled together and without speaking. They were all oppressed by what was to come, and the trivialities of conversation would have been grotesque.

They were admitted reluctantly by the footman, but no persuasion would cause him to show them into the withdrawing room. Instead they were left together in the morning room, neither cheered nor warmed by the fire smoldering in the grate, and required to wait until Her Ladyship should decide whether she would receive them or not.

After twenty-five minutes the footman returned and conducted them to the boudoir, where Fabia was seated on her favorite settee, looking pale and somewhat strained, but perfectly composed.

"Good morning, Mr. Monk. Constable."

She nodded at Evan. Her eyebrows rose and her eyes became icier. "Good morning, Miss Latterly. I assume you can explain your presence here in such curious company?"

Hester took the bull by the horns before Monk had time to form a reply.

"Yes, Lady Fabia. I have come to inform you of the truth about my family's tragedy — and yours."

"You have my condolences, Miss Latterly." Fabia looked at her with pity and distaste. "But I have no desire to know the details of your loss, nor do I wish to discuss my bereavement with you. It is a private matter. I imagine your intention is good, but it is entirely misplaced. Good day to you. The footman will see you to the door."

Monk felt the first flicker of anger stir, in spite of the consuming disillusion he knew this woman was shortly going to feel. Her willful blindness was monumental, her ability to disregard other people total.

Hester's face set hard with resolve, as granite hard as Fabia's own.

"It is the same tragedy, Lady Fabia. And I do not discuss it out of good intentions, but because it is a truth we are all obliged to face. It gives me no pleasure at all, but neither do I plan to run away from it —"

Fabia's chin came up and the thin muscles

tightened in her neck, suddenly looking scraggy, as if age had descended on her in the brief moments since they entered the room.

"I have never run from a truth in my life, Miss Latterly, and I do not care for your impertinence in suggesting I might. You forget yourself."

"I would prefer to forget everything and go home." A ghost of a smile crossed Hester's face and vanished. "But I cannot. I think it would be better if Lord Shelburne and Mr. Menard Grey were to be present, rather than repeat the story for them later. There may be questions they wish to ask — Major Grey was their brother and they have some rights in knowing how and why he died."

Fabia sat motionless, her face rigid, her hands poised halfway towards the bell pull. She had not invited any of them to be seated, in fact she was on the point of asking again that they leave. Now, with the mention of Joscelin's murderer, everything was changed. There was not the slightest sound in the room except the ticking of the ormolu clock on the mantelpiece.

"You know who killed Joscelin?" She looked at Monk, ignoring Hester.

"Yes ma'am, we do." He found his mouth dry and the pulse beating violently in his head.

Was it fear, or pity — or both?

Fabia stared at him, demanding he explain everything for her, then slowly the challenge died. She saw something in his face which she could not overcome, a knowledge and a finality which touched her with the first breath of a chill, nameless fear. She pulled the bell, and when the maid came, told her to send both Menard and Lovel to her immediately. No mention was made of Rosamond. She was not a Grey by blood, and apparently Fabia did not consider she had any place in this revelation.

They waited in silence, each in their separate worlds of misery and apprehension. Lovel came first, looking irritably from Fabia to Monk, and with surprise at Hester. He had obviously been interrupted while doing something he considered of far greater urgency.

"What is it?" he said, frowning at his mother. "Has something further been discovered?"

"Mr. Monk says he knows at last who killed Joscelin," she answered with masklike calm.

"Who?"

"He has not told me. He is waiting for Menard."

Lovel turned to Hester, his face puckered with confusion. "Miss Latterly?"

"The truth involves the death of my father

530

also, Lord Shelburne," she explained gravely. "There are parts of it which I can tell you, so you understand it all."

The first shadow of anxiety touched him, but before he could press her further Menard came in, glanced from one to another of them, and paled.

"Monk finally knows who killed Joscelin," Lovel explained. "Now for heaven's sake, get on with it. I presume you have arrested him?"

"It is in hand, sir." Monk found himself more polite to them all than previously. It was a form of distancing himself, almost a sort of verbal defense.

"Then what is it you want of us?" Lovel demanded.

It was like plunging into a deep well of ice.

"Major Grey made his living out of his experience in the Crimean War —" Monk began. Why was he so mealymouthed? He was dressing it in sickening euphemisms.

"My son did not 'make his living' as you put it!" Fabia snapped. "He was a gentleman — there was no necessity. He had an allowance from the family estates."

"Which didn't begin to cover the expenses of the way he liked to live," Menard said savagely. "If you'd ever looked at him closely, even once, you would have known that."

"I did know it." Lovel glared at his brother.

"I assumed he was successful at cards."

"He was — sometimes. At other times he'd lose — heavily — more than he had. He'd go on playing, hoping to get it back, ignoring the debts — until I paid them, to save the family honor."

"Liar," Fabia said with withering disgust. "You were always jealous of him, even as a child. He was braver, kinder and infinitely more charming than you." For a moment a brief glow of memory superseded the present and softened all the lines of anger in her face — then the rage returned deeper than before. "And you couldn't forgive him for it."

Dull color burned up Menard's face and he winced as if he had been struck. But he did not retaliate. There was still in his eyes, in the turn of his lips, a pity for her which concealed the bitter truth.

Monk hated it. Futilely he tried again to think of any way he could to avoid exposing Menard even now.

The door opened and Callandra Daviot came in, meeting Hester's eyes, seeing the intense relief in them, then the contempt in Fabia's eyes and the anguish in Menard's.

"This is a family concern," Fabia said, dismissing her. "You need not trouble yourself with it."

Callandra walked past Hester and sat down.

"In case you have forgotten, Fabia, I was born a Grey. Something which you were not. I see the police are here. Presumably they have learned more about Joscelin's death — possibly even who was responsible. What are you doing here, Hester?"

Again Hester took the initiative. Her face was bleak and she stood with her shoulders stiff as if she were bracing herself against a blow.

"I came because I know a great deal about Joscelin's death, which you may not believe from anyone else."

"Then why have you concealed it until now," Fabia said with heavy disbelief. "I think you are indulging in a most vulgar intrusion, Miss Latterly, which I can only presume is a result of that same willful nature which drove you to go traipsing off to the Crimea. No wonder you are unmarried."

Hester had been called worse things than vulgar, and by people for whose opinion she cared a great deal more than she did for Fabia Grey's.

"Because I did not know it had any relevance before," she said levelly. "Now I do. Joscelin came to visit my parents after my brother was lost in the Crimea. He told them he had lent George a gold watch the night before his death. He asked for its return, assuming it was found among George's effects." Her voice dropped a fraction and her back became even stiffer. "There was no watch in George's effects, and my father was so embarrassed he did what he could to make amends to Joscelin — with hospitality, money to invest in Joscelin's business enterprise, not only his own but his friends' also. The business failed and my father's money, and all that of his friends, was lost. He could not bear the shame of it, and he took his own life. My mother died of grief a short while later."

"I am truly sorry for your parents' death," Lovel interrupted, looking first at Fabia, then at Hester again. "But how can all this have anything to do with Joscelin's murder? It seems an ordinary enough matter — an honorable man making a simple compensation to clear his dead son's debt to a brother officer."

Hester's voice shook and at last her control seemed in danger of breaking.

"There was no watch. Joscelin never knew George — any more than he knew a dozen others whose names he picked from the casualty lists, or whom he watched die in Scutari — I saw him do it — only then I didn't know why."

Fabia was white-lipped. "That is a most scandalous lie — and beneath contempt. If you were a man I should have you horse-whipped."

"Mother!" Lovel protested, but she ignored him.

"Joscelin was a beautiful man — brave and talented and full of charm and wit," she plunged on, her voice thick with emotion, the joy of the past, and the anguish. "Everyone loved him — except those few who were eaten with envy." Her eyes darted at Menard with something close to hatred. "Little men who couldn't bear to see anyone succeed beyond their own petty efforts." Her mouth trembled. "Lovel, because Rosamond loved Joscelin; he could make her laugh — and dream." Her voice hardened. "And Menard, who couldn't live with the fact that I loved Joscelin more than I loved anyone else in the world, and I always did."

She shuddered and her body seemed to shrink into itself as if withdrawing from something vile. "Now this woman has come here with her warped and fabricated story, and you stand there and listen to it. If you were men worthy of the name, you would throw her out and damn it for the slander it is. But it seems I must do it myself. No one has any sense of the family honor but me." She put her hands on the arm of her chair as if to rise to her feet.

"You'll have no one thrown out until I say so," Lovel said with a tight, calm voice, suddenly cutting like steel across her emotion. "It is not you who have defended the family honor; all you've defended is Joscelin — whether he deserved it or not. It was Menard who paid his debts and cleaned up the trail of cheating and welching he left behind —"

"Nonsense. Whose word do you have for that? Menard's?" She spat the name. "He is calling Joscelin a cheat, no one else. And he wouldn't dare, if Joscelin were alive. He only has the courage to do it now because he thinks you will back him, and there is no one here to call him the pathetic, treacherous liar he is."

Menard stood motionless, the final blow visible in the agony of his face. She had hurt him, and he had defended Joscelin for her sake for the last time.

Callandra stood up.

"You are wrong, Fabia, as you have been wrong all the time. Miss Latterly here, for one, will testify that Joscelin was a cheat who made money deceiving the bereaved who were too hurt and bewildered to see him for what he was. Menard was always a better man, but you were too fond of flattery to see it. Perhaps you were the one Joscelin deceived most of all — first, last and always." She did not flinch now, even from Fabia's stricken face as she caught sight at last of a fearful truth. "But you wanted to be deceived. He told you what you wished to hear; he told you you were beautiful, charming, gay — all the things a man loves in a woman. He learned his art in your gullibility, your willingness to be entertained, to laugh and to be the center of all the life and love in Shelburne. He said all that not because he thought for a moment it was true, but because he knew you would love him for saying it — and you did, blindly and indiscriminately, to the exclusion of everyone else. That is your tragedy, as well as his."

Fabia seemed to wither as they watched her.

"You never liked Joscelin," she said in a last, frantic attempt to defend her world, her dreams, all the past that was golden and lovely to her, everything that gave her meaning as it crumbled in front of her — not only what Joscelin had been, but what she herself had been. "You are a wicked woman."

"No, Fabia," Callandra replied. "I am a very sad one." She turned to Hester. "I assume it is not your brother who killed Joscelin, or you would not have come here to tell us this way. We would have believed the police, and the details would not have been necessary." With immeasurable sorrow she looked across at Menard. "You paid his debts. What else did you do?"

There was an aching silence in the room.

Monk could feel his heart beating as if it had the force to shake his whole body. They were poised on the edge of truth, and yet it was still so far away. It could be lost again by a single slip; they could plunge away into an abyss of fear, whispered doubts, always seeing suspicions, double meanings, hearing the footstep behind and the hand on the shoulder.

Against his will, he looked across at Hester, and saw that she was looking at him, the same thoughts plain in her eyes. He turned his head quickly back to Menard, who was ashen-faced.

"What else did you do?" Callandra repeated. "You knew what Joscelin was —"

"I paid his debts." Menard's voice was no more than a whisper.

"Gambling debts," she agreed. "What about his debts of honor, Menard? What about his terrible debts to men like Hester's father and brother — did you pay them as well?"

"I — I didn't know about the Latterlys," Menard stammered.

Callandra's face was tight with grief.

"Don't equivocate, Menard. You may not have known the Latterlys by name, but you knew what Joscelin was doing. You knew he got money from somewhere, because you knew how much he had to gamble with. Don't tell us you didn't learn where it came from.

I know you better than that. You would not have rested in that ignorance — you knew what a fraud and a cheat Joscelin was, and you knew there was no honest way for him to come by so much. Menard —" Her face was gentle, full of pity. "You have behaved with such honor so far — don't soil it now by lying. There is no point, and no escape."

He winced as if she had struck him, and for a second Monk thought he was going to collapse. Then he straightened up and faced her, as though she had been a long-awaited execution squad — and death was not now the worst fear.

"Was it Edward Dawlish?" Now her voice also was barely above a whisper. "I remember how you cared for each other as boys, and your grief when he was killed. Why did his father quarrel with you?"

Menard did not evade the truth, but he spoke not to Callandra but to his mother, his voice low and hard, a lifetime of seeking and being rejected naked in it finally.

"Because Joscelin told him I had led Edward into gambling beyond his means, and that in the Crimea he had got in over his head with his brother officers, and would have died in debt — except that Joscelin settled it all for him."

There was a rich irony in that, and it was

lost on no one. Even Fabia flinched in a death's-head acknowledgment of its cruel absurdity.

"For his family's sake," Menard continued, his voice husky, his eyes on Callandra. "Since I was the one who had led him to ruin."

He gulped. "Of course there was no debt. Joscelin never even served in the same area as Edward — I found that out afterwards. It was all another of his lies — to get money." He looked at Hester. "It was not as bad as your loss. At least Dawlish didn't kill himself. I am truly sorry about your family."

"He didn't lose any money." Monk spoke at last. "He didn't have time. You killed Joscelin before he could take it. But he had asked."

There was utter silence. Callandra put both her hands to her face. Lovel was stunned, unable to comprehend. Fabia was a broken woman. She no longer cared. What happened to Menard was immaterial. Joscelin, her beloved Joscelin, had been murdered in front of her in a new and infinitely more dreadful way. They had robbed her not only of the present and the future, but all the warm, sweet, precious past. It had all gone; there was nothing left but a handful of bitter ash.

They all waited, each in a separate world in the moments between hope and the finality of despair. Only Fabia had already been dealt the ultimate blow.

Monk found the nails of his hands cutting his palms, so tightly were his fists clenched. It could all still slip away from him. Menard could deny it, and there would be no proof sufficient. Runcorn would have only the bare facts, and come after Monk, and what was there to protect him?

The silence was like a slow pain, growing with each second.

Menard looked at his mother and she saw the movement of his head, and turned her face away, slowly and deliberately.

"Yes," Menard said at last. "Yes I did. He was despicable. It wasn't only what he had done to Edward Dawlish, or me, but what he was going to go on doing. He had to be stopped — before it became public, and the name of Grey was a byword for a man who cheats the families of his dead comrades-in-arms, a more subtle and painful version of those who crawl over the battlefield the morning after and rob the corpses of the fallen."

Callandra walked over to him and put her hand on his arm.

"We will get the best legal defense available," she said very quietly. "You had a great deal of provocation. I think they will not find murder."

"We will not." Fabia's voice was a mere crackle, almost a sob, and she looked at Menard with terrible hatred.

"I will," Callandra corrected. "I have quite sufficient means." She turned back to Menard again. "I will not leave you alone, my dear. I imagine you will have to go with Mr. Monk now — but I will do all that is necessary, I promise you."

Menard held her hand for a moment; something crossed his lips that was almost a smile. Then he turned to Monk.

"I am ready."

Evan was standing by the door with the manacles in his pocket. Monk shook his head, and Menard walked out slowly between them. The last thing Monk heard was Hester's voice as she stood next to Callandra.

"I will testify for him. When the jury hears what Joscelin did to my family, they may understand —"

Monk caught Evan's eye and felt a lift of hope. If Hester Latterly fought for Menard, the battle could not easily be lost. His hand held Menard's arm — but gently.

THORNDIKE PRESS hopes you have enjoyed this Large Print book. All our Large Print titles are designed for easy reading, and all our books are made to last. Other Thorndike Press books are available at your library, through selected bookstores, or directly from the publisher. For more information about current and upcoming titles, please call or mail your name and address to:

THORNDIKE PRESS
PO Box 159
Thorndike, Maine 04986 ~~800~~
~~800/223-6121~~ 356-7220
207/948-2962

AOC